"SHE GAVE UP HER BABY!"

Nell's eyes looked deeply into his. "Sylvie's daughter. She must have told you. It was such an agonizing decision for her ... to give up her baby."

It was hard for Ty to breathe. Now Nell sat watching, waiting for his next move. He reached over and gripped her wrist so tightly it left it dead white like a corpse. "You know Sylvie doesn't have a daughter. Sylvie has never had a child."

"Ty, you're hurting me." The tears were gone from the devastating green eyes. Now they were wide, luminous, extraordinarily innocent. "I didn't mean to upset you. I thought you knew..." The wrench he gave her wrist could have broken it.

What was happening? Nell was Sylvie's best friend! What could she hope to gain from this? A throb began behind his right temple. Or was any of it true? Could it possibly be true?

Berkley books by Shirley Lord

GOLDEN HILL
ONE OF MY VERY BEST FRIENDS

SHIRLEY LORD
ONE OF MY VERY BEST FRIENDS

BERKLEY BOOKS, NEW YORK

This Berkley book contains the complete
text of the original hardcover edition.

ONE OF MY VERY BEST FRIENDS

A Berkley Book / published by arrangement with
Crown Publilshers, Inc.

PRINTING HISTORY
Crown edition published 1985
Berkley edition / August 1987

ISBN: 0-425-09702-1

A BERKLEY BOOK ® TM 757,375
Berkley Books are published by The Berkley Publishing Group,
200 Madison Avenue, New York, New York 10016.
The name "BERKLEY" and the "B" logo
are trademarks belonging to Berkley Publishing Corporation.
PRINTED IN THE UNITED STATES OF AMERICA

10   9   8   7   6   5   4   3   2   1

To Jane and Mark and Richard,
my very best friends

Acknowledgments

My thanks to Margaret and Bill Marquard, Jane and Guilford Dudley, Margaret Hodges, Iris and Emilio Gioia, Milton Gordon, Patricia and John Kluge, and Angel and Frank Wyman . . . as a privileged guest in their homes I was able to start, continue, and conclude this book during my vacations from *Vogue* magazine. Thanks to Charles Strouse for inspiration and information about the life of a composer; to William Garvin, the yachtsman, not the business executive, for "sailing" advice; to Martin Gersh for his expert knowledge on wine; to Freddie Gershon, Tony Fantozzi, and Ron Yatter for their unfailing encouragement; to my literary agent, Mort Janklow; and most of all thanks to my editor, Betty Prashker, for her unerring finger on the pulsebeat of the book and for all her excellent guidance; to my son Mark Hussey for his editing help; and last, but never least, to Ellen Sandles for her help in meeting this deadline.

Boca Raton,
April 25, 1975

I am a very happy woman. *(Pause for applause)* Not because, as you all know, I have just been elected Businesswoman of the Year—although for all our sakes I am naturally delighted that indisputable fact *(ironically)* has been so publicized. Thank you, *Fortune Magazine (humor)* for thinking of the award. It can only help what I am trying to do for women everywhere—right, girls? *(Pause for applause/laughter)* Okay. *(Modest resignation)* So I am also described as the most influential woman in the country today; more influential than our beloved First Lady *(pause)* . . . and Elizabeth Taylor. *(Pause for laughter. Change of pace—slow/serious)* It is a responsibility many women would tremble to contemplate, but I am proud of the distinction because of *(emphasize the next word) your* support, which brings me to the real reason *(stress slowly)* I am such a very happy woman *(even more slowly, with feeling)* . . . because I . . . know . . . you *(stress word forcefully)* all . . . love *(pause)* . . . me. . . . *(Throw arms out to the audience, allow at least ten minutes for applause, reception of gifts, flowers, messages delivered to stage before award ceremony. Check timing with Johnny at left)*

The woman in the wings allowed the typewritten speech to slip out of her hand. With a weary yet still graceful movement, she removed her glasses and, without turning, gave them to the man standing beside her, the man she knew would soon stoop to retrieve her speech from the floor.

"Mirror." It wasn't an order. It was simply a word spoken as effortlessly and thoughtlessly as breathing. The man held up a mirror at exactly the right angle for her to see her immaculately made-up face, yet she hardly seemed to look at her reflection. Her arms were limp at her sides. Her eyes appeared almost sightless, but suddenly a miracle occurred.

The woman began to smile. It was not the kind of smile usually given to a mirror to check that there is no lipstick on the teeth or to assess the reflection's impact on somebody else. It was the involuntary smile sometimes transmitted by the brain for those fleeting seconds when the body, out of control, is in ecstasy. Part animal, part human, it was a smile of glorious abandonment, charging the woman with high incendiary energy, breaking up her perfect mask of a face. With just the slightest movement, her body, too, changed. No longer aloof, she radiated an allure that was at once strangely vulnerable, even innocent, and so even more desirable.

The man beside her tried to suppress a sigh as he witnessed the familiar transformation. She heard the sigh escape. "Johnny . . ." She turned, still smiling the magic smile, lips parted, eyes glowing, loving and lovely.

"Oh, Nell . . ." He was a man in pain. She could hear it, see it. He hesitated before reaching out to cup her face in his hands. He was a second too late.

Just as quickly as the miracle came, it went. Nell Nesbitt switched off her smile and with it her magic. She turned away. "Leave me alone." These weren't just words. This was an order.

﹀

From the press box, high above the auditorium, the scene below resembled a tumultuous sea, as wave upon wave of bodies pressed forward, dressed in every hue of blue from turquoise to lavender, royal to navy to sky.

It was hard to see how more people could squeeze themselves into the packed throng, but every few minutes, like the force of the ocean only a few hundred yards outside, a new wave of blue-clad bodies would break the ranks, pushing those at the front nearer to the roped-off steps leading to the stage. From the soundproof booth it was intriguing to see the changes that were forever taking place below. Like animals sensing the increasing proximity of their prey, the packed crowd slowly ceased their restless head-turning, mouth-moving body gesticulations to become an almost amorphous, motionless blue mass.

"You could hear the proverbial pin drop. The silence was deafening. The atmosphere was pregnant with the desires and aspirations of eighteen hundred women . . ." Only clichés came into Kitty Stein's tired mind. She flagellated herself with them, each worn phrase rubbing like grit against her raw nerves.

As she always did when she was both tired and tense, Kitty unconsciously began to grind her teeth. She was jet-lagged to death, yet, *of course*, her darling boss and lover couldn't care less about that! Just off a ghastly, cramped, storm-ridden fourteen-hour—it had felt like fourteen days—flight from London to Miami, *he*, God bless his dedicated journalistic mind, had to make sure she didn't have a second to change her underwear, let alone her makeup. *He* wanted an eyewitness account of the fabled extravaganza of the Ready to Change annual sales conference and *he* wanted it *now*—not tomorrow or the day after. No, *he* didn't want to wait until she met Nell again after all these years. Kitty shut her eyes going over the long-distance conversation with her editor, Smith Maynard, parroting his voice, mimicking his instructions, knowing she was mentally doodling, her usual habit before writing a difficult piece.

Kitty tried to concentrate on the blue sea below, which was no longer fomenting but fixed in immobility, eighteen hundred pairs of eyes looking unblinkingly toward the stage.

Was something happening? Kitty couldn't see any reason for the arms below beginning to wave, why blonde, brunette, red, mousy, black, hennaed, and multicolored heads were tilting upward. For a minute, Kitty imagined herself onstage, visualizing the scene from there, wondering if eighteen hundred pairs of lips were open, like sparrows waiting for crumbs—but why was the Ready to Change brigade so obviously reacting to something she couldn't see?

Had somebody seen the curtains move? Even as the thought occurred, the heavy curtains opened just enough to reveal a spiral staircase which, with the benefit of the best theatrical lighting, looked as if it had been hewn out of mother-of-pearl. Kitty noted it was set against an ethereal blue-sky and white-cloud backdrop. Was Nell going to appear as an angel? If so, that was nothing new.

Kitty's lips pursed. She couldn't wait to see Nell with wings. She shrugged off her cashmere cardigan, relieved to feel her tiredness go with it. This wasn't a moment for jet lag.

She was suddenly totally alert, as out of a perfectly white cumulus cloud stepped a vision in silver—from the hair framing the beautiful, sensitive face, to the silver beaded dress faithfully following every curve of the slender body, to sparkling rhinestone-studded shoes. As the vision slowly descended the staircase and the blue sea of women surged and roared below, the soundproof box crackled into life and TV monitors showed the scene as it went out across the nation. From eighteen hundred throats Kitty heard an already familiar exhortation: "Financial security, emotional maturity, God-fearing, God-willing, we're Ready to Change the world . . ."

It was impressive, incredibly impressive.

Kitty shivered, looked for her cardigan, then decided against it. It wasn't her body that needed warmth; it was her spirit.

"Camera two . . ." The producer two seats away leaned forward, picking his nose. *He* wasn't impressed. Kitty felt a moment of affection for him—a man like Smith. He'd seen it all, met them all, and for the moment his nose needed his attention, not Nell Nesbitt and Ready to Change. Now Kitty could hear the voice-over of one of the TV commentators, pitched at just the right note of excitement. She wondered if she should write the piece as if someone with the pompous pride of the BBC were recording the moment for posterity; then the American commentator gave her another idea.

"Here she is at last, ladies and gentlemen, the Godmother—no sinister connotation to this label. Nell Nesbitt has given dignity and respect back to the word, as thousands of women all over America genuinely think of her with affection and gratitude as *their* Godmother, responsible for giving them their best chance in life with a career where, as you are all about to see, the rewards can be spectacular . . ."

As if on cue, the silver vision lifted her arms out to the audience, and the curtains opened to their fullest extent to reveal the rewards the TV commentator had in mind. One red, one blue, and one white Cadillac were in place onstage, their paintwork gleaming as no paintwork had ever gleamed before that Kitty had seen, each door embossed with a discreet American flag, surmounted by RTC and a miniature crown, the Ready to Change logo of Nell's unbeatable cosmetics empire.

As Kitty watched with growing, grudging admiration, Nell began to receive from the audience what appeared to be a never-ending procession of tributes. Flowers of every kind were being handed up to her, thrown or personally delivered onstage. Then there were baskets of letters and a bewildering assortment of objects, from a child's shoe to an orange wig to a bicycle wheel. "What on earth is that all about?" Kitty muttered to herself. The TV producer said in a stage whisper, "Symbols of past slavery, my dear. All Nell's disciples seem to go through withdrawal symptoms and have to hand over what best symbolized their problems . . ."

As the pandemonium below grew to hysteria, the silver vision put up a slender, restraining hand. On the TV monitor Kitty saw a closeup of her nails. Silver, too. A pretty color. She made a mental note to ask Nell when they got together what shade it was. Perhaps she'd even ask for a sample. Why not? Kitty was sure she was the same Nell inside, if not on the outside. The voice-over was getting on her nerves. ". . . this is the moment eighteen hundred women have been waiting for," the commentator burbled. "Soon eighteen hundred self-employed Ready to Change saleswomen, gathered here from all parts of the country, will learn who among them have best responded to the Godmother's crusade and sold the most Ready to Change products in one year . . ."

Kitty leaned forward. To her surprise she realized she *was* interested to learn who in the dense crowd below was going to drive away in a brand-new RTC award Cadillac . . .

Nell was a born showwoman, there had never been any doubt about that. A bad girl, but a born showwoman.

As press and cameramen crouched at the foot of the steps to record the award ceremony, Kitty started to scribble, hardly looking at what she was writing, her attention fixed on the tearful acceptances and dazed expressions of the top Ready to Change saleswomen. It was better than the Oscars . . . the suspense, the sudden second of silence after a name was triumphantly called out by Nell, the way spaces appeared in the crowd below as "disciples," as Nell herself described them, stumbled up to the stage and then back into the audience, holding extra large, special gold-plated car keys high above their heads like pirates' bounty.

The scenario was obviously planned down to the last detail, for soon, like the parting of the Red Sea, the crowd began to fan out with well-rehearsed choreography as Nell began a slow walk down into the auditorium.

God, she was still extraordinarily beautiful. Kitty caught her breath as she stared at the face on the TV screen of the woman she had once known so well. Not only beautiful but—Kitty searched for the right word—caring. Could it really be caring? She'd have to see the face in the flesh to see if Nell really had redeemed herself, really had become the good, all-loving, all-caring Godmother of worldwide repute.

Kitty reached the lobby of the auditorium as trumpets blasted and four sets of double doors were thrown open. She half expected the blue sea of bodies to flood out and engulf her, but the Ready to Change organization had thought of everything. As Nell Nesbitt stepped on a lipstick-pink carpet that led to the real world outside where her car was waiting, a battalion of beautiful young girls in white shorts and pale blue Ready to Change T-shirts surrounded her like Secret Servicemen around the president of the United States. All that could be seen of Nell was her dazzling silver head as she approached a stretch limousine convertible painted silver to match.

Kitty's press card didn't help her get any nearer to Nell. She made a mental note to add to her piece that annoying though it was, she was being obstructed in the most courteous, charming way.

Was it her imagination that her eyes met Nell's as Nell sat, poised and erect on the back seat of the limo, blowing kisses to those only now allowed to emerge from the great hall? There was no recognition in Nell's eyes, but why should there have been? They hadn't seen each other for almost twenty years. Whether their eyes had met or not—Kitty shook her head—there was no question that Nell's beauty no longer seemed just on the outside. Perhaps she really had been "born again," as had so often been publicized—perhaps she really had learned how to care. Well, she would soon find out.

‿‿‿

As the silver limo left the manicured grounds of the Boca Raton Hotel and Convention Center, it was both preceded and followed by a line of red, white, and blue Cadillacs, which echoed on their horns the chant being cried by the crowd left behind: "Financial security, emotional maturity . . ."

Fizz Campbell, Nell Nesbitt's personal assistant and chauffeur, drove at a snail's pace until she reached the bridge to make the left turn to Palm Beach. Fizz didn't need to look in the mirror to see her boss's expression. Fizz knew she would be smiling her special Ready to Change smile, a smile that still made Fizz's heart beat faster, even though she knew how quickly it would disappear once the Godmother turned back into a private citizen.

Where was Johnny? Odd that he wasn't in the car immediately behind. She'd heard trouble was brewing, but that was nothing new. There often was trouble between the two of them these days, but for all that Fizz knew, Mrs. Nesbitt couldn't do without him.

There was the last toot-toot from the convoy of cars, which were turning right, as instructed, toward Miami. Fizz could sense a change in the atmosphere—her boss, leaning back, letting down piece by piece until she seemed even to shrink in size.

"Okay, Fizz . . ." The directive was given in a confidential, "just between us" tone that indicated Fizz was part of a special inner circle. At that moment she would have given her life for the Godmother. Instead, she pressed her foot down on the accelerator to increase speed to sixty miles an hour. The "okay" also meant the Godmother was about to take off her halo and relax.

For once as she drove, Fizz didn't glance back at her boss as she was apt to do, subconsciously recharging the pride she felt to be chauffeuring a national figure. If she had, she would have been shocked to see undisguised fury obliterating the beauty that only minutes before had been shining with what newspapers often described as "a natural inner radiance."

As Fizz skillfully followed the twists and turns of Highway A1A, running alongside the stretch of Atlantic Ocean bordering the skinny east flank of Florida, Nell Nesbitt's hands became black with newspaper ink as she tore the front page of the *Miami Herald* to shreds. She looked at her hands with disgust.

How could she have been so stupid!

The headline and accompanying photographs still burned in her mind. She had made her hands dirty for nothing.

"Wedding Bells" . . . for those two! It was the second most ghastly shock of her life . . . one that could cause a seizure in most people.

Fate was conspiring against her again, strangling the life out of her as surely as a noose could tighten around a throat. A day that should have been one of her happiest had been destined to be ruined . . . ruined!

Again she could see the newspaper pictures in her mind, pictures of two such familiar faces . . .

Bile rose in her throat. Good God, she was going to be sick.

"Fizz, close the roof. Pull over . . ."

~~~

He'd allowed himself the luxury of daydreaming all the way from Miami, shutting his eyes to savor the memory of the night before: "I'm glad to see you can still derive pleasure from the simple things in life," he'd said, controlling his passion for just a few more minutes as, eyes shining, she'd moved into his arms, naked except for his latest gift, a rope of black pearls around her neck.

"Oh, darling, you're so . . . so amazing, so gener . . ." There'd been no more control. He'd stopped her mouth from moving another syllable.

"We're about there, sir."

He opened his eyes to look down from the helicopter in time to see a flash of silver, as eight hundred feet below the silver roof of a large convertible slowly closed over a head of the same color. Perfect match.

He wrinkled his nose superciliously. What would the bored Palm Beach matrons think of next?

Methodically preparing a cigar, piercing it with a gold piercer, he put it unlit into his mouth as the helicopter descended over the familiar roofs, gardens, and swimming pools of his neighbors and flew low over the golden palm beaches to land with precision in the center of a dark-green asphalt circle that was his private heliport.

The large expanse of lawn sloping gently from the white mansion to the ocean had been transformed since his departure at six that morning. As he jumped down, helicopter blades still whirring, he ignored the helping hand of his butler, taking in with one glance the yellow marquee that now commanded the lawn to the left of his property, the gaily striped yellow-and-white canopy leading to the west portico, and the exotic shrubs, trees, and flowers that had suddenly materialized to mark each stanchion. He found his hands trembling. The presence of the marquee seemed to make it all official. God, he was getting married in less than forty-eight hours. It was at once the most exhilarating yet disturbing thought he could remember experiencing. His self-mocking grin took years away from his face, and he ran like a youngster up curving steps into the black-and-white marble entrance hall.

"Sam . . . Sam . . . where are you?"

He took the stairs two at a time. He couldn't wait to see her, couldn't wait to hold her fast in his arms. Suddenly it seemed a lifetime since dawn when he'd left her sleeping. He could hear her laughter, so infectious, bubbling up from some inner well of stored humor—a well which, she'd told him, had saved her so often in times of crisis.

It was a sound he'd carried with him, that and the memory of her dark hazel eyes, so thickly framed with dark brown lashes. "I'm coming, darling . . . I'm coming."

As he reached the first-floor landing, Sam, a perfectly tanned size six in a diminutive bikini, rushed out of the bedroom so fast she collided with him. Without a pause he heaved her over his shoulder in a fireman's lift. Her dark hair, lightly flecked with gray, fell over her face, her arms and legs flailed ineffectually to be released. There was no need for words. They had been talking nonstop for weeks, throwing out the garbage—the misunderstandings from crossed wires, false trails, and innuendos—of years.

Late afternoon sunlight turned the king-sized bed into an arbor of gold. They were bathed in its warmth as they made love. He was unusually gentle but unmistakably possessive, she acquiescent to everything, all the storms passed, secure in the knowledge she was protected at last.

As the sun set, a soft wind from the Caribbean stirred the heavy silk curtains but failed to wake them from their exhausted emotional sleep. They slept on, unaware that high in the sky, catching the last light of the day, a skywriter was writing, "Congratulations, Sam. We love you. Your friends and fans at Channel 6."

It didn't matter. There had been similar messages delivered in the sky and on the ground for days. There would be more in the days to come.

As an unusually velvety night took over the sky, Sam returned to the typewriter she had left so hurriedly on hearing her future husband's footsteps. She could hear him singing dreadfully off-key in the bathroom, "Get me to the church on time . . ."

She laughed, cupping her freckled face in her hands, staring ahead without seeing the words she'd spent all day trying to find.

As the sound of the shower stopped and the door opened, she said softly, "Darling, come and see . . . I think I've got it at last . . ."

He draped a towel around his middle, to come and lean over her shoulder, depositing a kiss on top of her head.

She put on large tortoiseshell framed glasses, frowning, now studying every word intently. "What do you think?"

He tried to remove her glasses. "I think you should wear contact lenses . . ."

"Oh, you . . . you . . ." He tried to turn her face to kiss her again, but she resisted him.

"Darling, this is *serious*. Do pay attention. After all, it's going to appear in your papers . . ."

He turned the paper up in the typewriter.

> To be released *Tuesday, April 29*
> Palm Beach, Florida: SAM SAYS . . .
> "Financial security, emotional maturity, God-fearing,
> God-willing, we're Ready to Change the world . . ."

He sensed her intensity, knowing she was trying to penetrate his thoughts as he read on. The fear was still there in the eyes he loved so well, but he couldn't stop the bantering tone that belied his true feelings. "Will it ruin her?" he asked. "Are you sure you haven't left anything out? There's so much—it would be easy to do . . ."

She registered his sarcasm, his levity. She sighed.

Although he had actively encouraged her to write this, the last column they had both decided she would ever write, he was still not taking the subject seriously enough. Despite everything he knew, he still had not assessed adequately the full violent force of the enemy and, perhaps more important, the lengths and the depths to which she knew Nell would go to defend her kingdom and her saintly reputation.

She sighed again, thinking of the howl of protest that had gone up from the American public when they'd heard that after this "Sam Says" column, Sam would be "saying" no more . . .

Vogue had recently written, "A magical, mischievous mix of impressions, conjectures, and often uncanny prescience . . ." She had knocked Dear Abby off her "most widely syndicated perch." She was proud of that . . . prouder still that the American public avidly read her particular brand of journalism. Above all, however, she was *relieved*, oh, so relieved, that after this column, one she had waited years to be able to write, she would never have to meet another deadline, would never have to go "in search of the truth" again—which had been foisted on her as a vocation.

Sam felt her man's arm around her, saw his fingers twist the simple ring she'd worn since she was a teenager. It was an incredible feeling—this one of being so protected and loved.

Even as his grip tightened, her spirits lifted.

Why was she still worrying about Nell? The man she was going to marry could defend her against anything and anyone, even Nell.

She turned her face up to his, smiling radiantly. "Yes, darling," she whispered. "Don't worry. This will ruin her, all right. The facts speak for themselves."

2

London, E.10,
September 30, 1950

> *Dear Twenty-one,*
>   *Are you Mrs. yet? Or are you engaged? I live at 32*
> *Osborne Road. I hope I'm not too far away when I read*
> *this on my twenty-first birthday . . .*

The young girl put down her pen and stared angrily at the photograph of her mother by her bed. "Over my dead body . . ." she muttered, before dipping her nib into the ink to start to write again.

> *Nell O'Halloran is my best friend. I don't have a boy-*
> *friend yet. I wish I did. Nell has plenty, but she's very*
> *pretty. I'm not. I go to SWETC and I want to be an*
> *authoress, an actress, or a vet—in that order. I write a*
> *lot of stories. Do you still do that? I just had German*
> *measles and I've got a scar on my chin from scratching.*
> *I hope it's gone by the time I read this again. Do you*
> *wish you were me, nearly fourteen years old? Are you*
> *having a big birthday party with lots of boys and an*
> *iced cake with candles? Sugar's still rationed, though*
> *the war's been over for five years . . .*

She sucked the end of her pen reflectively and drew her knees up to her chest, rocking backward and forward. Nell thought she was mad not wanting to go and live in America, but who would want to live anywhere with *him?* How could her mother even *like*, yet alone *love*, such a monster . . . he was . . . gross!

A tear fell on the page, merging the O and the H in O'Halloran into a dark blot.

Life played such dirty tricks. Just when she was doing so well at school . . . just when she'd been made editor of the school magazine . . .

She heard a key turn in the front door and pushed her notebook under her pillow, blushing as she visualized the scene if her mother discovered she had written a letter to herself.

As far as her mother was concerned, it would be one more piece of evidence that she was "loony." She could almost hear her mother say with a long-suffering note, "Another nail in my coffin. Go on, Sylvie, just knock in one more nail with one more disappointment . . ."

"SYLVIE . . ." It sounded like an aria, but the reality of her mother's soaring summons cut sharply through her thoughts.

Well, her mother didn't sound unhappy. Sylvie corrected herself. Her mother sounded happy, not in a once-a-week, gin-and-tonic way. Sylvie groped for the right word. Mummy sounded ecstatic. That was ominous.

Sylvie unlatched the door to poke her head out into the five-by-six feet of space her mother referred to as the front hall, which separated the front door from her tiny bedroom, the kitchen, the "living room," her mother's bedroom, and the "front room," which was polished and vacuumed every other week but only used on Christmas Day and rare Sundays when they had visitors.

For years Sylvie had tiptoed past the room, constantly made aware by her mother that it was a room of unhappiness, terrified some unknown demon would spirit her bodily through the closed door. It had taken ages to piece all her mother's references together in order to realize it was the room where her parents had parted in anger in 1942 —"after a silly little quarrel," which to her mother's endlessly expressed regret she had never had the opportunity to make up. Peter Samuelson, Maud's young husband, had gone down with his ship soon after that forty-eight hour leave. Sylvie could hardly remember him, let alone the striking resemblance her mother insisted he'd had to Alan Ladd. Until "the monster" arrived on the scene, the tiny flat had been littered with pictures of Alan Ladd, torn out from newspapers and magazines, along with glossies from the Alan Ladd fan club her mother had joined. Now there weren't even any photographs around of her father, and all signs of Alan Ladd had also disappeared. "It isn't tactful," her mother had curtly explained, when Sylvie, knowing well the reason, felt she had to hear how her mother could explain away her treachery.

In the front hall, Sylvie found herself eye to eye with her mother. "Sylvie . . ." She could feel her mother's fingers trembling as they clutched her arm through her woolen jumper. "Sylvie . . . the date's set. Ed's asked me to marry him. We're going to be married in New York before he leaves for Korea . . ." Her mother spun her around in a crazy dance, her chignon unwinding to shower hairpins on the ground. Sylvie fought to break away, silent tears on her face. Immediately her mother saw the tears and all signs of joy disappeared from her face. Rage took its place. "You ungrateful bitch," she screamed. "After all Ed's given you—the chocolates, the nylons, the presents— you ungrateful . . ." Sylvie wrenched herself away to run back inside her bedroom, standing, heart thumping, against her locked door.

The memory of the first time she saw Technical Sergeant Edward Tramello, a security guard at the American Embassy, came with unwelcome, sickening familiarity in her mind. "One hundred, ninety-five pounds of mobile muscle reporting for duty, ma'am," he invariably said now on his arrival at 32 Osborne Road. How she loathed every ounce of him.

She'd first seen him on a bright-blue-sky Sunday, the day of rest, defined in Sylvie's mind by the gasometer's deflation at the end of their shabby street—the result, her mother had once explained with exasperation, of all the Sunday roasts being overroasted in innumerable gas ovens.

Choir practice had been unexpectedly curtailed, and Sylvie had returned home an hour early with a sense of apprehension she often felt when something unexpected happened.

She'd heard strange sounds, heavy breathing, groaning, panting, coming from her mother's bedroom.

Terrified, she'd pushed open the door, expecting to find her mother dying. At first she hadn't even comprehended what she'd seen, a sight she was now sure she would never forget.

Her beautiful mother had been sitting astride a man's lap, her back, caught in a shaft of sunlight, shining like silk; the man's hands— horrible, hairy hands—had been clutching, pulling, straining her mother toward him, his face hidden by her mother's hair that hung loose and lovely over her shoulders. Sylvie had been numb, opening her mouth with no sound coming out, quivering as they'd quivered, increasingly terrified by the tension, the sense of heat she could feel as with frenzied movements of her mother's behind she'd seemed to ride the man as if he were a horse, faster . . . faster . . . crying out urgently, "Oh God, oh God, oh God . . ." Suddenly the terrible ride had ended and—as if something had been torn out of them—their bodies had become limp and they'd clung weakly to each other.

The man had slowly raised his face to look straight in Sylvie's eyes. "What the bloody hell . . ." He'd let go of her mother so abruptly she'd fallen to the floor.

It was only then the full realization had hit Sylvie—that her mother had no clothes on. The sight of her mother's heavy, blue-veined breasts, the bush of smeared and sticky-looking black hair between plump legs, her stark nakedness, had shocked her out of her silence. She had heard herself screaming and screaming until the man—oh, how she'd hated him from the beginning—had smacked her so sharply her head had reeled back against the door.

"Ed . . ." Her mother's voice had sounded imploring, begging, all the fire Sylvie was used to hearing extinguished. "She's hysterical. Let me deal with her."

Nothing had ever been the same again. In a year, Sylvie had witnessed her mother change into a watching, waiting, hoping shadow . . . watching behind the curtains for the postman, hoping for Technical Sergeant Tramello's letters, then watching, waiting for his arrival. Now all her mother's hopes were going to be realized. She was going to become Mrs. Tramello.

Sylvie wrapped shaking arms around her chest. *She* wasn't going to become Sylvie Tramello. *She* wasn't going to New York. She couldn't, she wouldn't, live under that man's roof. Something had to happen.

She'd run away . . . hide in Nell's cupboard . . . stow away on an ocean liner. Sylvie's mind thrashed around to find a solution. One person would know what to do. Nell. She would talk it over with Nell, her best friend in all the world.

〜〜

It was an unlikely friendship—as Nell herself had pointed out. On the most wonderful afternoon of Sylvie's life, there had been a coming together of the minds in the dingy park behind the gasometer—when Nell O'Halloran, the acknowledged belle of the school, had asked her, Plain Jane also-ran, Sylvie Gertrude Samuelson, to be her best friend.

It was funny how a day could start out the same—dull, ordinary—and then, without any warning, something happened to make it the best day of your whole life.

On that special day, Sylvie remembered, she'd in fact been irritated with Nell. In typing class, Nell had deliberately stamped on her foot under the desk, making her cry out and punch the wrong typewriter keys. Despite her aggravation, she had also been flattered when she'd realized it was Nell's way of trying to get her attention to show her what she'd added to the business letter they were all typing in time to "On the Road to Mandalay" on the gramophone.

"Dear Sirs: We are in receipt of yours of the 15th instant. We wish to indicate our approval of the fact that Mr. Harold Pegler, the English master, has the hots for Miss Nell O'Halloran . . ."

Good thing old Withers, the typing mistress, had been in the process of winding up the gramophone, so she never saw a thing. Sylvie had found it impossible to concentrate after that. Later, walking home via the park with Nell—in a confused haze of pride that, for some unaccountable reason, Nell now wanted to confide in her—Sylvie had witnessed old Pegler make a fool of himself.

As usual, Nell had been followed by some of the boys from school. She knew how to handle them, ignoring their "Nellie-Bellie" cries, yet throwing devastating glances at them over her shoulder.

Sylvie had been impressed, despite blushing from a deep-seated sense of embarrassment.

Pegler had suddenly turned up, obviously furious with the boys, telling them to report to him at 8:00 A.M. the next morning.

Nell had handled that well, too, looking up at Pegler as if he were her savior, until Sylvie could see the man practically drooling with longing and lust.

It had been disgusting, but who could blame Pegler, or any man for that matter, wanting to get close to Nell?

It was a miracle, a bloody miracle, her mother said from time to time, that an old man like O'Halloran and his wizened little wife could have produced a raving beauty like Nell with her huge wistful green eyes, skin the color of magnolias, and glorious black hair, which even in two pigtails down her back was incredibly glossy and alluring.

The day Sylvie saw the look of abject devotion on Pegler's face and heard him say, "Oh sweet, lovely Nell, what am I going to do about you?" was also the day Nell had confessed what a miserable, straight-

laced life her parents forced her to lead. "I don't have a fraction of the
freedom you have," she'd told Sylvie, batting her eyelashes dramatically.

Her parents were so old . . . so old-fashioned. Nell had sat tearing
her handkerchief with frustration. "I'm in trouble even if I say hello
to the milkman!"

From then on, Sylvie had become a willing accomplice to Nell's
escapades, thrilled that God had singled her out to help, knowing with
satisfaction as time went by how much Nell depended on her. She
had become adept at providing Nell with imaginative alibis when she
wanted to go to the pictures with Bernie Trevis or George Bonnett.
What was the harm, in that?

Already in their forties when Nell was born, the O'Hallorans had
always guarded their beautiful daughter like a national treasure. Sylvie's appearance as Nell's "best friend" had come as a godsend, for
who wouldn't trust a girl with such honest, direct eyes, who blushed
when anyone took the trouble to compliment her on her warm, if
toothy, smile?

Who could doubt a youngster who rushed like a friendly puppy to
everyone's aid? They overlooked her clumsy side that toppled side
tables and knocked over lamps. Instead they were more and more
appreciative of Sylvie's patience, as she unscrambled the tangles in
Mama O'Halloran's embroidery silks and read the small print in the
newspaper to Pa O'Halloran when he mislaid his glasses, which was
almost a daily occurrence.

They soon treated Sylvie like "a member of the family," as Mr.
O'Halloran said. It made her squirm, particularly when she learned
Nell wasn't going to the pictures with Bernie or George but with old
man Pegler.

"I can't keep covering up for you, Nellie," Sylvie had told her
guiltily. "It isn't right. You're going to get yourself in trouble. I don't
know what you see in the old creep anyway . . ."

Nell had leaned back against a dead tree trunk, trying—as Sylvie
now knew so well—to look like an innocent babe in the woods. "I
think it's his voice," she'd said. "He makes me feel all funny inside
when he starts quoting poetry."

In a second, Nell's mood had changed. She'd yanked Sylvie's arm
fiercely. "He says he'll help me get a job on *Woman's Own* if I go up
to the West End with him one night to meet the editor. But you know
my dad will never let me . . ." Sylvie had tried to shut her ears to what

she knew was coming next. She hated the idea of lying to Nell's parents if Nell was going to waste her time with Pegler.

Seeing Sylvie's set expression, again Nell's mood had changed and she'd wheedled: "If I show you something, will you swear on our blood pact you'll never tell a living soul?"

Sylvie had stared ahead, a flush flooding from her collarbone to her neck and over her face, making it blotchy, fiery. She loathed the blood pact, which had been all Nell's idea.

"I don't need any blood pact not to tell. You know I never tell anybody anything you say," she'd mumbled. Nell had ignored her, searching inside her satchel to find her sewing kit. She had extracted a small pair of scissors and without speaking, as Sylvie had known she would, had stabbed them quickly into the cushion of her third finger, looking with fascination as a trickle of blood appeared.

Sylvie never understood why she felt compelled to cooperate, but she always did. She'd put out her finger, screwing her eyes tightly shut as Nell stabbed it. That wasn't the worst part. As usual, Nell had rubbed their fingers—their blood—together, then closed her hot little mouth around Sylvie's finger to suck away her blood!

Sighing, Sylvie had followed suit, sucking away Nell's blood as it had trickled from her finger onto her palm.

"Open your eyes. How can I show you something with your eyes shut, you silly twit." Nell had laughed shrilly—overexcited as she always was over the blood pact.

Sylvie had felt unclean, but Nell had this strange power over her—she had to admit it, reminding herself she was lucky to be that close to such an outstanding human being.

Nell had flung her head forward, one plait loosening from its clip to spill a cloud of dark hair toward the ground. On the back of Nell's neck Sylvie had seen a vivid mauve bruise.

"What is it?" Her stomach had knotted up with an unknown fear, while Nell had burst out laughing. "Don't you recognize it, you silly twit . . ."

She'd been so angry. "How can I know what it is? What have you been up to now?"

Nell had started to laugh so hard it had been difficult to understand her. "I didn't get 'up' to anything," she'd stressed the word deliberately, "but _he_ did." Seeing Sylvie's unhappy expression, she'd suddenly become serious. "It's a medieval sign of love, a poet's kiss, the secret sign of a man's hopeless passion . . ." She'd paused, waiting for

Sylvie's reaction, but Sylvie had refused to react, staring woodenly ahead, longing for the revelation to be over and done with.

Nell had stretched out the moment, arching back against the tree trunk. "It's a . . . love bite, Sylvie. Harry Pegler's love bite. It hurt but it was de-li-ci-ous." She'd poked her tongue out like a cat and rolled her shoulders suggestively.

It had been their first major quarrel, for, furious and upset, Sylvie had told Nell then and there that she was on a downhill path and that she, Sylvie Samuelson, did not intend to follow her there. But she could never stay angry with Nell for long. Nell's eyes only had to fill with tears and Sylvie immediately felt like a clumsy, unappreciative ox, insensitive to a wonderful wild spirit who, surely, deserved to be treated differently from anyone else.

~~~

Just as Sylvie expected, Nell had a solution. Even as Nell shook her head disbelievingly and muttered, "You must be out of your tiny asphalt mind, not wanting to go to New York," Sylvie felt her anxiety start to drain away in the silence of her friend's home.

The orderliness, cleanliness, and calm of the O'Halloran house always soothed her. She loved the fact that no doors were allowed to bang and no one screamed out names. Even Nell moved more quietly when she was home. Sylvie loved the whiteness of the linen table-cloth, scrupulously, almost invisibly, darned. The first time she'd been invited to tea, she'd even envied Nell because the neat crustless sandwiches, never overbuttered or sloppy, carried little flags to announce their contents—fish paste, cheese, and (that day) chicken spread.

Sylvie's mother did not believe in tea as a meal. Sandwiches were fattening, she often pointed out, eyeing Sylvie's boyish shape with suspicion, adding that as Sylvie was no beauty she could never afford to gain an extra ounce. It was an edict Sylvie had always accepted as being for her own good, supporting her mother's dislike of preparing anything to eat. Until she started going regularly to the O'Hallorans' she had never noticed the lack of food in their own larder—a situation that had begun to change after Technical Sergeant Tramello's arrival on the scene.

"It's a pity we can't change places." Nell wasn't joking. Sylvie knew Nell would have jumped at the chance to go to the States in her place.

It was ironic, because Sylvie wouldn't have minded living with the

O'Hallorans either, looking after them, doing their shopping, cleaning out the grate in exchange for Nell's room with its shiny linoleum, white-painted furniture, rosebud-printed curtains, and the cozy chair by the window, perfect for looking out at the stars. It was a beautiful but useless thought.

Once Nell finished berating her for "being so daft," she got down to business, as Sylvie knew she would, calmly and efficiently weighing the facts. Sylvie didn't want to go and Nell really didn't want her to go either . . . for what would she do without her? Nell told Sylvie to go downstairs and "check out the old folks." Sylvie was often shocked at the way Nell referred to her doting parents, but there was nothing she could do to change her, and deep down she was sure Nell really worshiped them. It was just that they put too much of a brake on her, which made Nell balk.

The following day, the two girls caught a number 38 bus to the home of Sylvie's Aunt Gert. Nell had decided that Gert (the younger sister of Sylvie's mother) would make the perfect chaperone for Sylvie when her mother left for the States with Ed—"until we leave school and you and I get a bed-sit together, when I get a super job on *Woman's Own*."

They giggled and screamed over the five-year plan Nell outlined as they bused, skipped, ran, and walked with their arms around each other from E.10 to E.6, oblivious to the dreary, nondescript, and identical East London streets, lost in a world of make-believe.

Only a headline on a billboard brought Sylvie back to reality and the purpose of their visit: "Korea . . . UN Forces Recapture Seoul from the Communists . . . Read All about It."

Korea. It was a foreign name that had become sickeningly familiar in recent days. To Sylvia, "Korea" stood for "Technical Sergeant Tramello," who was urgently waiting to join the "real action." Once the summons came, Ed would have a seven-day leave, after which Sylvie and her mother would be shipped out of the country with him. "As part of his chattels," Sylvie had told Nell despairingly. Her mother's wedding dress had been purchased, and many of her favorite clothes and pieces of furniture were already packed to be shipped to Patchogue, which was the part of New York that was Technical Sergeant Tramello's own and the place where his family of fine, Italian stock were apparently just longing to give his "lovely bride and her little gal a fine welcome . . ."

Sylvie doubted the welcome really included her. "There's never been a time we haven't had a fight," she'd told Nell, trying to make her understand for the hundredth time why the thought of leaving England to live under Tramello's roof was such a horrendous idea, "and my ma always sides with him, never me."

She didn't know how to explain to Nell the revulsion Tramello evoked in her when she saw his arm around her mother's waist, his hand on her mother's leg with his fingertips just edging under her skirt or, worse, familiarly holding her breast as if it belonged to him. She didn't know how to tell Nell about the nights she stuffed cotton wool in her ears trying to block out sounds from her mother's bedroom that were now all too familiar, bringing back the memory of her mother's heaving buttocks clutched by those horrible hairy hands. She didn't tell Nell because Nell probably understood what it all meant, whereas she didn't.

Aunt Gert had just started to work at Boots the Chemists in the makeup section, and Sylvie had been proud to see how quickly Nell had taken to her on their first meeting. Gert wasn't exactly pretty, but as Sylvie knew and was thrilled to hear Nell exclaim, "She's got style, that aunt of yours, real style."

Within minutes of their arrival, Nell asked, as she had done before, if she could "take a look" at the jars of cream on Aunt Gert's dressing table in the bedroom, trying out the lipsticks there, the powder in a pink box, as excited as a child in a sweet shop. As Sylvie well knew, Pa O'Halloran had threatened to wash Nell's mouth out with soap if he ever suspected a lipstick came near it.

It was only when the jam tarts came out with the silver-plated teapot that Nell seemed to remember why they were there and said all the things Sylvie couldn't say for herself.

Gert was silent. Sylvie didn't mind; she knew her silence was her aunt's way of sorting things out. Gert was the opposite of her mother, Maud, who never seemed to think before she spoke.

After about ten minutes, when she still hadn't made one comment and went to the kitchen to boil more water for the tea, Nell couldn't stand the suspense. Despite Sylvie trying to stop her, she went after Gert. They soon both came back beaming. The deal was done: Aunt Gert was going to intercede on Sylvie's behalf and "talk to Maud to see if you can't stay behind with me."

There were many arguments Gert intended to use, but when it came to it she wasn't surprised to find she didn't need one. She'd known for a long time Sylvie was a disappointment to her elder sister, but then Gert knew Maud felt her whole life had been a series of disappointments.

Maud had fancied herself an opera singer. She could still hit a high C with some accuracy, but she had never been able to make a career of it. "Not enough tenacity," in Gert's opinion, although to be fair, she accepted that Pete's death in the war had knocked her sister back for a long while, particularly since Gert knew that he and Maud had had such a row the day he left. Gert understood only too well the joylessness Maud had been living with. It took every bit of stuffing out of you. She'd been through it herself over a man. In her opinion it just wasn't worth getting too close to a man, any man. Here was Maud willing to try again, and good luck to her, but that didn't mean little Sylvie had to suffer. Such a sensitive, imaginative little girl, in love with books ever since she'd been old enough to hold one. Maud had never understood that. According to her, Sylvie was an impossible dreamer who scribbled rubbish in her exercise book when she could have gone dancing at the local tech, or who holed herself up in the local library with the old classics—Mary Webb, Jane Austen, all the Brontës. "She'll end up an old maid," Maud had said, as usual without thinking about what she was saying or to whom she was saying it. In a funny way—because it was Maud letting it all pour out—Gert hadn't minded her tactlessness. Gert was unmarried and getting on for thirty, but she knew she'd still sooner be alone than with the wrong man. Big Ed would certainly have been wrong for *her*. She could understand that Sylvie didn't want to get under his one-hundred-and-ninety-five-pound tread.

When Nell's parents made it clear how unhappy they were that her sensible friend and advisor was about to be whisked away, Nell announced grandly what she had achieved. ". . . And there's general relief all around: Sylvie's Mum and Ed are going off to live happily ever after in Patchogue, New York, but Sylvie's staying behind in England with Aunt Gert."

"Patchogue's just like Chelsea, ma'am," Ed had told an intensely curious Nell, "except instead of good old Father Thames, it's on the edge of Great South Bay . . ." More than that geographical detail he hadn't been willing to divulge, not even to a humdinger of a bird like Nell. Wow! What a body the young kid had, the Technical Sarge thought as he spoke; it was difficult not to get a hard-on just looking at her tits, even in her school uniform.

There were no tears, no recriminations the day Maud flew off with her fiancé, bound for Idlewild, and then to Patchogue, New York, and a new life in what Maud had learned was known as the Tramello Compound. There were too many hangovers in evidence after the farewell party at the local pub the night before. Nobody seemed well enough even to comment further on the behavior of Sylvie's best friend, Nell O'Halloran, and Technical Sergeant Tramello's boss, the dashing Captain Browne, who'd originally said he was only going to stay to wish the happy pair all the best in the world.

At midnight, to Sylvie's embarrassment, Nell's father had turned up to find out why Nell hadn't met her unusually lenient eleven-o'clock curfew. Nell had been nowhere to be found until Sylvie, anxious and apprehensive, heard her giggles coming from the lavatory behind the downstairs bar. "Nell . . . Nell, your dad's here . . . come to collect you," she'd whispered. There had been rustling, low voices, hiccups, more giggles. "I'm coming, Sylv . . . try to hold the fort." Out Nell had tumbled, barefoot, her lipstick smeared, the strap of her dress broken, followed by the captain, who on arrival had had such urgent business to attend to. Coolly, calmly he had been fastening his fly, all the while smiling at Sylvie as if to say, "Do you want some of the same?"

If Nell hadn't thrown her arms around the captain in full view of everyone when her father made it clear it was time to leave, it wouldn't have been so bad. Instead, it had turned into a terrible scene with old man O'Halloran trying to pull Nell away while Nell hung on to the American with her mouth, her arms, with every bit of her.

Aunt Gert told Sylvie to stop fretting over Nell's tarnished reputation. "It's already yesterday's news. Who cares what the neighbors think? Girls are only young once."

That evening, settling down happily with her precious books arranged on a new shelf in Aunt Gert's spare room, Sylvie found the letter she had started to write to herself, "to be opened when you're twenty-one."

When she had started the letter, autumn leaves had covered the ground and life had been full of dark uncertainties. Now it was nearly spring and, with Nell's help—Nell, the best friend anyone could possibly have—her problems were over. Sylvie felt safe and secure with Aunt Gert.

She only had a couple more years of school—not even that—and then she could start on her chosen career in journalism.

Journalism. It was a magic word and the route many of her favorite authors had taken early in life.

How to start? Where to go? *Woman's Own* with Harry Pegler's help?

Even Nell was bored with him now, although to hear her talk of him no one would ever guess it—least of all poor Pegler.

Sylvie picked up the new pen Aunt Gert had given her on her birthday and started to finish the letter.

> *A lot has happened since I wrote the last sentence. Mum's gone off to be married in America to Technical Sergeant Ed Tramello before he leaves for Korea. I don't like him, but I hope for Mum's sake he doesn't get killed. I'm living with Aunt Gert now at 10 Downton Street, Hackney Wick. No, not Downing Street, although maybe I'll go there one day to interview the prime minister, whom I hope will be Winston Churchill . . . if he's still alive when I'm twenty-one. My very best friend Nell has had her first proposal, though she's not yet sixteen. It's a secret, but as no one is going to see this letter except me, I'll write it down. It's from our English master, Harry Pegler, who's at least twenty years older (looks a hundred!). His wife died (no wonder) and he's got a daughter who's got a face, Nell says, like a rabbit. I hope she doesn't accept. I hope I'm in Fleet Street when I next read this.*
>
> *Love,*
> *Sylvie Gertrude Samuelson,*
> *fourteen years, five months.*

3

London, E.C.4.,
March 8, 1954

LOVE BY A TEENAGER

It's exciting . . . exhilarating . . . ecstatic . . .
exasperating . . . and, well, really extraordinary how *everything* changes about life
when . . .

It was like reading a love letter. It was more thrilling than the
moment she'd seen "A plus" on her English matriculation paper.
Reading it for the sixth time was as deliciously self-indulgent as the
evenings she ate chocolate fudge and curled up in Aunt Gert's only
comfortable armchair with a book by Simone de Beauvoir, her
current favorite author. Sylvie was so suffused with joy—a joy she
knew she had to hide—that it came out involuntarily, physically,
in a breathy sigh as once again she took a surreptitious look at her
first article in print. She could still hardly believe that *her* thoughts,
her words were there for all London to see on page ten of one of
England's most successful newspapers.

As she was about to open her desk drawer farther, where she'd
folded page ten of the first edition to show only her article, she felt
a tap on her arm.

The detested familiar blush made its way from her collarbone to
her hairline.

"Congrats, puss . . ."

Was she blushing because she'd been caught reading her own
article? Or was she blushing because it was Dick Kolinzcky who'd

25

caught her at it? Whatever the reason, she felt the redness spread across her skin like a disfiguring disease. She bent her head down, willing the color to subside.

"Kitty's back." He was gone before she could even give him a grateful nod. It was embarrassing that Dick had seen her reveling in her own success, small as it was. It would have been infinitely more humiliating if her boss, Kitty, had seen her. Sylvie smiled her little catlike smile, not aware she was hugging herself, a habit since childhood. She wouldn't allow anything or anyone—not even Kitty—to spoil this day of days. No, not even a hundred-percent genuine tantrum from a Kitty Stein three sheets to the wind after an alcoholic lunch at the Ivy was going to lower her spirits—or had Kitty gone with Smith Maynard to the Cock Tavern today? Then Kitty would be someone to deal with! Smith Maynard always put her in the foulest mood. Sylvie pushed all thoughts of fame and glory out of her mind and tried to concentrate on deciphering her shorthand.

In the year since she'd heard of and, with little effort, landed a job in the typing pool at the *Mirror*'s Readers' Service Department, Sylvie felt like Cinderella before midnight.

From the day she'd arrived at the drafty, grim box of a building in Back Hill, off the Clerkenwell Road, she'd been in paradise—as she frequently told Aunt Gert.

She had been intoxicated by the smell of the newsprint, packed bale upon bale right up to the ceilings. She was thrilled to be typing on paper headed *Daily Mirror* or *Evening Mirror*—depending on the problem. In her imagination she was typing hot copy to be delivered to the printer. Halfway through a boring, routine letter on rates or rents she would be daydreaming of great things for herself. It was hinted that Hugh Bartholomew, the omnipotent *Mirror* Group Chairman, had once been the office boy. But had he had a gasometer almost in his garden? One could willingly start at the bottom, Sylvie reckoned, if there was a top-class background to go home to every night.

From the beginning, she had been determined to be transferred out of the typing pool one day to work at Geraldine House, a mile or so away, the real home and heart of the *Mirror* group where she'd first been interviewed. She longed to be part of the unholy clamor made by the rat-a-tat-tat of innumerable typewriter keys, the rasping yells of "boy!" made by (mostly) unshaven men with (mostly) their shirtsleeves rolled up and—this had particularly thrilled her—eyeshades clamped to (mostly) scowling foreheads. In the distance she had heard the heavenly sound of the big press—Big Bertha, she'd heard someone call it—disgorging the end result of all the talent gathered under one roof.

And it hadn't taken that long for her to make the switch from the "back of beyond" Back Hill to "GH" as the HQ was called by its inhabitants.

Now she caught a number 6 bus from Hackney Wick every weekday morning. It was a journey of enchantment, through the financial old City of London, past St. Paul's Cathedral, down Ludgate Hill to Ludgate Circus, into skinny, scintillating Fleet Street, England's "street of ink."

The first morning on the way to "GH" the sun had been out and the huge black glasshouse of the *Daily Express* had glittered like the Wizard of Oz's palace and Sylvie was Judy Garland as she'd jumped off the bus to turn right to trip up the Yellow Brick Road, which was really Fetter Lane, to the *Mirror's* HQ.

It had taken six months to be exact—six months of taking dreary dictation from the *Mirror's* group of "experts," who answered readers' letters on subjects as varied as how to increase the size of tomatoes growing in what had been wartime garden allotments, to how to grow eyebrows faster, to where to go to learn French in a hurry.

After four months Sylvie had been promoted to join the select group known as "fillers-in," shorthand typists or secretary substitutes. It was a job that meant not only filling in at the *Daily Mirror* but at the *Mirror's* sister papers—the *Evening Mirror*, the *Sunday Pictorial*, and the weekend *Reveille*.

As Sylvie confided to her diary, "Filling in is really like fitting into Cinderella's glass slipper." She had spent two weeks as secretary to the celebrated sports editor of the *Sunday Pictorial*, endearing herself to him in only one day, making endless cups of tea, answering everyone's phone efficiently, and not muddling up the cricket scores phoned in from Australia—as the sports head's real secretary apparently tended to do.

As Sylvie told Aunt Gert, it didn't seem like real life at all, receiving a telephone call from the other side of the world. She had cried when the two weeks were up, although the fellows had sworn on their *Sunday Pictorial* sports caps they would refuse to consider any other filler-in when next the department became shorthanded.

After two days back at Back Hill, she'd been sent over to the *Mirror's* main darkroom, where the cameramen deposited their film to be developed. That hadn't been much fun. The man in charge was "a lech . . . watch out," she'd been told the first day by the about-to-vacation receptionist whose place she was taking for a week. "He'll try to pull your drawers down in the darkroom, but give him a kick and he'll stop." She had been so naive, so anxious to please, she hadn't even translated "drawers" to "knickers" until she'd felt loathsome fingers quick as a flash up her skirt and onto her camiknicker buttons when "the boss" asked her to bring in some film and "shut the door quick, my girl, or you'll be in for it." As she was momentarily blinded, her knickers were, sure enough, opened and his fingers were incredibly about to penetrate her private place when reflexively she'd lashed out, landing a lucky blow right to his solar plexus. She'd heard his muttered curse as he'd bent over, and she was out the door and the building "on the double." Aunt Gert had wanted to complain, but Sylvie had insisted she could handle it herself, although she hardly believed it. Cinderella's luck had been hers. The next day and all week, the dreaded lech had "phoned in sick with the flu," and a timid little man whose only vice was a day-long addiction to boiled sweets had taken his place.

By the time Nell dramatically announced she was "giving up Harry Pegler—one look at his father showed me what I had to look forward to—ugh"—Sylvie had, after four filling-in jobs, already gained the reputation of being a quick study and the most efficient filler-in of all.

The day the formidable, famous Kitty Stein, originator, heart, mind, and guts behind the wildly successful "Heart to Heart with Kit Carson" column, commandeered Sylvie's services sine die was the day Nell joined the Back Hill typing pool, sure from Sylvie's meteoric moves, she could do "even better, faster."

Kitty liked using a smattering of Latin in her column to give it "a bit of class," and it was she who explained to Sylvie that "sine die" meant she could stay at Geraldine House indefinitely—as long as she pleased her new boss.

"I'm no longer a filler-in and I've never been so happy. Thank you so much, Mum, for letting me stay behind with Aunt Gert," Sylvie dutifully wrote her mother in the States. She'd spent a few minutes wondering whether she should add a postscript and then, pressing her pen into the paper with intensity, wrote "perhaps one day you'll be proud of me after all."

She didn't tell her mother she'd turned down another job, as shorthand typist in the dispatch department of the publishers of *Hymns: Ancient and Modern*. It wasn't the hymns, but the word *publish* that had motivated her to try for that particular position, offering two pounds more than the three guineas offered by the *Evening Mirror*. She knew her mother would have been horrified by her lack of economic sense. She felt she had to tell the truth to Aunt Gert, who thankfully not only didn't mind her not telling her mother but actively forbade her to mention it.

Gert already sensed from Maud's infrequent letters that she was suffering from yet another "disappointment." Life in the Tramello Compound had not turned out to be a jolly bowl of pasta. Another crushing blow. Patchogue hadn't turned out to be New York City, either—or even an easy, near-at-hand suburb. It was sixty long miles away and "bears as much resemblance to Chelsea as Southend-on-Sea," Maud had scrawled on a postcard of a dreary-looking clam-digger, looking out at Great South Bay.

As Gert reasoned, money alone could never put the radiant smile she saw on Sylvie's face every morning, even Monday mornings. There were, God knew, few enough human beings in their hard-pressed, hard-up neck of the woods who actually looked forward to going to work as Sylvie did. So what if she only earned a pittance? She was exactly where she longed to be—and Gert, certain life would have some tough knocks in store for her sweet-natured but scarcely beautiful niece, was determined to let her enjoy her work as much as she could while she could—for who knew how long it would last? If she didn't get married—and there weren't any boyfriends on the horizon —Gert worried Sylvie would have to work for her living, just like Gert herself. If she could actually *enjoy* her work, then that was better than nothing.

Nell called Sylvie's determination to become indispensable to Kitty Stein "groveling," but for once Sylvie didn't care what Nell thought.

For some reason she wasn't afraid of Kitty as most of the other underlings were—and even some of the reporters and feature writers, too. Although Kitty let loose at her with a harangue once or twice a week, there was never any real heat in them. It was as if they shared an unspoken conspiracy—that in order to survive in the Fleet Street jungle, Kitty had to act like a prima donna, but as far as Sylvie was concerned, Kitty really didn't mean what she often felt she had to say.

"You're okay, kid," Kitty had told her once or twice, the only kind of compliment Kitty ever uttered. It was enough for Sylvie—"okay" meant "sine die." She could become a fixture in the "Heart to Heart" department, providing she continued to do as she was doing.

Even trivial things impressed Sylvie: a giant-sized coffee cup, for instance, belonging to the chief subeditor's secretary, Joanne, who had her name painted on it in bright blue letters. Joanne was a sunny person, liaising perfectly with the rest of the staff, placating those who protested that their "best lines had been subbed out"—cut—protecting her boss from the most vociferous. Sylvie stared at the "chief" whenever she was sure he wouldn't notice. He satisfied all her ideas as to how a newspaper chief should behave, shouting instructions into the phone, pushing his glasses forever onto his head, chainsmoking, sweating, growling.

"Gimme the lead letters . . ." Kitty didn't need to speak to announce her arrival in the glassed-off partition that was physical proof of her column's success and her eminence among the other "ink-stained wretches," as she liked to describe her colleagues in the largely unpartitioned newsroom. A strong gust of Shalimar perfume came in with her, as much a part of Kitty's "chic" as the snoods she invariably wore to the office, "to keep the hair right for the night," and the long fur tippet which, wrapped twice around her long neck, ended down her back in a fox's head with particularly vicious-looking eyes.

Sylvie passed Kitty a wire basket containing five or six letters. She'd quickly learned to cull what Kitty wanted from the hundreds arriving at the office every week. Lead letters had to be *provocative*, which meant *worth printing*; accompanied by Kitty's pungent, often unbridled answers, they would provoke a new deluge of letters, both for and against Kitty's advice, as well as letters from readers who thought they had exactly the same problems. When Sylvie pointed out how few people really had similar problems Kitty would snort and say— ambiguously as far as Sylvie was concerned—"Readers don't read!"

One of Sylvie's most important jobs was to keep count of the letters and in some way prove, no matter how many actually arrived, each month there was a ten- to fifteen-percent increase in volume. Kitty used this information in what Sylvie considered to be a masterpiece of a monthly memo to demonstrate how indispensable she was to the paper's continued prosperity.

"Controversy is grist to the mill," Kitty continually rammed home to Sylvie, pointing out that the more waves Kit Carson could whip up in the blue-collar readership—usually a sluggish sea of indifference—

the more Smith Maynard, the rakish features editor, would respect her and "build" her space.

"Any unmarried mothers, beaten wives, or won't-get-out-of-bed-sons?" Kitty lit a black cigarette and perched on Sylvie's desk.

"Yes, on top. An unmarried mother . . . she was in a convent. It's a beaut." It had taken Sylvie only a week or two to grasp the kind of letters Kitty was looking for in her mail. Privately, Sylvie knew she would never be able to assess letters with Kitty's cool disdain. Her stomach ached over some of them. She empathized with the lonely wallflowers, the unrequited lovers, the abandoned and seemingly hopeless. "You'll toughen up," Kitty would say, flicking cigarette ash onto a letter already smudged, Sylvie was sure, with the writer's poignant tears.

If she wasn't "toughening up," she was certainly learning fast about life. Too fast, Aunt Gert thought when, blushing and stuttering, going around the subject in circles, Sylvie tried to find out if Gert had ever heard of a man making love to another man and—worse—a woman loving another woman. How she'd hoped her aunt would agree with her—that Kitty's reaction to a letter received that morning had been the result of Kitty's overactive imagination. To Sylvie's horror, Gert had confirmed Kitty's carelessly tossed-off explanation. "Can't use it, it's from a fairy—homosexual—watch out for this kind of kinky sex letter, Sylvie. We can't risk being banned in Birmingham," Kitty had said.

Fairy! For weeks Sylvie couldn't get the word, with its new connotation, out of her mind.

Kitty often told her that "Heart to Heart with Kit Carson" had to stand for "good, clean sex." It was a mandate Sylvie initially found totally confusing, as Kitty came up with a headline like "Dirty Young Man" to accompany a salvo let loose on behalf of a new bride who, signing herself "Bewildered," sought advice on how to stop her nineteen-year-old husband from looking at other girls' bosoms and legs.

Nineteen years old! Sylvie could hardly believe she was almost in her nineteenth year herself.

She was choked with a mixture of envy and frustration when she read about the overnight success of another nineteen-year-old across the English Channel in France, Françoise Sagan, whose just-published *Bonjour Tristesse* was acclaimed as a runaway best seller, with film rights already sold.

What was wrong with her, that she couldn't write a word, let alone a book or best seller? When she got home at night her head was buzzing with readers' letters she knew could easily make dramatic plots. It wasn't as if she wasted time with a boyfriend, let alone a husband.

Although she knew it worried Aunt Gert, she really didn't want either—except on rare occasions when she ran across a school friend who asked her to admire a one-carat engagement ring or saw Dick Kolinzcky, the copy boy across the newsroom, chatting up Blondie, a pert, pretty typist whose sweaters outlined every ounce of her soft breasts.

"Stop mooning over that cheeky Czech. He's a nothing, a nobody." Kitty would break into her thoughts, and guiltily Sylvie would race her fingers over the typewriter keys.

Kitty said she had no time for men—yet she certainly spent enough time with them. How she had time to fit everything in never ceased to amaze Sylvie. Kitty was a daily lesson in organization, positive proof that time could be utilized to do more and more.

As Kitty told her one day, in a rare confiding mood, she even wrote an occasional column in Hebrew for the _Hebrew Times_, a column nobody at the _Evening Mirror_ knew anything about.

"Moonlighting," she laughingly explained.

It was another meaningful word Sylvie added to her rapidly increasing vocabulary, extra meaningful because it stood for extra money, something Sylvie was beginning to realize she badly needed. The whole idea of moonlighting increased Kitty's aura of success and added to Kitty's influence over her. To be paid for what one loved to do was all part of living in paradise. To be paid really well—not just three guineas a week—was so incredibly joyous Sylvie found it hard to contemplate.

There was nothing "cute" or attractive about her occasionally dropped "aitch," a definite sign she came from London's East End, the wrong side of the tracks.

For the first time she heard words and phrases that told of a style of life totally different from the one she was used to: "first night" . . . "cocktail party" . . . "fork supper," and of course, "lunch" for the midday meal and "dinner" for the meal after six. She still occasionally slipped up and called lunch "dinner," which raised an eyebrow or two, especially as her packet of sandwiches could hardly be called a meal, let alone dinner.

She didn't compare backgrounds in terms of money. She wasn't interested in amassing money. She _needed_ money to _spend_—on books, on clothes, and makeup—in order to deal with the fame she was determined to achieve. She already believed that writers, however successful, were unlikely to be rich, although she also knew successful writers never starved, because they were lionized and idolized.

She began to realize she was considered an oddity, because of her obvious ambition to work, to write.

The other girls in the office made no secret of the fact that they were only killing time with shorthand and typing until they found husbands to take care of them in the proper fashion.

In London in the 1950s, on both the wrong and right sides of the track, unless a girl wanted to be in show business—and, of course, wanted to be a STAR—the only well-understood ambition, particularly for someone like Sylvie with no money, no background, and not much education, was to be married. To become a wife was the only approved way to leave home and parents—to cut out—and sometimes move up a notch in the world.

Sylvie looked up one morning to see Nell—at Back Hill only two months—reporting for duty to the features editor, Smith Maynard, the man everyone said would one day be the youngest editor-in-chief in Fleet Street. Even in her sensible gray suit and ladylike white gloves, Nell looked like "somebody." Sylvie didn't even bother to ask how Nell had catapulted herself into such a fantastic spot. Nell was more beautiful than any pinup gracing the *Evening Mirror*'s page two. And she was not only beautiful, but also exceptionally brainy.

Sylvie stared into space, remembering that Nell had matriculated with honors, although she'd hardly studied for the grueling exams at all, frequently climbing out of her bedroom window for trysts with Harry Pegler when she was supposed to be swotting. Nell was a genius. No wonder Smith Maynard, the boy wonder of Fleet Street, had discovered her so soon. It took one to know one.

One summer evening when the pavements were so hot they scorched their way through Sylvie's thin soles, she saw Nell, her glorious black hair tied back with a big floppy ribbon, being ushered into a bright-red sports car. Sylvie did a double take. It looked like . . . could it be? Yes, Nell confided dreamily the next day. It actually had been Errol Flynn!

Where did they go? What on earth was Nell up to now? Was she about to become a film star? In her most aggravating mood Nell shook her head. "I can't tell even you, Sylvie." Her green eyes fastened on Sylvie intently. "You just wouldn't understand."

Sylvie was furious, but not jealous. How could she be jealous when she knew there was no way _she_ could cope with Errol Flynn for even a second, let alone the hours she was sure Nell had spent with him.

"What time did you get home? Did _he_ take you home?" Sylvie had visions of old man O'Halloran fainting on his doorstep as the sleek car arrived with such a celebrity behind the wheel. "How did you meet him?"

Nell laughed an infuriating light tinkle of a laugh. "I'll tell you on your birthday, Sylvie, when you're a whole year older."

"Oh, go and jump in the lake. I'm not that interested."

She _was_ interested in Dick Kolinzcky though—more and more so as she shyly accepted his invitations to have coffee at Jimmy's Sandwich Shop. She would choose coffee with Dick over a fast ride with Errol Flynn any day. She tried to figure out what it was she saw in someone Kitty always dismissed either as a "nothing" or "that wild Czech gypsy."

His hair was too long. He was very dark-skinned and she had to admit he wasn't good-looking in a conventional sense but, Sylvie sighed as she wrote in her diary late at night, "We're linked by something more important than looks. We're linked by our ambition." She'd soon discovered Dick's was as large and as hungry as her own.

"Did you read this?" He'd pushed an unfamiliar pink-colored newspaper in front of her the evening before. The _Financial Times_. "Can you believe such a brilliant idea, yet so simple . . ."

She'd tried to be enthusiastic over the article about an American publisher named Walter Annenberg, who'd just started a pocket-sized weekly called _TV Guide_ that carried nothing but program listings. She couldn't grasp why Dick thought it showed such brilliance. He had stressed that Annenberg had bought out many small publishers who already had TV listings in various American cities, and so had ten regional editions to start with. "No wonder his circulation is already nearly two million. He had a million and a half by the end of the first year. He can't fail. You only have to compare how many TV sets there were before the war, just after the war, and now . . ."

He hadn't expected her to answer. He _had_ the answers, all of them, which he'd supplied at breakneck speed. He'd then shown her pages of figures he had worked on to prove where _TV Guide_ was likely to be in a decade. It had all been very impressive, but she hadn't been able to see how it was going to help Dick in his plan to build what he called a "conglomeration of companies, each contributing to the others' growth . . ." particularly when after their third coffee date she learned that he, as a copy boy, earned little more than she did.

"He's a loser. Don't waste your time with losers," Kitty told her sharply as she picked up and read without compunction a badly spelled note from Dick inviting Sylvie to queue up for "the theater . . . a seat in the gods to see Eric Portman in *Seperet Tables* after work on Friday."

"For God's sake, Sylvie, he can't even spell!"

Blushing, Sylvie looked straight ahead and muttered, "He's Czech . . . he's only learning to spell English now."

Kitty ignored her, not altering her tone as she read aloud a reader's letter on ghastly violet-colored writing paper, then said in a bored voice, "How can we cope with this man with his attraction to women in see-through plastic macs? The drop-dead basket, don't you think?"

Sylvie took the letter as if it were poison and dropped it quickly in the wastepaper basket. How dare Kitty talk about Dick in the same breath as a pervert! Whatever anyone said, she *was* going to queue up with Dick for a "seat in the gods," as he had described it. So Nell had already seen *Separate Tables* from the stalls with one of her admirers. Who cared? A bird's-eye view of London's historic St. James's stage with Dick holding her hand was all she wanted.

She was so nervous all day Friday that she kept running to the ladies' room on the fourth floor. She couldn't think what was wrong with her. It was her first real date with Dick, but why couldn't she take it in her stride? Why couldn't she be like Nell—cool, calm, and collected, handling several dates a week? Why did she feel so flustered and—worst of all—why on earth were her waterworks so affected?

She knew she'd put on too much lipstick, that her hair was straggly because she'd combed it too much, but when she finally met Dick as planned outside Swan & Edgar's at Piccadilly Circus and he tucked her arm through his, everything started to get back to normal.

He himself looked tidier, more grown-up. She was proud of the masterful way he escorted her across the busy streets, felt she was singing inside when, maneuvering her through the crowded foyer of the theater, he put his arm firmly around her waist. At the top of the theater—"in the gods," the cheapest seats jammed tightly together—Sylvie was forcibly aware of Dick's presence. He's so close, she thought to herself, it's as if we're joined at the hip like Siamese twins. She could hardly concentrate on Rattigan's play about tortured relationships.

Her head spun ecstatically when toward the end of the first act Dick brushed her forehead with his lips, and holding her hand tightly, moved it to rest on his thigh. She longed for him to kiss her on the mouth . . . longed to be sitting next to him for the rest of her life. She was throbbing with something that was so precious she couldn't bear the thought of the evening ending.

It was still warm when they left the theater, although there was the scent of autumn in the air, a smoky haze that usually gave Sylvie a melancholy feeling . . . of days passing too fast . . . of memories not yet lived.

When they passed a dark narrow alleyway on the way to her Haymarket bus stop, Dick stopped and wordlessly pulled her to him. It was the first time she had ever felt a man's body so close to her own. She knew what to expect, had always thought she would be terrified to feel a man's strange lump or bump pushed up against her, but she didn't feel terrified at all.

"Oh, Dick . . ." He stepped back into the darkness of the alleyway, not loosening his grip, and she followed him awkwardly, stepping on his toes as if she were learning to dance. Out of nowhere came a memory of the first time she waltzed, standing on her father's shoes when she was a little girl as they'd danced around the tiny kitchen. But now she wasn't dancing. She was loving—loving a man.

"Sylvie, you're so . . . so pretty . . ."

"Pretty?" There was such a note of amazement in her voice that Dick laughed in the way she loved to hear him laugh, with real merriment, like a rascally little boy. His mouth was on hers, hard, forceful, yet despite its power to bruise, to make such an indelible impression on her senses, she found herself opening her mouth, knowing what to do without being told, some instinct encouraging his tongue to come inside, while her body naturally moved toward the wonderful growing hardness that sought the soft nest between her legs. As Dick moved against her, her head spun again with a mixture of joy and confusion as she felt her private parts get wet, soaking wet. Was it her period? She knew it couldn't be. She was wet with longing.

His hands, beautiful hands she'd always thought, long with fine fingers like a concert pianist's, were seeking her breasts and she wanted them there. Emotions she'd never experienced came like waves, one after the other. She wanted his mouth on her breasts, too, and her abdomen. She wanted his tongue to lick her belly button. His tongue to explore her. . . . But even his hands couldn't get near her bare skin. Why, oh why, had she worn a dress that had to go over her head? Nell would never have dressed in such a frumpy, spinsterish way. Nell! Why on earth was she wasting time thinking about Nell when at last she was living the way Sylvie imagined every girl, except herself, lived? Dick was stroking her with tender loving strokes so that her small breasts seemed to respond as if they would grow, flowering just from his touch. She could hear their breaths, urgent, fast, panting toward something, and she wanted it . . . oh, she wanted it; but she was scared.

Just when his tongue was at its most searching, when she felt her knickers soaking with her wetness, when his hand had crept down under her coat, under the skirt of her dress, was unbelievably on the bare part of her leg between the top of her stocking and the lace of her camiknickers, his long sensitive fingers touching her pubic hair, edging toward the hot dark place she longed for him to find, a brutal beam of light intruded, breaking through their joy, their privacy.

They jumped apart guiltily as a firm yet somehow still-kind voice said, "Now, what's going on here, you two. Move along now, young man, young lady. Isn't it time you were on your way home to your mum and dad?"

Sylvie's heart thumped painfully in her chest all the way back to Aunt Gert's. She couldn't bear to think of Dick's embarrassed, guilty expression. Had she looked the same to him? She hoped not. As she went over the evening in her mind, she felt defiant. All right, perhaps if the policeman hadn't come along, if he hadn't shone his flashlight into the alleyway and interrupted their lovemaking, she would *really* have something to feel guilty about, for would she have stopped Dick touching her *there?* And once he'd touched her, would she have touched him . . . and . . . perhaps actually let him enter her?

She was certain she wouldn't, not for any high moral reason but because she would have been too scared of the consequences. So she was determined not to feel ashamed, although they'd hardly spoken as they'd emerged sheepishly from the alleyway to half run, half walk to her bus stop.

At first she'd been relieved her bus had come along almost immediately. It was only when she'd curled up in bed in the dark at Aunt Gert's that the longing had come back and she'd started to wonder and worry how Dick would treat her when they saw each other again at the office on Monday.

It was the longest, most painful weekend of her life. Until she saw Dick again—about 11:00 A.M. on Monday—she suffered from the same feelings of agitation she'd experienced on Friday, before their date, feelings that came and went with increasing intensity. Just when she thought she'd go crazy, apprehensive that Kitty would arrive before she could find out how Dick was going to behave, he came whistling into the office and with his usual cheeky wink said, "Hi, Sylvie. Coffee after work?"

What a beautiful day it suddenly became. When Kitty arrived fifteen minutes later, even she commented, "What's up, Sylvie? You look radiant. Have you won the football pools?"

~~~

Aunt Gert had big news for Sylvie—news that unfortunately meant a change in their living arrangements. If Nell hadn't been there when Aunt Gert started to explain, Sylvie would have been crushed, but in two seconds Nell had turned what should have been the worst news into the best. She danced first with Sylvie and then with Aunt Gert, round and round the tiny sitting room, singing, "I could be happy with you . . . if you could be happy with me . . ."

In the middle of it all, there had been a ring at the doorbell and in had come the reason for the upheaval, Pierre Repelle, the French chemist Sylvie knew Aunt Gert had met months before at a Boots' function and had been corresponding with ever since. She'd brought his name into the conversation more and more in recent weeks. Now seeing the man—blond, stocky, looking more Swedish than French— Sylvie realized (noticing the blush on her aunt's face) Aunt Gert had to be in love! Well, that was great; but was love the reason she needed Sylvie's room?

Of course not, Sylvie told herself a week or two later. If Aunt Gert was going to marry Pierre, he would surely move into Gert's room— if he didn't have a home to offer her. Apparently he didn't, for Aunt Gert told her that Pierre had lost everything in the war. Sylvie totally understood Aunt Gert's blushing explanation. Ambition was behind the big change—something Sylvie understood only too well. Pierre and Gert were one day going to start their *own* beauty business, because Pierre had a unique formula for helping the skin stay young, using, of all things, silk from the silkworm.

Sylvie hadn't taken any of it seriously. Now she started to listen, for Gert and Pierre were going to use her bedroom as a lab—once Sylvie found a place of her own.

And that apparently wasn't going to be long, either . . . nor was it going to be a place on her own. It was going to be a bed-sit with Nell!

A conspiracy had been going on, Sylvie realized without anger, for it was a conspiracy between the two people she loved most in the world, Nell and Aunt Gert.

Nell had wanted to move away from her parents for years. (Sometimes, hearing her vehemence on the subject, Sylvie thought the idea must have been there since Nell was old enough to talk.)

In Gert and Pierre's grand plan, Nell had seen the perfect opportunity and the best excuse. As Sylvie now learned, Nell's parents had already been told that as soon as a suitable place was found, if they didn't allow their darling to move there with Sylvie, she was going off on her own and they would never hear from her again.

Could they afford it? That had also been well discussed—and solved. Aunt Gert was doing so well she was going to subsidize the two of them. Everything moved so fast, in only another two weeks Gert announced she had seen an affordable possible place in Hammersmith.

There were tears in Sylvie's eyes, tears she didn't understand as she followed Nell, Aunt Gert, and Pierre to the bus stop the next night. It was as if one chapter of her life were over and another were about to begin. It was thrilling; it was also terrifying in a way she couldn't explain.

There was obviously no confusion in Nell's mind. Her arm familiarly tucked through Pierre's, Nell was so excited that one word ran into the other and Sylvie learned for the first time that Nell had plans to join Pierre and Gert in their business once they "made it big."

"Make it big." Sylvie smiled indulgently, hearing Nell use the phrase three times in as many minutes. It was Nell's favorite expression at the moment. Just like Dick, Nell had even begun to clip stories out of newspapers—but the reason was different. Nell's file of clippings concerned only the males of the species who'd made it big.

Howard Hughes, for example, who, it had recently been reported, had written a personal check for $23,489,478 to buy RKO Studios.

There were clippings about lesser-known men, too—Earl S. Tupper, who'd made millions out of plastic canisters called Tupperware that you could store upside-down. Nell forced Sylvie to read every clipping in the collection, animatedly pointing out that it only made sense to be interested in *multimillionaires*. "Why go for less, when there's more to be had?"

As they neared Hammersmith Broadway, Sylvie began to share Nell's enthusiasm. They were going to be nearer Fleet Street—and, as she might have expected, Aunt Gert had found not only an afford-able bed-sit but a cozy one that could even be made pretty. Admittedly it was down outside steps, in the basement of a big old Victorian house, but Sylvie described it to herself as a secret cave.

"We can check out everyone's ankles . . . shoes! Anyone in ugly cheap shoes won't be allowed in," Nell cried, as she realized that, once inside, their eyes were on a level with the pavement outside.

Pierre explained in fascinatingly broken English that Gert had heard of the place through one of his colleagues, who somehow had managed to get the impossible—a phone—which was still there.

Eureka!

When Sylvie told Kitty of her impending move—to a bed-sit that actually had a _phone_, Kitty, in a burst of generosity, said she would pay for the phone's rent in exchange for some occasional dictation over the wire on weekends.

If Kitty can ever get through, Sylvie thought grimly the first week-end in residence, when the phone hadn't stopped with calls for Nell. Where on earth did she meet all the boys—or were they men?

As the weeks went by, despite nights that got later and later and the quantity of champagne that was poured down her willing throat, Nell looked more gorgeous than ever.

There was one call she waited for; she even broke dates at the last minute in the hope it would come through.

She wouldn't tell Sylvie who it was she was actually willing to wait around for. "The Spaniard who blighted my life," she would sing out sometimes. Other times, moody, morose, she would go out of her way to shock. "He's married, tied up with a dozen kids . . . you know the old heartbreak story . . ." Then seeing Sylvie's worried face she would throw contrite arms about her. "I'm lying, Sylvie. You know I don't mess around with married men"—then, slyly—"unless they're in show biz. That doesn't count. Marriage is just make-believe to them. They're all swine."

When the longed-for phone call came, Sylvie knew. Nell was ra-diant. Meeting the "mystery man"—as Sylvie began to call him—was the only time Nell ever expressed any doubt about her appearance. She would put things on, tear them off, pin her hair up, brush it down, add lipstick, wipe it off. In fact, Sylvie told her she acted like a mad person . . . and still Nell's questions never stopped. "Do I look slim in this, Sylvie? Is my hair okay? Should I add rouge? Do I look too young in this dress?" On and on until she left, a disheveled, glorious mess. She was always back early from the mystery dates, usually depressed, certainly never elated, growling in response to anything Sylvie said, which made Sylvie think the mystery man *had* to be married . . . otherwise why the early return home?

"Can't win them all!" Nell would throw an unusual look of defiance at Sylvie over a breakfast of a cup of tea and a digestive biscuit.

Often there was a swift and fierce determination to be out doing, *achieving*, after a date with the mystery man.

"I'm going out with a knight—a knight of the theater, me girl, so watch me bring back a tiara," Nell announced with an exaggerated Cockney accent one morning after returning particularly early—about 10:30 P.M.—the night before.

The next morning Nell told her that her problems started when she decided not to wear a bra. Sylvie screamed out "Nell!" finding her in the kitchen, with their precious piece of prime beef out of the larder clapped to the blackest eye Sylvie had ever seen except in the movies.

The appalling sight kept her anger from boiling over, even as she thought, "Can I still use the meat for our Sunday lunch?"

As Nell well knew, the beef had been bought for a special lunch to say thank you to Gert and Pierre. Just as important, Sylvie had invited Dick to the bed-sit for the first time.

"What on earth has a bra or no bra got to do with your eye? What a sight you are!"

"My tits, you twit." Nell winced as she spoke. "I didn't realize a knight in shining armor would get so worked up. After all, I *was* wearing my boring old blue blouse." Nell turned innocent eyes on Sylvie as if expecting her to agree that there had been no attempt on her part to lead anyone on. Sylvie snorted. Even with her eyes shut, she could visualize how Nell must have looked in the clinging, thin silk blouse which, as Nell well knew, emphasized her breasts and large nipples, bra or no bra.

With no response from Sylvie, Nell went on, "Well, I s'pose he was so strung up after his performance he wanted to let it all hang out . . ."

"What are you talking about?"

"It was a classic seduction scene, my love. After two glasses of champers and a fairly amateur lunge in his dressing room, he took me to this club off the Haymarket for dinner. Then he asked if he could come back to my place—he's married, you see, but only to keep up appearances. I mean they don't fuck or anything . . ."

"Nell!" Sylvie was scandalized.

"Oh, sorry, Sylv. But I'm only telling you what he said. Anyway, he drove me halfway home, then turned onto this bomb site off the Bayswater Road. Sylvie, stop staring like that. Your eyeballs will pop out . . ."

Nell started to laugh as Sylvie tried to grab the beef away.

"Don't worry. I'll wash all the bugs off. Aunt Gert and her froggy Frenchman will never know, or your darling Dick either." Nell pressed the beef so firmly to her eye that its blood started to run down her cheek. "They say Cleopatra bathed in beef blood, too. Very messy, I think, don't you?" Nell nonchalantly wiped the blood from her face with the edge of the tablecloth. "Anyway, this famous blankety-blank knight had such a hard-on he kept trying to press my face down onto him . . ." The more shocked and tense Sylvie became, the more Nell seemed to enjoy telling her story. "He got quite violent. I couldn't fight him off. He just tore my knickers apart, ripped my blouse in two, and kept muttering, 'I thought so, you little tramp, no bra, eh . . . I thought so.' He almost bit my nipples off, he sucked so hard. Boy, they're sore. I really tried to enjoy it but just when I was going to let him do it, I saw his cock. It was an awful color . . ."

Sylvie screamed, putting her hands over her ears. "Don't tell me any more . . ."

"Oh, don't be such a milksop, Sylvie. Be your age. Haven't you ever seen your Dick's cock? It's about time!"

"Shut up. Shut up," Sylvie screamed. "How can you talk that way?" Sylvie had never told Nell what had happened after the theater. The moments spent in the alley with Dick were sacred, tucked away in a special place in her mind, only taken out and relived when she was in bed in the dark, moments she felt sure would be repeated one day when the time was right.

"You're an idiot." Nell seemed totally unconcerned that Sylvie was so upset. "I haven't said I did it, have I? You can let them get it in a little way, then tell 'em you're a virgin and scare them off forever. To stop *him* pushing me around, I said I'd suck him off, but instead I bit him hard." The word came out venomously. "That's when he socked me in the eye. Somehow I got out of the car and ran."

"With no knickers on?" Sylvie's question came out so innocently that Nell started to laugh until she cried, tears mingling with blood from the beef still trickling down her face. "You're too much. Yes, I left my rags in his car and, guess what, I even got a lift from a respectable insurance agent who never even tried to put his finger in. If he'd only known what was under my skirt, all wet and gooey . . ."

Sylvie banged out of the house in a fury. Nell was getting too difficult to handle. She wasn't going to put up with it. If Nell didn't change, she was going to—well, what could she do? She couldn't afford any place on her own.

Later that morning, Nell, wearing overlarge summer sunglasses despite a wintry downpour outside, tried to placate Sylvie in the office, leaning over her desk with what Sylvie called her "pussycat" smile.

"I'm busy," Sylvie said. "Kitty wants five columns in advance."

Nell kept on talking, but Sylvie ignored her, typing furiously, knowing she was bound to be making mistakes. No matter. She'd sooner do everything over than say another word to Nell—at least until Nell promised to reform.

Sylvie worked late, almost until the daily paper's night shift came on, and was amazed to hear a familiar French accent when she wearily let herself into the bed-sit.

What on earth was Pierre doing there? Was Aunt Gert there too? She could feel herself blushing, thinking of the unmade bed, the untidy jumble she'd left behind that morning as she'd slammed out in anger. But Aunt Gert wasn't there. She didn't like the way Nell was looking up at the Frenchman, sitting on the floor at his feet. What did it remind her of? Sylvie searched her memory. Nell was wearing her old look of Pegler adoration.

Pierre jumped up as she came in. "Ah, Sylvie . . . 'ow 'appy I am to see you. Are you 'appy 'ere, *ma chérie*? Your *tante*—aunt—is worried about you, *mais* I tell 'er she is silly to worry. You are both big girls, *n'est-ce-pas?*"

Later Sylvie was furious that she had answered in monosyllables and hadn't asked Pierre point-blank why he was there. Although he left behind a large book on botanical history, presumably for Nell to study, Sylvie wasn't about to give either Nell or him the benefit of the doubt and ascribe the visit to furthering Nell's interest in the cosmetics business.

In all the time Nell had been at Geraldine House, Sylvie had never once felt a twinge of jealousy over her conquests or exploits. The exquisite ruby-bead bracelet Nell received, she said, from an unknown admirer, the violets that arrived every two hours at the bed-sit one day with only one word on each card until the words made up a flattering invitation to dine with an Italian film producer, the phone calls, the first nights, the glamorous parties Nell increasingly went to—none of these things evoked Sylvie's envy or jealousy. Then twice in one week Sylvie was overcome with the disease, all the more sickening because it descended so unexpectedly, so rapidly.

It started on Sunday at the lunch Nell and she prepared together. Nell had been behaving particularly sweetly, trying to show she was sorry for upsetting Sylvie, bringing her a morning cup of tea, making the bed they shared together, even vacuuming the whole room without being asked.

It should have been a wonderful day. It had stopped snowing and the sun was shining so brilliantly it lit up the basement, particles of snow glittering like diamonds on the windowsill. With typical flair Nell had tied red-and-white checked bows on the water pipes that lined one wall, and lit red and white candles, so that everything ugly in the room faded into insignificance.

Just before their guests arrived, she even splashed the bedspread and curtains with a scent she said Pierre had recently formulated for her to try. Sylvie was in such a state of nerves over Dick's first visit that she wished she hadn't invited him. As she checked the roast, burned her fingers on a saucepan, and tried to calm down her hair, which was behaving in a particularly unruly fashion, she felt hot and bothered and was sure everything was going to be a disaster.

But at first everything was fine. Nell was a born hostess. With cheap cooking sherry poured to the rim of their new glasses from Woolworth's and hors d'oeuvres, shrimps on sticks, Nell made everyone feel relaxed.

It was only when Sylvie dropped her napkin during lunch at their makeshift dining table—the sewing machine covered in a red-and-white checked cloth—and bent down to retrieve it, that for her the whole atmosphere changed. She couldn't believe what she could see. Dick's leg firmly rested against Nell's, so close there was no space between—and, worse, Nell seemed to be rubbing her leg up against his. Sylvie was so confused, she got up too quickly. Her chair crashed back against the side table, sending two of the new sherry glasses smashing onto the linoleum. Tears came to her eyes. She hurried into the kitchen, sure that Dick would come after her, but he didn't. She clenched and unclenched her hands, remembering the Nell of a few days before, sitting with the beef they were now eating clamped to her black eye. Sylvie hoped it would poison her!

When she returned with clean plates for the trifle, she saw Dick gazing into Nell's eyes as if Nell really were Cleopatra and he Mark Antony. Could he read her mind? Dick turned to look at her and—Sylvie couldn't believe his cheek—winked.

The rest of the day passed in a blur of incidents that might have seemed trivial if her emotions hadn't been so painfully raw.

Why did Dick and Nell volunteer to wash up so quickly? Did Dick's hand linger on Nell's as she passed him with wet soapy fingers pieces of china to dry? Did Pierre actually put his arm around Nell's waist as she asked him a question about the botanical book? Why did Dick and Nell go into the kitchen again just before his departure? Sylvie forced herself not to follow them, her stomach churning so badly she had to rush to the lavatory in the dark and now-freezing yard at the back.

Only Gert seemed unaware of the tension Sylvie felt was building up in the room. Relaxed, her feet up on their footstool, Gert fell asleep, a look of contentment on her face as if to say, now that she had seen for herself how happy her two little charges were in their bed-sit nest, all was right with her world.

Sylvie was cool to Dick the next morning when he came into Kitty's office with a note. No matter what apology he tried to make, Sylvie vowed not to accept it—but there was no apology. To her increased unhappiness, it was a thank-you note to both of them. She received little satisfaction from the fact he spelled Nell's name with only one *l*.

Was life going to continue to hurt like this? she asked herself three days later when Nell told her casually that Smith Maynard intended to send her out on her first interview.

Jealousy was well named the green-eyed monster, all right. Sylvie could feel it eating away at her intestinal tract. First Nell's beauty had stolen Dick's heart; now Nell's brains were going to sweep her into the editorial job Sylvie longed to have herself. Sylvie knew Nell would carry it out with brilliance, probably without even trying or caring, while she herself watched from the sidelines, trapped at the "Heart to Heart" desk, buried under the weight of readers' problem letters. Sylvie bit her lip, trying to subdue the very real pain she felt, knowing it was unworthy, knowing she should congratulate and encourage Nell, who was, after all, her best friend. "That's wonderful, Nell, really wonderful. Who . . . are . . . who's the interview with?"

"Oh, no one important. A deb's delight, a photographer bloke who lives in a swinging studio in Pimlico, said to be a boyfriend of Princess Margaret's. Can't even think of his name, something like Armstrong-Smith . . ."

A week later Nell was full of the smashing time she'd had with Tony —"Armstrong-Jones. He's sexy, Sylv. His visitor's book is a great big mirror—you scratch your name on with a diamond. Nobody pinches it because it's attached with a chain. He was in bed when I arrived, although he was expecting me. His charlady let me in after I'd rung the bell dozens of times. I was so mad. She pointed the way down this spiral staircase . . . which he built himself. He's ever so clever. When I knocked on the door, he said 'come in.' You could have knocked me down with a feather. There he was as large as life, sitting up in bed. We had huge cups of tea. I tell you, he's _really_ something."

As Sylvie predicted, Nell's interview was given a prominent spot in the paper. It was lively, fun, as irreverent as Nell herself.

Soon Nell was writing about personalities on a regular basis—and sometimes not coming back to the bed-sit overnight at all, or appearing in the office for days.

Once again Sylvie found herself covering Nell's tracks whenever the O'Hallorans called up from a street-corner phone box. Nell's father called at the crack of dawn one day and Sylvie could hear herself becoming more and more desperate. "She's on an early day shift— you know, six o'clock she has to be in. Yes, I know it's early—but she works for one of the most important men in Fleet Street."

As she hung up, she thought bitterly, "He's so important I've never yet managed to say more than good morning to him." It was not likely that Smith Maynard would ever offer _her_ anything. He obviously regarded her only as Kitty's slave.

It was general gossip around the office that Kitty had the hots for Smith, who also had a ladies'-man reputation but didn't seem to reciprocate Kitty's feelings.

On impulse one Sunday, Sylvie decided to visit Aunt Gert and discuss her painful jealousy and the whole Nell situation.

As the bus lumbered toward the East End of London, Sylvie wondered why Nell had become more evasive lately and more uncommunicative. On the few evenings she had been home, she'd hardly spoken, refusing all calls, apparently not even expecting one from the mystery man. She'd even gone to bed without eating, turning her face to the wall. Sylvie decided it just showed how spoiled Nell really was. Only a year older than herself, Nell already had a promising future with several by-lined pieces in print and even her photograph running with two of them. Yet now she was sulking like a child over something or other, while she, Sylvie Samuelson, who longed to be a writer, had no hope, no prospects. Her one stupid piece printed without her name, "Love by a Teenager," all seemed so very long ago, and nothing had happened since.

Sylvie tried to stop thinking about herself. Only the week before at Lyons' Corner House restaurant, Aunt Gert had told her things were moving ahead much faster than planned. It wouldn't be too long before Pierre and she would be ready to start their company. Blushing as vividly as Sylvie, Gert had also intimated in her usual modest fashion that perhaps she and Pierre were ready for something else too. "We're really very fond of each other. Perhaps . . ." she'd faltered, "perhaps we'll get together. Yes, we may get married before we launch the company."

All thought of discussing Nell disappeared when Sylvie arrived at Aunt Gert's house. Luckily she still had a key; otherwise, as she thought later, Aunt Gert probably would never have let her in.

As it was, Sylvie would always remember she heard the news of Churchill's resignation and the appointment of Anthony Eden as the new prime minister as she walked into Gert's little house to find the radio on full blast, although no one appeared to be at home to listen.

"Is anyone at home? Aunt Gert, are you there?" Sylvie heard an unfamiliar sound. What was it? Memories of her mother and the dreaded Technical Sergeant Tramello came into her mind for the first time in ages—but it wasn't *that* kind of sound. Someone was sobbing and trying not to be heard. Muffled sobs.

Sylvie had never seen Aunt Gert out of control. She could hardly believe that the red-rimmed eyes, the crumpled, wrinkled face, the soiled dressing gown belonged to her trim, stylish aunt.

"What's happened, auntie? What is it? It's Pierre, isn't it? Oh, God, has he been in an accident? Oh, auntie . . ." Sylvie tried not to cry, but her tears splashed on her aunt, even as Gert tried to turn away.

"Go away," she moaned. "Leave me alone. Go away." It was all she would say, over and over again. Sylvie sat beside her for what seemed like hours, until, not knowing what else to do, she went to make a cup of tea. Where was Pierre? She didn't even know if he lived with her aunt. Knowing Gert, Sylvie was sure he did not.

When she went back into the bedroom, Gert was half sitting up, slumped against the bed back, eyes closed, clenching and unclenching her hands. "Please talk to me, auntie. Please . . . please . . ." Something in Sylvie's voice penetrated. Gert opened her eyes, such sad, mourning eyes.

"Has Pierre—is he—?" Sylvie was frightened to hear the answer.

"He's gone. Don't ask me about it. It's all over. No marriage. No company. It's over."

"Oh, auntie, it can't be. Why? It's hardly a week since you told me —why?"

"I don't want to talk about it."

Sylvie knew her aunt. There was no way at that moment she was going to learn any more.

She stayed the night, phoning the bed-sit in case Nell might be worried about her, but up until midnight there was no reply, so she gave up. She rocked her grieving aunt to sleep, whispering "sleep . . . try to sleep," as if she were a baby. In the morning, Sylvie said she would move back again into her old room if that was what her aunt wanted.

"Let's wait and see, Sylvie." Despite her words, there was hopelessness in her voice. Gert, the feisty aunt whose shoulder she had always leaned on, now looked old, defenseless.

"Oh, Aunt Gert, I hate leaving you," Sylvie cried. "Should I call Kitty and take the day off?"

"No, no, no." Aunt Gert practically shooed her out of the house. "I'm going away tomorrow—to see my friend Betsy up north. I don't want to be in this house for a while. I promise I'll call you when I get back but I won't be in any hurry to return. I'll drop you a note with my address. Betsy doesn't have a phone." She paused. "Thank goodness." There was a trace of the old vehemence in her voice.

As Sylvie made the early-morning journey to Fleet Street, she realized how much she would loathe giving up what she supposed was her newfound independence in the bed-sit, however aggravating it was sometimes to live with Nell.

The whirlwind of activity that was Nell's life was like living with a kind of music, always stimulating, often nerve-wracking, yet Sylvie suddenly knew how much she would miss it. Nell made life exciting with one bat of her long lashes. All the same, Aunt Gert's happiness had to come first.

What on earth could have happened to cause such a terrible breakup between Pierre and herself? Before Sylvie left the house, she had glanced into her old room, which she'd grown used to seeing transformed into a small laboratory with bottles and jars all neatly labeled on shelves, microscopes, measuring jars, weights, and measures on a pristine counter.

Test tubes, jars, lotions, potions—everything seemed smashed, mangled on the floor. A chair was overturned. Even books had been wrenched apart. It looked as if a tornado had rushed through—a human tornado. The shambles had shocked her almost as much as the sight of her aunt. Head down, deep in thought, Sylvie walked into Geraldine House.

Smith Maynard's secretary had deigned to call to ask where Nell O'Halloran was. There was no answer at home, and Nell hadn't turned up for an important assignment. Where was she?

Jolted out of her concern over Aunt Gert, with no word from Nell all day, Sylvie couldn't wait to get back to Hammersmith.

Had Nell been at home last night and not answered the phone?

The flat was in darkness as Sylvie let herself in, yet heart pounding, Sylvie felt someone was there. Sure enough when she switched on the light, there was a lump in the bed which had to be Nell.

What on earth was happening with the world? Nell, who *never* really cried, had been crying too. But what a difference there was between her and Gert. Aunt Gert had become old and ugly with tears. Nell simply looked like a little child, softer, more vulnerable, her green eyes luminous, glistening. But she *was* pale, unnaturally pale, and there was a sickly smell about her.

"What on earth's wrong, Nell? Are you ill or something?"

As upsetting as Aunt Gert's tears had been, Sylvie felt terror as copious tears flowed down Nell's cheeks. "Nell, I can't stand it. What is it?"

"I'm pregnant."

"What . . ." The word came out like a long, low whistle. "Oh, Nell." Now *she* was sick. She retched, staggering to the sink to plunge her face in cold water, before rushing back to Nell's side to cry, "Are you sure?"

"Of course I'm sure." The old Nell broke through for a second. "I've been drinking gin for hours. 'Mother's ruin,' but no luck."

"Why are you so sure?"

"Ducky, I'm nearly three months late with my curse, doesn't that tell you anything?"

"Does he know?"

"*He?*" Nell scowled. She bunched her dark hair on top of her head, throwing Sylvie a disgusted look.

"Yes, _he_," Sylvie yelled. "He—the father—have you told him?"

Nell stayed silent.

A terrible thought occurred to Sylvie. Did Nell know who the father was?

She had asked the question before she could stop herself. She could have cut her tongue out, but to her fury Nell started to laugh, a harsh, humorless laugh.

"I know you think I've been busier than a whore, but in fact I haven't. There's only ever been one."

Sylvie looked Nell straight in the eyes. "Who is it?"

Nell jumped out of bed. "I'm going to be sick for the fifteenth time. No wonder, with the gin, the castor oil . . . oh, my gawd . . ." She didn't reach the sink in time.

Nell wasn't going to tell her who the father was, Sylvie was sure of it. No matter how much she threatened not to help unless she knew, Nell knew _her_ too well—knew she'd help her down to her last penny. Pennies were about all she had.

"I want you to tell Kitty." Nell paced up and down the linoleum until Sylvie thought she'd go crazy.

"What!"

"Yes, of course I want Kitty in on this." Ironically, Nell's irritability calmed Sylvie down.

Nell went on. "It's obvious Kitty is the one person who'll know what to do—where to go for a nice, safe, unmessy abortion. That's what her column's all about, isn't it? Helping those who've lost their way?"

Sylvie ignored Nell's obvious sarcasm. "Abortion's against the law."

"Yes, but so's Kitty! You should hear what Smith—Smith Maynard —says about her. He says she knows every trick and trickster in the business."

Nell was right. Kitty did know whom to go to. Dr. Payne across the river in Streatham, but Nell had left it too late. Careless about dates, she was near the end of her fourth month, not third.

"Stupid bitch," Kitty said, visiting their bed-sit for the first time.

She looked like someone from another planet, Sylvie decided, totally out of place on their faded chenille chair, with her burgundy snood matching her burgundy velvet suit by Hartnell, the Queen's dressmaker.

Kitty tapped long fingernails—burgundy-colored, too—on the wobbly side table. "So you won't tell us who the unlucky man is, Nell?

You don't want a penny from him, is that right? So who *do* you want a penny from? Sylvie? Your decrepit old parents? What are they going to say about this unexpected grandchild?" She glared at a morose Nell, whose face still reflected the pain she'd endured without the expected result in Dr. Payne's surgery.

"I'll make out," Nell snarled.

"Yes, you probably will. A devil like you with the face of an angel . . ." Kitty sucked reflectively on her black cigarette, then threw out a command, "Stand up!"

Like a sleepwalker Nell slowly rose, staring stonily at the feet she could see walking by on the pavement outside, feet often in down-at-the-heel shoes—slingbacks, wedgies—nothing smart, not in their poor neighborhood. The shoes emphasized her misery.

"You don't show yet," Kitty decided after a hard look. "That's lucky —but it won't be long. About another month at the most. You'll have to leave the *Mirror* . . ."

"I won't, will I?" It was a wail, the first sign of the child inside the woman's body, the child being denied something she wanted. Nell turned bleak eyes on Kitty. "Can't I take a leave of absence like Tilda, the ad manager's secretary did—a family emergency, or something?"

Nell started to cry silently, her shoulders heaving. Sylvie could hardly believe her eyes and ears as Kitty moved to put her arms gently around Nell, whispering, "Look, kid, I've been there. I know what you're going through. Yeah, that's what you can do—a leave of absence. Not yet, though. Come back to work for a few weeks—probably no more than three. I'll watch you like a hawk. I'll decide when you're to receive the call from your poor old Ma, summoning you home to help with poor old Pa. They don't have a phone, right?" Nell nodded. "So no one will bother you. Then a week or so before delivery I'll check you into a convent I know . . ."

"No . . ." Nell was drained white. "No, I'm . . . I'm frightened of nuns, Kit . . . Miss Stein. They're witches. They might cast a spell on me."

It was amazing. Kitty was still sympathetic. "I'll be with you, Nell, don't worry. They won't dare cast any spells with a good Jewish girl like me around." She forced Nell to look at her. "Do you want to keep the baby?" The question shot out the way a seasoned reporter knows how to throw one to get a straight answer. Nell looked at the floor, her hair glorious and lustrous, shining in a sudden ray of sunlight.

"I don't know, Miss Stein. I don't think so." She suddenly looked vindictive. "I think I hate its guts . . ."

"Nell!"

Kitty silenced Sylvie's cry with a withering look. "Well, we'll wait and see. We'll discuss it nearer the time."

But it didn't turn out that way. Certainly Nell followed Kitty's instructions, going back to work diligently, writing a couple of good pieces—one on Anna Massey, near Nell's age but already a star in *The Reluctant Debutante* at the Cambridge Theater; the other, a tribute to James Dean, killed in a car crash, at twenty-four.

One Thursday Kitty said to Sylvie, "It's curfew time. Go and tell Nell her mother has just called you on the phone . . . and will now be calling her . . ."

Nell acted out the anxious daughter to perfection, even asking Smith Maynard's permission to consult Kitty for advice.

But did Nell have to spend so long that lunchtime talking to Dick in the cafeteria? Sylvie could have thrown the basket of stale ham rolls at them, not sure even that kind of disturbance would have broken their concentration on each other. What were they talking about? What did it all mean? Was Nell actually telling Dick her dark secret? If so, why?

"Of course I didn't tell him," Nell said grumpily on the bus going home. From now on she would refer to the bed-sit as the "prison," because Kitty's edict meant that was where she was going to stay put, except for car-hire rides, courtesy of Miss Stein, to Streatham twice a month for medical checkups.

Sylvie couldn't stop herself from asking Nell again if she'd told Dick, until Nell lost her temper, which she did easily these days, and yelled, "Shut up! Once and for all, no, no, no! I have not told your loved one *anything*."

Nell's stomach now stuck out with a funny little lump. "As if you've swallowed an olive, trust you," Kitty said with asperity. "You'll be back to your svelte, bloody sexy shape in no time . . ."

Armistice Day, November 11, 1955 . . . would she ever forget the scream for help in the middle of the night? Sylvie fought to keep her eyes shut, trying to block out sounds she was sure had to be part of a bad dream. There it was again. Nell's hands suddenly clawed, clutched her. "Oh God, oh God, oh God . . ."

Sylvie became wide awake. Nell was thrashing about the bed like somebody drowning. "It's coming, Sylvie, oh God, the brat's coming.

Oh, oh, oh . . ." The screams were interminable, perforating Sylvie's eardrums into a thousand holes.

"It can't be, it can't be . . ." Sylvie switched on the light to look at the clock on the mantelpiece, as if knowing the time would reaffirm that Nell's baby wasn't due for at least another five or six weeks.

She heard the sheet rip. Nell suddenly had manic strength, tearing at the cloth with her teeth, her hands, obviously in agony.

Sylvie's fingers trembled so much she misdialed Kitty's number twice. Her boss's voice, caked with sleep at first, was soon alert. In a second she was all business. "I'll be there."

Sylvie hardly recognized the Kitty Stein who arrived nearly an hour later. Without makeup or her famous snood, with thick hair down her back in a careless, unraveling plait, she looked younger, no longer intimidating, in fact as nervous and as vulnerable as Sylvie felt herself. Her spirits sank. She desperately needed the familiar, tough-as-boots Kitty to lean on, to follow. Her teeth chattered with fright as Nell's screams reverberated through the room. Thank God the rooms immediately above were without tenants for the moment. Vulnerable-looking or not, Kitty took in the situation and took charge.

It was still the beginning of hell, torture. Was childbirth always like this? Sylvie frequently asked herself as the hideous night went on. If so, God certainly knew how to punish Eve.

Kitty, anxious but authoritative, got through to Nell. "Do what Doctor Payne taught you. Remember your natural-childbirth exercises—take a deep breath, that's right . . ." Whimpering like a baby herself, after an hour of following Kitty's forceful instructions, Nell began to scream again. The baby was coming out.

"Push down. Push down." Kitty's face dripped with perspiration. "Sylvie, use that big saucepan to boil more water. Yes, fill it up. Push, Nell. C'mon . . . imagine you're on the loo . . . push the baby out . . . go on, girl, you can do it. It's coming, Nell . . ."

"Oh, oh, oh . . . ." The agonized wail was more than Sylvie could bear. She ran into the kitchen, averting her eyes from the bed where Nell lay spread-eagled, her hair matted, moaning, groaning, turning her head endlessly from left to right, right to left, beating at the wall with her fists, leaving bloody stains on the wallpaper as she heaved with desperate, agonized thrusts.

Sylvie buried her head in her hands. Would the nightmarish ordeal never end?

She heard a loud slap, then a weak, lonely cry, followed by another and another until the sounds engulfed her ears—a baby howling. The baby had arrived.

"Nell, you have a beautiful . . ." Sylvie heard Kitty start to say, a foreign note of awe in her voice.

She was interrupted.

Nell screeched, "I don't want to know. Take it away. I hate him, I hate him. I'll never forgive him . . ." A storm of sobbing and screeching followed, mingled with the mewing of the baby—a horrifying mixture of ugly decibels.

So this was the result of love, of lovemaking. Sylvie tried to be sick, but she retched emptily.

Now Kitty was screaming. "Where's that water? Where are you, Sylvie? For God's sake, we still have work to do. Come back in here at once . . ."

~~~

With the dawn, they all slept. Nell, her face to the wall, uncaring that the sheets were stained with blood, refused to move, pushing Sylvie away as she tried to clean her up. Wrapped in a blanket on the floor, Sylvie watched Kitty, curled up in the armchair, jump and shake in her sleep. No wonder. After this ghastly night, would sleep ever produce anything but bad dreams?

In seconds, however, she fell into a deep, dreamless sleep.

Ten o'clock. Sylvie jumped up incredulously when she saw the time, forgetting for one second what had happened, thinking she'd overslept. Kitty, her hair neatly back in its usual chignon, looking as if she were ready to give dictation, sat at the sewing machine which was now doubling as Kitty's desk. Nell still lay as Sylvie remembered her from hours before, inert, face to the wall, the sheet drawn up to her chin with clenched hands.

"She hasn't budged," Kitty clipped. "And neither has the little one, poor thing. I'm just writing some facts down for the convent. I only hope they'll take the poor, wee mite . . ." Kitty had emptied out the smallest drawer of their tallboy to use as a makeshift crib. Sylvie looked at the minuscule scrap of humanity for the first time and saw Kitty had wrapped the baby in the shawl Nell had crocheted for her the Christmas before, embroidering a fancy initial "S" on the corner.

"Baby S," Sylvie said shyly. "What on earth is going to happen to poor little Baby S? Will the convent arrange the adoption?"

"If Nell gives permission . . . which she will," Kitty answered grimly.

After coffee and toast, Kitty was ready to leave. "Stay here," she ordered Sylvie. "I'll be back later when I've made arrangements with the mother superior." She paused reflectively, looking at Sylvie. "No hope, I'm sure, of your persuading Miss Movie Star here to use her celebrated tits to give her baby some milk?

Sylvie blushed. It sounded degrading to her, yet looking at the baby, so defenseless and unbelievably tiny, she irrationally wished she herself had the milk to give. She couldn't imagine Nell breast-feeding.

"I called Doc Payne while you were asleep," Kitty said from the front door. "He'll be here within an hour, so wake up the sleeping princess before he arrives, and get some clean sheets on the bed and fresh air in the place." Kitty winked, and Sylvie remembered how Smith Maynard had apparently once described Kitty to Nell: "She's an alleycat with a lopsided halo." Sylvie blinked back tears. Lopsided halo or not, Kitty Stein in her eyes was now a saint.

The silence was oppressive after Kitty's departure. Sylvie dreaded having to contend with Nell's mood when she had to wake her up but, as had often happened in the past, Nell surprised her. She woke up herself after only a few minutes, docile, even passive, allowing Sylvie to wash her, only crying out when she lifted her arms over her head to slip on a clean nightdress. "I ache all over. If only men had to go through this. Blast and damn them all to hell and back . . ."

"Don't you want to see your . . ."

"Shut up," Nell said furiously. "The answer's no, no, no! Don't ask me again."

When Dr. Payne had been and gone in only forty-five minutes, making what in Sylvie's opinion was an altogether too rudimentary checkup of both baby and mother—although Nell's hostile attitude obviously hurried him along—Nell asked for a cigarette and, to Sylvie's surprise, a drink.

"We don't have either," Sylvie said.

Nell pouted. "Won't you be a love and go to the off-license for me . . ." The nearest off-license, as Nell well knew, was a bus ride away. Sylvie started to remonstrate, then thought better of it. They needed so many things now—sanitary towels, baby powder, nappies, baby clothes. Kitty couldn't very well deliver the baby naked to the convent.

Before she went anywhere, however, Sylvie was determined to find out exactly what was going on in Nell's head. Adoption? Or did she want to keep the baby? Knowing how Nell abhorred nuns and the Catholic church, how would she react to Kitty's actions?

Nell changed the subject skillfully, suspiciously thoughtful of Sylvie's welfare. "Don't let's discuss any of that now. You look dead beat, Sylvie. It was a rough night for you, too. Why don't you get some sleep. Don't worry about the cigs and the booze. I can do without."

"Well, I'd love to collapse, but we need some things urgently. Will you be all right for an hour or so?"

Nell smiled sweetly. "Yes, darling. Get a small bottle of Gordon's, will you? I've grown to fancy 'mother's ruin' . . ." She started to giggle, then seeing Sylvie's exasperated expression, stopped short.

It was strange, Sylvie thought later, how her feeling of apprehension built up during the time she was away from Nell. Just her luck, she missed the bus both going and leaving the shops, which added a good hour to her absence. By the time she dragged herself back to Hammersmith, it was afternoon and the day was darkening.

"Here I am at last, Nell." She tried to sound cheerful, but there was no answer. There was no Nell either—or any baby sleeping like an angel in the bottom drawer.

A chill seeped through her body. She could hardly summon up enough energy to phone Kitty. The room was spinning around as she clutched the receiver, hearing the phone ring and ring in the glass-partitioned office where she longed to be, with life going on normally again. Kitty wasn't there to answer it, and it seemed no one else was going to bother to answer either. Again, Sylvie blinked back tears. Crying wasn't going to get her anywhere.

It was then she saw Nell's note, propped up on the sewing machine. "Gone to see the man who did it to me. Don't worry, I'll be back. SWALK, N." Signed with a loving kiss! If Nell had been there Sylvie would cheerfully have hit her. By the time Sylvie reached Kitty it was evening. "What are we going to do?"

"Nothing." Kitty's matter-of-fact voice calmed her for a second, until she added, "If the baby dies as a result of this, Nell will go to jail. Manslaughter."

"Oh, Kitty . . ." Sylvie couldn't control her tears any longer. They raged out in a torrent. "Don't say that, oh, please don't say things like that . . ."

"Sylvie, be quiet. Take hold of yourself. Go to bed; that's where I'm going. Neither of us can afford to lose two nights' sleep over Miss O'Halloran."

Nell returned the next morning with the morning paper, but without the baby. Wan, grubby, with a defiant expression Sylvie knew well, Nell handed her the *Daily Express*.

"What's this for? Where's the baby?" Sylvie screamed.

"Read all about it," Nell said weakly.

"Baby S on Hospital Doorstep" was the headline halfway down page one. "A baby girl weighing 4 pounds, 8 ounces, no more than a few hours old, was found yesterday evening in the doorway of the Hospital for Sick Children at Great Ormond Street by hospital porter Ernest Dudley. Wrapped in a shawl, embroidered with the letter 'S' . . ."

Sylvie put the paper down, her hand starting to shake. "I can't believe you did this. There's no way you won't be found out . . ."

Nell leaned back against the front door, eyes closed, deathly pale. "Who's going to tell? You? Kitty? Doc Payne? With his reputation, he wouldn't dare go to the police. He knows I'd tell them he butchered me . . ." For a second the old Nell surfaced. "I wasn't going to let those crows in black put their noses in my business! Before I could think straight, they'd have me in the confession box . . ." Nell shivered dramatically.

The doorbell rang as Sylvie started to reread the story. It was Kitty, anger steaming out of her, as tangible as steam from a kettle. "You callous slut," she cried, brandishing a rolled-up *Daily Express* like a truncheon. "What do you think you're accomplishing with this? I'm taking you straight to Hammersmith police station . . ." She went to grab Nell's arm, when Nell fainted. It was no fake faint, as Sylvie first thought. She fell straight forward so quickly they couldn't stop her cutting open her head on the edge of the sewing-machine.

For a few frightening moments, they both thought she was dead. She came around only to faint again, blood pouring from her head and from between her legs like water from a tap. Fate was on Nell's side, Sylvie reckoned, for by the time they managed to carry her back to bed and revive her with smelling salts, only to see her faint one more time, Kitty's fury had abated to be replaced with her usual common sense. She sat as she had two nights before, curled in the armchair, saying her thoughts out loud as Sylvie crouched beside her on the footstool, Nell apparently asleep, the sheet again clutched tightly up to her chin.

"There's only one way I can live with this," Kitty said for the fifth, or was it the sixth, time. "Only one way my conscience can justify keeping quiet. What good would it do to tell the police anyway? What good would it do prosecuting *that* . . ." She turned a baleful eye on the prostrate Nell. "Sending *her* to jail won't help the baby, and it's only the baby that counts. You heard what Nell said about nuns. The cunning little she-devil probably heard me telling you yesterday about going to see them. It's lucky for her and me that I couldn't see the mother superior until today, so she doesn't know what I was about to spring on her." Kitty pursed her lips together, an idea formulating in her agile mind. "The paper will have to go to bat for Baby S . . ."

Sylvie sat up quickly. "What do you mean?"

Kitty excitedly started to outline an idea. "We'll start an editorial crusade—a terrific idea. Smith will love it. We'll adopt Baby S until we find the right loving parents, that's what we'll do. And if the authorities won't let us adopt, we'll adapt . . ." She laughed sardonically. "We'll act as sponsors or something. I know it can be done—then we'll run a daily or twice-weekly report on Baby S's progress. It's a circulation builder. I love it." Kitty clapped her hands together. "Back to work for you, Sylvie my love. We've got a lot to do. I'd better leave now. Make some soup. Leave it for Sarah Bernhardt here—she can warm it up. I'll send Doc Payne back to make sure she really isn't dying. No such luck, I'm afraid . . ."

"I knew I was right! Smith's crazy about the idea." Kitty's uncharacteristic sotto voce murmur into Sylvie's ear was so close that Sylvie could feel Kitty's breath uncomfortably warm on her skin. She shifted miserably in her chair. She couldn't remember when she'd felt more confused. She knew she should feel impressed—even grateful for Kitty's quick thinking to save the baby and to salve their consciences (giving Nell the benefit of the doubt that she *had* a conscience to salve), but again and again the same sentence rang in Sylvie's head. The baby's going to be exploited.

Soon she was sure she was right as she was swept up in the fervor of the *Mirror*'s adoption campaign, working right in the center, in campaign headquarters, having to follow the general's—Kitty's—orders every minute.

Kitty changed her tone and attitude depending on who she was talking to on the phone. She discussed with hushed reverence the editorial plan with officials of the Church of England Adoption Society; used a cozy, "old shoe, we're-Cockney-mates-together" attitude as she interviewed the porter, Ernest Dudley, who'd almost "stumbled over" the tiny white bundle . . . and the nurses now caring for Baby S, who cooed over the meager scraps of black hair, the porcelain skin, the fragile tiny fingers.

It was incredible how Kitty was literally able to put the words into people's mouths that she most wanted to use in her column. Only a few days before, Sylvie would have marveled at this facility. Now she cringed at the hypocrisy of it all.

Even Kitty's back-to-business immaculate appearance stung; the way she puffed away on one black cigarette after another, discussing the baby—Nell's baby—as if she were merely a good "lead letter" subject. Sylvie tried, but she couldn't stop thinking of the terrible scream-filled night that had brought Baby S into the world, a baby now discussed minute by minute like a piece of unwanted merchandise.

Twenty-four hours after the *Express* had printed the news of the discovery of Baby S on the hospital doorstep, the *Evening Mirror*'s public-spirited crusade to find a wonderful, loving home for the abandoned mite stretched over three columns carrying Kitty Stein's bold by-line. Sylvie's hand trembled as she carried out Kitty's instructions to put six copies of the first edition onto her desk to await her arrival.

Kitty's wide grin when she saw how her story was displayed increased Sylvie's unhappiness. All her joy in her job, in being part of the newsroom's maelstrom, even in journalism itself, was spoiled. She felt drained, dispirited; she couldn't even finish reading the tearjerking story that wallowed in sentiment, dramatizing what Porter Dudley first thought when he saw the odd-looking white bundle on the porch. Sylvie choked back an angry cry when she read Kitty's stitch-by-stitch description of the crocheted shawl, including the few dropped stitches and the fancy embroidered "S," posing the question, "Whose fingers worked so lovingly on this shawl . . . probably crocheted for a christening that was never to be . . . instead used to wrap the child up like a parcel to leave on a cold, wintry doorstep, as the mother crept away into the shadows. Whose heart is breaking tonight reading my words? Whose heart . . ." Sylvie threw the paper into the wastepaper basket.

"S for smashing Sylvie." She could recall Nell's laughing remark, see Nell's sparkling eyes as she'd watched Sylvie open the tissue paper to find her gift. She remembered how proud she'd felt that Nell, despite her giddy social life, had taken the time and trouble to crochet the shawl _and_ even embroider her initial.

"Whose heart is breaking tonight?" Sylvie felt that heart was hers. Against her will she started to brood over remarks she'd heard and discarded when she'd first started to work for Kitty—how other secretaries had warned her that Kitty would sell her grandmother down the river for a good story. Now their words had new relevance.

All week long Kitty plugged the crusade, adding a new "revelation" each day—and not a word of truth, Sylvie thought bitterly. She spent long days answering the phone, sifting through letters and telegrams from people "anxious" to be considered as parents, or "genuinely concerned" about the baby's welfare. More likely "anxious" or "genuinely concerned" to get their hands on the money, was Sylvie's cynical opinion of the majority of inquirers, following the announcement that the paper had started a trust fund for Baby S, inviting readers to contribute "even as little as half a crown or a couple of shillings" for the baby's future.

As the public lapped up the story, the paper's sales soared every day, and the hyperbole increased until Sylvie thought she'd go crazy. She could hardly speak to Nell, who seemed totally unaffected by all the fuss.

"Have you seen this?" Sylvie pushed the _Mirror_ under Nell's nose, so she couldn't avoid seeing the four-by-six grainy photograph of Baby S held in a pretty nurse's arms.

Nell coolly pushed the paper to one side. "I've seen it. The paper's doing a good job. It's a good story."

Sylvie could have throttled her. Not trusting herself to speak, she rushed out into the night and walked around and around the block until her fury abated. She couldn't understand why she felt so bitter. It was as if it were her baby the paper was "giving away"—for that was how the adoption scheme seemed to her.

Just as suddenly as it began, it was over with a bombshell announcement arriving by phone from an official of the Church of England, who, Sylvie thought with a rush of relief, had suddenly awakened from their deep sleep to realize exactly the amount of exploitation going on.

All along it had been agreed that the Church of England Adoption Society would make the final decision as to whom the adoptive parents would be. Because of the *Evening Mirror*'s trust fund, an agreement had been reached that the paper's senior executives would also take a personal interest in who would provide "the perfect home for Baby S."

Sylvie knew something untoward had happened when—knowing Kitty was talking to the Adoption Society as she had been doing every day for the past couple of weeks—she suddenly lost her "holier than thou" voice to screech "What the hell!" Sylvie turned in alarm to see the usually imperturbable Kitty turn pale. No wonder. The Society was adamant that only the sketchiest details of the chosen parents could be released. No names, no address, not even the neighborhood. The only facts they would allow to be printed were the parents' ages (father, thirty; mother, twenty-eight), their health (excellent), the father's occupation (owner of a small grocery shop).

Sylvie forced herself not to smile as she heard Kitty try every kind of argument to be able to release more information that Sylvie knew the paper was counting on to continue the circulation build for at least a few more days. But, no, the official stood firm. Finally defeated, Kitty finally put the phone down, swore hard and bitterly for a few seconds, before screaming at Sylvie, "Bloody stupid idiots! Why didn't they tell me this last week!" Sylvie longed to say, "Because you never asked them. You didn't want to hear anything that would upset your story . . ." But she knew to keep her mouth shut. Instead she shook her head, attempting to look as sympathetic as possible. Kitty swallowed, then marched across the newsroom to break the unwelcome news to Smith that although the parents had been chosen, the paper was not going to be allowed to release their names, because "it would not be in the best interest of the baby."

~~~

Had only two weeks passed since the end of the adoption crusade, only fourteen days without a mention of Baby S in the paper? It didn't seem possible, but when Sylvie saw the date she realized with shock that along with everyone else she had already stopped thinking about the story; and to her shame she had hardly even given a thought as to how Baby S was getting on in her new home. It was "business as usual," and although she knew Smith had given Kitty a hard time for not sewing up the story the right way from the start, Kitty was not totally in the doghouse because the adoption crusade had boosted sales to an all-time high, and a murder in Oxford Street, conveniently occurring the day after the adoption story petered out so feebly, had kept them there.

It all added to Sylvie's cynicism but, she reflected, it was probably all for the good. She would never look at life so naively again. All the same, she felt isolated, longed to talk out her feelings of sadness and disillusionment with Aunt Gert, who had always been the one able to put things in perspective—but now it was impossible. She'd heard only recently through one of Aunt Gert's business friends that Pierre had left England to make a "new life" in Canada, and Aunt Gert's lost, hopeless look certainly seemed to confirm it was true, although Gert still refused even to mention Pierre's name. In any case, Sylvie knew she couldn't, wouldn't *ever* betray Nell's secret—not even to Gert. So, she decided, the pain she felt inside was a "growing up" pain and one she'd have to deal with all by herself.

As Kitty saw it, doom was inevitable for Nell.

It could come about violently. "That gorgeous neck can easily be wrung one night by some oversexed, double-crossed monster," or through oblivion—"Married or unmarried, Nell's quite likely to get stuck with a brood of runny-nosed kids in an East End council house. She's obviously highly fertile." These were Kitty's predictions frequently expostulated to Sylvie in the weeks following the adoption campaign. "She'll get pregnant again, mark my words, and I don't want *you* around to get involved next time."

"She's off men." Sylvie tried to get the conversation back to the column, sensing where Kitty was headed. "Did you see this one?" Sylvie endeavored to make the letter she was holding sound like an Oscar-winning script.

Kitty waved it away. "After all this I hope you realize how easy it is to get into trouble. I don't want you mooning after that Czech anymore. He's bad news."

"Why do you say that?" Sylvie was defensive, although hardly sure Dick was worth defending. She wasn't sure of much anymore after Pierre Repelle's defection to Canada and the terrible episode she had just lived through with Nell.

In one of her worst moods, after an obviously fractious lunch with Smith Maynard, Kitty had been picking on Sylvie for at least an hour until, as often happened, she had a swift—and contrite—change of mood, sensing Sylvie's depression. "We're both overwrought—emotionally exhausted after all we've been through this year."

Sylvie didn't answer, her feeling of desolation growing as the newsroom outside grew quieter and she realized once again she hadn't spoken to Dick all day.

Kitty was a witch. She seemed to read Sylvie's mind. In quick, staccato sentences she started to tell Sylvie in a rare illuminating moment of intimacy why Dick Kolinzcky troubled her so much. He apparently bore an uncanny resemblance to a man she had once loved, a man who had let her down ten years before, and the father of a baby she had lost in childbirth. "So can you understand, little one, why I feel so protective. It's too close for comfort, after all that happened to Nell. Seeing the way you moon over Dick, like I used to moon over . . . well, never mind. It's as if God has given me a chance to look after you."

Across the newsroom, Smith Maynard came out of his office and Kitty shut up abruptly, her soft manner disappearing as she went to check her looks in the mirror balanced on top of the filing cabinet. "Now perhaps you can understand *why* I get so concerned . . ." were her parting words as she headed out in Smith's direction.

Yes, I *understand*, Sylvie thought, but it's totally unfair.

She'd been brought up to think her father looked like Alan Ladd, but that hadn't meant her father had ever been invited to Hollywood or had ever stepped onto a film set, for that matter. So why should Dick's resemblance to a man in Kitty's past mean Dick had to be endlessly run down? Kitty was exasperating!

Nell never returned to her job at the *Evening Mirror*. For some reason, although no one ever questioned her three-month leave of absence to look after her elderly parents, she told Sylvie and Kitty she couldn't face going back.

She took a job at Selfridges in the cosmetics department and to Sylvie's amazement seemed to love it as much as she'd ever loved her journalistic job at the *Mirror*. It didn't make sense to Sylvie.

"Aren't you wasting your brain, Nell?"

"No, I'm not," Nell answered with every bit of her old fire. "I'm learning. I love the cosmetics business, you know that. One day when —if—Gert and Pierre get back together, I'm going to join them."

There was defiance in Nell's voice, but as usual, Sylvie thought, Nell had been too preoccupied with herself to question the breakup. She had to admit that this time Nell had certainly had *enough* to preoccupy her. In any case, she didn't want to talk to Nell more than she had to about Pierre and Gert.

"A lover's tiff?" was all Nell had asked, and Sylvie had just nodded, still seeing in her mind Aunt Gert's tear-swollen, unhappy face. Would she ever know what had really happened? Finally, Gert had opened up enough one day to say Pierre had tried to make up but that she'd made it clear she didn't want anything more to do with him, and it was true—he _had_ emigrated to Canada.

"I ran into Dick in Oxford Street today," Nell told Sylvie one surprisingly warm spring evening when they were sitting together on the steps leading down to their bed-sit. "We had a cup of tea together."

"What—what did he say?" Sylvie could hardly get the question out, but not knowing what they'd talked about was worse than having to ask.

"Well, I can certainly see why you're so hung up on him. He's as smart as a whip . . . attractive, too. Funny, I never noticed it when I was at the _Mirror_." Nell leaned back languorously, wetting her lips— her movements, her smile, all suggestive of a special secret kind of intimacy. "But you're still too nice for him, Sylvie." Nell sprang forward, bringing her face close to Sylvie's as she continued, "He's got big plans—he won't be around here much longer. He knows of some opportunity opening up for him in the States—or Canada, I think he said—he's so ambitious, _too_ ambitious for you!"

Sylvie didn't answer, her pain on hearing this from Nell and not from Dick growing, as she remembered Dick's intensity, his dark eyes looking into hers, the way he often unnecessarily brushed his hair away from his forehead. Had Nell looked at him the way she looked at other men—most men—with moist, inviting lips, slightly parted, "to make them think of French kissing," as she'd once told Sylvie? Had she leaned her beautiful shapely body back as she was doing now, as an invitation for exploration? Sylvie shivered. "I'm going inside."

Surely Nell had to know she had hurt her? Didn't Nell care? Her best friend and her only beau? Sylvie told herself she was exaggerating their relationship as she lay awake in the dark, but it was hard. As she listened to Nell's steady breathing, so easily able to sleep the sleep of innocence, it was very hard.

When Sylvie arrived at the office next morning she decided to summon up her courage and ask Dick out for coffee. It wasn't the right thing to do. She knew her mother—and probably even Aunt Gert—would be scandalized at her forwardness, but she didn't care. She had to find out whether her suspicions about Dick and Nell were justified—suspicions about what, though? She hardly dared think what she was really suspicious of . . .

Dick came into her office as she was opening the morning mail.

"Sylvie . . ." Dick's earnest manner, his eyes intently boring into hers, made her think of Nell's description—"as smart as a whip . . . attractive, too."

To her horror she found herself snapping: "What do you want?"

His dark skin seemed to darken still more—as if he were blushing. "Well, it sounds as if you're not very interested in anything I have to say. Nell told me . . ."

Sylvie interrupted excitedly, "Yes, she told *me* . . . you're not going to be here long, are you? Got big plans, I hear."

He became agitated. "What's wrong with you?"

She didn't know why she was burning inside, why everything was coming out the wrong way—the green-eyed monster revealed in sharp ugly sounds.

Now he sounded angry. "Well, at least your *best friend* has something intelligent to say. She even knows something about the Canadian economy . . ."

They were having a row. It was incredible. Here she was hearing he was going away—to join a development group in Canada—and instead of encouraging him, wishing him well, she was quarreling with him.

"Kitty's right about you. You're an opportunist!"

"Kitty!" he snorted sarcastically. "I should have my brain examined for thinking that you were my . . . my . . . kind of person. Kitty! That overrated, oversexed joke who dresses up in her mother's clothes, who thinks she's sophisticated with her ugly long nails, chignons, black cigarettes, and too many gin and tonics . . . hmph!" He went on, gathering steam, with an amazing revelation. "Miss Kitty Stein is not that much older than Nell—or you, for that matter! Not even ten years . . . I've seen her birthdate in personnel. Yet you believe every stupid thing that comes out of her overpainted mouth!"

Sylvie shrieked at him, "How dare you speak like that. Kitty has got more brains, more thought, more . . ." To her horror Kitty suddenly materialized in the doorway, a malevolent look on her face.

"What are you doing here? What do you want?" There was a "get out" sign in every icy syllable.

"I came to see Sylvie . . ." Dick's voice was just as insolent as Kitty's.

"I suggest you forget about seeing Sylvie. She's not interested."
Kitty lit a cigarette and blew smoke in his face.

He lost his temper. "You phony bitch," he cried. "I'll decide
whether I forget Sylvie or not. Don't you try to stand in my way. Who
do you think you are, you phony . . ."

Kitty flew at him like a virago, her nails ripping his cheek.

"Oh, no, no . . ." Sylvie tried to pull Kitty away, but there was no
need. Dick backed out, wiping his cheek, his eyes narrowing. "I'll
never forgive you for this, Kitty Stein, never, ever."

Then, "I'll call you later," he hissed at Sylvie.

"Don't bother." She didn't mean to say it . . . didn't mean it. Her
emotions were all mixed up, as she recalled how Nell's leg had rubbed
against Dick's, remembering the cup of tea the two of them had had
together only the afternoon before. She didn't see him looking back
at her; she was too busy fussing over Kitty, calming her down. She
was crying inside, but through the glass her face was a mask of indifference.

By the time Sylvie left the office that evening it was buzzing with
the news of Dick Kolinzcky's outburst in Kitty Stein's office—and the
consequences.

"Poor kid, he's been fired for insubordination," Sylvie heard Sid,
one of the reporters, say as she passed his desk.

Tears came to her eyes. "You mean Dick . . . Dick Kolinzcky?" she
asked tremulously.

Sid didn't bother to look up as he answered. "Yeah . . . well, you
were there. Nobody talks to the great Stein like that and gets away
with it. It's a shame, but at least he was going to leave the country
anyway. Now he says he's going sooner . . . without a reference or his
holiday pay, either."

Sid abruptly turned his attention away from Dick's problems and
stared moodily at the paper in his typewriter.

"Is . . . is he . . . still here?" Sylvie dared to break through Sid's
musing.

Sid shook his head irritably. "Long gone . . . long gone . . ."

It's all my fault, Sylvie thought, as she ran to catch her bus to
Hammersmith. All my fault. Why did I say all the wrong things?

Because you're jealous, she told herself fiercely, jealous that Dick
likes—perhaps even loves—Nell. But if he loved her, did it mean
they'd 'made love'? "Despite what you think, there's only ever been
one," Nell had said. One man, one baby.

Sylvie bit her lip to stop herself from crying out, conscious that people were looking at her. She felt she was going mad.

Dick was packed and ready to go; his cousin Peter was sending him off in style in a hired car. He looked around the room that had seemed such a haven when he'd first arrived in England as a refugee after the war. The lump in his throat had nothing to do with the room. He'd always hated its shabbiness; memories from his earliest childhood kept tormenting him, reminding him that life had once been different. He could still remember that the sheets touching his skin had been soft, soothing, that nannies had bathed and dressed him, and that his shoes had never hurt his feet. Now his feet hurt all the time. Cheap shoes.

It had been Nell's remark about the shoes passing by on the pavement above their heads that day that had first made him realize she wasn't just a dolly bird after all, but had a quick wit, a colorful imagination, and perhaps a brain, too. Nell. Strange girl. Sylvie, stranger still.

Dick felt his anger at Sylvie start to rise. Damn and blast those cool, reserved English girls with their quiet, mouselike ways. They were more misleading than flamboyant beauties like Nell, a type he'd always stayed well away from.

There was a knock at the door. Who on earth . . . for a wild second he thought it might be Sylvie come to wish him bon voyage and tell him she really believed in him after all.

The sight of Nell disarmed him, her actions more so. She flung her arms around his neck, making his cravat tighten so he was almost throttled. Despite himself he could feel his penis stir. She was so lovely, so luscious . . .

"Dick, I want to come with you . . ." To his horror, he saw a suitcase behind her in the hall.

"You're crazy . . ." he began to say.

Nell moved her body against his. He halfheartedly tried to withdraw.

Her eyes filled with tears. "No strings, Dick. I've thought of nothing else since I found out your plans. I'm not expecting anything. I promise you, I won't be a burden. I'm your kind of person. I want a new life in a new country where a girl's given a chance because of her brains, not her body. Oh, Dick . . ." She looked so helpless, he involuntarily drew her inside and put his arms around her, not knowing what to say or do.

"Nell, I only have my savings. I couldn't possibly look after you, too," he said helplessly.

"I've got savings, too," she said proudly. "I'll give them to you . . . look." She broke away from him, opening her handbag.

To Dick's amazement, it looked stuffed with pound notes—five-pound notes. "I've got dollars, too." Nell threw her arms around his neck again. "I found out which ship you're on . . . I've got my ticket. I've thought of everything—my passport—even a reference from Smith Maynard—but I can't go alone. I'm too scared. Oh, Dick, please . . ."

The clock on the mantelpiece showed him time was getting short. Even as he saw the minutes ticking away, the downstairs bell rang. That had to be the hired car. "It's no good, Nell. No good." He shook his head.

Nell looked up at him beseechingly. "I'll get a job. I won't hang around once I've found something, but . . . but . . . please let me come with you now. I'll help you. You'll be lonely in a big new country like Canada. I'll sew your socks, cook for you, help you spell . . ." She was laughing, but in a sweet, kind way, not sarcastically. He remembered Nell telling him how Kitty and Sylvie had laughed at him behind his back, laughed about his looks, his ambitions, his poor spelling.

The sweetness of Nell. He could smell something like lilacs on her skin. Again his penis started to throb.

Here was this exciting, truly beautiful young woman saying she wanted to be with him, help him, keep him company on his great adventure—Nell, the beauty he'd always deliberately avoided, sure she would be the one person who *would* ridicule him. He'd been wrong. He felt a surge of elation. He turned to lift her off her feet, finding his hands on her silk-clad legs.

"Anyone at 'ome up there, mate?" The driver of the hired car was shouting upstairs.

Dick hurriedly opened the door again. "Yes, sir, those bags down there; can you start loading? I'll be down to help." He gave Nell a searching look before he ran downstairs.

It was fate—on her side for once—Nell thought, that the phone on the landing started to ring as soon as Dick went out the front door with the driver.

If *he* had answered the phone, but she did, intuitively sensing danger, still not expecting the rush of guilt when she heard Sylvie's timid voice ask if Dick Kolinzcky was still there . . . Sylvie at the office . . . Sylvie, who had obviously just learned from Sid or one of the other hacks that this was the day that Dick was departing on the high seas to find fame and fortune in Canada.

"Sylvie, it's me." Guilt, tension, and anxiety that Dick might suddenly reappear made Nell's voice harsher than she intended.

There was a gasp from the other end.

There was no time to explain that she meant Sylvie no harm, no time to make her understand Dick was not for her . . . that she, Nell, was out of his type of mold, not Sylvie. "I've wanted to tell you for months, Sylvie. I'll write."

"What d'you mean?" Sylvie's voice was low, controlling a sob. Nell knew exactly how Sylvie must look, feel.

She stifled her fragile conscience. "Dick's asked me to marry him —at last. We're going to Canada together to make a new life. One day we'll get our baby back. I'll write, Sylvie, I promise. You'll find someone . . ."

"Who is it?" Dick called. Nell carefully replaced the receiver as he ran back up the stairs.

"Wrong number."

Dick bent down as if to pick up her suitcase, but then straightened up to hold her fiercely by the shoulders. "No strings?"

"No strings." Nell looked into Dick's dark eyes and felt her stomach lurch. Canada with Dick Kolinzcky. Canada, next-door to America, what a way to go . . . what a stepping stone to step on. It was going to work. It *had* to work.

4

Paris,
October 11, 1957

naxim's

3 RUE ROYALE

UN DINER POUR CELEBRER

LE VINGT-ET- UNIEME ANNIVERSAIRE

DE LA NAISSANCE

DE SYLVIE

11 OCTOBRE 1957

MENU

Terrine de poisson avec son coulis de tomate

Canard rôti à l'aigre-doux

Granité de poire

Le gâteau de Sylvie

LES VINS

Bâtard-Montrachet 1950

Château Haut-Brion 1945

Krug 1947

Twenty-one years old at Maxim's in Paris—it wasn't a dream come true, because she had never dreamed that particular dream, but it certainly represented some of her "dreams"—catching a plane to a foreign capital as easily as catching a bus to the West End of London, just to eat an extraordinary gastronomic dinner with magnums, not ordinary-sized bottles, of champagne, served by attentive but never obsequious waiters who looked like film stars. There had been presents, too, in discreet velvet boxes. Her mother had been right for once. Good things could come in small parcels. Above all, her dream had always been to be able to display a kind of nonchalance when accepting privilege and luxury. Not indifference—which was rude and not the way to "win friends and influence people"—but a charming nonchalance she felt she would never be able to adopt. Nell would be able to do it, even if she were given the crown jewels. Sylvie dragged her mind away from Nell. She had forgiven her, would probably always forgive her *anything*, but she couldn't allow her thoughts to dwell without some pain on the person she still considered, in some deep-rooted and perverse way, to be her best friend.

Kitty, sitting at one end of the long table, really acted like a best friend. Yet Kitty would always be the "boss." Sylvie couldn't regard her any other way. She stifled a sigh, but in seconds she was blushing as a huge cake, ablaze with candles, was set before her.

"Wish! Wish!" They were all crying out the same thing, but Sylvie knew only Aunt Gert was really wishing with her—for her to gain what she wanted most in life—not that wishing had ever got either of them anywhere, although since Aunt Gert had become an Avon lady she seemed much happier, thank goodness.

Sylvie blew out all the candles but one. Was it a sign? Proof there would always be one stumbling block? Swiftly she extinguished the remaining flame and jumped up to kiss first Kitty, then Aunt Gert, and her mother and Ed. It was ironic to think she was sitting there as large as life in the most exclusive restaurant in Paris *because* of her mother and Ed.

Her mother's letter had emphasized that they were spending Ed's "hard-earned savings to return to Europe for the first time since our marriage, just to be with you on your twenty-first . . . but we'll get to London a day or two late because we're on a package tour for Korean veterans that goes first to Paris, then to London . . ."

Kitty thought that was typical of Sylvie's mother. Determined Maud was not going to steal Sylvie's thunder with a big homecoming scene, Kitty had come up with the idea that Sylvie should join *them* in Paris actually *on* her twenty-first birthday, rather than wait to celebrate a few days late in London. Again Sylvie found herself stifling a sigh, along with the thought that planning the idea had been much more fun than actually living it.

It hadn't taken more than twenty-four hours for the dreaded Ed Tramello to start criticizing her as he had always done, for her mother to join in, and for Aunt Gert to tell them both sharply to "shut up."

Gert's fierce protective manner had stunned her sister Maud into silence, until Maxim's champagne had untangled her vocal cords and —with the appearance of the cake—opened her tear ducts.

Ed snorted with exaggerated scorn and announced he was going "to take a leak." Her mother, apparently used to this reaction to her tears, wiped them swiftly away with the heavy linen napkin, smearing her mascara onto her over-rouged cheek.

Sylvie was about to jump up again to give her mother what she knew would be a useless kiss of comfort, when Smith Maynard said dryly, "Don't I get a kiss? After all, I'm the guy who's paying the bill . . ."

Sylvie knew she was blushing again, but who cared? Ungrateful, *unthinking* wretch that she was, so conscious of her mother's every move, incredibly she'd forgotten momentarily that she had a life of her own to attend to and that included paying special attention to the man sitting at the opposite end of the table from Kitty.

"You really don't know how pretty you are, do you, Sylvie?" Smith pulled her face down so that instead of her timid kiss landing on his cheek, she found her mouth on his.

"Steady there, birthday girl . . . even birthdays don't get you that far!" Kitty was laughing, but Sylvie knew she meant every word. Kitty had worked relentlessly to become "Smith's woman" and she was holding on grimly to a fragile, up-and-down relationship. Forced to hear endless details, ironically Sylvie now often found herself in the uncomfortable position of advisor to the advice maven.

Sid, dear Sid, the reporter she had clung to the terrible day Nell had told her she was leaving with Dick—how could she have sat down without giving Sid a kiss? He had made such a loving toast, too, before the cake arrived, calling her "Miss Indispensable Ray of Sunshine." Life would be so simple if only she could fall in love with Sid! But love wasn't simple. It was a disease, the kind you could only catch when you least expected it. You couldn't inject it, force it, even hypnotize yourself out of it. She knew, she'd tried.

There was a sound of breaking glass, then "oh, shit." Kitty had knocked her glass of red wine to the floor, spilling much of its contents on the way into the trouser cuff of the paper's leading Paris correspondent sitting on her right. Instead of apologizing, Kitty started to giggle. "Even Houdini couldn't have done that! Now you'll have something to drink when you get home," she slurred. "A little unorthodox, but just lap it up like this . . ." Kitty tried to look coquettish as she wiggled her tongue in an imitation of a cat lapping up milk. She merely looked grotesque.

Sylvie glanced at Smith. He was scowling as she knew he would be. How could Kitty act so stupidly? Smith had been warning her to lay off the booze. She always promised him she would—"cross my heart and hope to die"—but there was a gremlin inside her, she'd told Sylvie, that forced her into self-destruction.

In a detached way, Sylvie saw a familiar scene ensue. Smith Maynard looked at his watch, then beckoned Sid, talking in a low monotone. She could guess what he was saying, appointing Sid as "keeper of the Kitty . . . and her slave," ordering him to get both of them safely back to the hotel, while he, Smith, went gallivanting somewhere else. It had happened before. It would happen again until Kitty stopped losing control of herself. Smith Maynard was not prepared to be a nursemaid and put Kitty to bed until she sobered up; he was a tough editor who would never put up with Kitty's attention-grabbing antics.

"She's out of control, Sylvie. This is getting to be a bitch." Smith Maynard whispered across the table. "I'm going back to the Paris office to work." Sylvie tried to smile, to make light of the situation so that Kitty would not guess what he was saying, but she couldn't cover her anxiety.

"Where're you goin', Smith?" Just as Sylvie dreaded, Kitty had seen Smith stand up, obviously getting ready to stride out. Kitty tried to grab his arm as he passed, and missed. Her chair listing to one side, she ended up with her head in the by-now thoroughly aggravated Paris correspondent's lap.

Out of control. The words rang in Sylvie's ears later as Sid, who had become Smith's right-hand man, helped Kitty into a cab. She'd hated the sneer so apparent on her mother's face, the "I-told-you-so" smugness on Ed Tramello's. What a miserable end to Kitty's generous, joyous gift.

Impulsively Sylvie put her arm around Kitty, who immediately fell asleep on her shoulder, every few minutes emitting a soft, low snore.

As the taxi crossed the Place de la Concorde, Sylvie closed her eyes. Out of control. That had been the verdict on Pa O'Halloran's sudden death, a heart attack brought on by grief that had grown out of control.

"He never got over Nell going off like that without saying good-bye or anything." Mrs. O'Halloran had looked smaller, more wizened than ever, after the funeral when Sylvie and Aunt Gert had each held a work-worn hand. Even then, when her own wound was still fresh and deep, Sylvie had found herself sticking up for Nell. "She didn't mean to hurt you, Ma. She loves you. I know the news is going to really . . . really upset . . ."

"No, it's not." The little lady had sounded emphatic for the first time in Sylvie's memory. "She won't care. Nell hasn't got a heart—doesn't know what the word means—not like you . . ." Mrs. O'Halloran had reached up to pat Sylvie's cheek awkwardly. Sylvie had longed to explain just why Nell had had to go with Dick, why she'd had to follow him wherever he went because he wanted her with him. But she couldn't. There was no way she could hurt the lonely old lady further by telling her about Nell and Dick's baby. It was still too hard for her to think about coherently, let alone talk about it.

Then there was the money. Mrs. O'Halloran had started to tell Sylvie about some missing money, her savings in fact, but with tears in her eyes she'd obviously thought better of it. Despite Sylvie's prompting, she would say no more.

For a time Sylvie had moved back to Hackney with Aunt Gert, but she'd felt both in the way and claustrophobic at the same time. One day Aunt Gert, who was getting over her own sorrow by worrying about Sylvie, suggested perhaps they should both move to a totally new place together. They'd found an airy, first-floor flat at the poor end of Chelsea Embankment.

It was just as well that Sylvie had moved closer to town, because it was then that Smith Maynard started to take Kitty out on a more regular basis and Kitty began to behave so erratically.

She'd been madly in love with him for years, she'd told Sylvie—as if Sylvie needed to be told. Love *was* madness, when it wasn't pain—the mental kind of pain from betrayal, the physical kind as a result of making love with a man.

When the "dates" first began everything was fine, except that Kitty arrived in the office later and later, as if going out with the real decision-maker on the paper gave her the right to cut corners and slack off.

There were rumors around the office that Smith was soon going to be made editor, that the present incumbent was longing to retire after a lifetime's combat in the hot seat, taking the fire either from the government or the public, whenever either or both thought the paper transgressed its boundaries. Life at the office had started to become uneasy when a couple of times Sylvie had had to ghostwrite Kitty's column, feeling that though she was protecting her boss's reputation, she was also shortchanging the paper. When the columns appeared without comment—except from an embarrassingly appreciative, so-bered-up Kitty—filling-in *as* Kit Carson had begun to become a habit.

If only she'd felt better about it. If only she'd been able to view it as the heaven-sent opportunity an understudy longs for when the star fails to appear. It never felt that way. It felt instead like a hole-in-the-corner exercise. She had grown more and more guilt-ridden.

At first Sylvie had told herself it was good practice as she'd tried to copy Kitty's aggressive style. Sometimes she had found it too difficult to do—and hadn't even tried. A certain reader's letter had struck too much of a chord in her own life. She'd taken the letter home to answer, endeavoring to deliver an urgent message via the column that "life can go on. Life does have meaning. There is hope after . . ." The next morning, about to give the copy to the subeditor, she'd found she'd written ". . . Dick." A Freudian slip that she didn't need Freud's help to understand.

During the last three months things had grown worse. Life at the office was no longer just uneasy; it was unbearable. Smith was obviously trying to cool his relationship with Kitty, who seemed oblivious to his slights and constantly threw herself at him. In the past, when-ever Kitty returned from lunch a trifle high, she'd nevertheless brought back an aura of glamour from the two or three hours spent at the best table in the best restaurant. Sylvie had always thought of ice cubes clinking in crystal glasses, could almost smell the exotic gust of Shalimar mingling with the plat de jour. Now, Kitty's drinking evoked a different picture. She was a sad spectacle; drink added to her gloom, instead of washing it away.

If it hadn't been for Sid, Sylvie wouldn't have known what to do. It was Sid who'd told her, even as they'd driven to London Airport for her first trip abroad, that unless Kitty changed her ways, she was headed for big trouble.

"What trouble?" Sylvie had asked, sure Sid had to be wrong, and overexcited about her wonderful birthday treat. She was happy to see Kitty's head close to Smith's in the front seat of the company limousine. Sid had hesitated, then whispered, "Smith puts the paper first and last. Anyone who doesn't measure up doesn't get a second chance."

"But . . . but . . . isn't it wonderful he agreed to come with Kitty to Paris?"

Sid as usual had tried to be diplomatic, not realizing that Sylvie had never been able to understand how Kitty had persuaded Smith to host a birthday dinner for her at Maxim's, as well as insisting that Sid come, too.

"He likes you, Sylvie. He knows more than you realize." Seeing Sylvie blush, Sid had squeezed her hand tightly. "He knows you're a trooper—we all know it—but he had to be in Paris anyway. Kitty knew that. He's setting up a series on the Common Market, taking potshots at France in particular. You know the sort of thing—'The froggies have no shame, only envy, are now trying to ruin us tradewise, tying up with the Germans in the European Economic Community . . .' "

As their taxi went up the Champs-Elysées to turn left onto Avenue Georges Cinq, Sylvie wondered if Smith really had gone to the Paris office to work. She doubted it. Paris at night was too seductive. She suddenly longed to be part of its seduction, going somewhere in a décolleté dress, scented with Shalimar, for an assignation with someone special.

"Do you want to go to a nightclub?" Was Sid able to read her mind too? His earnest scrubbed face came close to hers. She instinctively tried to retreat but Kitty, lying heavily to one side of her, blocked her way. She couldn't budge. A waft of garlic from Sid's breath demolished all further thoughts of assignations.

"No, I'd better not, Sid . . . another time."

"Oh, all right." He scowled in the dark of the taxi, thinking that Dick Kolinzcky had probably been right after all to go off with the beauteous, sexy Nell. Sylvie was a cold fish. He doubted if anything, or anyone, could ever turn her on.

~~~

11 October 1957

Dearest, Darling Sylvie,

I've just realized today is your twenty-first birthday. Sorry you won't get this for a couple of weeks, unless the mail pulls its socks up. I've been so busy fixing up the

apartment—it's huge, near the Royal York—that's To-
ronto's best hotel. I love it. It's "neat"—no, not tidy—
you know me! "Neat" is a word they use over here to mean
"trendy," "with it." We'd say "super!"

Dick is also frantically busy. Right now he's up in
Saskatchewan on some uranium deal—he has a deal a
minute. I hate to say it, Sylvie, but you spotted him all
right. He is brilliant and so sweet. I hope one day we'll
all be one happy family again when you've found Mr.
Right—I know you will—he's going to be wonderful—
just like you.

Nell put her pen down and once more studied the bracelet with the
one gold charm she was sending to Sylvie. It was the perfect present.
Nothing could remind Sylvie more of their tie to each other. Nell
pinched her lips together as she started to elaborate on the "exciting
life" she and Dick were living together in Toronto.

Toronto. Exciting! Hmph! It was dullsville personified, where emotions only erupted over ice hockey! One day she would buy a stick just
to break it over the next hockey moron's head. If Sylvie only knew
what a travesty of the truth her letter was . . . the laughs were certainly all on her.

"Exciting" with Dick meant checking his spelling for mistakes and
his socks for holes. When he was actually present in the three-room
apartment they shared, actually miles away from Toronto's prestigious
Royal York Hotel, Dick studied most of the night, but most of the
time he wasn't there. He was traveling, God knew where, to parts of
Canada that were "no place for a woman." At least that's what he said.

It was funny how she missed him when he was away—even though
by now she'd learned to live it up a little in his absence. Even in
dullsville, there were always one or two kindred spirits who knew
where the action was.

But when Dick was in the apartment there was an electricity about
the place, one she easily plugged into, hating to leave, encouraging
him in his ideas, certain he was going to make it big.

Nell quickly scanned the evening paper to add a few restaurant
names to the letter. "We love trying new places every week . . ." She
then wrote a rapturous, entirely fictitious report of the places Dick
had taken her to—"to Stratford, Ontario, two hours' drive away, for
the opening night of Tyrone Guthrie's Shakespeare Festival in a mar-

velous modern adaptation of an Elizabethan playhouse overlooking—
yes, you've guessed it—a river called the Avon . . . sailing on a big
shot's yacht on Georgian Bay and Lake Muskoka, where those that
count have mansions they call 'cottages' and often own whole islands,
too! Yes, Sylvie dear, there's plenty of life up here north of the Forty-
ninth Parallel." Nell thought for a moment, then added, "When
they've made it big, it's *very big* up here!" She signed, "Lots of love,
Nell," with her usual flourish, then picked up Sylvie's present once
more, letting the gold charm swing from its anchor. Yes, it was the
perfect choice.

As she wrapped the bracelet in tissue paper, then folded the letter
around it, the phone rang. She hoped it was Dick telling her when
he'd be back. In one way, she liked the freedom his absence gave her.
In another, she longed for his return, especially this time. He was still
unfinished business, an elusive, strange personality that defied pin-
ning down. She wasn't about to give up on that.

She'd surprised him the night before he'd left on this trip up north,
going into his room at midnight in a negligee she'd bought expressly
for the purpose of seducing him. The roses over the bosom that were
so demure when seen on the hanger didn't hide her nipples but emphasized their deep color, making them look darker, bruised, even
painted, as she'd heard the whores painted theirs in Quebec City. The
rest of the slim pink sheath was transparent so he'd had to realize she
was naked underneath. But she'd been smart enough not to choose
anything that gaped open, giving away the goods with no trouble, no
anticipation. She knew that wasn't the way to get a man like Dick.
Little pearl buttons linked the two sheer halves together from top to
toe—little virginal buttons that just asked to be ripped apart.

"Hello." Her voice was breathless, overanxious. She frowned into
the phone. "Dick?"

Despite a bad line, nothing could hide the unusual excitement in
his voice. "I'm going to a . . . *crackle, crackle* . . . I'll meet Joseph
Hirschhorn at last . . . a great coup . . . *crackle, crackle* . . ."

The interference grew worse, but Nell hardly needed to hear any
more. Dick's interest in Joseph Hirschhorn had become obsessive.
She was sick of hearing his name, sick of learning how five years
before Hirschhorn had organized a search with eighty men using
Geiger counters in Ontario's Algoma Basin and found a giant uranium
deposit, that he'd staked claims covering fifty-six thousand acres, had
then moved on to obtain rights to mine uranium on four hundred and

seventy square miles to establish the first Canadian uranium mine. So what, Nell had been responding for months. Uranium wasn't gold.

"Where's the meeting?" she screamed down the phone.

He wasn't listening, or couldn't hear, for suddenly his voice came through with clarity, not answering her question. "He's looking for new ventures, and I know just what they should be. This could be the turning point."

"Where are you meeting?" she attempted again.

"With the first group in Winnipeg, then Chicago." His voice was all business.

Nell pouted, the pout conveyed by her tone. "I'll meet you there— in Chicago." A wheedling note affected her voice. "You promised the first time you crossed the border you'd take me . . ."

"Impossible."

Nell stamped her feet in fury. She had heard that inflexibility before when they had been face to face in the same room. Despite every ploy, every effort, Dick had always been immovable whenever they fought. What hope had she now when he was nearly three thousand miles away?

"How long will you be gone?" She was seething with anger but knew better than to express it.

Again the line deteriorated at the crucial words, "about a month to . . . *crackle, crackle* . . . come back to Toronto immediately."

"You can't be serious!" Nell exploded.

". . . may be able . . . this is the best chance I've had . . . let you know next week . . . *crackle, crackle*." She heard the receiver go down with a decisive click and she burst into furious tears. Damn and blast him. Who did he think he was? The tears didn't last long. As she looked up she could see her reflection in the mirror above the phone. A red-eyed, pale-faced Nell O'Halloran stared back.

Crying over a man? She'd have to put a stop to that. But she needed money to go back to the fast track. Should she risk her meager savings at the club? The thought of poker, blackjack, and the men that went with it made her spirits rise. One man in particular, Joe Diaz, who looked as Hispanic as his name, yet was as Canadian—and as obsessed with ice hockey—as the Canadian prime minister.

Joe Diaz. Nell ran her tongue over her lips, remembering the way he'd stared at her steadily the first time she'd been taken to the Apollo, the secret gambling club, by Cliff Atkins, one of the more hip guys at the advertising agency where she typed from nine to five.

Used to attention all her life, she had been surprisingly unnerved by Diaz's unwavering stare at first—although he'd made no move to come closer. Then she'd forgotten about him with a winning streak at roulette taking all her attention. When her luck turned and her winnings disappeared along with all the money Cliff was willing to provide, Nell had looked up with eyes about to brim over with frustrated tears; she locked into Diaz's gaze as securely as if their eyes were a pair of bar magnets.

It had been easy to give Cliff the slip. She'd gone to the ladies' room, knowing Mister Hispanic Hypnotic Eyes would be waiting for her when she came out—and he was, acting the way she loved a man to act, silently, masterfully taking her arm and leading her out by a back door to a long dark limo.

"You're a beauteous creature," was all he'd said on their drive through dark empty streets to the edge of town. After parking beside a clump of trees, he'd offered her a drink from a heavy silver flask. She'd been prepared to fight off the usual pass, had been vaguely disappointed when it hadn't come, and had wondered what all the fuss was about and why he'd even bothered to pick her up at all. An hour later without much conversation he'd driven her back to the flat without touching her once. But he *had* given her a special pass to the club and suggested she come as his guest as often as she liked, "because you've got star quality, Miss Nell O'Halloran . . . you can be a very special attraction."

Cliff Atkins hadn't spoken to her for at least a week—as if she'd cared—but when he finally did, she'd used all her guile to find out more about Mr. Hispanic and was all the more intrigued when Cliff had warned her to beware. "Joe Diaz is a dangerous fella; he's part owner—maybe the sole owner—of Apollo, but everyone says he's really part of the Mafia, the Canadian branch. Why do you want to know, anyway?" It had been easy to fob Cliff off with a vague excuse, and the next night, not a little scared, Nell had gone to the club alone. It was as if Diaz had been waiting for her, expecting her. She was given a great chunk of chips and a spot at the table, where she was literally the center of attention. Nell had lapped up every moment—especially when after an hour or two Diaz had led her to a back room for some caviar and champagne, his eyes never leaving her, looking her over slowly as if she were a masterpiece about to be put on exhibit.

It was the first of many solo visits—and irritated that Diaz always seemed in such total control of himself, she'd decided one night to make the first move, deliberately pushing her body against his as they'd gone toward the back entrance for her usual limo ride home. Instead of opening the door Diaz had swung round to face her, as inscrutable as ever, maneuvering her into a dark corner. "You like to fuck, don't you, Nell?" he'd hissed, ". . . but there's a time and a place for everything. We'll make it together, baby, and I promise you, it will be worth waiting for. But I have big plans for you . . . and, for me, business always comes before pleasure." She'd seethed with fury but she'd still listened as he'd outlined the kind of future he had planned for her, *if* she was prepared to follow his directions. Thank God a warning bell had sounded in her head. He'd made the hotel job of luring wealthy, bored businessmen to the Apollo sound tempting for a few minutes. Then she'd seen right through it. She would be little more than a hooker, without any real share in the profits. That wasn't the way to get rich—and certainly it wasn't how to get rich and respectable. After her ordeal in Hammersmith, Nell was determined never to be trapped by a man or men again.

When she'd refused even to consider it, Diaz had told her not to come back to the club until she changed her mind.

Now she pummeled her hands on the kitchen tabletop. There had to be a better way to the top, and it wasn't in her dreary job at the agency where all the women were jealous and all the men scared shitless that she'd make them lose their cool in business hours.

Her anger came back as she saw the letter she had just written to Sylvie, a letter full of lies about a happy, exciting life with Dick— Dick, who was now going to the States without her, who might be away a month. Hell and damnation! She couldn't risk losing the little she had. Even if she were allowed into the club, she might get in debt to Diaz and end up getting laid for a pittance.

Nell went into her bedroom and took a letter out of the shoebox where she'd hidden it a week or so before. He was obviously still in love with her. The "froggy" with the magic formula hadn't been able to get her out of his mind, even though he'd gone as far away as he could to forget her. His letter was so predictable that every word reminded her of Harry Pegler; she'd thought when she'd made love with him at Aunt Gert's house that he'd be able to teach her some fantastic, erotic French tricks without actually fucking. Instead, he'd slobbered like a dog in heat and she'd had to turn into the teacher to keep him on a rein until she could come. Until now, she had never thought it worth losing Aunt Gert's friendship. Nell could still remember the poor woman's face when Gert had come home unexpectedly and found her dull, pompous little chemist Pierre Repelle sucking her dry on the floor. What a scene that had turned out to be. She would never have guessed Gert could get so steamed up. It had been a revelation to see her go to work destroying Pierre's treasured *laboratoire*.

That was the trouble with the working class. They had such boring ideas, such a stereotyped, narrow vision of life. Just because Pierre had given in to what he called his "beeg lust for 'er," Gert had had to play Sarah Bernhardt and break up *everything*—literally *everything*—the lab, the company, the entire relationship. Such a waste, for they had had something going that could have really produced. At least Pierre had provided the spur to send her running to Dick. The day she'd received Pierre's first letter from Canada was the day she'd learned when Dick Kolinzcky was leaving. It had been a definite signal that Canada was where she ought to be headed, too.

She hadn't given Pierre or his formulas a thought until now, but the more her rage grew over Dick, the more she kicked herself for wasting time. She loved the beauty business, always had since she'd been old enough to open a jar. She could run rings around Gert in the sales department. She reread Pierre's second letter once more and made up her mind. She would give it a try. With a sure, steady finger she dialed information to try to obtain a Montreal number.

"Pierre, *c'est moi* . . ." Her voice was soft, sad, wistful. "Yes, at last . . ."

There was a long sigh at the other end, then an excited babble of French. She interjected, "I've missed you, too. I've tried not to—but—" It was her turn to sigh.

"Oh, Nell, *ma chérie, petite* Nell . . . I want you so badly . . ." It was a case of Harry Pegler all over again. Like Harry Pegler, he didn't stand a chance. By the time Nell hung up, she was sure she had him masturbating for relief, and everything was arranged. She would arrive on Friday for the weekend—which, she knew with resigned boredom, would certainly be spent in his bed. But then on Monday she would begin her apprenticeship in the beauty business in earnest. Her timing—or rather Dick's, if he but knew it—was extraordinary, for Pierre had just told her with pride that since his arrival in Montreal the year before he had been working nonstop and he had just landed an important free-lance job as consultant on a pharmaceutical project. "I am earning a lot of money—you'll be surprised, *ma chérie*. I now 'ave a research lab of my own. Zis is ze land of opportunity. And now, *ma belle*, you will be my inspiration . . ."

There was one more thing she had to do. She wasn't about to put herself in the Frenchman's hands without escape money.

She brushed aside the knowledge that it would mean burning her bridges with Dick forever as she tried to open the box where she knew he kept an emergency fund.

Finally, frustrated and irritable, after trying in vain to force the box open with a knife, she once again unwrapped Sylvie's present. She would use the charm for the job—the charm that would remind Sylvie of the promises they had made to each other long ago. The gold scissors with knife-sharp blades were tiny but they could cut, pierce skin, bring blood. They would remind Sylvie of their childhood blood pact.

Nell forced them into the small aperture and easily pried open the box.

She gasped. Dick was a sly one, always pleading poverty when she asked him to take her out. Inside the box was a fat bunch of banknotes, easily five hundred dollars—and underneath was an old memo from Sylvie accepting Dick's invitation to see *Separate Tables* "in the gods."

Sentimental fool. Nell cut the memo in shreds with the tiny scissors and flushed the pieces down the toilet. Then she neatly tucked the dollar bills into her purse. "Thank you, Dick," she said sardonically to the snapshot propped up on her dressing table. "I hope you agree this *is* an emergency. I promise you, you'll get it back in spades one day . . ."

∿∿

Inadvertently, Sylvie's mother had done her a good turn for once. How irritated Maud would have been to know how far off target her poisonous darts had landed.

Maud had written—ostensibly "full of a mother's natural concern" —to warn her about tying herself up with an alcoholic. "Kitty's going to ruin herself and pull you down with her if you don't watch out. Her advice column is a joke when you compare it with what we have here in the States."

She had enclosed a few clippings of advice columns called "Dear Abby" and "Dear Ann Landers," apparently written by identical twin sisters, who were intensively competitive. In emphasizing how paltry

Kit Carson's advice was in comparison to the two American dread-
noughts—both fast appearing in papers all over America—her mother
had hit a nerve, not so much rattling Sylvie's loyalty or love for Kitty
but appealing to her common sense and natural antenna for what
readers everywhere were beginning to want. Sylvie immediately saw
that both Abby and Ann prided themselves on "telling it like it is."
They were both warm, witty, and straightforward, with no emphasis
on *themselves* as all-seeing, sophisticated seers. The overall feeling
Sylvie received from reading the columns scrupulously was that if the
advice mavens weren't sure about something themselves, they sought
advice from experts who did know. Above all, she found their honesty
wonderfully refreshing.

Of course, Maud didn't know what had been happening since her
return to the Tramello Compound in the States. There had been a
steep escalation in the number of complaints—about letters not answered, about glib, reckless advice handed out "with no real heart."
This was all a result, Sylvie knew, of Smith's impenetrable coldness
since their return from Paris. He was no longer "available" for Kitty's
calls, and he didn't return them. There had been one or two embarrassing scenes at the office when Kitty screamed at Sue, Smith's secretary, to no avail.

One morning Sue called Sylvie and asked if she could have lunch
with Smith that day.

"Lunch?" Sylvie repeated incredulously.

"Yes, at the Ivy at one o'clock. Can you make it?" Sue's tone was
impatient, just verging on sarcastic, implying she knew, as everyone
in the office knew, that Sylvie would have climbed Mount Everest to
be there.

Sid certainly knew what it was all about. He came in to wish her
good luck just as she was contemplating going home to change, conscious that her military-style overcoat was old, even missing a button,
and that her simple jumper and skirt did nothing for her; but Sid told
her, "Don't change a thing. Just be yourself."

In two seconds at the Ivy, she'd known if she had been wearing rags
it wouldn't have made any difference. Smith didn't see her as a
woman. She was an appendage of the paper and, it appeared, was now
going to be a valuable one.

"Kitty's taking a leave of absence—enforced by me."

Sylvie looked down at her shrimp cocktail, not knowing what to
say, a lump of pity clogging her throat.

"I've been worried about her—about the column for some time

now." Smith thrust his hand beneath Sylvie's chin, forcing her to look at him. "Don't think I don't know what's been going on. I'm not that much of a dunce, little one."

Of course she blushed, and went on blushing as he continued, "You can write, Sylvie, and under my direction you're going to write a helluva lot. You've got what it takes. As Beaverbrook says about his star Godfrey Winn, you can bloody well 'shake hands with people's hearts.' "

It was the most exciting meal of her life, and it went on and on until the restaurant emptied and waiters started to reset the tables noisily for dinner.

Suddenly unafraid, Sylvie told Smith about the columns she had been studying from America—compassionate, full of integrity, yet entertaining without going overboard. Smith watched her carefully. He was seeing a young Kitty all over again, pulsating with enthusiasm and motivation. Goddammit, why the hell had Kitty had to fall in love with him? Stupid bitch, taking him seriously. She, of all people, should have known better.

In the car on the way back to the office Sylvie again returned to the ideas Ann Landers and Abby had given her. "There's no reason, is there, why we can't use big-name experts? They can only publicize the column." Eyes shining, Sylvie didn't see that Smith was preoccupied with other thoughts. "We can give the reader free advice that would normally cost a fortune . . ."

He interrupted her. "I know. I know. We'll develop that idea, but enough of that for now. I want you to do some special pieces, too. Don't you want your own by-line? Do you want to be Kit Carson all your life?"

"Oh, yes, oh, no . . ." Sylvie was so overwhelmed that without thinking she kissed Smith's weatherbeaten cheek. "I won't let you down."

"I know you won't. There's no chance of that." He winked, the kind of conspiratorial wink Kitty would have given her. Kitty! What about Kitty? Sylvie was contrite. How could she have gone through a three-hour lunch thinking only of her own future, now so incredibly, un-expectedly bright with promise. "Where is Kitty? What about her?"

As the car scraped through a light change from amber to red, Smith scowled. "She's drying out in a clinic." He looked out the window so Sylvie couldn't see his expression. "I put her there myself. She knows this is her last chance. If she doesn't shape up this time, she'll be fired. She's lucky to have another break."

"Can I go and see her?"

"Better you don't. Not yet. In a week or two. I'll let you know when." And, Smith promised himself, that was going to be a long, long time coming. Sylvie was going to go far, and he didn't intend to let Miss Stein put any roadblocks in her way.

Under Smith's direct tutelage, Sylvie took over the Kit Carson column from that day on. Little by little she incorporated new ideas, but more important was her natural ability to convey a sense of caring.

It wasn't always easy. There were quick tears in the ladies' room after Smith threw a column back at her, covered in blue pencil. "Quit trying to be Bob Hope, for God's sake, Sylvie. Wit, yes, sometimes. Not all the time—this is putrid. Where's that famous sensitivity of yours? Don't fuck yourself up."

He was always right, his pencil marks showing her immediately where she'd gone off track. She grew to learn that whenever she was doubtful over the choice of a word, a reference, a pun that sounded too slick, the blue pencil would flush it out. She would take a breather and rethink it over a coffee at the nearby Kardomah Coffee House in Fleet Street. She now had not one but two young assistants, because the Kit Carson mail was increasing at a tremendous pace. Now they delved into the pile to come up with possible lead letters, just as she had once delved. She welcomed their ideas but left nothing to chance, going through the discard basket in case something might trigger an interesting new slant. Borrowing the American idea, she called on outside experts from time to time to get the benefit of knowledge the readers would normally never be able to afford. It worked wonders. The paper's circulation grew as readers became aware they now had the chance to air their problems to the best brains in the country—and for free!

However, as Smith freely admitted at executive editorial meetings with the proprietor, it was Sylvie's unique, wise, yet young-womanly approach that was really giving Kit Carson a new lease on life and was responsible for the record-breaking mail.

True to his word, Smith saw to it that Sylvie had the chance to write pieces under her own by-line.

"How d'you have the time to do all this?" Aunt Gert marveled, seeing a three-column story with "By Sylvie Samuelson" in bold type.

Sylvie chuckled. "You've chosen the right piece to ask that question about, auntie. If you want something done, ask a busy person!" She had established an immediate rapport when she interviewed Cyril

Northcote Parkinson, creator of Parkinson's Law, which satirized the growth of bureaucracy: "Work expands so as to fill the time available for its completion. Expenditure rises to meet income . . ."

". . . And expense accounts . . ." Sylvie had added in a burst of wry self-accusation. Reimbursed for business expenses now, she realized how dangerously quickly she'd come to depend on taxis instead of buses or the tube.

A zany, three-way conversation about fate with John "Look Back in Anger" Osborne, Ian "James Bond" Fleming, and herself . . . a contemplative look at the future of a fifteen-year-old "self-made" millionaire rock star called Paul Anka . . . a hilarious description of America's twin "advisors," Abigail Van Buren and Ann Landers—these were vivid, acerbic pieces that made other journalists take notice of Sylvie. She was being talked about. Where had she sprung from? How had Smith Maynard managed to pull yet another talented rabbit out of his well-worn hat?

It was heady stuff, only occasionally countered by Nell's glowing letters about the marvelous life she was leading with Dick. After a fairly regular flow, the letters stopped coming. Was it because at last Sylvie had been able to write something positive about her own life? She'd played down her success, attributing her new position on the paper to "extraordinary luck." Oh well, she had too much to do and too much to worry about to give Nell's silence much thought.

At last Smith Maynard was officially named editor-in-chief, and to Sylvie's surprise, at the party thrown to celebrate the appointment, Smith himself toasted her as a star in ascendancy. How guilty she felt the next day when he casually told her that now he was the boss, he had no intention of reinstating Kitty.

"But she's okay now," Sylvie pleaded.

Smith was adamant. "I don't care whether she's become a whore or a nun, m'dear. There's no place for her on my ship. Don't worry, I'll see to it that she finds something—maybe in features on the *Sunday Pic* . . ."

Soon after, Sid told Sylvie to stop trying to help Kitty. It was the third time in as many weeks that Kitty had broken their date to meet for lunch. "I'm sorry, Sylv, you've got to face it. Kitty thinks you're public enemy number one. She's around the Street doing the whole Bette Davis number from *All about Eve*. And you, my pet, according to Kitty, have to be the original Eve who gave Joe Mankiewicz the idea in the first place! It's all dagger-in-the-back stuff, but . . ." Sid stopped, seeing Sylvie's anguished expression. He patted her awkwardly. "Hey, listen, don't take it so badly. You've done everything to help her—she's lucky she lasted so long. All that prima donna stuff from a kid born in Birmingham."

"Oh, Sid, underneath all the phony baloney Kitty's wonderful. I *know*."

True to his word, Smith managed to arrange for Kitty to join the women's page of the Sunday paper, and Sylvie went over to welcome her back to Fleet Street.

There was the same velvet snood, the Shalimar, the long, perfect, burgundy-colored nails—Kitty *looked* the same, but there was an icy edge to her voice when she saw Sylvie.

"Ah, my protégée, come with burnt offerings to the altar of knowledge. And how is Monsieur Maynard's latest *folie?* . . ." Kitty looked Sylvie up and down slowly. There was no mistaking her implication, but Sylvie decided to ignore it. She tried to put her arms around Kitty, but Kitty pushed her rudely away, rage and humiliation breaking through her frosty demeanor. "Get away from me, you two-timing little bitch!"

Now Sylvie heard for herself what everyone had been telling her. "Don't think I don't know now what you were really up to behind my back. Yes, Miss Stein, thank you ever so much, Miss Stein, three bags full, Miss Stein," Kitty mimicked, batting her eyelids. "Oh, yes, Mr. Maynard, thank you, Mr. Maynard, yes, I'll open my legs for you, Mr. Maynard, any time and anything you say, sir . . ."

Sylvie ran out of the office in tears. Kitty *was* insane. As so many had tried to tell her, Kitty believed her newfound success and ever-increasing space on the paper was because of a new "hot affair" with Smith Maynard. It was degrading, stupid—but Sylvie had to accept that there was nothing she could do to convince Kitty otherwise.

It hurt. Oh, it hurt a great deal that Kitty seemed to hate her so much—but that was what always happened when you allowed yourself to have feelings for other people. Sylvie gritted her teeth. Work was the only antidote—the only way to live with comparative peace of mind.

⌇

There were no more letters to Sylvie from Nell because living and working in Montreal as Pierre Repelle's "assistant," Nell rarely gave Sylvie a thought, and when she did, she had no enthusiasm to write even a fictitious account of her new life with Pierre.

She occasionally thought about Dick . . . usually when Pierre made love to her, as he did night after grinding night. It helped her get through the monotony of the same wham-bang routine to fantasize that it was Dick on top of her gasping, "Nell, oh, I'm coming . . . oh, Nell, Nell, Nell. . . ." At first she'd pretended to possess a passion equal to Pierre's as his overactive penis so quickly contracted and semen squelched between her legs. "Yes, ohhh . . ." she would moan, "don't go . . . oh, oh, oh," her face a mask of indifference at total variance to her frenzied movements and agitated voice. She took pleasure after a while in tugging Pierre's short blond curls to simulate a building ecstasy that she had once experienced only too well. But it was rage she felt, not ecstasy, as Pierre pumped away. She longed to hurt him, to punish him, to punish all men—especially the one who had exacted such a terrible punishment from her.

She vowed she would never be pregnant again. The new secret wonder pill, obtained, Pierre told her, "with great difficulty and expense, *ma chérie*," took care of that possibility. It was ironic, Nell thought, that although the pill was obviously a godsend, precluding the dreaded "end-of-the-month" anxiety, it also meant she had no more excuse to stop Pierre's passionate bulldozing.

When, raw and sore after a four-hour marathon Sunday session, she fought against resuming on Sunday evening, Pierre locked himself in the bedroom, refusing to come out to go to work on Monday. It took twenty-four hours of coaxing to persuade him that she was longing for him just as much as he was longing for her.

If anything could be worth the nightmare nights, it was the long, if arduous, days learning from him in the lab. She was beginning to understand the essential differences between product formulations. Although Pierre still hadn't revealed his most prized formula—the one with which he hoped to build his own cosmetics empire one day— little by little he had allowed her access to other secret files and formulas.

It hadn't taken Nell long to realize it wasn't so much Pierre's original ideas that counted; it was what he could do, and *did*, to clarify and improve on other people's. Even his "secret" formula using silk was, Nell now knew, somehow based on a silk makeup Helena Rubinstein's chemists had created.

He talked in riddles when she tried to find out what he was so excited about. So far she didn't know enough to interpret his mysterious statements, which, summed up, indicated that it was time for a new skin-care miracle. There hadn't been one since the early forties when a Dr. Blank had brought into being the first moisturizer, proving that despite his unassuming name, he really knew a thing or two about keeping skin young. According to Pierre, he had proved that to achieve such a remarkable thing, it wasn't so much a question of _adding_ moisture to the skin, as _trapping_ the skin's own supply.

Up to then the heavy oils in use hadn't helped the skin at all and could even be detrimental. Dr. Blank had invented a unique "moisturizer" using an oil-in-water emulsion that was so soothing and smoothing it was believed that women would begin to moisturize their skin (and help it stay young) as regularly as they brushed their teeth. Of course, women had to believe in it first, and that, Nell realized—although Pierre obviously didn't—could be a much more difficult task.

Pierre reminded Nell of a magpie. He stole ideas as that sly bird stole bits and pieces from other birds' nests, only to use them more imaginatively.

If only he was more imaginative in bed! If only she could feel even a flicker of desire for him. As it was, for the first time in her life, Nell began to understand her mother's opinion of sex, expressed so often as "It's a duty, Nell. Somehow you have to force yourself to give it to get a roof over your head, food to eat, clothes on your back."

She remembered how shocked her mother had been when, twelve years old, Nell asked if what she had just learned at school could possibly be true? That a man and a woman . . . surely it couldn't be true of her ma and pa? Or could it?

Even now, with a cynical twist to her mouth, Nell remembered her mother hadn't let her finish the sentence. Her face cold and angry, her mother had blurted out, "It doesn't last long, love. It's all over in a few minutes, then he goes to sleep and you can forget all about it."

Her mother hadn't known what she was talking about. She'd never been near a drilling machine like Pierre Repelle. All over in a few minutes? What a joke that was!

It was funny how studying shoes walking by on the Hammersmith pavement had taught Nell what a giveaway they could be. It was amazing the number of people who fussed over their top halves, yet let their bottom halves go to hell. Color, condition, fit . . . Nell prided herself she could even detect the kind of fit that separated "expensive" from "superexpensive." In London she'd described it as

"Lobb over Lotus": one extreme—custom-built and custom fit—to the other—mass-produced pavement loafer.

As it was, later she would describe in an irresistible, little-girl way, how she'd first fallen in love with his shoes. In a way it was true.

Nell dropped her handbag outside Montreal's Chez Delmo Restaurant, as she rushed to the bank to deposit some money for Pierre. It was chaos. Laboratory vials rolled into the gutter as if they were on an assembly line, followed by keys, coins, lipsticks . . . it was all too much. Nell could feel angry tears pricking her eyes as she scrambled vainly to retrieve her possessions. As she lunged to grab one vial, she stumbled, went down heavily on her knees, a new pair of nylons laddering from top to toe like a zipper unzipping.

As she swore under her breath, she became aware of a pair of slim, highly polished black shoes blocking the vials' crazy roll. *Super*expensive shoes. She raised tearful green eyes as a hand with a plain gold band on the third finger supported her elbow and helped her to her feet. "Are you hurt, little lady? Here, let me help you . . ."

A rosy-cheeked, rotund Santa Claus, with fluffy gray-white hair surrounding a shiny bald pate, beamed at her.

Shit! Why couldn't he have matched his elegant shoes? Santa Claus began to pick up her scattered items. Nell's disappointment irrationally boiled over into rage. Why couldn't the shoes have belonged to a Mr. Tall, Dark, and Handsome?

Without warning, for once in her life unpremeditated tears flowed down her cheeks. Life was so unfair, so diabolically unfair. Here she was in the land of opportunity with *no* opportunity to make it big, as she deserved.

Santa Claus was actually pulling out a white linen handkerchief. "Wipe your eyes, pretty one. Here . . ." Nell took a delight in blowing her nose heavily on its pristine whiteness, handing it back to him disdainfully.

"Say, perhaps you need a drink. Would you like something to steady your nerves—you seem all upset? I think I've got everything . . ." Again he gave her an avuncular smile.

She had never been inside Chez Delmo, although Pierre had often promised to take her there. It was known to be the city's finest seafood restaurant, run by the Perissets, who knew food as only the French seemed to know it. Cheapskate that Pierre was, he'd never kept his word. He hardly took her anywhere—except to bed.

Her depression deepened. To hell with the bank and his deposit.

She would have a champagne cocktail, perhaps even two or three to drown her sorrows.

It was the wisest decision of her life. Before the restaurant closed for the afternoon, Nell had learned that Santa Claus was none other than Wallace Wainwright Nesbitt, the subject of one of her clippings in her "make it big" file, a west-coast Canadian who shuttled between Vancouver and Los Angeles when he wasn't shuttling between Los Angeles and New York, New York and London, and the rest of the world. An early supporter of the DuPont chemist Earl S. Tupper—"the first polymer-age saint," he called him—Nesbitt told her he'd found that instead of getting less busy "in my dotage," he'd become more and more involved in the Tupperware revolution.

Nell was a marvelous listener and a tiger when it came to getting a good story. She wasn't interviewing Wallace Nesbitt for any paper. She was interviewing him for herself, particularly when she learned he'd become more and more of a workaholic since his wife's death the year before.

What did Wallace Nesbitt see? What so many men before him had seen—a tremulous, fawnlike beauty with huge, lustrous green eyes that seemed as if they might flood with tears unless one trod very, very carefully, to protect what surely had to be the most sensitive, delicate soul. There was a streak of silver in her dark hair that strangely moved him. She must have been through very hard times.

As Nell placed long pale fingers for a second on his pinstripe sleeve, he groaned inwardly. If only he were younger, if only he could be injected—if even for an hour—with some of her youth, enthusiasm, and vitality, and not have to think about blood-pressure pills, checkups, and lonely, impotent nights.

Nell smiled at him with her eyes as she raised the champagne glass to her lips. "Thank you so much for coming to my rescue." The restaurant was dimming its lights to show them they should be leaving. He was intrigued with her, this girl who was apparently a chemist herself, in the newfangled cosmetics business.

When she shyly asked him if they could meet again to discuss the marketing of one of her ideas, he was momentarily taken aback. It wasn't his style to talk business with women—yet there was something about her. She liked him, he could see that. She needed help; she was an English girl trying to make it in a wild, buccaneer country. He handed her a card, saying gruffly, "Call Miss Gerard. She'll know when I'm next going to be in town."

"Oh, are you leaving?"

"Yep. Got to be back in Vancouver for the weekend, but I'm in and out all the time."

He didn't dare ask for her address or phone number. What could he possibly need it for? He would look like a ridiculous old man. If she called, well, he'd think about seeing her. If she didn't, it would all be for the best.

～～

Six weeks later, Nell had the silk formula. It had taken all her guile, all her acting ability. Above all, it had taken a patience she hadn't even known she possessed. She was learning. Oh boy, she told herself grimly, she was learning fast.

Since meeting Wallace Nesbitt, an idea had been growing and growing until it consumed her. First there was Plan A, to be followed by Plan B, and—if things went miraculously according to both plans —finally Plan C. But how to accomplish A and obtain the silk formula, which despite his demonstrated lust and often-proclaimed love for her, Pierre still kept under strict lock and key?

Ironically, in the end, visible symptoms of the ambition burning deep inside her led naturally to her goal. Her appetite gone, her concentration on her usual lab work waning, her dead dull responses to the usual nighttime routine began to concern even the obsessively self-centered Pierre.

"What's wrong with you?" He sulked. He cajoled. He cried. He raged, coming to a conclusion that was one hundred and eighty degrees away from the truth. He always knew when Nell had been through his papers. In a perverse way it pleased him, thinking she was looking for evidence of his infidelity or more knowledge about his past life, which he had never been too eager to divulge. Subconsciously, did he want her to find the document he had only recently received, which told him he could now consider himself a widower? It proved enough evidence had been gathered to assume his young wife had died in a concentration camp. Now as Nell seemed to pine more every day, Pierre was sure she had found the proof that, despite what he had told her in the past, he was, in fact, free to marry.

It was a moment of exaltation. Until that second when he had realized what was really responsible for Nell's strange transformation, he'd never been sure of her. Half angel, half witch, he had never been totally certain that his body, masterful though he knew it to be, was enough to keep her obediently in check.

He mentally drew himself up, cocksure, strident. "So zat is ze reason you are so un'appy, *ma chérie*. You are, after all, like all ze other women. You want me to marry you. You 'ave read that I am a free man, *n'est-ce-pas?*" He enjoyed the feeling of supremacy, proud that despite the urge to ravage her, he was going to let her suffer for a while. How abject she looked, turned to the wall, only her heaving shoulders showing the amount of her emotional distress. He decided to keep her guessing . . . longing to see her grovel. He knew he would marry her in the end. It would be ridiculous not to. She was the most brilliant student he'd ever known, naturally gifted and innovative in the lab. She would also be a superb advertisement for his masterwork —for the silk products that could revolutionize skin care. His spirits soared at the thought of her by his side bringing them into being, selling them. She even had good marketing ideas, for a woman. Yes, he would make her his wife.

Nell didn't know how she managed to control herself. She had to turn to the wall, her shoulders shaking with suppressed laughter. As Pierre had gone on with his monologue, it had all fallen into place. What a respite it was. How wonderful to lie awake in the dark, pretending to sniffle and snivel, while he, the bastard that he was, talked about wrestling with the decision of whether to marry her, that until he had made that decision he couldn't touch her.

Unfortunately—as she guessed—his self-imposed celibacy wouldn't last long. She gave it a maximum of twenty-four hours.

As they sat at the dining table after working together in silence all day, Pierre started to complain, half accusing, half self-pitying, " 'Ow can I keep my mind on my work when you are with me all day, worrying me all night about zis marriage?" He shot his hand under the table, under her garters, between her legs, forcing his fingers into her, withdrawing to suck them with sounds of gluttony. He pointed to the bedroom door, his hand shaking. "Get ready for me." His voice was unsteady with anticipation. "You do not need to worry—to weep anymore. I will be your 'usband."

It was child's play from then on for Plan A to move toward fruition. Whereas before she had begun to be careless in her responses to Pierre, hardly bothering to conceal her increasing boredom, now with a small diamond engagement ring on her left hand, she showered him with expressions of love and contentment, eagerly agreeing to go for instruction in the dreaded Catholic church, in preparation for her "conversion" into the faith and a Catholic wedding in the fall.

Pierre's insistence on her religious conversion was hardly consistent with his other, usually erotic requests. One day he demanded she meet him for lunch in Montreal's old quarter wearing one of his favorite outfits, a demure shirt, Scotch kilt with knee-high stockings —"But nothing underneath, my darling." At a dark corner table at the back of the restaurant, beneath the cover of the long tablecloth, she worked him into a frenzy, contracting her wet hole tightly around his probing fingers while she masturbated his swollen penis. She knew now exactly how to time him. A second before he was about to come, she stood up, smoothing down her skirt, one hand forcing him back against the banquette, his eyes closed, his forehead damp with perspiration. "Oh, darling," she whispered, agonized, "I have to go to the loo . . . get the bill quickly . . . let's go home."

Later that night, sated with lovemaking and champagne, made to feel like the king of France, Pierre lay naked while Nell slowly massaged every inch of him with sensual-smelling essential oils. She was naked, too, her full breasts brushing his skin as she leaned over him, whispering details of her magical plan for the launch of his silk skincare line. It should coincide with their wedding, she said, when she would be at her most radiant, when she would make sure that buyers from Eaton's and all the important Canadian stores would be there, and the press, and Radio Canada and . . . There was all the erotic appeal of a thousand and one nights in her voice. Half asleep, Pierre agreed to everything she said. It would all come true and they would live happily—richly—ever after.

~~~

Fate, Nell breathed, fate again was on her side. "Please ask him if I can see him. It's urgent." She replaced the receiver, leaning back against the wall of the phone booth until her heartbeat slowed its too-fast pace.

Mr. Nesbitt was arriving in Montreal on Wednesday. Wednesday was the day Pierre had an all-day meeting with one of his pharmaceutical clients.

Two days later, at noon precisely, Nell was on her way to lunch with the man who'd "made it big." She winced as she moved her shoulder bag from one side to the other. She hurt, but it was going to be worth it. It *had* to be worth it.

At two o'clock, Wallace Nesbitt leaned foward with his most Santa Claus–like smile. "You're an amazing young lady." Nell modestly looked down at the figures she had so laboriously compiled, calculations and estimates that she had spent the last half hour of her presentation explaining. Inside there was a sigh of relief bursting to be let out. Patience, something told her, have patience. Say nothing.

"It only took you two years to devise this formula and marketing plan? It's ingenious." He didn't seem to see her quick nod. "And you're only twenty-four? . . ." He sounded skeptical.

"I'll be twenty-five this year. Do you want my birth certificate?" She moved as if to open her bag.

Nesbitt roared with laughter. How wonderful to be young enough to want to be older. Nell frowned, lowering her eyes.

Oh, Lord, he'd hurt her feelings. Nesbitt stood up, pushing the dining chair away to pat her shoulder. Nell cringed, smothering a cry. "Whatever's wrong?"

To his horror, the beautiful eyes started to water again. "Nothing . . ." He could see *something* was wrong. He hadn't risen to be a leader of men for nothing. With a few more words of gentle persuasion he started to learn more about the vision of loveliness sitting beside him. She was engaged to a fiend. She wanted to break it off. This was the reason she'd decided to tell him, trust him with her formula. Her fiancé, also a chemist, was jealous of her talent. He was trying to take credit for her work.

Why, it was a crime against humanity! So the fiend was French, was he? Without proper papers? Well, deportation could easily take care of him, and solve this beautiful young lady's problems pronto.

Wallace Nesbitt could never remember the sequence of events that day. Did Nell take off her jacket and slip her blouse off her shoulder to show him the ugly bruise at the top of her arm where the French brute had hit her? Did he kiss her out of sympathy, or did she kiss him to thank him for it?

It really didn't matter, because a miracle occurred. She *did* inject him with her youth and vitality, as weeks ago he had longed to be injected.

For the first time in eight years, as her petal-soft lips and the merest tip of her tongue touched his, he felt his penis stir faintly into life— just like the old days.

It was Nirvana or was it his Nemesis? He was so excited he hardly dared look at the angel who had brought about such a miracle. He shut his eyes. There it was again, the same petal-soft kiss . . . and . . . a recurrence of the miracle. His horn was hardening. Little did she know what she was doing.

He shifted awkwardly in his chair. He longed to capture her lovely pale hand and force her to stroke him back to life as a virile man once again. If he had a heart attack he didn't care. It would be a wonderful way to die. It was a miracle the way this angel had come into life . . . a miracle.

5

The phone rang as he lifted his hands from the keys. His concentration was so intense on the segue just completed that for a moment he didn't realize the unwelcome extraneous decibels were in his room, intruding on his carefully imposed hours of solitude.

Damn and blast the Italians! Someone on the switchboard had fucked up again. It had to be some *bullo, cafone,* from the Palazzo de Sporto, full of *folie de grandeur* and horseshit, trying to inveigle him back to witness yet another sweaty session at the Olympic Games.

His fingers crashed down on the piano to produce chords as discordant as the mixture of languages running through his head. How the hell had he allowed himself to get swept up in this athletic fervor? He didn't need to *see* any jocks—or jills, for that matter—to create the music for the musical about the Games. If Osborne needed "flesh" for his words, that was his problem. He hadn't needed to go to a girls' school to write *Holy Cow,* still SRO on

Broadway after 676 performances. He hadn't even gone to sea to get "inspired" for *Schooneroo*, which was about to open in London. Even in dock he felt seasick.

The phone went on ringing as he lit a forbidden cigarette. He knew all right why he was still in the hundred-degree heat, stifling in the city, when he could have been beside the Mediterranean at Porto Ercole. Well, he'd soon be there—*with* the cause of his travail, Fiametta D'Orso, who could inspire Nero to give up his fiddle . . . Fiametta, the cutest little hurdler God had ever made, with legs that started under her armpits and bosoms that fitted exactly in each one of his hands. As he stretched one hand to take the phone off the hook, he grinned at the thought of the lady's tempestuous tears on the track the day before. She'd learned the hard way that when you're at the top, you have to work even harder to stay there and not allow yourself the luxury of hoping for the best. So the best hadn't happened. She'd escaped from her chaperone one night too soon, to practice some unorthodox "hurdling" with him—and lost the preliminary race she had expected to "walk" to win. She was out before she'd even begun . . . out to go to Porto Ercole with him, where he'd lick her wounds. The memory of her taut, lean flank made him feel pleasantly aroused. In one way he hoped it was Fiametta calling, although in another he knew he would be irritated that she'd ignored his orders not to disturb him for twenty-four hours.

"Ty, it's six o'clock. Miss Samuelson's here."

Jesus Christ. It couldn't be six o'clock! When he'd last looked at his watch it had been three-fifteen. He put down the receiver on the table and went back to the piano to pick up his watch, shaking it in disbelief. Time evaporated when he was working. Music was the ultimate seduction. Nothing and no one could—or would—ever take precedence in his life. The thought was strangely comforting. He ran his hand over his chin. He hadn't shaved. He hadn't even eaten lunch. He hadn't read the list of questions he'd insisted on seeing before this interview with London's leading hotshot columnist.

Ty Caplan, America's most colorful, controversial, and successful composer, said into the phone, "Be a sweetheart, Dottie. Put her off until tomorrow."

"Can't do that, Ty. You did that yesterday. You promised Lionel—remember?"

Lionel Bart, his close English friend, creator of a new breed of musical, *Fings Ain't Wot They Used T'Be*, and *Oliver*. Ty Caplan's mind immediately went in the direction it most wanted to go—to music, the new kind of music and musical that Bart had made so enormously popular. Bart was a bloody marvel.

"Are you still there?" Dottie's voice was soft but there was no mistaking its sense of purpose. "I'll bring her up if you're halfway decent . . ."

Decent? His shirttail was out. Hair on his chest was bursting through the place where the shirt buttons were supposed to be. His mouth felt like a Roman sewer and his chin could easily be used as a scouring pad . . .

"What's she like?"

"Your type," Dottie replied succinctly. "Small ass, good tits, a light tan, freckles, and ferocity."

"Okay," he sighed. "Put her on a leash and bring her up in ten minutes. Order some more Campari—I'm almost out."

He ran a razor inadequately over his stubble, brushed his teeth, and changed his buttonless shirt for a *Schooneroo* T-shirt. Might as well publicize the show for the English hotshot. Whatever her name was, Samuelson had to have something on Bart, he reflected. It wasn't like Bart to ask favors, although he certainly did plenty for others. Ty couldn't think of many of his fellow composers who would go out of their way to spare him embarrassment and humiliation. He couldn't think of one, in fact, yet Bart had covered up Brenda's last alcoholic rampage and somehow kept the scene at London Airport out of the press. Being married to Brenda meant Ty had long ago run out of favors—the quid pro quo kind of favors he could call on to be repaid. Now *he* was forever repaying them. Oh well, he'd promised Bart he would give one of his rare interviews and so he would—in fifteen minutes flat. He had to get on with his work.

He'd never met a female journalist who asked a single intelligent question about his work. Why should this one be different? He glanced at the list of questions. No apparent reference to his marriage to an older woman, an aging star, a superstar, in fact, and the woman who'd discovered him playing his own pieces in a west-side bar and started him on his way up. Brenda—the woman he'd allowed himself to love so much that he'd revealed his hunger for the home he'd never had.

He shut off that train of thought as decisively as he now shut the lid on the piano.

Before the doorbell rang he called Fiametta and arranged to pick her up that evening at nine-thirty, ". . . to lick your wounds and relax your muscles, *bambino*."

At five past ten the phone rang and rang and rang. When it finally stopped, Ty Caplan picked it up. "Take my messages from now on. I'll tell you when I'm available."

"Signore, shall we say you are in or out? Signorina D'Orso, she say . . ."

"Out! Out!" he yelled. He turned to look piercingly at Sylvie as he replaced the receiver. "Out of my mind, I think."

It was true. What had happened to him? And where, for God's sake, had four hours gone? Slipped into space like four minutes.

He returned to the sofa where before the phone rang he had been about to hold the small workmanlike hand of a young woman who a few hours before he had never heard of, let alone met. Now he examined her short unpolished nails as if they were pearls, and tried to rub an ink stain off her thumb as if it were a blot on a priceless heirloom.

It was lunatic, implausible, a plot he would never have agreed to support with his music. He tried to classify his feelings as relentlessly as he pursued elusive chords for his music. A curious mixture of awe . . . and . . . compassion—that was it. . . . He wanted to wrap this girl up in his arms and not allow the world in to hurt her.

First it had been her voice. A good voice with a hint of Bart in it . . . lurking Cockney? Right the first time, he'd learned, pleased to note how easily he'd turned inquisitor, strangely eager to know from the minute he saw her who and what she was. After an hour he'd even chided her for her lack of tenacity in getting answers from him, instead allowing him to interrogate her.

He'd found himself pointing out he didn't give interviews. He had a reputation for being extremely difficult with journalists. He'd only agreed to see her because a friend had asked him to. Was she on an assignment? Or was she there under false pretenses?

She'd replied gently—could it be lovingly?—like the mother he'd never known, that with his questions he'd actually been very revealing about himself. Motherly, sisterly . . . hell! Whatever it was, she was a natural psychologist.

Ten o'clock became eleven, then twelve, and the traffic outside became increasingly noisy. In foreign cities he always liked to live on "nightclub" streets—quiet by day when he worked—noisy at night when he was out.

He showed her his inner anger, sorrow, attitude about the world. He went to the piano to play something for her. It was as natural as breathing.

He came back to the sofa to stand over her accusingly. "Do you always have this effect on men? Is this your trick?" He knew he was sneering. Jealousy—on the few occasions he had experienced it— always ruined his cool, twisted his emotions so that the most unlikely, bizarre thoughts were translated into bitter words.

Before she had time to answer, he snapped, "I should have known from the rag you work for with its million circulation. You must have a Ph.D. in brainwashing . . . give a little . . . gain a lot." He hardly knew what he was saying, but in any case she smiled what he would later call her "girl-scout smile," her freckles amazingly apparent on her cheeks and snub nose. Her apparent serenity stung him further. "So, Nell, your best friend, stole Dick . . . good, wholesome Dick, from under your nose and never said good-bye to her poor old parents —broke their hearts, and yours—but you made it big in Fleet Street and . . ."

Her freckles were shining with tears. A lump rose in his own throat; his cynicism died a swift death. His skin wanted to dry her skin. There were tears in his eyes that she never saw as he took her in his arms. "Sylvie, oh, Sylvie."

～～

"Where the hell is she?" Smith Maynard was on the warpath, a path that stretched at least twenty feet wide and long through the newsroom. The tension made typing faster and phone calls shorter, everyone aware that _something_ was wrong and _someone_ was going to pay for it, not necessarily the transgressor.

Sid scratched his head and looked out of Smith's window, one of the few on the floor. In the distance he could see the gold symbol of justice on top of the Old Bailey, where England's major criminal cases were tried. Justice? There wasn't any justice. Why should _he_ be in the hot seat, taking the full blast of Smith's fury for one of Sylvie's worst pieces ever? He, of all people, who had never even reached first base with the woman? At that moment Sid felt so sour toward her he even tried to think of Sylvie as Kitty did. Could Kitty be right? Was Sylvie the original Eve? She hadn't returned from Rome, even though she was one of the few on the staff who now had company-car status. That was what worried Sid the most.

Sylvie wasn't the kind of girl who wasted other people's time, even the time of company chauffeurs, well used to waiting around. She probably was no longer impressed by the fact that she had a driver at her disposal to fetch and carry her—it never took *anyone* long to get used to convenience—but Sylvie was usually more thoughtful than she needed to be. Sid had even heard her apologize to a charlady for being in the office so late, helping empty her own wastepaper basket so the old girl could clock off and get home to bed.

When Sylvie's secretary told him she'd checked out of her hotel two days early and nobody seemed to know where she'd gone, including Ty Caplan's infuriating girl Friday, Sid had started to quiz one or two of her girlfriends, who were as mystified as he was. He finally called Gert, not wanting to worry her, yet desperate to talk to someone. Gert knew something, that was sure. The fact that she was so obviously *not* worried infuriated Sid. He could sense her embarrassment, her suppressed excitement and apprehension right through the phone wire.

"Well, she sent in the piece she was supposed to send, didn't she? Perhaps she's sightseeing. I don't think she's ever been to Rome." Gert was really on the defensive.

Sid was surprised at how angry Gert's words made him. He snarled down the phone, "You know damn well Sylvie's been to Rome before. What about her piece on *La Dolce Vita?*"

Gert didn't answer, and he didn't trust himself to say any more. But what on earth was Sylvie up to?

~~~

And she had thought Pierre was such a genius, obtaining the "never-ever-pregnant" pills from an alchemist who brewed in some magic lair what every woman wanted. As Nell brushed her hair, noticing without alarm a few more silver threads, she laughed out loud at her lovely reflection. Fifty cents each, eleven dollars a month, the Pill was easily available to every woman in the United States—and probably always had been in Canada, too. What a lot of wool the "froggy" chemist had pulled over her eyes, but she'd got even. As she sprayed her favorite lilac scent over her shoulders and breasts, she muttered under her breath, "The cheapskate."

Now she knew for sure every man had his price. How she had

hoped to hear that the arrogant prick had been deported back to the rubble and dust he came from, which turned out to be Belgium, not France! The fact that it had taken Wallace only about five minutes to find out Pierre wasn't even French had upset her more than anything. It hadn't taken much longer to learn that unfortunately Pierre Repelle's papers *were* in order. Nevertheless Wallace had scared the shit out of the yellow-livered beast. After receiving an official-looking letter from the Chief of Immigration, Pierre had packed up and gone, bag and baggage, one, two, three. Wallace had explained that one of his people had made it well worth Pierre's while to book a one-way ticket back to Europe.

Nell had consolidated her position with Wallace, despite the barely concealed loathing of his desiccated spinster sister, who obviously longed to put poison in her soup. Now it was time to put Plan C into action.

Nell shut her eyes, stroking and savoring the feel of her own silky skin. Tonight was the night to put a flame to the torch Wallace had been carrying for her for weeks . . . a flame no amount of frost from his sister could put out.

As Nell heard a gentle tap on the door she threaded her arms through the sleeves of the short housecoat on the back of her chair.

"Come in."

In the mirror she saw Wallace's face as he entered. It was as anxious as a child's, tentative, not sure of his right of admission.

She leaned forward to be sure her breasts, full, heavy, could be seen as she moved. So far she had not allowed him to see her naked. Now that Pierre was no longer a threat, she would allow him a tantalizing glimpse of what was in store *after* their wedding. The wedding had to be soon, before her own restlessness loused up everything. God, she was horny for a real man, a virile mountain of strength, not a worn-out sugar daddy, but someone who would force her to give what she was capable of giving.

"Nell, my baby . . ." Wallace Nesbitt stood back, looking with reverence at the amazing treasure that had literally landed at his feet only six months before.

"Good evening, Wallace. How was your day?" Nell's voice was as soothing and as soft as the coo of a dove.

"I missed you, as always . . ." He hesitated. "My angel, the Kennedy-Nixon debate is on tonight. I'd like to see it . . ."

No member of his family, no employee, not even a close colleague had ever heard Wallace Nesbitt speak like this. Wallace Nesbitt gave orders, commands. He never requested or entreated—not until now.

But no member of his family, colleague, or employee could ever say Nell did anything to bring about this unusual behavior. Except for Anne, Wallace's frostbitten sister, whom everyone expected to be jealous of such a glorious creature, everyone saw Nell as that rare member of the human race—born singularly beautiful *and* modest at the same time. She had been the soul of propriety ever since Wallace Nesbitt had taken her under his considerable wing, rescuing her, it was said, from a very dangerous man.

"I've missed you too, Wallace. It seemed much longer than forty-eight hours . . ." Nell looked lovingly into the mirror, directly into the reflection of Wallace's eyes. She leaned forward still more, knowing Wallace would be able to see the crease in her bare buttocks as the housecoat left the chairback to settle on her shoulders. She was gratified to see his mouth quiver. Absence was a good tonic for any relationship, but particularly an unfulfilled one.

Her actions had been well thought out. Now she leaned her head on her hands, sighing, knowing he would come nearer. He came swiftly, kneeling to place a well-manicured hand on her bare thigh. "Nell, baby, what is it?"

"I missed you," she whispered.

"You *really* missed me?" There was no mistaking the astonishment in his voice, a reflection of the suspicion Nell knew had been well nourished by Anne.

Well, Anne, dear, she said to herself, tonight is the beginning of the end of your influence. Soon you will no longer be in a position to affect your brother's opinions about anything or anyone.

She lowered her eyes, noting with satisfaction that even though she hadn't touched the man, there was an unusual bulge in his crotch. She moved her body imperceptibly so that her housecoat opened still more and he could see how near his hand was to her black bush of hair protecting the lips she knew he longed to enter.

"Little Nell." He was actually blushing.

She bit her tongue to stop the laughter that would ruin everything.

"Oh, Wally." She covered his hand. It was trembling. No wonder. To her surprise she felt her vagina begin to dampen, to throb. She couldn't believe it. She had gone so long without sex that she actually even wanted this old man to bring her off. But that was too easy, she told herself fiercely. She must never again appear "easy." Wallace was so old-fashioned she knew he would only propose if he firmly believed her story that she'd fended off with difficulty everyone who had tried to get near her. It was vital he believed that she hadn't slept around like every other young chick he'd run across. Now she knew there had been quite a few other young girls. It was no wonder, with his incredible wealth. No, she had to remain a madonna in his mind, worthy of the pedestal he'd placed her upon.

As Wallace's hand moved across her thigh she fought the temptation to push his fingers inside her, almost writhing to get relief.

Help came from an unexpected quarter. There was a rap-rap-rap on the door and Wallace's dear sister—little did she know it—saved the situation.

"Wallace, are you there? You said you wanted to see the debate, so I arranged dinner early." Anne's voice was sharp with irritation and aggrieved lack of appreciation. He stood up so fast the blood drained from his face and he had to hold onto Nell's chair.

"We'll be there—we'll be there in fifteen minutes." There was no mistaking the cold reproof in his voice. His disappointment was so intense that the dizzy spell which had come out of nowhere as he rose to his feet stayed with him. "Must sit down," he whispered apologetically.

Nell was all caring, all loving, tying her housecoat tightly around her, leading him to the chaise lounge. Even though he felt faint, his penis stayed hard as he saw her bare behind peeping from below the silly housecoat as she ran to the bathroom. She returned to unfasten his collar, take off his shoes, and, kneeling, gently began to stroke his forehead, wrists, palms with a towel soaked in eau de cologne.

"I'm sorry, Nell."

"Wallace, you work so hard. I wish you'd let me travel with you all the time—to take care of you . . ." She was hesitant, shy. He could tell she was frightened of intruding. How typical of sweet Nell. He didn't answer, thinking deeply. Surely they were the thoughts of a foolish old man, he told himself, yet what was holding him back?

His sister's warning hadn't been ignored. She'd distrusted Nell from the moment they'd met. It didn't surprise him. He had never brought anyone home since Shelagh died and Anne had taken over running the place—yet Anne was the only one who suspected Nell's motives.

What had Nell really gained that other women hadn't gained before her? In fact, others—the few mistresses he had had during Shelagh's lifetime and one or two prostitutes he'd kept on ice—had gained infinitely more. A small apartment in Vancouver, the use of a secretary in the Vancouver office, one or two trips overseas, a guest room reserved for her exclusively in the main Vancouver house . . . that was all Nell had gained. She wasn't like other women—or was she? There hadn't been any "others" for so long; had he forgotten what women were really like? He didn't think so, although until Nell came along he hadn't been able to perform.

As he'd jokingly discussed with his doctor and friend, Jed Baxter, even a eunuch would have been stirred up by the sight of Nell one spring day in a pretty white blouse which in some way had emphasized her amazingly large nipples. In her most headmistresslike manner, Anne had told Nell to change because the blouse was in such poor taste. He'd longed to intervene when the poor girl, obviously distressed, had run upstairs without a word, to return looking like a nun! He'd been so full of longing to run his tongue around each pink areola, to roll each exquisite plump point between his fingers, that he hadn't been able to speak let alone stop Anne in her tracks.

There had been other wonderful, unexpected moments when, like teacher and pupil, he would be answering her questions—always so many questions from such an agile mind. He remembered one occasion when she'd been sitting in his Los Angeles office, dressed so simply and decorously that not even Anne could have faulted her for her appearance, although even with her hair combed straight back, and wearing little makeup, she had still looked ravishingly beautiful. She had wanted to understand more about direct selling, which Tupperware had pioneered to bring about their early phenomenal success.

"The whole direct-selling approach is contingent upon networks of relationships," he'd begun to explain patiently, "with women selling to their extended families—friends, neighbors. That's the reason Tupperware does so well in close-knit working-class and ethnic areas . . ."

"Give me an example," she'd broken in eagerly.

"Well, like the South Side Chicago neighborhoods, dominated by Lithuanians, Polish-Americans . . ."

Her fervor for facts had touched him and he'd gone on to explain in more detail. "Direct selling depends on constantly replenishing the sales force. New salespeople place big initial orders, which generate a high proportion of annual sales and of course healthy commissions for the sales directors, who are then motivated to bring in other recruits. And so the system perpetuates itself."

"So without a successful recruiting program you mean sales would sag—profits would go down? Do people get commissions just for recruiting people even if they don't sell products?"

He could still remember smiling at her intensity, as with pen poised she'd waited to write down his answer. Then to his shock and embarrassment he'd found his penis swelling just from looking at her.

To punish himself—which unfortunately meant punishing her too —he had had to pretend to be irritated by her questions. He'd answered sharply, "Of course salespeople's commissions go up according to the number of recruits they obtain. That's obvious. I've got to start my meeting now, Nell. You go off to the plastics factory. I've arranged a meeting with the head of research and development, as you requested. I can't do more."

She'd known his meeting wouldn't start for another twenty minutes. She'd looked hurt that he was getting rid of her when he'd promised her a full fifteen minutes without interruption. What she didn't and couldn't know was that in another five seconds he'd have had her on the floor of his office to strip her naked and probably fuck himself to death.

Well, it had never happened, and tonight, when to his amazement she'd allowed him to see more of her than ever before—her ridiculous housecoat hardly covering her breasts or even her velvet-smooth behind—Anne had rescued him from committing an indiscretion. But did he need to be rescued?

He could still feel his heart thumping unpleasantly, his pulse racing, his head perspiring while Nell, darling that she was, administered special loving care.

Perhaps repressing his feelings was worse for him than acting on them. Perhaps he should jump on her here and now. Wallace opened his eyes to see a look of such sweet concern on Nell's face that he was ashamed. How could he even think of behaving like such a lout? Nell was so lovely. He'd always despised old men who ran off with beautiful young girls, but Nell wasn't just young and beautiful. She was smart, incredibly smart—incredibly thoughtful too—and as beautiful inside, if it was possible, as she was out. And when they'd met that day—she an orphan in a strange country—she'd had no one to turn to except for the Belgian fiend, who had kept her almost a prisoner.

Unconsciously Wallace clenched and unclenched his hands. He couldn't allow that ever to happen again. Initially he'd thought he would give Nell encouragement and perhaps some financial aid to get her clever beauty idea off the ground. If it worked—and if his people saw fit—he then intended to take a small interest in the business to help in its expansion, but he had been deluding himself.

The thought of Nell going out into the world, perhaps moving away to establish the business seriously in the States (which they'd both agreed made more sense than Canada) was agonizing.

He needed her. He needed her gentle hands, her pale beautiful body.

He shivered at the thought of the breasts he'd just seen, full, maternal breasts that he now knew he had to suck soon or go mad. He made a decision as he always made decisions, firmly and with a map of action rapidly forming in his mind. He would involve himself personally in her business, work by her side, guide her, and lead her to the top as if she were already a member of his own family. They would be partners forever—professionally *and* privately.

He got up slowly. "I feel better. Get dressed, Nell. I want Anne to like you, little one. Don't let's upset her by being late for dinner."

He tried not to look at her as he left the room. It took all his will power not to ask her to take the housecoat off, so that he could commit to memory every aspect of the body he was now determined to possess. He longed to memorize it in the way he'd always memorized anything that fascinated him, an intricate piece of machinery, a complicated formula. It was his phenomenal memory that had catapulted him to the top at school and in business.

He smiled as he went downstairs. Being able to memorize Nell's body would help him get through the hours without her.

"Anne, I want to talk to you." Wallace shut the library door. Anne blanched. She guessed what was coming.

"Don't do it, Wallace." They had never needed to explain much to each other.

"I'm in love with her. I know I'm a fool in many ways, but I think she genuinely cares for me. I know she needs me. I thought at first I just wanted to rescue her—to protect her. Now I realize I want her to protect me too."

Anne knew better than to laugh the harsh sarcastic laugh she had ready. "Is there nothing I can say to stop you? She's after your money, Wallace. You can't see it, but I can. She's a brilliant little chiseler who'll ruin you."

"Anne, don't make it hard on yourself. You're my sister. I'll always stand up for you, but if you want me to continue to see you, to *love* you as a sister—then you *must* respect Nell and respect my intelligence." He poured himself an unusually large Scotch and soda. "I haven't been wrong before, have I?"

Anne shook her head sorrowfully. "No, you haven't, but you never had time for women before." As he raised a wry eyebrow in her direction, she smiled thinly. "All right, you never had time in an *emotional* sense. You never showed Shelagh much love—or gave her that much time. You were too busy working." Anne hesitated. "Promise me one thing . . . you won't sign away your fortune or change your will until you are sure she loves you and not what you can provide."

He sighed. "Anne, how much of a fool do you take me for? I haven't worked my tail off all these years to give it all away. And in any case . . ."

Anne interrupted, not able to suppress a flash of anger. "What about Johnny? What's he going to say?"

Now it was Wallace's turn to be angry. He flushed. "Why on earth should Johnny have to 'say' anything? It's none of his business. He's my stepson, my friend, not my priest or advisor. I've always done my best for him. He'll want the best for me. I'm the only father he's ever had. I know how much you love him, but Johnny's well taken care of, don't worry about that."

"Pour me a drink, will you? I don't usually want one, but I feel very shaky about all this . . ." She paused. "Have you asked her yet?"

Brother and sister looked at each other and the deep bond between them meant they both started laughing even before Wallace began to shake his head ruefully. So no proposal had been made. Anne hoped it was because Wallace was still not totally sure deep down what he was doing.

"Promise there will be some sort of prenuptial agreement, won't you?"

Wallace winked. "Pre- and post-, but it will never be needed. My judgment's right, I promise."

There was a light knock at the door. "Come in."

Wallace beamed, recognizing that Anne's voice was softer, kinder than it had ever been before to Miss O'Halloran. Her mistrust was as great as ever, but by her tone Wallace knew—as usual—Anne was willing to give him the benefit of the doubt.

Later that evening as Nell and Wallace watched Senator Kennedy and Vice-President Nixon debate on television for the most influential office in the world, Anne carefully observed the young woman she was now sure would one day become her new sister-in-law.

Nell *was* extraordinarily beautiful, there was no question about that. Better dressed, too, than she had been when they'd first met three or four months before. But covered up or uncovered, there was a sensuality about her, an animal grace that made her movements fluid, yet suggestive. Couldn't her brother see that? Her movements alone belied the gentle, caring, madonnalike person Wallace seemed to perceive.

Yes, Nell brought her brother an ashtray without being asked to, adjusted his footstool, looked at him with huge, wistful eyes, her mouth slightly open, as if awed by the height, breadth, and width of his magnificent intelligence—but was her admiration genuine? Did Nell really worship her brother as she seemed to do? For the first time Anne wasn't sure. Her doubts were still more on the negative side than the positive, but now she hoped she was wrong.

She loved her strong-willed brother, who'd dominated everybody he'd ever known, including their own mother, herself, Shelagh his first wife, and Shelagh's son, Johnny, who had been born after his father had been killed in a mining accident, and the son Wallace had adopted and raised as his own.

"It's giving him the edge, there's no doubt about it," Nell said excitedly. "It isn't what he says. Nixon's just as smart, and probably much more knowledgeable, but physically look how miserably he measures up against Kennedy . . ."

Wallace beamed at Nell as she spoke, as if she'd just explained how *Echo 1*, the world's first communications satellite, worked. The man was really out of his mind over the little witch.

"You're right, Nell. Kennedy's good manners, his movie-star looks —these TV debates are going to change the whole structure of electioneering. Boy, does it show the power of TV"—Nell and Wallace exchanged glances and said together—"to sell a product!"

Anne sank back in her chair with a shiver of foreboding as Wallace and Nell laughed and exchanged radiant smiles.

"Two minds with but a single thought . . ." Wallace said; then earnestly, "At least I hope so . . ."

Anne's sense of dread increased as she saw her brother do what he never did—demonstrate his feelings in public, taking Nell's hand and pressing it to his lips.

There was no stopping the relationship now. Anne gripped her chair with a sudden premonition. Nobody stood a chance against Nell. No matter what Wallace said, she would probably end up with the lot.

Three days later Nell was smiling broadly as she sat in the plush back seat of one of the Nesbitt company limos en route to a very important "interview."

It had worked! Her plan of letting the old boy _see_ the goods that could be in store for him without letting him actually _touch_ had worked. Nell knew she was grinning idiotically, even as she sat in the limousine taking her for her first meeting with the world-famous Hungarian-turned-Canadian acting coach, the tempestuous Violana. Nell felt the limo taking her to Violana's restored, eighteenth-century stone townhouse in Old Montreal was really a golden coach on the way to the stars, for she was certain that at last she was on her way. She wanted to sing out at the top of her voice, "I'm going to make it big, big, big . . ."

Even as she bubbled over with the thought that she had the old boy in her clutches, she ran her hand over the soft sleeve of her black ranch-mink coat. "The best skins . . . a coat made of the best skins . . . and that's the way it's always going to be from now on—the best of everything," was the message relayed so satisfyingly to her brain by her possessive fingers. At her throat were the best pearls. She looked down. And on her feet? She had trouble suppressing a giggle as she remembered her foot fetish, if that was the right description for her old preoccupation with the feet and shoes that had passed by at eye level in such melancholy procession in Hammersmith. The shoes she was now wearing were one hundred and eighty degrees removed from the Hammersmith variety. They were black crocodile, real crocodile from the swamps of the Amazon. She grimaced self-deprecatingly as she bent to touch the skin that in the pictures she'd seen looked so hard on the reptile's back, yet had been fashioned—sculptured, she corrected herself—to her feet so expertly that the shoes both fitted and felt like soft silk gloves.

Wallace was meeting her at Violana's townhouse to carry out the introduction. That in itself was an achievement. Wallace Nesbitt did not leave his office in the middle of the afternoon simply to fulfill social niceties. Wallace Nesbitt rarely left his office in the afternoon for any reason. People came to him. It has been Wallace who had suggested Violana could be "useful." Although Nell knew Violana's reputation for making stars in show business—her teaching of voice projection, role portrayal, film and stage techniques were legendary— she had been enthralled to learn that Violana had another, more closely guarded claim to fame, one that the beneficiaries were not too eager to broadcast.

"She's done a number on several of my business associates." The wry note in Wallace's voice had been unmistakable. "I know person-

ally some lackluster guys she's transformed into leadership material."
Nell recalled how lovingly the old boy had looked at her. "If she thinks
you have it, she'll teach you how to motivate people fast . . . how to
lead people by the nose . . . how to hypnotize a crowd into buying
when they've come along determined not to put their hands in their
pockets. But no matter how much money is offered, she won't take
anyone on unless she thinks the seed of something—leadership—is
there." Wallace had patted her adoringly. "She'll see the seed in you,
my darling. She'll make it blossom overnight."

The Violana conversation had come at the end of a meeting a few
days after the Nixon-Kennedy debate, a meeting that had made all the
effort Nell had been pouring into the relationship with Wallace so
worthwhile. He was going to support her all the way, he'd said. He
was going to be at her side, building her beauty business into the best
there could be—the way he'd been at the side of the plastics genius
Mr. Tupper. He was going to guide her, but most important of all he
was going to give her the crucial financial support.

He hadn't proposed but, as Nell almost purred to herself as the limo
started climbing the steep slopes of Montreal's old quarter, he hadn't
needed to. He was going to ask her to marry him when the opportunity
was most appropriate. It would be boring and predictable, as romantic
as a box of fattening chocolates with a heart on the lid and a rosy red
ribbon around the box. Nell Nesbitt. She liked the sound of the name.
Alliteration had always been one of her favorite writing devices, but
the best thing about a life spent as Nell Nesbitt—as Mrs. Wallace
Wainwright Nesbitt—was the name's ability to command attention,
to open doors, to make other lesser fry circle her as minnows circled
whales, minnows that she could—and would—use for her business
and for herself.

My God! There was Wallace standing in the doorway of a narrow
five-story building, much of it covered in ivy and, as far as Nell could
see, with each window shuttered and barred. It looked more like a
private prison than the elegant townhouse that had been written about
in every interior decorating magazine she could think of. Wallace was
frowning, looking at his watch. She wound down the window as the
limo pulled up. "Am I late, darling?" There was just the right amount
of guilty deference in her voice, not too much, not too little. She
could see the old fool's face visibly soften and relax as he hastened to
help her out, waving the chauffeur away. "Traffic?"

As far as her watch was concerned she was on time, but Wallace was a stickler for seconds, let alone minutes. Inwardly she sighed at the tedium inevitably ahead. "Yes, a little. Sorry." She was two and a half minutes late but, what the hell, until the ring was on her marriage finger she would go along with the charade of pacifying Big Daddy.

The front door was opened by a woman with the face of a pig, but a beautifully coiffed and dressed pig. There was distinct condescension in the way she introduced herself. For a moment Nell's irritation at the cavalier manners of the pig was lessened because she thought the woman said her name was "Maple Syrup." But when Wallace asked her courteously to repeat her name, she learned Violana's assistant was called Mabel Stirrup—certainly there was nothing sweet and cloying about Mabel.

Nell wanted to kick herself for the quiver of anxiety which momentarily assailed her deep down in her gut. Anxiety about what? Who the hell was Violana, let alone Miss Pig Face? All the same she held on to Wallace's arm to help her sail into a reception room on the first floor.

It was as dark and as forbidding as the outside of the house. Where were the rooms dancing with candlelight that Nell had seen in *House & Garden?* The silver room where the Russian ballerina Ulanova had been photographed, eating gulls' eggs served in baskets of bluebells? For a moment the old fear of being considered second-best made her think that perhaps they were sitting in the second-best reception room.

Then Violana suddenly came in and electrified everything. It was the only way to consider her entrance. One moment the room was dark, empty; the next it seemed full of something "happening." God, Violana was just as ugly as Mabel, but like a shiny black crab she scuttled everywhere at once—to a hidden switch box to illuminate the room with five-foot high skinny electric candles that showed off a glorious coromandel screen and a huge white marble fireplace where to Nell's astonishment some definitely questionable couplings were carved in stark relief. She had no time to study the pornography. Violana was speaking, her voice as angry as her eyes, which reminded Nell of nothing more stimulating than a pair of shiny black olives soaked in oil. "You have been neglecting me, Vallace. Vy? You did not send me your usual so kind donation for my scholarship fund? Yet ven you call me, vot do I do? I send avay my gifted adorable student" —the words sounded like gunshots—"in order to meet this young lady that you seem so interested in?" She never once looked in Nell's direction. Nell could feel her own anger build like a fire that might easily erupt if she was going to be treated like a child at her daddy's side. Perhaps, like the animal Nell decided instinctively she was, Violana could smell her animosity; suddenly Violana became as fey and as charming as a vicar's wife at a tea party. Had she seen Wallace's hand go to his checkbook? No, it wasn't a checkbook he was bringing out. It was an envelope, probably with a check already in it. So she was going to be "sold" as a possible "seed" after all—it would have nothing to do with her potential?

Violana took the proffered envelope with hardly a thank you. Ignorant cow, Nell thought. An ignorant cow with a pig for a secretary or assistant or doorkeeper. "I think, Vallace, my dear, your outsize"—the way Violana pronounced the word made it more *outsize* than it deserved—"personality means if you stay I vill not be able to make contact with this beautiful creature." Nell bristled, touching the sleeve of her mink to remind herself of what she had achieved and where she was going. Creature, indeed!

But Wallace was getting—could it be *apologetically?*—to his feet, a dazed look on his face when he looked at Nell. "She is indeed beautiful, Violana, and very, very smart. You'll find out. But you're right, I mustn't stay, mustn't get in your way. I know you have your own very exceptional methods of discovering talent. As you know, I've never brought you anyone before—have never, in fact, been in your gracious home."

Nell fumed again. Why did he have to sound as if he were making a speech? Why did he say things like "gracious home" when anyone with half an eye could see they were in a drafty, dreary barn, that only Edison's invention in the form of dozens of lightbulbs made tenable? All the same, Nell jumped up to kiss him fondly on the cheek. "Thank you for sparing the time. You are so wonderful to me, darling." Nell was well aware Violana was looking at her with no attempt to disguise her contemptuous amusement. All right, Violana, old girl, she said to herself, you can laugh at me all you want to now. When I've sucked you dry of whatever you have to offer, you'll have to go down on your knees to *me* if you want to see another cent of Wallace's money for your old scholarship fund.

Pig Face was back to escort Wallace downstairs. When the door closed behind him Violana strode toward her like a matador entering a bullring. She was wearing a brilliant red top with huge bat-wing sleeves, so that as she approached and swung one arm across the other, it was as if she were literally confronting the enemy, the bull, herself. If Violana thought she was going to demoralize _her_ she had to think again . . . as Nell knew well whenever she felt in a tight corner, and God knew she had been in a few, she was always at her best.

As Violana stood over her, Nell looked at her steadily from top to toe, then leaned back in the armchair and slowly slipped the mink coat from her shoulders. She was pleased she had decided to wear the simple white wool dress . . . simple on anyone else. On her it was dynamite, emphasizing the amazing smallness of her waist, the sensuous curve of her bosom. Violana's eyes creased in an appreciative smile and when she spoke her voice was softer, kinder, which in one way was even more undermining.

"Vould you stand up, child?" Nell forced herself to be calm, to nod her head in acquiesence, and slowly stood up to find even in her beautiful high-heeled crocodile shoes she still had to look up at the old witch. Violana brought her face close to hers, so close Nell was uncomfortably aware she must have eaten garlic at lunch. Now it was Violana's turn to take time over a visual inspection.

Nell gritted her teeth, determined not to take her eyes away from the face coming nearer and growing more imperious and frightening. "You are _very_ beautiful, you know that, don't you, darlink?" Nell remained motionless, silent, certain the question was a trick. "Vy then do you vear that sick green eye-makeup? It makes you look like an Irish peasant who doesn't know anythink . . . and I believe you know a great deal, don't you, darlink?" From that moment on Nell loathed Violana but nothing showed on her face. She continued to remain motionless, expressionless, as Violana delivered what Nell realized must be her usual pep talk to anyone she was prepared to take on.

"From vat your protector told me on the telephone you are about to embark on a new business venture together. You are going to use vomen to sell other vomen the idea that they can be as beautiful as you, is that right?" Nell smiled a slow affirmative smile that deliberately carried a derisive note.

Violana turned on her heel and walked to the other end of the long room. "Valk toward me . . . slowly . . . more slowly . . . stand still. Valk! Yes, I know, beautiful vitch, you are beginning to hate me, but believe me it is just a beginning. You vill hate me much, much more next veek and by next month . . . my God . . . I vill be vatching my vhiskey to see it is not poisoned . . ." Violana laughed so heartily Nell could see the black fillings at the back of her ugly mouth. "But it is very funny, my beautiful vitch, because by then you vill know that you need me, that only Violana vill be able to show you how to use that . . . that"—she searched her mind for the right word—"I think you say in English 'sensuality,' to harness it and then direct it to *attract* in a vay that is unthreatening to vomen. It is vomen you vant to like you, *n'est-ce-pas?* To respect you, to adore you? No?" The guttural accent was beginning to grate on Nell's nerves, to wear out her energy, and drain her adrenaline, but Violana's next sentence inflamed her so much she knew she was likely to be blushing like Sylvie used to blush. "Or do you vant to be a hooker, my dear? Your tits are already too vell developed. They hang from your shoulders like signals telling the vorld you are desirable, desiring, vanton—that you vill give yourself easily."

Nell lost her control. She lunged out at the evil, leering woman, screaming, "How dare you, I'll tell Wallace. No, no, no . . ."

Violana easily sidestepped, going on as if Nell hadn't even spoken. "Ve have to be sure they do not send the vrong signals to the vomen you vant to sell your products to. Ve don't vant them to be frightened of you, locking up their husbands, their teenage sons, vhenever you appear."

Nell drew herself up loftily, about to make bitter retort and leave the wretched woman, never to return, when she realized she was being dismissed anyway. "Come back, Vednesday. Ve vill begin. Ve vill do some marvelous magic together. You are a star. You are going to become the greatest star of my life. Three o'clock Vednesday vithout eye-makeup please and never, never *green* eye-makeup again!"

Pig Face came back and Nell, feeling she was in a trance, followed her downstairs, trembling at the ignominious dismissal, yet aware deep inside of another emotion—elation. Violana had recognized she was *already* a star; Violana would make her the greatest star, and for that Nell would endure the learning process ahead . . . endure and then, later, after her graduation, she would wreak her vengeance on the old cow for the insults she had suffered today. Nell smiled slowly to herself. It would be well worth the effort.

~~~

Brenda Caplan stared at the portrait through an alcoholic haze. She lifted the revolver and despite a slightly shaking wrist took aim with accuracy, leaving gaping holes in the forehead, the eyes, the mouth, the crotch. "So you want a divorce now, do you? You lying, cheating bastard . . ." She sprawled back on the couch, throwing the revolver to the floor like a discarded toy.

As she poured herself a large gin, she decided she would make sure a picture of the disfigured portrait of her husband appeared on the front page of every major newspaper in the world. She would write the caption herself. She started to compose it out loud.

"I shot the bastard in the brain—where he hatches his plots to sleep with every available piece of tail in town. I shot him in the eyes to stop him seeing what he most lusts after; then the mouth to stop his lies . . ." She stopped, pleased with her train of thought, ". . . and finally his prick to make sure he has nothing left to live for."

A horrifying thought struck her and she bent forward to retrieve the revolver, this time not bothering to stand up to shoot. "Eureka!" This shot carved a hole through the one hand visible in the portrait— the right hand. She had to make sure Ty's composing days were finished, although with no brain he'd sure find it hard to create any music.

That thought struck her as particularly funny and she threw herself back on the couch in a paroxysm of giggling, drinking gin as she laughed until she tossed the glass away and started to drink from the bottle.

At four-thirty the doorbell rang. She tried to get up to answer it, but every time she tried to stand the damned floor gave way beneath her feet. These bloody English apartments! Just riddled with dry rot!

As she made a third attempt, a key turned in the lock and in came Stan Piro, her faithful hairdresser and traveling companion.

"Why'd you ring the bell, Stan?" she slurred. "What's the matter with you?" His arms full of parcels, he didn't bother to explain it hadn't been easy to find the key as she'd obviously changed its hiding place again.

"Sooooo, wot 'ave we 'ere, then," he cried in an attempt at a Cockney accent. "Madame's been at the gin again, 'as she? Daddy won't like that, will he?"

"Don't mention 'daddy' to me," she screamed. "Look what I think of daddy . . ." She pointed dramatically at the portrait. "Next time I'm going to finish him off in person."

Stan was used to Brenda's tirades, but the gaping black holes in what had been a remarkable Bernard Buffet portrait of Ty Caplan made him feel inexplicably sick. It was inexplicable because he loathed the man's guts. "Oh, my gawd, Brenda, you have been a naughty girl. What did you want to do that for?" The words came out automatically. He didn't listen to her rambling reply.

He knew he would like to see Ty Caplan dead as a dodo—God knew he had put up with enough crap from him when he'd been in residence as master of the house. Caplan had never made any pretense about his feelings, looking down his perfect nose, implying that homosexuals were the scum of the earth, not fit to set foot in his home —which Brenda's money had bought in the first place! But, luckily, even when Brenda was crazy about Ty and could hardly bear him out of her sight, she had always had her own way. It meant he'd stayed around because in her opinion only Stan Piro's talented hands could bring any life to her thin hair and produce a semblance of the abundance and glory that her fans remembered from her heyday in the 1940s.

As Stan looked at Brenda now he thought dispassionately that it was still possible to see why she had been a superstar. The soft lighting in the Eaton Square apartment didn't show the myriad fine lines around her fabulous slanting eyes. In fact the lighting made even her alcohol-ridden, drab skin, usually overpowdered and overrouged, look soft and subtle.

"Come on, my lady . . ." Stan was bored to sobs at the thought of the evening ahead, but Brenda was his only meal ticket these days, as he constantly had to remind himself. "Let's get you ready for the the-a-ter."

To his horror Brenda started to sob. If there was anything Stan didn't know how to cope with it was tears, especially a woman's tears. A man's were bad enough, but tears from a fag-hag! "Shut up, Brenda. Shut up," he screamed. He hovered over her, wondering whether a few sharp slaps to the jaw would stop her.

"Ty wan' . . . wants a divorce," she moaned. "My baby want . . . wants to leave me . . ."

"Whatever for?" Stan was genuinely surprised. He knew the composer that the world hated to love, the bad boy of Broadway, probably screwed around by now, but he couldn't blame him for that. He'd been present at enough of Brenda's ugly scenes and sojourns with the bottle to know that any man would have to be a saint to put up with it forever. Her breath was enough to make a man join the Foreign Legion. All the same, he'd thought Ty Caplan was too self-centered, too in love with his blasted music and himself to let anyone *else* interfere. So why the divorce, when his marriage to Brenda worked so well as a safety valve?

Stan suddenly remembered something Kitty Stein had told him—

about Ty and her little brown mouse. He hadn't taken it seriously. What was it? This kid, Kitty's protégée, someone Kitty had even taken abroad for the first time, had treated like her own daughter or sister or something . . . helping her get some education . . . a Cockney with no money, no chance of anything . . . as he groped to remember the full story he absentmindedly rocked Brenda back and forth until her heavy sobs ceased, to be replaced by a low purr like a cat.

She was asleep. Well, that meant the opening night of _Stop the World, I Want to Get Off_ was off for them too. He didn't care. He was sick of carting a drunken old woman around, even one as famous as Brenda.

After he'd undressed her and put her to bed, Stan dialed Kitty's number. As he heard her phone ring he thought to himself, "Now, Kitty's a fun girl who appears to have her drinking under control—although she can certainly put enough of it away, too."

The call from Stan Piro was the call Kitty had been waiting for all her working life. A disloyal, dishonest slave, or an abandoned, heart-broken lover or mate were always good for a plate of real dirt, and this dish was gold-plated—perfect for the unspeakable Sunday rag she now worked for—the "Sunday Filth," as Fleet Street had long ago nick-named the paper.

When she put down the phone, Kitty stared out of her top-floor window on Pont Street, across the rooftops of the mews below, beyond the gold glitter of Harrods, as if she could will her eyes to see across Knightsbridge all the way to Montpelier Square where Smith Maynard now lived in the style to which his editor-in-chief position entitled him.

Was this the story to win back Smith's respect? Would he view it as sour grapes, or was he human enough to want to get even with the star-who-got-away?

Kitty's stomach churned with anger and envy as she thought of Sylvie, the little brown mouse of Fleet Street, or "Eve," as she usually described Sylvie to her closest cronies.

Everyone in the Street knew how irate Smith was over Sylvie's behavior, yet he insisted she was only on a leave of absence and still ran occasional pieces from her, which infuriated Kitty even more.

How Smith could go along with the hypocrisy, she didn't know. There was Sylvie, holed up with a famous celebrity—had hardly left his side, according to Sid, since she'd interviewed him in Rome in the summer of 1960—and Smith never printed a word about it, although their names had been linked by the competition.

And now, according to Stan, who was privy to Brenda Caplan's most unguarded moments, America's most famous and successful composer wanted a divorce and Brenda was brokenhearted. That could only mean one thing as far as Kitty was concerned. Sylvie had to be pregnant. Why else would Caplan want to marry her? What did he *need* to marry her for when he got everything he asked for without marriage? Sylvie had probably learned enough tricks from the dreaded Nell—and whatever had happened to *that* pin-up girl of the fifties? Kitty stopped daydreaming and went to her typewriter.

The only way to convince Smith she could still write was, of course, to write something wonderful. She was unbelievably inspired on this subject! The shooting of the portrait would make a wonderful beginning. Thank God she'd befriended the fairy hairdresser who, lonely and depressed on his first trip to England, had run into her in a pub one day and turned out to be a wonderful source of gossip from then on. This was really a bonanza.

Kitty almost didn't answer the phone when it rang at nine o'clock that evening. She hadn't stopped working for three hours, finishing a piece she knew was one of the best things she'd written in years.

Her prose was spare and taut. She described Sylvie's journey from the East End of London, carrying with her such a burning ambition it had transformed her nondescript personality into a scheming, stealthy one, capable of moving mountains. Her article was a tour de force. Smith had to like it. Kitty had already decided she would risk humiliation and take the story personally to Smith the next morning before he left home to become incommunicado behind his office door, guarded by Sue the watchdog.

But thank God she answered the phone.

It was Stan, a terrified Stan screaming at her that there was something wrong with Brenda. "What shall I do? That shit Ty called. I listened on the other phone. He told her he wanted out—he was going to go into seclusion to write serious music. She screamed and ranted, but he never budged, said he was going to see a lawyer in the morning. She's locked herself in the bathroom and I can't get an answer out of her."

A picture that had come in from a photo agency the month before flashed into Kitty's mind. It was of Ty Caplan and Sylvie holding hands in the main square in Capri. There was no mistaking the look on their faces: they were in love. She could just visualize it now on the front page of the *Evening Mirror* beside a picture of the disfigured portrait. She could see the headline—"Brenda Caplan Commits Suicide"— and her by-line, "by Kitty Stein," big and bold, just beneath . . . if Brenda Caplan was dead. She sounded dead.

"Wait there, Stan. I'll be right over." Kitty rushed to collect her camera and flash. She wasn't going to entrust this picture-taking to anybody else.

Kitty guessed Smith would be unlisted in Montpelier Square, but that didn't faze her. In the States she would have a hard time getting through to an unlisted number, but in England if you knew what to say, it was easy.

"The ex-directory operator, please. Hello? Yes, this is Kitty Stein of the *Sunday Globe*. Please call and ask Mr. Smith Maynard of 40 Montpelier Square if he will accept my call. It's a matter of extreme urgency."

Please, God, let him be home, she prayed. Please let him be home and say yes.

"Yes." Curt, brusque, Smith sounded as unkind and as unwelcoming as ever, but at least he'd agreed to talk to her.

Fear of rejection made her timid. It helped that she had facts, not emotions to pass on. A hard-nosed reporter first and editor-in-chief second, Smith Maynard listened attentively.

They worked out everything together. Sid was called and given the story. Kitty loved how it sounded as she dictated every word succinctly. When a story *sounded* good, it always meant it *read* even better. When she reached Eaton Square she would call in the final paragraph. She had two versions ready—one with Brenda dead, one with Brenda a pathetic ghost of her former self. Either way, Sylvie was to blame.

She caught a cab to Eaton Square. The police were there before her, questioning a still-hysterical Stan.

An ambulance arrived soon after, although the police pathologist told her on arrival that Brenda was very obviously dead from a huge overdose of pills and booze.

Was Smith grateful—appreciative—that she'd handed him for free the major scoop of her career, a scoop that would obviously cost her her job on the *Sunday Globe*?

Yes, she thought, as the long night filtered into a smoky gray dawn, he was appreciative, showing it in the only way that mattered to her. He agreed she could come back to the *Mirror*.

They didn't discuss salary. It wasn't money Kitty wanted. She knew Smith would see her right on that. She wanted to be back where he was only a desk or two away—working her guts out for *him* and *his* paper and nobody else's.

It was Sid who reminded her that she had to resign from one paper before rejoining another. She did it right away, waking up her about-to-be ex-boss before he could see the early edition of the *Mirror* where, just as she'd visualized it, her story was the lead item on page one; her by-line was big and bold, and the two pictures emphasized that every word she had written was true.

Her story with the two pictures went around the world, getting a particularly big play in the American press—but that didn't thrill Kitty nearly as much as knowing she was the number-one topic of conversation in Fleet Street bars for at least a week.

Were Smith and Kitty back together again? If not emotionally or sexually, they were at least once again an editorial team.

Would the "Sunday Filth" sue? Could they sue? What would be the grounds? Breach of contract? Kitty, like most hacks, had never had a contract. Alienation of affection one wag suggested . . . but of course the lowly *Sunday* didn't sue. "We wouldn't give Kitty Stein the satisfaction of thinking she's worth suing over," said one Global goon.

In a few days, it was all old news.

Kitty was back in harness at the *Evening Mirror*, trying to find a corner in the newsroom to call her own.

All she cared about now was that Ty Caplan had seen her story, the true story of Miss Nobody Goody Two Shoes who had always been determined to be *somebody*, no matter what it cost or who got hurt.

Then Kitty prayed that Ty Caplan, known for his irrational behavior, would abandon Sylvie, preferably on a lonely highway miles away from anywhere, so that Sylvie would have to walk . . . and walk . . . and walk . . . until her shoes became as down-at-heel as once they had always been.

6

Nassau,
February 25, 1966

THE WALL STREET JOURNAL.

After four years of phenomenal growth that propelled a 400-percent jump in its stock price, the Phoenix-based direct-sales Natural Beauty Cosmetics Company has run into hard times. Last week a 42-percent drop in third-quarter profits was disclosed—and investors had soured on its prospects long before the announcement. Over the last nine months Natural Beauty's stock has plunged 69 percent in value.

The company's main problem, according to industry analysts, is competition from a new company, founded by Nell Nesbitt, who four years ago married Canadian businessman Wallace Nesbitt. Wallace Nesbitt, an early supporter of Earl S. Tupper of Tupperware (one of the first to believe in the direct-sales marketing idea), bought for his wife a small, California-based direct-sales company with one major asset, a sales force known as "cerebral housewives," brought together by a mutual longing for more education. Attending school at night, during the day they created and ran the California Color Makeup Company, selling the products in local neighborhoods. "To express the spirit behind the sales force more adequately," as Nell Nesbitt told a press conference at the time of the acquisition, she renamed the company Ready to Change.

In the last two years the Ready to Change Cosmetics Company has made extraordinary inroads, not only into Natural Beauty's territory but into that of other small, direct-sales cosmetics companies. With a zealot's zeal and apparently unflagging energy, Nell Nesbitt is, as she describes it, "now engaged in an expansion program which will concentrate on igniting ambition in American housewives everywhere." So far, she has certainly proved she is cast in the same mold as her pioneer husband . . .

Nell laughed self-deprecatingly as she pushed the paper away and leaned her head against the plane seat. If she *really* had unflagging energy, even Avon would have to sit up and take notice; but, as she was now only too aware, she could only do so much herself, and these days her energy seemed to have been put on hold.

Across the table Johnny's eyes met hers. He winked at her. Goddammit. Even one look from those intense dark blue eyes of his made her wet, and he didn't even know it.

Her trained sense of caution went into operation. Could Wallace, sitting apparently so serenely beside her, possibly know how Johnny affected her?

Certain her husband was looking at her, Nell turned to give him her most radiant smile.

It was the smile Violana had coached her long tedious hours to produce.

"Vot turns you on, Mrs. Nesbitt? Peanut butter? Butterflies? Testicles? . . ." Nell could hear the loathsome guttural voice even now. "Go on, think about vot turns you on and smile, *smile*, Mrs. Nesbitt. You look like the Virgin Mary ven you smile. Now let's forget the Virgin and get the sex across. It's a tool—a selling tool that you're blessed to have. Get it out . . . out. Give vot's inside you—you'll get everything you vant in life . . . those ads for your products . . . yes, that's right. Smile . . ."

Canada's most brilliant acting coach had been right. Her smile had even penetrated Wallace's pocketbook and he had coughed up money for the first Ready to Change TV ads, the ads Nell knew would start the business rolling.

"Have you read this?"

Wallace nodded and patted her hand. Nell's stomach churned. He was *so* condescending. Did he really believe that *he* was responsible for the meteoric jump in sales, telephones ringing off their hooks with women clamoring to join her Ready to Change brigade? If he did, then it was all her fault. She had laid on her gratitude with a trowel. "Oh, darling, you're such a visionary." Visionary, her foot! Once upon a time, maybe. Wallace Nesbitt was now just an old man who needed to be suckled like a baby, who hadn't had an original idea in years— except to marry her.

"It's on the way, baby. It's on the way . . ."

Even Wallace's voice grated on her, but she continued to smile as he went on: "But you promised me you wouldn't talk or think about business for the next week. You've got to relax, baby. Charlotte's looking after the store. You've got nothing to worry about. The first lesson in running a *big* company is to learn how to delegate. You *must* learn how to de-le-gate . . ." Wallace smiled at his adopted son. "Right, Johnny? And it's easy with another workaholic in the family. Someone you can trust not to cook the books or put a knife in your back."

To Nell's irritation, Johnny smiled his agreement.

He *always* agreed with Wallace. At first she'd thought it was because he lacked guts, had no backbone, was just one more interminable "yes man" around Wallace Wainwright Nesbitt.

Now she knew differently. Johnny Nesbitt was no "yes man." He simply loved the man who had brought him up as his own son. In Johnny's opinion, that man could do no wrong. No wonder in the early days, when they had first met, he had been so suspicious of her. Even more suspicious than Anne, who of course had set out to poison his mind against her from the beginning. Not so long ago Johnny had admitted he *had* once believed Anne—that she was little better than a whore, and after only one thing, his stepfather's money.

Nell twisted her emerald engagement ring restlessly, remembering those days—Johnny's coolness, his studied avoidance of her until, just as suddenly as his suspicion was there, it was gone, to be replaced first with an amused respect, then a growing admiration as he saw how hard she worked for Ready to Change when she didn't need to work at all.

Why had his opinion of her changed so radically, so quickly? It was nothing she had done—or could have done—to convince him she genuinely loved the old geezer. Wallace had simply told him to believe in her—and so he had.

How hard she'd had to work to keep the lid tightly shut on the tempestuous Nell O'Halloran. How difficult it had all been to develop the slightly shy, but always charming persona that was now so perfectly in place. She'd had to pay for it in an extraordinary way. Her hair had turned almost white, almost overnight.

Of course she'd wanted to dye it back to her original dark brunette, but first Wallace and then Johnny had pleaded with her not to do it, both of them backed up by Johnny's dreary wife, Charlotte.

At the time, to go against their wishes had seemed tantamount to revealing everything about herself. It was as if with every drop of Miss

Clairol's Loving Care she would be proving everything Anne had ever said about her was true—that as a "restored" brunette she would stand exposed as a gold digger, a vulture just waiting to pick the flesh from Wallace's bones. The final decision had been Violana's, who had called on Kenneth, a brilliant, young New York hairdresser who, acting on her directive to "bring out the angel, play down the vitch," had turned the white into silver, a silver halo which had become her trademark.

It had taken her time to realize that as usual Violana had displayed uncanny genius. Once she'd grown used to it, Nell had seen that the silver hair made her look even more outstanding and unusual. She looked older without looking old, beautiful without looking sexy, dignified but not stuffy. Her hair, as Violana had intended, was a great deceiving act.

Nell shut her eyes, savoring the thought of the week ahead in Nassau as guests of Wallace's multimillionaire chum Eddie Taylor. Although Wallace was chiding her for thinking and talking about business, she knew one of the reasons they were going to Nassau was for Wallace to further his involvement in a massive new casino complex being planned for the island. She hoped Wallace would have long business sessions behind closed doors with Eddie Taylor, while she walked on a golden beach, slightly ahead of Johnny, her bikini exposing the round firmness of her behind. She hoped she would be free to go dancing with Johnny under the stars at the new resort Eddie Taylor had created out of swamp and marsh. She wanted to dance not like the decorous wife of the chairman, but *close*, so close her breath would mingle with Johnny's in the tropical night, while her thighs insinuated the magic their bodies could make together.

When had it all started? Perhaps from the very first day they'd met, the day Johnny had returned from his sheep farm in Australia. Looking back, Nell realized now his presence had been disturbing and distracting right from the beginning, forcing her to work harder to keep up the pretense of being totally devoted to Wallace.

As she looked out at a blameless blue sky, Nell recalled, as she often did, how she'd dreaded Johnny's reappearance in Wallace's life, knowing how Wallace and Anne doted on him. Of course at that point, even though Wallace was obsessed with her, he was still irritatingly holding back from the commitment of marriage.

May the fifth, 1961, had been an epoch-making day for the world; U.S. Navy Commander Alan Shepard had made the first U.S. expedition into space. Wallace had taken her along on a business trip to the States, where he was completing a deal with Spencer Love, the founder of Burlington, America's leading textile company. Everything had gone so well that Wallace had accepted Spencer's invitation to celebrate at the Loves' Palm Beach home, and they'd hopped on a Burlington jet as easily and effortlessly as catching a cab.

The trip had intensified Nell's determination to become a real part of it all, not just as a guest, an appendage of Wallace, a bystander at the feast. She'd wanted desperately to be like Martha Love, the one who gave the orders, issued the invitations, arranged the "placement."

How chagrined she'd been, placed at the "baby table" one lunchtime—as Martha herself had called it. Despite the fact that Martha had seated herself there, Nell had not been placated. She'd known then, as she'd always known instinctively, the difference between first and second class, the head table and the table for those less important. The increased spur to her ambition had perhaps been necessary. She had been tiring—despite Violana's incessant hiss in her ears to "have patience, darlink, patience"—perhaps even visibly, of her Little Miss Muffet role.

On May 5, along with the Love family, they had been breakfasting in the garden patio. A few minutes after the Loves' black butler had plugged a small television into what appeared to be a socket in a tree trunk to witness Shepard's takeoff from Cape Canaveral, Nell had heard a man's voice cry "dad" and seen Wallace jump out of his chair, his face unusually red with emotion.

Johnny had traced Wallace to Florida and, as Nell had quickly learned about Johnny, he was unwilling to waste even a minute after five years away and had flown overnight on a company plane to get to Palm Beach in time for breakfast.

Before Johnny's arrival Nell had been skeptical about everything she'd ever been told about him. "He wouldn't be dissuaded—no matter how hard I tried to stop him. He left the family business to prove he could make it on his own," was the well-worn way Wallace had described Johnny's sheep-farming venture to her, his eyes lighting up whenever he mentioned his adopted son's name. "He's a hell of a fellow, Nell. Although I can tell you I was really mad at the time, I understand now why he felt smothered by me and couldn't get a sense of his own identity."

Nell had thought all that was hogwash. She hadn't been able to understand how the adopted, much-loved son of a multimillionaire would go to such a godforsaken spot as Australia where, according to the letters Wallace occasionally passed to her, he was living like all the other roughnecks. The only explanation Nell could accept for anyone to exchange the comfortable, effortless expense-account life Johnny had always lived, for the rough, raw, backbreaking tour of duty "down-under" was *failure*. Johnny Nesbitt had to have been a failure in the Nesbitt empire and he'd gone as far away as possible to hide the fact.

All she'd needed was one look at Johnny to know she'd been wrong, totally wrong. Johnny exuded vitality, enthusiasm, honesty, purpose-fulness. As she'd studied him from behind dark glasses, she told herself that Johnny Nesbitt was the kind of man they could easily have been watching on television—making history like Alan Shepard, a pioneer in space. Now she believed what Wallace had told her—that instead Johnny had pioneered on earth in a desolate part of Australia and made his investment pay off a hundred times.

"Now he's ready to come home and take over the reins from me. He's made his point." Wallace had chuckled with pride, while his eyes had moistened with sentimental tears.

Hogwash. Hogwash. Nell hadn't believed a word—until she'd set eyes on Johnny Nesbitt for the first time. What a man!

Johnny had been eager to introduce Wallace to Charlotte, too, standing so awkwardly beside him that day. Charlotte was the rangy Australian girl he'd met and married in Perth. Nell had set out to befriend Charlotte, who had easily fallen under her influence, excited to be in at the beginning of a new cosmetics empire—just as Sylvie would have been—Sylvie, who, Nell had learned only recently, had made a surprising, happy marriage to a wacky, bohemian, but suc-cessful Broadway composer.

Nell shut her eyes, telling herself fiercely one day she would be happily married, too—to Johnny. If she'd met Johnny first there never would have been a Charlotte—and one day there wouldn't be a Char-lotte around either. She would have given up the unequal battle and gone back down-under where she belonged.

Down-under! How Nell longed for Wallace to be literally down-under, underground. How much longer could he live with what doc-tors called his "tired heart"? If she heard him whisper, "let's go against doctor's orders," one more time, she swore she would suffocate him with the pillow he liked to prop under her.

As Derek the steward removed the seafood platter to replace it with one of fresh fruit, the plane lurched, sending everything sliding to the floor. "Sorry, Mr. Wallace, sir, Mr. Johnny . . . a bit of turbulence. Buckle up for a few minutes, sir." Nell burned as she heard the obsequious note in Derek's voice. No matter where they were—in the Canadian houses, the California ranch, the New York penthouse, the sloop, or, as now, on the company jet, it was always, "Yes, Mr. Nesbitt, no, Mr. Nesbitt, three bags full, Mr. Nesbitt," for Wallace and Johnny. Never a word to Mrs. Nesbitt. She didn't count, even if her Ready to Change company was beginning to beat the knickers off the competition. As far as the Nesbitt organization was concerned she was a nobody. Well, she would show them. She *was* showing them!

A sudden wail reminded Nell it wasn't only the power of Johnny Nesbitt's looks and personality that made her foolishly—occasionally —lose sight of the role she had to play so carefully.

Johnny's daughter, the adorable doe-eyed Lucy, was waking up, her six-year-old face blurred with sleep, blinking, grimacing, wrinkling her pert little nose as she wondered for a second where she was.

Nell's imagined scenario on the Nassau beach changed to include Lucy. How charmed Johnny would be to see the two of them collecting shells together, racing each other in and out of the surf. Surely he *had* to be charmed? Why should he be different from other men? Was he? Could it be she was destined to love only those who for some unaccountable reason would never love her? Her mouth went dry. She'd never stood much of a chance with the only man she'd ever cared for until Johnny came along. She'd lost all chance when the baby came, born out of her ignorance and naivete.

Now she looked lovingly at Lucy. Lucy could be the perfect replacement for the baby she'd lost. Lucy was the prettiest, sassiest little girl she had ever known, like the little girl Nell was sure she must have been herself—with one insurmountable difference. Lucy was already an heiress, used to the best things that life had to offer, whereas she had had to start by learning what the best things *were*.

Nell leaned across to clasp Lucy's hands as the jet dipped and plunged as if it were in an acrobatic display. "Shall we go shelling, shilly, shally, Lucy?"

It was a familiar conversation and Lucy immediately lost her look of fear, giggling as she replied, "Shilly, shally, shilly, shally, Auntie Nelly. We're silly, shilly, shelly people . . ."

They made up words, played pat-a-cake and "I Spy" until Jeff Boyd, the company's chief pilot, announced, "Landing in five minutes, folks. Check seat belts."

The sea below was more brilliantly turquoise than the necklace and bracelet Wallace had given her the month before for an "unprecedented increase in Ready to Change sales." She hadn't been expecting jewelry. She hadn't even wanted it, hard though she would have once found that to believe. She had only wanted expansion money—big money for the Ready to Change movement to open up across the nation, not leave it "to grow naturally," as Wallace always replied so casually to her pleas.

The vivid color of the sea burned her eyes. They smarted with angry, frustrated tears. She knew the company couldn't move forward without a new influx of capital—money that Wallace would hardly miss; yet he continued to be obstinate, merely patting her hand, telling her not to work so hard. She inwardly seethed. He wanted to keep her in harness and prevent her from the great success she knew she could achieve. Even if Wallace died, as by right he *should* have done by now, she couldn't be sure of inheriting the amount she needed.

The agreement she'd signed couldn't have been clearer. For every year Wallace lived after their marriage, she would receive more money —although during the last three years, whenever she'd particularly titillated him, Wallace had intimated that he'd increased her inheritance. She had known not to ask by how much. Now, Nell reflected grimly, every year Wallace lived, the faster she would turn into an old crone, separated from Johnny—whose own inheritance from the Nesbitt estate could make all the difference to Ready to Change.

Violana was right as usual. It wasn't the chronological passing of time that aged you; it was the way you lived your life—and for a woman *that* meant enough sex with the person who turned you on the most. Without it even the youngest, most attractive woman could shrivel up like an old pea pod.

Violana's black-olive eyes came into her mind and she shifted imperceptibly in her seat, remembering the thundery afternoon in Violana's studio when, bored out of her mind with Wallace, she'd been in a particularly foul mood, acting like a spoiled child, imitating Violana's broken accent in an insulting way, refusing to follow instructions, becoming ruder and ruder.

Without warning she'd burst into angry sobs. To this day she didn't know what had caused her to lose control so absolutely. Before she'd known what was happening Violana had lifted her up in her brawny arms. Nell could feel her insides tremble even now at the thought of them. She had carried her, still whimpering like some idiot child, to the huge couch onstage where much of Violana's unorthodox lessons took place.

"You need fuckink, darlink . . . by an expert . . . you vant it, it vill be vonderful, you know that, don't you, darlink. You need to come again and again and again until you scream . . ." Violana's voice had dropped so low she'd sounded as she looked, more male than female. "Turn over." There had been a note of command in her voice that couldn't be ignored. Nell's every pore had throbbed with excitement as she had obeyed her. Lesbian love. Violana, she'd realized for the first time, had to be a lesbian. She'd never given it a thought before, so obsessed had she been with learning everything she could from the old crow. It had taken much longer than she'd expected to learn how to handle—control—her speech. It had been a struggle, first to realize that she still could give away her poor East End of London beginnings, not with anything as obvious as a Cockney accent, but by putting the wrong emphasis on words, using "poor-qvality expressions," as Violana described them, as well as making grammatical mistakes. What a joke that a Hungarian who still couldn't—or wouldn't—say her _w_'s had alerted her to a stupid wrong use of the word _ought_; Nell had been forced to realize that for years she had been using it too much and with the wrong tense.

The memory of the "first time" with Violana came sharply into focus. Nell contracted her vagina, struggling to stay calm, yet closing her eyes as she relived what had turned out to be the most mind-bending sensation she had ever experienced.

Violana had undressed her, but only from the waist down, taking time to slip her long sinewy fingers around her waist to release the belt of her skirt, then slowly . . . slowly . . . agonizingly slowly slipping it down. There had been no sound from either of them, only the soft swish of silk as next she had slithered off Nell's panties. Nell had felt that her heart was going to stop beating. Although she still had on an angora sweater and her bra, she had never felt more naked, lying on her stomach as Violana, now each touch a caress, had unclipped her garters and removed her garter belt and each stocking with exaggerated care.

Her bottom bare, her top covered, she—who always reveled in her nakedness—had felt strangely indecent. "Don't look at me." Violana had sounded as low and guttural as usual, but with—Nell had noted with acute suspense and excitement—a tremor of desire. Violana was aroused. It was the last time she'd thought about how Violana felt.

With deliberate strokes the famous teacher had begun to massage her from the soles up, her hands surprisingly soft, but her fingers, her long fingers hard and prying, opening her buttocks, inserting one, two, three cold fingers as sharp as steel deep into her rectum, while the other hand had crept around her thigh to pierce her now-oozing cunt, the fingers working masterfully in tandem. One hand had hurt so much that Nell had started to moan, until other sensations took over as Violana manipulated her so expertly, penetrating deeper, deeper until just as she was on the verge of coming, the crescendo of a mind-bending orgasm about to be reached, the old witch had abruptly withdrawn both hands, and without warning Nell had felt an astonishing sting across her bare behind.

It had taken her a minute or two to realize she was being whipped, but by such a fine silk cord, the sensation each blow produced had increased her wetness, made her pant more with longing, not less. "No, oh, yes . . ." she'd cried, as much for Violana to put her magical fingers back as for the stinging blows to stop. They had stopped, to be replaced with a soaping and sponging she would never forget, a flannel as soft as a baby's diaper pushed and squeezed inside her, water squelching and always Violana's fingers in and out, water, soap, flannel, sponge . . . she had felt like an erotic baby. "Now you can turn over, you glorious vitch, you beautiful evil baby vitch . . ." Violana's voice had been thick with lust and longing and soon her tongue had been everywhere, flicking like an asp's. She'd burrowed her face between Nell's legs, forcing them wide, wider apart. Even as her tongue had licked, her teeth had fastened on the soft flesh . . . again the pleasure mixed with pain had started her body to shudder with orgasms . . . again and again . . . she had been drowning in orgasms as the old woman had once more invaded her rectum and with cruel forceful thrusts pushed her body up to receive in full the force of her animal mouth.

"No more, no more . . ." She had tried to cry weakly, wrenched apart, in real pain as Violana's fingers had become more and still more demanding. The more she'd cried, the more savagely Violana had worked on her, and, opening her eyes, full of painful tears, Nell had seen Violana strap on a huge dildo before she'd brutally turned her onto her stomach again and with crazed wild thrusts had shot the blunt-nosed instrument into her behind. Nell had screamed out in agony, but even as the pain of breaking flesh had scorched her mind, a tremendous rush of other feelings—ones she'd never experienced before—had overwhelmed the pain. Agony and ecstasy had mingled, taking over every cell of her body. She had given herself up to the sensations, sure she was going to die, drowning in her own sweat and mucus and blood.

The first time was something she would never forget—never—but there were many variations on the theme that excited Violana the most . . . leaving her half dressed, usually naked from the waist down, which never ceased to make her feel vulnerable, like a small child again, crying in a wilderness of loneliness and frustrated emotions . . . sometimes following Violana's orders sulkily, but *always* following them—to stand face-to-wall in a corner, her breasts bare, naked beneath a rough skirt that scraped her flesh, which later Violana would soothe for an ecstatic hour with honey and beeswax and wine. . . . "You are my feast tonight, my evil baby vitch . . ."

"Why are you sighing, babe?" Wallace squeezed her hand, bringing her back to reality and to the bittersweet knowledge that Johnny and Lucy were so near, yet so far.

"Was I? I didn't realize. Sorry." It was the truth. She hadn't even realized she'd been sighing. She had to be more careful, but perhaps it was fortuitous. Should she try to tell Wallace one more time? She had to convince him that Ready to Change could be as big as Tupperware, or bigger, if only he would properly capitalize it. Inwardly she found herself sighing again. It was useless. She'd already asked too many times in too many different ways. Wallace didn't want the company to grow bigger. Not if it meant *she* was running it. In his mind she was his property, and Ready to Change was merely a hobby he allowed her to enjoy.

Nell smiled at him again while her brain ticked over. If anything, she knew Wallace was beginning to resent the company's demands on her time, although he had never actually said so. What a farcical situation it was. Little did Wallace realize why she'd jumped at the idea of Charlotte "minding the store," as he'd put it, while she had a "well-earned rest with the family." She could see right through his plan, encouraging Charlotte to do more, to release her of responsibility, so that eventually she would be free to devote more time to him.

What a terrifying, stultifying thought. She would sooner be dead.

Building the company meant more to her than anything—even a life with Johnny and Lucy. But she wanted both and she would get both. Johnny would make the ideal partner in business, too—and one day Lucy would join them, learning, working, side by side. Little did

Wallace realize . . . or did he? A shiver went through her, knowing how quickly and efficiently Wallace Nesbitt dealt with anyone who—in his opinion—transgressed or opposed his authority.

She could feel her panic rising, blind panic at the thought of being trapped with Wallace and Anne for life, while Johnny and Lucy lived their lives without her.

"What *is* it, Nell?" Wallace rarely used her name. His tone was searching, more definite now.

Nell swallowed hard. She had to invent something fast.

She leaned over to whisper in his ear as the Gulf Stream made a rapid descent over the vivid sea and barren scrubland of Nassau. "I think my curse has come early, dammit. I feel strange, queasy. I hope I'm wrong." She delicately traced his earlobe with the tip of her tongue and sensed his body stir.

"Daddy, where's Auntie Nell?" Lucy scuffed her toes in the sand restlessly. "Can't she come shelling with me now?"

Johnny tweaked his daughter's pigtail, unraveling still more of the already unraveling braid. "Auntie Nell's with granddad. You'll have to put up with your poor old dad for company . . ." Lucy giggled as a tickle accompanied his last words.

"Auntie Nell's a great shilly-shelly person . . ." Lucy took off like a baby gazelle across the broad expanse of beach below Eddie Taylor's magnificent terrace. "Bet you can't catch me, daddy . . . catch me . . . " Johnny acted like an old man, puffing and blowing out his cheeks until he caught up with her, hoisting her onto his shoulders, then charging down the beach like a jet engine, pretending to be frightened of the waves, jumping in and out until finally, with Lucy still clinging to his shoulders, he plunged into the turquoise waters up to his waist with Lucy screaming joyously.

From her bedroom window Nell watched the scene, a warm glow spreading through her as she saw the happiness on the faces of father and daughter. Out of nowhere darkness obscured the glow, darkness that was never far away these days. Was it the cause or the effect? Would she always be cursed with this dark sense of desolation when she saw so much evidence of Johnny's tenderness, gentleness toward Lucy—because she was *not* Lucy's mother, not Johnny's wife? Or was her despair a curious jealousy that Johnny so obviously loved being with Lucy more than with any other human being? When he was with Lucy, his often "all business" attitude disappeared. He became the gentlest, most compliant of human beings, a kind of man-boy, the most perfect shoulder to rest on, yet full of pranks and fun.

"Nell, where are you, Nell?" A bitter expression obliterated Nell's beauty, an expression that would have told even the village idiot that here was a wife who loathed and detested the man who had just spoken, despite the cooing sounds that emanated from the generous, curved mouth. "Yes, beloved. I'm here. Would you like to take your morning swim? The ocean looks quiet. Perfect for you, I think."

Wallace Nesbitt beamed as he came out of the marble bathroom to see his treasure standing by the window in a ridiculously small peach-colored bikini, which emphasized the whiteness, the paleness of her glorious skin. It was the kind of skin any man would want to get lost in, to sink his teeth into. What an extraordinary cannibalistic thought . . . as if he would dream of marking her beauty in any way. Wallace suddenly wanted to feel her close to him again, to press his aging tired body on her vital, still so youthful one. He thought she backed away as he went toward her, but it was so slight a movement he knew he had imagined it. Nell had never denied him once—not once. Would the miracle happen today? As he drew her toward him, maneuvering his penis to the glorious valley of his dreams, the miracle *did* happen. His flaccid penis imperceptibly started to harden. He took her exquisite hand and placed it on his horn. She didn't start stroking as she usually did. "Are you still tired, hon? You told me your period hasn't started yet." He could never get used to the fact that the modern woman could be wearing a pair of minuscule pants or a minute bikini, yet still be flooding with blood. The tampon was certainly as big an achievement as anything Tupper had created.

"No, darling, I'm not tired. It's just that Johnny and Lucy are on the beach. I thought you might like to swim with . . ." Wallace shut her mouth with his.

"I'm horny for you, babe. I'm sorry I fell asleep so fast last night. Hell, we're on vacation. How about a little fuck before lunch . . ." A scream built inside her as out of the corner of her eye she could see Johnny and Lucy splashing each other in the ocean, could imagine the ripple of firm muscles as Johnny moved his arms, his legs, could see him now lift Lucy high above his head. The scream was building but wouldn't surface.

Without a word Nell went back to the king-sized bed and, shedding her bikini pants, put a pillow beneath her buttocks, opened her legs, and closed her eyes as she felt Wallace's weight descend.

After the unexpected, unwanted session of sex, Nell was delighted to find that Wallace remained uncharacteristically lackadaisical for the rest of the day. Usually the proof that he could still "perform his duty as a man" (as far as Nell was concerned, that was a particularly irksome expression of his) meant he ran around like a two-year-old, but not this time. After an early lunch Wallace sat on the terrace like a Winston Churchill Buddha, his face shaded by a sombrero, puffing away on a large Havana, benevolently watching Nell, Johnny, and Lucy cavort about in the surf, dozing and reading.

By the time shadows crossed the lawn and Lucy, exhausted, went docilely to bed, Wallace suddenly announced he didn't feel up to the planned evening activity—going to the Bahamian Club for dinner, followed by gambling in the private room at the back.

"When Eddie comes in I'd like to spend a quiet evening with him. I want his input on the hotel-casino complex I'm interested in, and I'd like to get his opinion of some of the government people I'll be meeting tomorrow . . ."

Nell pouted, just enough to let him know she was disappointed but not enough to show her very real passion for baccarat, blackjack, and every other kind of gambling. All the same it stopped Wallace short. Before he could say anything, to Nell's joy Johnny interjected, "Why don't I take Nell? She's probably never seen the sharks in action. She'll get a kick out of seeing how easily some people lose their money . . ."

"Do you really want to go, hon?"

"Not without you." How she got the lie out she didn't know. For once she doubted her ability to be convincing, but Wallace insisted she go and soon she felt like seventeen going on eighteen, setting off with Errol Flynn . . . except she'd never felt anything for him, whereas here she was with Johnny, whom she loved.

As they left the Lyford Cay grounds, Johnny at the wheel of a Jaguar convertible, Nell sat as close to him as she could, her hair flying loose in the breeze. Suddenly for some inexplicable reason her happiness was tinged with a sense of danger. It was uncanny. She should have been in heaven going off alone with Johnny, yet a premonition gnawed at her. Was it because she was frightened of her own emotions? Was she frightened she wouldn't be able to hold them in check—that she would break down and reveal how she *really* felt? Nell heard her heart beat so loudly that she tried to hold her breath to calm down, jumping uncontrollably when Johnny put a restraining hand on her knee as he pulled up sharply to avoid a car coming out of nowhere. The strange, uneasy feeling stayed with her all through a magical dinner, when Johnny alternately flattered and teased her about her incredible ability to motivate women into selling other women "powder and paint," as he put it. The feeling persisted even when he threw a casual arm around her waist as they went into the private room where the gaming tables were just beginning to swing into action. The touch of his hand at her waist, the closeness of his tanned skin: Nell had just started to dream about kissing him on their drive back through the warm tropical night, when she saw Joe Diaz a split second before she was sure Diaz saw her. It was the worst shock of her life.

Her legs went weak. It was all she could do to move, but move she must. She turned abruptly away from Johnny. "I've got to go to the ladies' room, Johnny. Sorry."

It wasn't surprising that he looked puzzled. "Are you all right?" Nell didn't answer, rushing, running back to the restaurant, not knowing what to do, where to go, whether to hide or not to hide.

Joe Diaz from Toronto, friend of the big guys in the Mafia, the man who eight years before had offered her what had been little better than a hooker's job. All right, she hadn't taken it, but he'd offered it, because he'd seen right through her—he'd known without knowing her that she'd often _acted_ like a hooker.

She'd even been attracted to him for five minutes—attracted because of his apparent indifference. Had it been indifference or had it been his iron control? How furious she'd been, despite the fact that he'd hinted they could and _would_ have a future if she followed his orders, which meant first luring wealthy businessmen to the Apollo, to the gaming tables, and later, as a consolation for losing a considerable amount of money, into her bed.

And now she was Mrs. Wallace—above reproach—Nesbitt, a reformed whore in discreet couture clothing. Nell locked herself in the lavatory, her mind rebelling against the unexpected, dreadful intrusion from her past. What if Diaz was talking to Johnny now, telling him about the girl she used to be? She pressed her head against the cool tiled wall, trying not to be sick. She was overreacting. Perhaps Diaz hadn't even seen her. She couldn't risk going back to the tables. She'd send a message to Johnny saying she didn't feel well. That was it. She'd go outside and ask for their car, to save time. Better to be safe than sorry.

Nell peered out of the ladies' room, looking up and down the passageway. No one in sight. Her confidence returned. She _had_ overreacted, but she still had to get away fast. She started to tiptoe warily toward the foyer, half expecting Johnny to appear to take her in his arms to protect her.

As she went past a door marked "No Exit," a pair of arms came out and grabbed her inside before she knew what was happening. She was numb, unable to speak as a familiar voice said, "Good evening, Miss O'Halloran—Miss Nell—or should I call you Mrs. Nesbitt now?"

She was in what looked like a storage cupboard, so dimly lit at first she could see no faces, only bodies, one, two, three. Thugs. They looked like thugs. She remained silent as Joe Diaz went on speaking.

He knew everything. Quietly, coolly, a manner she remembered well, he ran through the major events of her life during the last few years as if he were reading her curriculum vitae for the benefit of a review board. The date of her marriage, where she'd spent her honeymoon, the Nesbitt homes, the Nesbitt friends she saw in Canada and the U.S., and the birth and spectacular rise of her Ready to Change Cosmetics Company.

By the time Nell left the room she felt an hour had passed and she'd aged a hundred years. In fact only twenty minutes had elapsed which, with a mixture of relief and aggravation, Nell found Johnny didn't appear to have noticed; he was enjoying a winning streak at the blackjack table.

Twelve hours later, like a sleepwalker, Nell started to follow Diaz's orders for the first time—orders of a very different, much more momentous kind than those issued years before. She was amazed that what she had viewed as a most unsavory, dangerous association from her past should have presented her with the opportunity she so sorely needed. If she helped them, they would help her—more than she could ever realize. And if she didn't help them?

Joe's implication had been clear. Blackmail. Her seedy past life exposed. He knew all about her association with Pierre Repelle. "Little Orphan Nellie—the rip-off artist of all time," was the way Joe Diaz had described her, touching her cheek with the cold surface of his signet ring.

So here she was walking to a rendezvous along the fine white beach stretching from one end of the island to the other. With her was darling Lucy. Incredibly they knew about Lucy, too—but luckily not the way she felt about her. Lucy was her "cover"—she was shelling with Lucy, while Wallace and Johnny attended an important business meeting in town to discuss the Nesbitt participation in the planned casino complex with the Bay Street Boys, as members of the Nassau government were apparently called. Again it was a meeting that Joe Diaz knew all about.

Why was she following his orders? Nell's mind churned even as she called out to Lucy, "Here's a pretty one. Come and see, Lucy."

Out of fear? Yes. Out of greed? Yes. Out of a sense of destiny, fate? Yes, yes, yes—that was how life always dealt its cards to her. Nell looked back to see Lucy lagging farther and farther behind. There were now a couple of men, incongruous in business suits, strolling on the beach just behind Lucy. "Hurry up, darling. There are some lovely shells here . . ." She stood, her feet in the surf, looking out to the horizon, waiting for Lucy to catch up with her. Joe had outlined an exciting challenge, with an enormous reward if she could meet it. Now she was going to learn *how* to meet the challenge.

For only one or two minutes she was deep in thought, forgetting to urge Lucy once again to catch up with her, as the little girl dawdled gathering shells and pieces of coral, skipping in and out of the ocean. One minute Lucy was there—the next? Nell's scream was primeval, agonized from the very pit of her being, for when she turned for a split second of disbelief she saw the beach was empty. Lucy was gone, nowhere in sight—and neither were the men in business suits. She heard a car engine start on the road above the beach. "Lucy! Lucy!" Her screams were mimicked by the sea gulls as she tried to run up the sloping beach to find the gap in the sea-grape hedge which ran beside the beach for a few miles, obscuring all signs of the road. She fell and picked herself up as sobs wracked her body. What had happened? What did it mean?

By the time Nell reached the outskirts of the Taylor Compound her fear had changed to hysteria. She was incoherent, shaking, her feet lacerated by coral. She had been used as a dupe. They hadn't wanted to help her. They hadn't arranged their meeting to discuss a big scheme to outwit Wallace in his negotiations for part of the gambling complex. It was a scheme they had intimated she could help scuttle; she would receive in return all the money she would ever need for Ready to Change. They had been lying. It had all been a trick. Lucy. Lucy. Lucy. They had wanted Lucy.

Going out of control for the first hour before Wallace and Johnny returned to the house saved her. By the time they arrived to listen as she told the police everything she could remember of the morning walk, a store of strength had surfaced to save her from spilling out the truth. Johnny's tortured face and his efforts to make her feel blameless were the worst of all.

By the time the ransom note came she had shut the lid remorselessly on the feeling, caring woman. A million dollars for Lucy. A voice that sounded scorched told Johnny, "Lucy's safe—will be safe. You'll get her when we get the money. No tricks, no worry. Then we want a guarantee that you and your pop leave the island for good. Stay away from our business. The casino deal is all locked up and doesn't include you."

Now Nell knew what hell on earth was all about. During the days that followed she lived in fear that somehow, something would link her with the kidnappers, that Joe Diaz would saunter along the beach and in his usual laconic fashion tell Johnny or Wallace or *anyone* who would listen that "little orphan Nellie" was a one-hundred-percent fraud, who had "used" Lucy—a child of six—as her "cover," while she went to plot her own husband's downfall in order to satisfy her insatiable greed for more money and power.

Every time the phone rang she froze.

The nights were worse. She would wake screaming, struggling to be free of the straitjacket she was sure she was locked in, about to be carted off to a mental home. Instead she found she was locked in an old man's arms, her husband's arms.

If living with Johnny's anguish was torment, living with Charlotte's silent reproach was worse. Charlotte, whom she'd seen rush into Johnny's arms at the airport the day after the kidnapping, crying hysterically, her arms flailing about as if they didn't belong to her and she didn't know what to do with them . . . Charlotte who had begun to look at her warily, eerily, as if she could read her mind.

Perhaps it was because as the days went by with no news, as Charlotte grew uglier, making no attempt to cover her red-rimmed eyes or comb her unruly hair, Nell if possible looked even more beautiful. With her appetite gone, the pounds fell off, adding to her ethereal appearance, highlighting the exquisite shape of her face, while her skin, paler than ever, was almost luminous in its transparency.

A week after Lucy's disappearance—the most agonizingly slow week of Nell's life—came another call, "miraculously traced," as Wallace and Johnny exclaimed, to the Bahamian Club. Nell shivered as she sat in on their conversation with the chief of police. There was nothing "miraculous" about it, of that she was sure. Diaz left nothing to chance. For some reason—and she was sure there was a message in it for her—he had *wanted* the call to be traced.

Just as she felt her complicity in the kidnapping was about to burst out of her, she fainted without warning—as she'd fainted the day Kitty had been about to take her to the Hammersmith police station.

When she recovered, Wallace and Charlotte were sitting at her bedside, Wallace visibly concerned, his plump hand shaking as he attempted to stroke her head, Charlotte, her lips clamped together in a disapproving line, staring at her with fixed intent.

"Thank God, my darling—I thought you'd never come around. The doctor's on the way . . ."

It was getting dark. "Where's Johnny?" she cried, knowing the answer, not needing Charlotte's low hoarse whisper, "He's gone to deliver the ransom money . . ."

Nell turned beseechingly to Wallace. "Surely he hasn't gone alone?"

He patted her as if she were a tiny child or a beloved puppy. "There, there, don't get agitated. Of course, he's protected. We're setting a trap for the bastards. Don't worry, my darling. Don't worry—it's all going to work out . . ."

But it didn't work out. Johnny, ashen-faced, shoulders hunched, came back a few hours later. "We were duped. They smelled a rat. The car was there all right, just as they described—but no occupants. No Lucy . . . no one . . ." His voice broke and he ran into the study, locking the door behind him.

The next day came a warning. A lock of Lucy's hair, one sleeve of her dress, and a terrifying note. "No more tricks or next time we'll send you a slice of Lucy."

As Nell heard Johnny and Wallace discuss sending Charlotte and herself back to the States, Nell agonized over what she could do to make sure there were "no more tricks"—to make Johnny and Wallace understand they were dealing with men who put little value on life, particularly a child's life. How could she convince them without implicating herself?

The more she thought, the more convinced she became that she *had* to contact Diaz herself—to beg, to plead, to swear she would do anything he asked her to do if only he would release Lucy. But how to get to him, let alone convince him she meant what she said?

It was taken out of her hands. Both Wallace and Johnny were adamant that she had to return to the States. "Why should you live with this? Charlotte refuses to leave, but you *must*." Johnny's face was twisted with pain. He gripped her shoulders as if to steady himself. "Dad's agreed to return because he knows this is killing you. You're going to be ill, blaming yourself day after day. Get back to work. It's the only medicine that's going to help." He turned to look out over the ocean. "I'll get the bastards." There was a frightening, menacing note in Johnny's voice. Nell shivered again as he repeated, "You'll see —I'll get them and Lucy's going to be saved. She *has* to be saved."

When the phone rang in the Los Angeles Ready to Change office a few days later, Nell had a sudden premonition that Diaz was going to be on the other end.

"Mrs. Nesbitt . . ."

"You low, scheming, rotten . . ."

"Save your emotion for your sales pitch." Diaz didn't raise his voice, didn't sound affected by the hatred that was impossible to miss. "Daddy's going to cough up plenty and I give you my word, Miss Lucy is as fit as a daisy."

To her horror Nell broke down, sobbing into the phone, "Don't harm her, *please*! Take me, harm me . . ."

There was a stifled sound, then a low whistle. "So the ice lady does have a melting point. Well, who would've guessed it." Before she could reply, Diaz snarled, "I wouldn't harm a hair of your beauteous head, lady. You're far too valuable—or you're going to be—but . . ." —for the first time Nell heard what so many had heard in the past, a note of venomous intent in Diaz's voice—"when our little transaction is complete—and we're going to make them sweat for another forty-eight hours—it's up to *you* to see that big daddy and little daddy stay away from our island in the sun. Otherwise I can't answer for the consequences . . ."

When Nell put the phone down her fingers were numb. How was she going to live through the next forty-eight hours knowing that Lucy was going to be returned, providing Johnny did nothing rash? Should she tell him the kidnappers had contacted her? But why would they have called her in Los Angeles, knowing Lucy's parents, Johnny and Charlotte, were waiting so desperately for news over three thousand miles away? It would be a certain giveaway that she was implicated.

She felt ill, physically as well as mentally, incapable of another minute's work. She called the chauffeur to take her back to the house. The only way she felt she could endure getting through the next two days waiting for the outcome was to feign illness—to go to bed and curl into the fetal position, doped with a strong sedative, so that the time would slip by while she dozed in a never-never land.

By the time she reached her bedroom she knew she didn't have to feign being sick. She *was* sick—vomiting, a pulsating pain above her temple.

Two days later, pale and strained, she lay in the lacy king-sized bed, propped up on pillows, going through the motions of reading the latest Ready to Change figures. They were so healthy that in usual circumstances she would have leaped up to join the frantic fray, urging her fast-growing numbers of Ready to Change consultants on to bigger and still-bigger sales. Even the proof that they were hurting the competition in the Midwest and as far southwest as Houston didn't penetrate the deep freeze she had forced onto her brain in order not to break down.

The expected phone call came at five-ten, but not from Nassau directly—from Wallace. It was the first time Nell had ever heard him sound agitated, even inarticulate. "Charlotte—she—Lucy . . ." Had Joe Diaz kept his word? Nell was so obsessed she didn't think about guarding her tone, let alone her words. "Get to the point, Wallace. What are you trying to say?" Her coldness and sharpness were unmistakable. Nell swallowed hard. Despite Violana's training, for the first time she had actually allowed the real Nell, and the real Nell's feelings, to emerge. Before Wallace could say another word, Nell poured honey onto the wound she was sure she had caused. "Wallace, I'm out of my mind. Forgive me, darling, for sounding so, so . . . I didn't mean to sound so harsh . . ."

"Forget it." He sounded his old self—in control, in command. Whether she had caused a dangerous question mark in his brain she didn't know and at that exact moment didn't care as he went on, "Another call came this morning. Johnny paid up—plenty —and . . . " His voice broke. "Lucy just came running in from the beach. She's safe, Nell. She's safe. Thinner, scruffier, but safe, safe . . ."

Although Nell could feel tears pouring down her face there was no trace of them in her voice. It was back to business. She had to eradicate every vestige of her first cold hard words from her husband's brain. "Thank God. Thank God, darling," she breathed heavily. "Oh, darling, I can't be here without you for one more moment hearing this news. I'm getting up. I'm coming to the office to bring you home. Let's have dinner in bed. I can't wait to hold you—to comfort you—

and to be comforted by you . . . " The huskiness that suddenly welled up in her throat didn't hurt. "Oh, Wallace, thank God . . . can I . . . can I call them?"

"Oh, do, darling. Use Eddie Taylor's private line, otherwise you won't get through. Apparently the press are already swarming all over, tying up the usual lines."

Charlotte, damnable Charlotte, answered, but at least the wariness and watchfulness were out of her voice. She sounded so ecstatic that she was almost hysterically yelling out her joy. The Australian accent seemed accentuated over the wire. "She's fine, Nell. I can't believe it. We've all been crying and laughing at the same time. Eddie's doctor's here from Canada and he's just examining her now. It seems physically she's really okay. Of course, she's nervous. It's going to take months . . . years, perhaps, for her to get over the trauma . . . " Nell was just going to ask to speak to Johnny when he obviously took the phone away from Charlotte.

"Your shilly-shelly little pal is doing fine, don't worry, Auntie Nell. We're going to have a big celebration dinner with Esmeralda's white chocolate cake—Lucy's favorite and yours, too, no?"

Jealousy as thick and heavy as an English fog clouded Nell's senses for a moment. She felt a wild urge to rush to the airport to catch the first plane out to New York and Nassau. She should never have let them send her back to Los Angeles. She longed, yearned, ached to be with Johnny and Lucy and share in the white chocolate cake and all that it stood for.

"Nell, are you still there?"

The fog lifted. She had to remember Violana's instructions—and more important her prediction. If she was ever going to be bigger than the biggest star—"the most influential, powerful voman in the vorld, my darlink"—she had to submerge the instincts that ordinary women allowed to govern and often wreck their lives.

"I'm here, Johnny. I'm so overjoyed I find it hard to find the right words. I'm just going to pick up Wallace. It's all been such an ordeal for us, I think we'll stop by a church and offer our thanks to God."

~~~

The favorite moment of Sylvie's day every day came when she opened her eyes either to see Ty studying her with his little-boy look of wonder or to see him still fast asleep, his face in repose. Then he was "ironed out," Sylvie would tease him, gentle like the lion in the *Wizard of Oz*.

There was such joy in waking up, knowing that she was his and he was hers, that theirs was one of the real loves that just seemed to grow and grow, turning life into more and more of a glorious adventure.

Sylvie knew they were envied; many people even tried to spoil what they had, but it was impossible. "That's why I don't mind the fact that Ty doesn't want any children," she'd written in her last letter to Aunt Gert. "He's frightened a baby will change everything. He's wrong, but it really doesn't bother me. He's my baby and I'm his."

All the same, Sylvie did get a funny unexpected tug at times when she saw a beautiful baby on TV or out in Central Park. Not often, just sometimes, usually when Ty was rehearsing. Never when he was home. His presence consumed her.

She could hear the faint sound of his piano from the room where he worked, although he always said he couldn't hear one tap of her typewriter. "Are you sure you're really writing the great American novel?" He wouldn't believe she was serious about it, but how could she be when hardly an hour passed without his walking in to kiss the top of her head, to ask her opinion about something, to stretch her shoulders back, warning her not to get the "pianist's disease" of a bad back from her crouch over the typewriter. They were so happy it was indecent—as the world at large had tried to convince them in the dreadful days following Brenda Caplan's suicide.

Kitty's piece had devastated Sylvie. While she stayed in Europe with Ty that summer and fall, the story seemed to follow her everywhere like a curse, parts of it reprinted in papers where she least expected to find it, or plagiarized, usually in gossip columns and show-biz magazines, with exaggerated descriptions of her femme-fatale ability.

If it hadn't been for Ty's apparent lack of concern, Sylvie was sure she would have crept into a hole and waited to die.

She knew only too well about newspaper morgues, the files where she knew her "story" would now be available forever as a perfect example to pluck out and refer to whenever another story called for an "Eve" type or a "little brown mouse," as Kitty had described her, who through her "insatiable ambition and greed" had turned into a "superstar rat."

Ty had just about convinced her he really wasn't affected by it, so neither should she be, when she'd overheard him dictating a letter to his faithful secretary, Dottie.

She had never heard such a harsh, unrelenting note in his voice as he directed his lawyer, Jerome Mossop, to see if there was any way he could sue Kitty Stein into the poorhouse, where he hoped she would rot until her dying day.

Later that night he'd revealed more about his early life . . . his mother dying at his birth . . . his father certified as insane when he was twelve . . . the lonely, unloved years in an aunt's house, miserable years except for the time he was allowed to spend at the house next door where there was a piano the neighbors wanted to keep in tune . . .

Music was the only constant in his life, he'd told her, until that six o'clock one hot August evening in Rome when she'd walked in. He'd talked about Brenda, capricious Brenda, the big star of the forties, who had taken him literally out of poverty and obscurity, who had realized he had a special talent, who had fallen in and out of love with him and so many others, and who had quickly grown to resent and then detest his music. He'd told her about the rows, the fights, the meanness, as his success had grown and other stars had beaten a path to his door, hoping his music could help their careers. Then Brenda's drinking took over their lives. The bruises, the knocks, the pain had flooded out and Sylvie and he had cried together, locked in each other's arms.

That night Ty had told her they were going to be together forever. "You're not going back to London until Kitty Stein is ruined and/or dead and buried." His hands had stroked her hair, his mouth close against her cheek. "I'm taking you back with me to America. We'll be married in Mendocino where the Pacific comes crashing in. We'll be married just before sunset. You'll wear a simple white dress, my young virginal bride . . . and everyone will start to applaud, you'll see . . ."

And it had all taken place just as he had described, with no more ugliness, no more false accusations. To Sylvie it was really incredible. As soon as they had become Mr. and Mrs. Ty Caplan, the world had indeed started to applaud—even Smith Maynard had cabled congratulations! But there had been no word from Kitty. No congratulations. No apology—and there never would be, Sylvie was sure of that.

Ty couldn't understand why she didn't hate Kitty. Whenever she thought of her, after they were married, it was with a surge of pity, not hatred, not even anger. She was sure Kitty didn't really hate *her*. She had been jealous and, as Sylvie remembered only too well, jealousy was a self-destructive force that swallowed up all the good in someone and emphasized all the bad. Jealousy wasn't so much a green-eyed monster but the devil itself, ruining every good intention, every moral instinct, until life could only be viewed through dark sinister eyes. That Kitty had been jealous was more than obvious—so her vicious article written in a jealous storm could not be judged by normal standards. She had been sick when she wrote it. She was to be pitied. And if Kitty was still jealous, Sylvie reckoned it was lucky they lived so far apart, for that made it unlikely Kitty would ever hear about the fantastic, exotic life she was now leading.

Ty needed her—she needed him, too—but he could hardly bear to have her out of his sight. She was so proud to hear his cronies marvel at the change in the "loner," as they described Ty pre-Sylvie. She was so happy when he insisted she go with him on recording sessions. She never ceased to marvel at the acuteness of his ear, his ability to dissect an orchestral recording, to hear every instrument individually. "The sax missed a note . . . it's missing a D-flat . . . take out the trombone . . . take out the strings . . . the sax is leaking through too near the mike . . ." It was a foreign language in a foreign world. She tried to be helpful when Ty asked her opinion, but it reminded her of the old days when Dick Kolinzcky had reeled off financial statements to her, hoping for an intelligent reaction. Then, as now, she had been out of her depth—but *now*, unlike then, Ty, unlike Dick, wanted her reply and listened intently to everything she said, however feeble she felt it was. He not only listened, but took notes. He continually said she was making an unbelievable contribution to his work. From being social outcasts—as Sylvie had once told Ty she felt their relationship had made them—from the very first week after their marriage, they became the toast of every city they visited in America. It was intoxicating. It was also frightening.

If waking up was Sylvie's favorite part of the day, Ty always said breakfast with her was better than dinner at the White House.

Although Sylvie still felt all thumbs in the kitchen, especially in what she considered to be the most spectacular, electronic, and awesome kitchen in New York, she was happy to cook what Ty referred to with pride as "Sylvie's English breakfast" every morning.

He was so possessive of their privacy he had imposed an inviolable rule—that the "help," their live-in maid and houseboy, should *not* put in an appearance until Sylvie summoned them.

Their living arrangements were certainly different from most people's, she often reflected, and certainly different from those of all rich people she had come across. They acted more like a couple of kids playing at being grown up—but who could complain about that?

As Sylvie prepared eggs, bacon, mushrooms, toast, marmalade, and tea in the eighteenth-floor kitchen with a view of Central Park that stretched all the way to Harlem, she hoped she would hear from Aunt Gert soon.

It was time Gert wrote to say she agreed with Sylvie's advice. If only Aunt Gert could be a fraction as happy as she was, Sylvie told herself as she bustled around the kitchen, it would still be a thousand times better than her present introverted state.

Pierre Repelle had returned, endlessly repentant over the past. Aunt Gert still hadn't told her what Pierre had done to cause such a major upset; but whatever it was, Sylvie had written firmly that it was time for Gert to forgive and forget. Pierre had apparently sent flowers, managed to persuade her aunt to go out to lunch and dinner, and had practically camped on her doorstep begging forgiveness—but Aunt Gert hadn't as yet decided to give it.

As Sylvie heard Ty's footsteps she energetically whipped up four eggs in the pan, still thinking of Aunt Gert. She decided she would write again to stress that it was time Gert started all over again. It was never any good brooding over past hurts.

It was eerie, Sylvie realized later, that Nell and Dick's relationship had flashed into her mind at that moment for the first time in months just as Ty had come in with the mail—which to Sylvie's delight contained the hoped-for letter from her aunt, but enclosing a newspaper clipping, which soon overshadowed even the decision Sylvie had been longing to hear.

"I think you're right," Gert had written. "Pierre and I are going to get married in the new year. I chose that time hearing that Ty has forgiven the British press at last. I'm so thrilled you are coming back for the opening of his new symphony, because of course, I couldn't get married without you being here. Now you've got to be my matron of honor, as you can't be my bridesmaid."

Happy tears had bubbled up in Sylvie's eyes, soon to be dried with shock when she opened the newspaper clipping to see Nell's face staring up at her.

It was an old photograph taken, Sylvie dimly remembered, at some charity function Nell had been sent to cover by Smith Maynard.

As Sylvie read the story her tears returned.

Poor Nell.

How terrible.

What an amazing chapter of events.

She passed the clipping wordlessly to Ty.

Canadian Financier—Celebrated Entrepreneur Wallace Nesbitt Dead at 74

Qualicum Beach, Vancouver Island, 7 August 1967—A tragic sequence of events led to the sudden death here early today of Wallace Wainwright Nesbitt, who apparently suffered a heart attack while bathing at a secluded cove near his island home. A family spokesman confirmed that Mr. Nesbitt had been in poor health since the kidnapping last year of his only granddaughter, Lucy Nesbitt, during a family vacation on the Bahamian island of Nassau. The seven-year-old child was returned to the family after an absence of six weeks, following the payment of a ransom said to be as high as one million dollars. At the time it was reported that the kidnapping was intended to deter Mr. Nesbitt from pursuing certain gambling concessions planned for the island.

The kidnappers have never been apprehended.

Mr. Nesbitt also leaves a widow, the former Nell O'Halloran of London, an adopted son, Jonathan, and a sister, Anne. Wallace Nesbitt founded and at the time of his death was chairman of the board of the WW Nesbitt Group, a multimillion-dollar business conglomerate with huge holdings in Canadian and American real estate, oil, and heavy machinery. An acquisition made in 1962 focused his attention on the cosmetics industry for the first time, and it was his considerable experience in the direct-selling area which led to the immediate success of his Ready to Change Cosmetics Company, where all products are sold by independent contractors . . .

Ty stopped reading to watch Sylvie as she looked stonily out at the park.

"What are you thinking?"

"I was wondering what happened to Dick."

"To good old Dick? . . ."

To Sylvie's surprise, Ty's lighthearted banter hurt. She didn't understand why. Everything was so long ago. She hardly ever thought about Dick, yet only moments ago she had been thinking about both Dick and Nell. She'd heard a couple of years ago from Aunt Gert that

Pierre had somehow found out Nell had made a spectacular marriage to a multimillionaire, who was obviously this old Canadian. Sylvie remembered she had laughed at the time, for the news had been so expected—with her beauty and brains, Nell had always been destined to make it big. For some reason she hadn't given Dick any thought then, wondering only about Mrs. O'Halloran, hoping that if the poor old lady was still alive, Nell had made peace with her, and that with her new affluence, Nell had made sure her mother would never want for anything again.

But what shocking news this was—first a mysterious kidnapping and now a sudden death. Again Dick came into her mind. Whatever could have happened to the love between Nell and Dick, a love that had been so great it had produced a child?

Ty turned Sylvie's face to his. He looked anxious. "You're not still thinking about Dick, are you?"

Sylvie shook her head, forcing herself to smile. "Of course not, darling." She tried to change the subject. "Don't you want your scrambled eggs?"

Ty pulled her roughly onto his lap. "Do you know what I really want?"

Sylvie kissed his nose. "I can guess." He covered her face with kisses, scraping her skin with the rough stubble of his unshaven chin. "Can you believe you made me jealous, Mrs. Caplan? . . ."

She laughed again at the earnestness of his expression. "How crazy . . . I . . ." Ty didn't let her finish, kissing her more and more passionately, until he ignited a soaring need in her, a need she knew was going to be gloriously fulfilled.

His beautiful long fingers were under her skirt, slipping off her pants, feeling the wetness that he so quickly aroused.

"Turn around, darling. . . . " For a split second Sylvie hesitated, an unwelcome memory from long ago sliding into her mind like an unwelcome snake . . . her mother on a man's lap, her legs wrapped around his waist, her back shining in a ray of sunlight as she "rode" the man with relentless urgent movements. Sylvie mentally shook herself. How could she compare the great love between Ty and herself with her mother's now endlessly acrimonious relationship with Ed Tramello. She slipped off Ty's lap, let her skirt fall to the floor, and tenderly unzipped her husband's jeans, sitting and facing him on his lap, inserting his huge wanting penis deep into her. As his hands clasped her to him and she hooked her toes into the back of the kitchen chair, the memory came back one more time, immediately to be erased by the growing, building joyfulness that his searching penis and probing tongue caused in her. "Oh, darling, my darling . . ."

They sang out the ecstasy of their orgasms together over and over, until, spent, they rested on each other, his mouth still softly kissing her cheek, his beautiful fingers now stroking her hair. The aftermath of his love, as Sylvie so often told him, was to her as beautiful as the intensity of their passion. Every touch told her how deeply, sincerely, he cared.

Now, with eyes closed, she drifted on a cloud of serenity. Ty whispered in her ear, "I want to have a baby."

"Oh, Ty . . ." Sylvie pushed away to be able to look him searchingly in the eyes. Suddenly the way he'd said what she'd been longing to hear for so long hit both of them and they started to laugh.

Sylvie felt choked with happiness as she said, "Masters and Johnson would really have something to say about your having a baby . . ." Then she whispered, "Oh, Ty, do you really mean it?"

"I really mean it. I mean I want *you* to have my baby."

~~~

"*Vive la femme libre* . . ." The noise from five hundred screeching, cheering women was execrable. Every blood vessel in her head was about to burst, but Nell went on smiling and smiling, knowing that in the wings of the great Expo Pavilion both Johnny and Charlotte were looking at her.

How different their thoughts would be. One would be so full of love; the other now so full of hate and suspicion.

Behind the rehearsed, extraordinarily powerful public smile, Nell nursed another intensely private one, so private and intense she could feel its heat rampaging through her body. It was a smile of anticipation, of hope, most of all of relish, as she remembered once again the moment Johnny had let his guard down, had made her realize he *did* care, was attracted—was, after all, no different from all the other men who had longed to possess her.

Nothing had happened since—but it would. She would make sure of it. And *then*, not before, she would decide whether Johnny really did have the caliber to be her partner for life.

Even just a few weeks ago she would have sworn her life on it. Now she wasn't sure. After all, he had once chosen Charlotte. How could *any* man of his caliber choose a woman like Charlotte?

Her wonderful Ready to Change women were pressing forward to the stage, showing their adoration, proving once again how well she understood women and how adept she had become, thanks to Violana, at taking her public's pulse. Her decision to go ahead and use those controversial words, despite Charlotte's damning, critical rejection of the whole idea, had as usual been right. Because *she* had said them. If Charlotte had tried to parody "*Vive le Quebec libre*," the now-famous words uttered by de Gaulle only three months before, it would have been a catastrophe, probably setting off another international incident!

The world's press would have interpreted them as a terrifying sign of female support for de Gaulle's right to interfere in Canada's affairs and move for an independent Quebec. But *she* had said them with exactly the right inflection, endearing herself to every woman out there . . .

Charlotte was stupid, slow, like the Australian kangaroos lumbering across the landscape she came from—in the wrong place at the wrong time.

Out of the corner of her eye Nell saw Johnny looking at her with something approaching awe. Charlotte had obviously told him she was cooking up something to attract press attention—something that could backfire and ruin the business.

Instead, even an idiot like Charlotte, let alone someone as smart as Johnny, could see how much those four little words had increased the love her girls felt for her, if that was possible.

Roses, violets, peonies, hyacinths—the heavy scent of the flowers being thrown or handed up to her onstage was making her feel faint, but she would never faint again. She was determined about that. She was a leader like de Gaulle. She was in charge.

Every one of the women out there needed her, looked to her for guidance to obtain a life of her own without the sinister downward pull of a man's influence. That was why the man she chose to be her right-hand man *had* to be worthy of her. If any man could be. Could Johnny?

The fact that she could even ask herself the question was exhilarating. Was she already over his deteriorating sexual effect on her, before she had even had a chance to drain his body into hers?

The atmosphere in the car leaving the World Exposition grounds was tense. Nell retreated from it, leaning back against the upholstery, her eyes closed, knowing she was still in a privileged position as a grieving widow who had somehow summoned up an inordinate amount of strength for the sake of her business.

It was accepted she could now fall apart—whichever way she chose to do it—and not keep up pretenses while she was with her "family." She didn't have to speak or even look at either of them. She could pretend they weren't there.

There was a problem with keeping her eyes shut. It often triggered off the same set of slow-moving pictures in her mind's eye—the eye she *couldn't* shut, however hard she tried.

Every night when she went to bed—and it was getting later and later—until a sleeping pill took effect, she was back on that gritty beach, with the cool wind whipping her flesh. Every morning when she first woke, until she forced herself to face the day, she was in the ocean, swimming behind Wallace Wainwright Nesbitt as he carried out his morning constitutional, the slow swim out to the point agreed to and in fact encouraged by his doctors.

Yes, goddammit, she should have been in earshot of Wallace Wainwright Nesbitt's cry for help. Charlotte, looking through her damn binoculars, knew that—she hadn't had to ask the question, but Charlotte had asked it the day Wallace died, despite Johnny's look of fury and his attempt to silence her.

And why was Charlotte looking at the beach and sea through binoculars? As Nell had tried to point out to the silly cow, for the same reason she had swum *away* from Wallace and not toward him.

She could hear herself patiently repeat the same lie, over and over again to Charlotte. "I didn't hear Wallace because all my concentration was on Lucy—just as yours was—watching her with your binoculars!"

Of course she'd heard Wallace suddenly shout out. She would never forget the sudden agitation . . . the splashing behind her . . . the spluttering . . . the gasps and "help me, Nell, help me . . ." followed by a horrible gurgling. She'd heard everything but she'd swum steadily toward the shore and precious Lucy—who'd just come into the water—Lucy who since Nassau had become more precious than ever.

Charlotte had actually cross-examined the child as to whether she remembered calling out, "Auntie Nell." So Lucy couldn't remember. What did that prove? According to Charlotte it proved she had witnessed through her best Bausch & Lomb an act of manslaughter!

Had Charlotte actually said the word? Later she denied she ever had said it that gray un-August-like morning. In fact she hadn't said it. She had *screamed* it out, but what else had she seen?

Not only a drowning, dying man with a heart that had decided to stop at an inopportune moment—not only her sylphlike daughter running out of the water, chased by her laughing aunt, apparently impervious to the cries of her dying husband.

Had Charlotte seen Johnny run with them, Aunt Nell and Lucy, along the beach until—aware Wallace was in the water—Johnny had stopped to look out toward the point where he'd expected his father to be?

Surely by then Charlotte could have tried to do something *herself* about Wallace's travail? Or had she been frozen into immobility, glasses to eyes watching Johnny and her swim out to attempt to rescue the unrescuable—to see Johnny bring back not Wallace's body, but hers in a state of collapse?

Had Charlotte seen Johnny cradle her in his arms on the beach, wrapping up her body with his body, suddenly giving her the closeness she'd longed for for years, his tears falling onto what he thought were her tears? Had Charlotte seen her turn to cling to him so suddenly that her bikini straps had snapped to release her breasts? If she had, she had never said so—and even if she had *seen*, she didn't, couldn't know that as their wet bodies had melded together on the beach, Nell had felt the urgent throb of Johnny's penis growing, growing, despite the melancholy of the moment.

Late at night and early morning the dark memories—of the grayness of the water and sky, the whip of wind across her shoulder blades, the hoarse cries for help from her drowning husband—were strangely never ameliorated by the memory of Johnny's sudden surge of passion that day, even as he cried bitter tears over the loss of his father.

It was only at other times—like the exhilarating occasion just passed, the first major meeting in Montreal of leading Ready to Change saleswomen—that she could savor the memory of Johnny's moment of weakness.

Whatever Charlotte had witnessed, Nell knew Charlotte now distrusted and hated her with a deep unmitigated hatred. She was taking Lucy back to Australia for Christmas. Naturally she expected Johnny to accompany her—but it wasn't going to happen.

Was that the reason for the extreme tension in the car now? Had Johnny already told his wife he felt he couldn't leave his father's widow alone at Christmas, after all she had been through? That it was thoughtless, heartless, and all the other words Nell had infiltrated into his mind, to go so far away when Nell needed the family the most?

There was no question as to whether Nell should accompany them down under. As Charlotte had said in clipped, bitter sentences, Lucy hadn't seen her other grandparents in far too long. Australia was healthy, open, fresh. She wanted Lucy to have that kind of change of scenery after all the child had been through, with *no one* around to remind her of what had happened in Nassau.

And where would Johnny and Nell spend Christmas and the New Year? Nell wasn't sure if she could continue to hide her private smile, the one that was warming every inch of her inside. Johnny didn't know it yet, but they weren't going to Vancouver or even New York. She hated their California place, too. She didn't want to be anywhere that reminded her of the last five years in purgatory with a spent old man.

As the limousine approached Montreal's celebrated Ritz Carlton Hotel, Nell allowed a little moan to escape to show she was about to reenter the bitter, real world. Her eyes remained closed. She imagined the reactions to the only sound she had made for the last forty-five minutes. Johnny would be looking anxious, concerned that she might have driven herself too far this time. Charlotte—who knew better— would be her now-usual tight-lipped, scowling self.

Nell opened her eyes to reward Johnny with a sweet lingering look. Soon, only days away, with Charlotte and (unfortunately) Lucy en route to the other side of the world, she would tell Johnny she could not face Christmas, even with him at her side, in the Vancouver house looking at Anne's disapproving face. Too many memories—and New York and Los Angeles wouldn't be any better.

She would tell Johnny what was almost totally the truth. She needed to go *home*. She ached for double-decker buses, London cabs, young British bobbies with their pink-and-white baby skins, soft rain, and crocuses in the snow. Most of all she needed to go home with Johnny at her side—devoted, compassionate, caring for his "step-mother"—for a very special reunion. She would tell him it was the only way to get through the trauma of her first Christmas without Wallace.

Again fate had decreed what was going to happen.

Trust Sylvie to send a letter of condolence to the Ready to Change headquarters in California, the one address where her mail was care-fully sorted so that she had a chance of receiving what her excellent staff knew she would want to receive. And Sylvie's letter had been so

typically Sylvie. It didn't sound as if she'd changed or matured at all.
It had been a little-girl letter, with her attempts to comfort—"in your
most desperate hour." What a joke!

All the same, the letter had been a signal from fate. Sylvie had
written to say she was going to London for Christmas to stay at Ty's
favorite hotel, the Savoy, and later would drive down to Surrey for
the New Year to see Ty's old friends, the Frank Forresters. "How
wonderful it would be to catch a glimpse of you after all these turbu-
lent years. I'd love you to meet my husband, and he longs to meet
you, my oldest and still my best friend." To see Sylvie happy, loved,
with a brilliant husband at her side would have been impossible unless
she, Nell, had a brilliant, loving man at *her* side. And Johnny was
going to be at her side, although he still didn't know it.

In her lavish hotel suite Nell looked at herself long and hard in the
mirror. How would Sylvie look eleven, or was it twelve, years older?
How would Sylvie think she looked? She would be shocked by the
silver hair but, Nell flashed a sample of her famous smile at her reflection, Sylvie would have to admit she still looked awfully good—better
than ever, in fact. Her skin had the kind of glow rich girls were born
with. There was an effortless style about her. It had always been there,
but now the style was backed up with the best clothes and care money
could buy.

The dark green velvet of her Chanel suit, the fire of her emerald
ring, and her brilliantly made-up eyes (soft gray or brown, never any
more green shadow) added up to—Nell sighed—there was no better
word for it than class. She had always had class naturally. Now it was
honed to perfection with the right choice of possessions. And what
would be the best possession of all? Johnny, without question. Johnny,
the perfect combination of rake and gentleman. She separated the
word in her mind to make *gentle man*—that was Johnny, the perfect
husband, the perfect father.

How amazed Sylvie would be when she called her at the Savoy to
say she was staying there, too. Christmas in London. Mimosas and
violets sold in magnificent profusion from barrows on street corners.
Tea at Fortnum & Mason's. She would buy Johnny a marvelous
Christmas present at one of the great men's shops in Jermyn Street.
Hot chestnuts on the Thames Embankment.

Nell's stomach did a somersault. She *was* still affected by Johnny.
Was it because she still hadn't slept with him? Whether that was the
reason or not, she had to overcome that wearisome hormonal weak-

ness. It didn't add up to what she had planned for herself—to be the first *real* leader of women, the first woman to show other women that being Ready to Change meant *everything* was possible; to show them that freedom from a man was the best goal a woman could set for herself.

Nell had long ago met the challenge. She had been ready to change herself, and *had* changed out of all recognition. Now that Diaz had given her the money and blessing to go ahead—Diaz was "pleased," he'd said with laughable understatement, that she had turned her back on Wallace at the crucial moment—there would be no limit to what her Ready to Change movement could accomplish.

As she heard a tap on the door and Johnny's voice say, "It's me—can I come in?" she once again flashed her secret-weapon smile at her reflection and whispered, *"vive la femme libre,"* before going to open the door.

7

London, W.C.2.,
New Year's Eve, 1967

Sagittarius: As a Sagittarian, you are the original charmer. Your nature radiates self-confidence, making you a desirable presence in any
crowd. However, the same elements that attract admirers bring jealous rivals, so be on
your guard, especially as the calendar year
comes to a close and Jupiter moves into Scor-
pio. In the new year you can expect some up-
heavals in career matters, but Uranus, a
positive influence, will spur you on to new
heights of creativity, providing you pay attention to what motivates you—your work—and
not what distracts you—your love life . . .

Nell threw the horoscope on the floor and languorously
stretched out her body to its fullest extent, arms above head, toes
pointed toward the end of the bed. Magazine horoscopes were a
joke in one way, but in another it was uncanny how often there
was a sentence that *galvanized* because it hit a nerve so accurately.

After last night with Johnny—her first night with Johnny—it was
difficult, if not impossible, not be distracted by love.

She could still feel his mouth on her breast, her abdomen, his
tongue on her clitoris. Her vagina throbbed at the thought of him,
and as she moved her arms down over the pale pink Savoy blanket,

her blood raced as she saw a faint blue bruise where he had gripped her wrist in his passion.

He had left guiltily, his face pale, strained, at two or three in the morning, although she had pleaded with him to stay. He would probably never understand that despite her need of him, she had been pleased he'd resisted her, crying out that his mind was in turmoil; he didn't know what had overtaken him, how it had ever happened, what it all meant.

Through slightly parted curtains, Nell could see a weak sun turning old Father Thames into a streak of silver as it stealthily sneaked between the London Embankments. How wonderful it was to have been fucked by Johnny for the first time in London of all places. It was so good to be back. Nell mentally corrected herself. It was so *satisfying* to be back in London as a great success—not as the chattel of a man, but to be able to afford the Savoy herself, to have the black-coated front-desk men bow and scrape to her because of who *she* was and not because of whom she was married to or living with.

Funny to think that the men behind London hotel front desks had ever intimidated her. They were only minions, all of them, despite their fancy dress. The world was divided into minions, masters, and mistresses, and she was both a master and a mistress! She laughed, her mind returning to savor the memory of what had happened after her return from the theater with Sylvie and Ty.

She had been ominously quiet. Johnny knew she was upset but didn't know why, didn't know she was trying to quash the gnawing old jealousy that had surfaced out of nowhere as she had seen how obviously in love Sylvie and Ty were. She'd felt all the worse because Johnny hadn't been demonstrative at all—in fact, he'd been almost offhand, just when she'd wanted him to be his most doting.

She had grown quieter and quieter, totally unlike herself, to teach him a lesson—but it hadn't had the desired result.

Sylvie had been the one to worry about her, not Johnny. Trust Sylvie. It had been just like the old days.

In the ladies' room at Les Ambassadeurs, where they'd gone after the show, Sylvie had continued the conversation they'd started the day before, at their first lunch together in over ten years.

Nell had sat staring moodily at the mirror, oblivious of her reflection, which radiated such beauty, despite her look of despondency.

Sylvie had put her arm around her. "What's wrong, Nell? Well, I know, of course, what's wrong. How *could* I ask such a question—but

you have *so* much going for you. You're so brilliantly successful, still
so incredibly young-looking. There'll be others—another man who'll
love you like Mr. Nesbitt loved you." Nell had let her rattle on, hardly
paying attention until, hesitating, Sylvie had said, "I wanted to ask
you yesterday . . . what . . . whatever happened to Dick and you?
Whatever happened to Dick?"

Nell had been proud of her performance. It had been Oscar caliber.
She'd turned to look at Sylvie, her eyes flooding with tears. "He turned
out to be a fiend, a real fiend, Sylvie. He . . ." She had looked down
at the floor, her shoulders shaking. "He stole my savings and just left
me one morning—abandoned me in Toronto without a penny, without a friend in the world . . . without a word." She'd paused, wondering for one perilous moment if Pierre had ever mentioned their
relationship, but when Sylvie obviously believed every word she was
saying, Nell had elaborated on Dick's cruelty. "He wanted me to do
. . . to do . . . all sorts of things, kinky sex, you know. . . . If I hadn't
met Wallace . . ." Her voice had become thick with emotion. "Wallace was *so* wonderful—he made me see how wrong I'd been all these
years, turning my back on God. Dick was a nightmare. You were so
lucky, Sylvie, that he seduced me and not you. You would've never
been able to cope—would have never recovered . . ." Nell had seen
with satisfaction that Sylvie still blushed in the same unbecoming way,
color flooding from her collarbone to her forehead. "How terrible.
How terrible." Sylvie had put her arms around her so tightly that Nell
had been sure she was wrinkling her new Christian Dior faille. She'd
pulled away, reminding Sylvie they were keeping the men waiting
upstairs. As they'd begun the slow walk back, Nell had commented
that the life Sylvie was leading with Ty seemed to suit her. "For the
first time I can ever remember, Sylv, I think you're putting on weight."

It was then that Sylvie had told her "their secret." It had been the
final crushing blow of the evening Nell had looked forward to so much
—the evening when she'd wanted to show Sylvie and her wunderkind
composer/husband how far she had traveled from the slums of East
London; when she'd longed to prove how successful and at the same
time how loved she was. Instead, when with a shy smile Sylvie had
whispered, "I'm pregnant," she had felt as she'd used to feel as a little
girl—misunderstood, unappreciated, in the wrong place at the wrong
time. "I'm going to have a baby in June." Sylvie's news had stabbed
her as surely as if a stiletto had been pushed in her stomach. She
hadn't been able to enjoy one mouthful of the superb dinner ordered

in advance by Ty. Instead, every touch of Ty's hand on Sylvie's, every proud note in his voice as he'd boringly raved on about Sylvie's perfection as a wife, had added to her torment.

Now as she rang for room service, suddenly ravenous for breakfast, it was hard to believe she had suffered so much between 10:30 P.M. and 12:30 A.M. the night before, because by 1:00 A.M. all her dreams had come true.

She would have a baby, too. Yes, Nell decided, she would, despite swearing never to let a man's seed make her belly swell again. For Johnny it would be worth it. She would make him her slave and they would make love every day of the wretched nine months. Step by step she went over the events of the night before in her mind—the way she'd barely said good night to him at the door of her suite, angry tears glistening in her eyes, her fingernails digging into her palms to stop herself screaming as she'd heard him haltingly try to explain why he felt he had to leave at the end of the week to fly to Australia to join Charlotte and Lucy; how seeing Sylvie's obvious love and concern for her had convinced him she would be well looked after in London. Sylvie could take his place as loving companion until she returned to the States. "*His place!*" No one could take his place, but as he'd tried to tell her his plans, she'd been paralyzed, unable to tell him or show him her terrible aching need.

Fate had been kind to her. As it happened, her aloof coldness had been the best way to deal with Johnny.

Fifteen, twenty minutes later had come a knock at her door, a knock she hadn't expected. She hadn't been ready, her makeup but not her dress off, her hair tousled, disheveled as she'd run her hands through it again and again as she'd furiously paced the floor, wondering how on earth she would ever be able to get through the New Year's Eve festivities watching the Caplans' joy in each other, knowing that Johnny was going to leave her like some unwanted old relative to Sylvie's "tender care."

When she'd opened the door to see Johnny standing there she'd run to collapse on the bed, suddenly dead beat, worn out with the pretense of years, crying noisily like a child, not caring how she looked. And incredibly—just as if she'd planned it—he'd lain down beside her, his hardness growing against her thigh just as she'd felt it that day on Qualicum Beach. She couldn't remember how her dress had come off so quickly but her nakedness had made him go berserk. He'd lifted her to him so violently his shirt had ripped, and as she'd responded to his passion they'd rolled onto the floor where they'd stayed, it seemed for hours, making the most tempestuous natural love of her life.

"Oh, Johnny," Nell moaned out loud. Her appetite disappeared. She didn't want breakfast. She wanted Johnny—big, oh, so big, inside her, rocking her crazily down onto him until she could feel her insides split in two.

The phone rang.

"Johnny . . ." she gasped, then, "oh, it's you, Sylvie. I thought it was . . ." Nell yawned as Sylvie babbled on about having to go for one more fitting for the fabulous dress she was going to wear that night to the New Year's Eve party. "Elizabeth Wondrak is a marvel, Nell. You must go to her. She can rustle up something to out-Paris Paris even in a day! I can never give her much time, but she seems to thrive on it, never complains, always delivers. Will Johnny and you have lunch with Ty while I go over to Elizabeth about twelve-thirty? She's going to finish the dress while I'm there. I should be able to join you about two-fifteen for coffee, then, what do you think . . . we should be able to check out and be on our way to Surrey about four? Does that suit you?"

Nell was hardly aware of her answer.

Johnny. Johnny.

She couldn't wait to hear his voice, to feel him close to her, to know that all thoughts of Australia were as distant as the godforsaken place itself. She knew she brushed Sylvie off too quickly, but she didn't care. "Yes, yes, Sylvie, whatever you say. I've got to go. Ask Ty to call when he's ready for lunch. Let's meet in the American Bar."

Johnny's line was busy. She was about to ask the operator to interrupt when she heard the key turn in her lock and her breakfast arrived. It was just as well. She had to stay cool. But who could Johnny be talking to? She tried to drink her tea slowly, to observe the rules that Violana had taught her to calm her nerves and charm any audience in the world; rules that she'd even introduced when making love—making her wait to come when she was on the verge of coming—rules to build "self-control."

One, two, three, four, five . . . Nell counted to ten slowly, taking deep breaths from her abdomen every other count, exhaling in a long low whistle, then she ran her tongue briskly over her top teeth, "like a vind-screen viper, my dear . . ." Violana had never even tried to say her w's—or had she really enjoyed calling her a "viper"? Certainly that wasn't the only derogatory name the wicked witch had used to describe her.

Nell deliberately tensed every muscle in her body, one by one, starting with her toes, until she reached her forehead, the crown of her head. When she felt herself become as rigid as a board, she let go quickly, collapsing on the bed like a "veak voman . . . veak . . . veak. You have no energy, no spine, nothing . . ." She shut her mind to what had invariably followed with Violana. Still her breath was too fast, her hands clammy, her mind full of Johnny. Oh, it was sick!

"Johnny?"

He answered. "Nell . . ." A sigh inherent in the way he said her name traveled through the wire into her ear and down to her viscera. She pushed the fingers of her left hand into her thick wetness, winding down on them as she clutched the receiver with the other hand. "Johnny, I miss you. I need you. Come and have breakfast with me. I don't even know what time it is."

"I can't, Nell. I shouldn't. I don't know what to say to you. Last night should never have happened. Don't hate me . . ."

Hate him? Was he crazy?

"Hate you, Johnny?" Nell lingered lovingly on his name. "Hate you? I love . . ."

"Don't say it." He interrupted sharply. "Don't say anything you'll . . . I'll regret. It was a crazy evening. I lost control. Forgive me."

She tried to persuade him to come to her room but he wouldn't be persuaded. He sounded desperate, abject. Nell couldn't believe he really felt as unhappy as he sounded. "Ty wants us to have lunch with him . . . Sylvie's going to join us for coffee. She suggested we should be on the road about three or four." She could hear the anxiety in her voice, realized she was talking too quickly, trying to tie him to her by confirming the mundane arrangements.

He hesitated. God, he was hesitating. Blind panic rose in her as Johnny sighed again down the phone. "Nell, my . . . my being here . . . I don't think it's helping you—or me—or anything. Last night . . ."

She was screaming now in real pain. "Johnny, come here, please, please, don't say this to me . . ."

His tone changed. She knew how quickly he made up his mind. "I'll contact you in an hour."

"Johnny . . ." But he was gone.

An hour. A whole hour. How could she get through the next sixty minutes? Nell found her watch. It was only nine-thirty. One more hour to ten-thirty. Two hours before lunch . . . two hours to make love again and force Johnny to realize there could never be a woman to measure up to her.

Nell pushed the breakfast tray away so violently that orange juice spilled over the pink blanket. Shit. She ripped the blanket off, then decided against trying to make the bed look alluring herself. That was the housekeeper's job. Swiftly she dialed to ask for a maid to come to change the bed, then rushed to the bathroom to soak in a hot bath redolent with her favorite lilac scent.

Ty Caplan was on his second Manhattan when Nell finally arrived in the American Bar. He didn't usually drink at lunch but it was New Year's Eve, and life was so unbelievably wonderful, and the barman at the Savoy had to be the best Manhattan-maker in the world, so what the hell.

Sylvie had been right about her best friend. Nell Nesbitt was undoubtedly a gorgeous-looking woman, there was no doubt about that. Smart as hell, too—which just went to prove how supersmart his own little brown mouse was. Ty chuckled to himself as he watched Nell approach.

Kitty Stein would hate the fact that her insulting metaphor for his beloved had become his own special form of endearment for her. Sylvie *was* his little brown mouse, which meant the world was really just one big cheese and he wanted to give her all of it all the time.

Nell was tense. She'd been "unnaturally quiet" the night before, according to Sylvie, and now Ty supposed Sylvie would consider her best friend was unnaturally quiet again, which apparently was not her usual style.

She ordered a champagne cocktail, drank it down like a truck driver, and ordered a second before she told him Johnny would not be joining them for lunch.

Ty idly wondered if they'd had a fight over money. The Nesbitt estate would be something to fight over. It was uncanny how many rich-as-Croesus guys liked to leave the wires crossed when they finally bowed out. Probably old man Nesbitt hadn't been any different, especially when it came to deciding whether or not to leave his dough to such a good-looking broad as Nell . . . quite possibly for some loser to get his hands on later.

As they made desultory conversation on the way into the restaurant, Ty decided to ask Nell at some point if Johnny—low key but obviously supersmart himself—was one of the executors of the Nesbitt estate.

Seated at a corner table, he didn't like the look on Nell's face when he asked her what time Johnny would be back.

"Is something wrong, Nell? I mean, I just hope we can make an early start this afternoon. There's bound to be traffic . . ."

God almighty, Nell's eyes were filling with tears. He covered her hand. It was quivering. "Can I do anything?"

"No, nothing." Her voice was unsteady but she didn't take her tear-filled eyes away from him. He found it unnerving. "Johnny's had a cable from . . . from Australia. His daughter's sick—Lucy—he's had to . . ." The tears started to pour down her face so fast it was like a waterfall. For one bizarre moment Ty thought of the Fountain of Trevi in Rome . . . Rome and Sylvie. God, how he wished Sylvie would walk in and rescue him right then. He didn't know how to cope.

"Well, that's awful but obviously I can understand why he had to—had to . . ."

"Oh, so can I . . . a daughter . . . a child . . ." Nell looked down at the tablecloth. "I'm sorry to be so emotional. It's just the cable and the prospect of Johnny leaving . . . then seeing Sylvie again after all these years. I never realized London would make me so upset. Does Sylvie ever mention her little girl?"

Ty shook his head quickly as if to clear away a fog that had just landed. "What did you say?"

Nell's eyes, still wet and shiny, looked deeply into his. "Sylvie's daughter. She must have told you . . ." Even as Ty felt his stomach churning, he registered the fact that Nell was moving her hands like a puppet, opening her purse with stiff staccato movements, taking out what looked like a picture frame, except where the picture should be was a newspaper clipping under glass. "Baby S on Hospital Doorstep . . ." The woman was still speaking. "I brought this over with me. I wanted to ask Sylvie if she'd kept in touch. It was such an agonizing decision for her . . . to give up her baby. She wrapped her in a shawl I'd made for her for Christmas—with her initial S embroidered in the corner—that's where 'Baby S' came from. . . . The paper we worked for—*The Mirror*—helped to get the baby adopted." Ty shot out his hand to cover Nell's mouth. He could actually feel blood draining from his face. It was the same sensation he'd had the morning they'd taken his father away. It was the same sensation he'd had on hearing the news of Brenda's death. He swallowed hard. It was even hard for him to speak. Life was draining out of him. When he was sure she had stopped talking, he took his hand away. Now she sat watching, waiting for his next move. He reached over and gripped her wrist so tightly it left it dead white like a corpse. He summoned up all his will power not to put the same pressure around her neck. "You know Sylvie doesn't have a daughter. You know Sylvie has never had a child." He knew his voice was too high. God, he sounded like a hysterical fag.

Nell was answering back, words pouring out fast. "I'm sorry, I thought . . . I thought Sylvie had told you everything. Good God, I can't believe it. . . . She loves you so much . . . she told me so again and again yesterday. Ever since I've been here she hasn't stopped telling me how she loves you—how she never thought she would ever love anyone again after what Dick did to her." She tried to pull her hand away but Ty held on.

"What are you trying to say to me?" The bitch, he thought, the unbelievable stinking evil bitch. "What are you trying to *do?*"

"You're hurting me." The tears were gone from the devastating green eyes. Now they were wide, luminous, extraordinarily innocent. "Ty, you're hurting. . . . I didn't mean to upset you. I thought you knew Sylvie had had a baby with. . . . Oh . . ." The wrench he gave her wrist could have broken it. He hoped he had. He didn't care. A veil of fury obscured his vision. The Thames outside the lofty Savoy windows was a sheet of pointilism. He dragged Nell to her feet. He didn't speak. She didn't speak at first. Then through clenched teeth— "What are you doing? Where are you taking me?"

She knew enough not to make a scene. His hand encircled her wrist like a handcuff as he walked her through the restaurant up the stairs into the front lobby. "I'm taking you to Sylvie—to repeat your filthy lies to her face . . ." He found he still had trouble getting his words out. He wanted to throw up all over the bitch's Chanel suit. He couldn't believe any of it was happening. Sylvie's best friend, indulging in the biggest act of calumny any woman on God's earth could perpetrate. What did it all mean? What could she hope to gain from it? A throb began behind his right temple. Or was any of it true? Could it possibly be true? There was so much pain from the thought of ever doubting Sylvie that Ty shut his mind before the pain could grow.

The amazing thing was that now the bitch was as cool as the coolest

English cucumber. The green eyes were cold like the emerald rock on her finger, her demeanor that of a girl with the best lineage in town.

There was a crowd in the lobby already high with New Year fervor, back-slapping, kissing.

He lost hold of her as he pushed her into the swinging door leading to the courtyard and was pushed himself by one of the merrymakers. His attention faltering for the wrong second, by the time he swung himself back inside the lobby she was out of sight but Johnny was there, coming toward him, asking in his well-mannered voice if everything was all right. All right!

"Where's the bitch? Where is she? She's coming with me. She's coming with me."

"Now wait a minute. What's going on here?" Johnny put a restraining hand on his arm. "Are you out of your mind?"

Ty didn't know what stopped him from lashing out and landing one on Johnny's well-bred nose. The fire was still in his groin, but suddenly so was a pain, blotting out everything else. He had to get to Sylvie to wrap her in his arms, to see the childlike look on her sweet-tempered face, to feel the slight swell of her belly with *his* child inside her. He would be comforted just by looking at her before he even breathed a word of the incredible scene that had just taken place. He pulled away from Johnny. "Tell your stepmother she hasn't heard the last of this. The only thing that will save her is a straitjacket. I'm not sure she doesn't need one right this minute . . ."

Ty ran out into the Savoy courtyard. Thank God the Jaguar was there, ready for what was to have been a happy, leisurely drive with the Nesbitts down to the Forresters' country estate in Surrey. Happy? Leisurely? Vomit rose in Ty's throat. He collected the keys from the doorman, tossed him a five-pound note, then still in shock opened the wrong door for the driver's seat. "What's the quickest way to Chester Street?" he cried as he started to edge away from the curb.

Johnny had come through the swinging door, was looking at him as if he'd gone mad. Well, he'd learn soon enough who the mad one was.

"Turn left, go down the Strand, sir, through Admiralty Arch, down the Mall . . ."

"Hyde Park Corner?" Ty interrupted impatiently.

"Right, guv . . . sir, I mean. Turn left by the Palace and Chester Street's the third turning on your right . . ."

"Take it easy," Ty heard Johnny say.

"Go to hell." He eased the lovely machine out of the courtyard, feeling his heart beating so fast it was all he could do not to lean back to recover, but his overriding anxiety to be with Sylvie didn't allow him any time for that. The Strand and the Mall were amazingly empty. Thank you, God, for these empty streets. . . . He drove fast up along Constitution Hill to join a heavy swarm of cars at Hyde Park Corner. As he turned left, making a wide sweep into Grosvenor Place to get ahead of the traffic, he didn't realize he was turning into a two-way street with traffic coming up from as well as going down toward Victoria Station. The right-hand wing of the Jaguar hit the right-hand wing of a Sunbeam Talbot racing up the slope to one of London's busiest and most dangerous intersections.

The impact sent the Jaguar spinning around to face the traffic it had just passed. It hit first a baker's van and then a 1956 Renault, the collisions forcing it across the pavement to imbed itself in the eight-foot-high wall surrounding the garden of Buckingham Palace.

Drenched with sweat, Dr. William Carlisle stepped away from the operating table in Theater C of London's St. George's Hospital to make a quick phone call to his wife. "I'll be home late. We have an emergency. I'm sorry, dear. No New Year's Eve for me. You go to the party without me." He then rejoined the team of green-gowned surgeons who for the next five and a half hours would attempt to repair Ty Caplan's seriously injured body.

As Dr. Carlisle tried to explain later to the American's brave little English wife, "We have been successful in the most urgent task— stopping the internal bleeding." He didn't go into details. Mrs. Caplan *seemed* composed—but there was no point in alarming her further, telling her they had been appalled to find that about four and a half pints of blood, approximately forty percent of the body's total supply, had drained into the abdominal cavity. They had set to work with swabs and suction devices to remove it, and during the operation Ty had received six pints of Rh-negative blood. His condition was far from good, but in some ways, as Dr. Carlisle reassured Sylvie, he had actually been lucky. There appeared to be no damage to the spine or to such major organs as the liver, the spleen, or the pancreas.

She began to ask intelligent questions, so the doctor decided to answer them. The pancreas was important because, lying deep in the left side of the abdomen, it secretes insulin as well as potent digestive enzymes which if released into the abdominal cavity "can damage tissue and cause dangerous inflammation." He didn't tell her of the meticulous examination they had made of the twenty- to twenty-five-foot small intestine, that they had used saline solutions laced with antibiotics to flush debris out of the abdominal cavity to reduce the risk of infection.

More questions? He sighed. "We found a large wound in the sigmoid colon and several lesions in the small intestine, which necessitated removing certain segments and stitching the ends together." Repairing the damage to the large bowel had been much more complicated. "When injured, the large bowel tends to stretch so that its blood vessels become less efficient in maintaining circulation. The large bowel doesn't heal as easily as the small intestine—for this reason we decided to perform a temporary colostomy, removing the damaged segment of the sigmoid, sealing off the lower end of the bowel.

"In six weeks, if all goes well," Dr. Carlisle told Sylvie with a note in his voice to say that this was the end of their conversation for the night, "another operation will give your husband normal bowel function once again."

"What's the prognosis?" Sylvie's voice was so low that Dr. Carlisle had to bend his head to hear her, but he didn't need her to repeat the question. It was an unusual way for a wife to ask about her husband's chances, but then one never knew how a woman was going to phrase anything or how a woman was going to react. He'd seen rum reactions in his day.

"The most perilous time will be in the next week to ten days." There was no point in giving this one platitudes or soothing answers. He hated having to pass on the huge question mark that was in all their minds after having worked so hard on the fellow, but he had to do it. "The most serious threat we face is infection of the peritoneum, or lining of the abdominal cavity . . ." There were other life-threatening possibilities he wasn't going to go into, such as the nasogastric tube running from the patient's nose to his stomach to remove digestive juices that could force gas into the intestine and strain the stitches. Caplan was of course going to be fed intravenously, and eventually if all went well he would be able to take liquids. If . . . if . . . if! The doctor sighed again. His work was his life and his life was full of "ifs" and "buts." He suddenly realized how exhausted he was. Thank God he didn't have to celebrate New Year's Eve.

He looked at the white face staring up at him. He sensed she wasn't registering what he said. He led her over to a nurse. "Who can we call, Mrs. Caplan, to come and take you home?"

"Home?" For an insane moment Sylvie couldn't remember where she lived, where "home" was. She shook her head. "I . . . we . . . I live in America now."

The nurse helped her along. "Mr. and Mrs. Caplan were—are—staying at the Savoy Hotel. That is where we managed to reach her this afternoon . . ."

"Well, then . . ." He could hear his voice growing terse. He didn't want to be bothered with logistics. It was going to be enough of an effort to get himself home, let alone Mrs. Caplan. He turned to the nurse. "We must arrange for Mrs. Caplan to be taken back to her hotel."

She interrupted, as he'd known she would. In slow measured tones she told him it wasn't that she wouldn't—but that she *couldn't* leave the hospital, the place where her husband's life hung so tenuously in the balance.

As Sylvie spoke she was thinking whether she should call Nell again. There had been no answer, not from Nell or from Johnny's suites. She couldn't remember now what kind of message she'd left because then she hadn't understood what had happened. An accident. She remembered she'd left word that there had been an accident, that they should call the Forresters in Surrey and get the directions to go on ahead, that she would call later if and when Ty and she were able to join them.

How long ago it all seemed. Like another life. Sylvie felt she was acting in a play, that none of what was happening was real. Her senses were reacting *so* slowly. Far away—at least she thought it was far away —she could hear a radio announcer describing the scene in Trafalgar Square as the old year crawled into oblivion. Good-bye 1967. . . . Every minute of 1967—until this dreadful day—had been so packed with magical happiness.

Sylvie knew there were tears on her cheek. She hadn't realized she was crying silently. Why was she crying now when Ty was receiving the best attention, was in the best care? When every minute from now on was moving toward his recovery? She hadn't cried once during the long hours waiting for him to emerge from the operating theater. How had it all happened? Why had Ty so obviously been on his way to collect her from Elizabeth Wondrak's when their plan had been for her to return to the Savoy to join the group for coffee? And where were Nell and Johnny? Why hadn't they come to the hospital or at least called? Her head ached with questions, yet none of them mattered. Nothing mattered except Ty's recovery. All the answers couldn't change the most terrible day of her life.

The nurse led her to a cot in a ward two or three wards away from Ty's. Sylvie knelt on the cold floor. "Oh, God, oh, God, please God . . . let him recover. Our Father who art in heaven . . ." She couldn't finish the Lord's Prayer. Recover. Recover. She clung fiercely to the word, willing every second be spent in aiding his progress.

Sylvie remembered other New Year's Days. They had nearly always been a letdown, arriving with the "Monday morning feeling" other people apparently experienced. She had never experienced it on a Monday, because going back to work after the weekend had always been such a joy for her.

The first day of 1968 began for Sylvie at 4:00 A.M. when she awoke, every inch of her aching, throbbing. Her baby. Their baby. She could hardly believe she hadn't given a single thought to the life growing inside her.

She cautiously began to stretch out on the cot, half expecting not to be able to; but bit by bit, as her muscles contracted and relaxed, her aching ceased.

Her mind cleared and the full horror of yesterday's events sent her thoughts into a tailspin of activity. She tiptoed out into the dimly lit corridor to find the lavatory. Anxiety made her heart beat faster as she inspected her knickers and wiped herself, terrified in case there was blood—but there was no blood. The baby was safe. Her aches and pains, her uneasiness, she told herself fiercely, were psychosomatic. She had to take herself firmly in hand.

"How is my husband?" she asked a nurse she hadn't seen before. "Mr. Caplan in . . . intensive care? Can I see him?"

The nurse shook her head brusquely. "Not now. The doctor's with him." The nurse suddenly smiled an unexpected smile, which took away the moroseness of her expression. "He's conscious. You'll be able to see him in the morning after Doctor Carlisle's been back."

Sylvie checked her watch. It was four-ten. How could she get through the rest of the long cold night? "Has there—is there a message for me?"

The nurse shook her head, the weight of her responsibilities back on her face. "Nope." Then just as quickly as before she relented with another smile. "Do you need something to help you sleep, Mrs. Caplan?"

It seemed the only solution. She had to make sure she slept because of the baby. "I'm pregnant—three and a half months . . ."

The nurse looked concerned. "You shouldn't be here sleeping on that uncomfortable cot. Why don't you go back to your hotel? We'll call you if there's any change."

Sylvie shook her head adamantly. "I can't leave until I've seen—spoken—I just can't leave . . ." She allowed herself to be led back to the cot like an obedient schoolgirl and took a mild sedative with a glass of milk. Soon she was dreaming she was sitting beside Ty at the piano as she had so often sat while he played his latest composition, but now Nell was sitting there, too, smiling her alluring catlike smile, gazing at Ty with a Harry Pegler look of devotion. As Nell devoured him with her eyes, Sylvie looked down to see Ty's foot pressing close to Nell's, except now it was Dick Kolinzcky's and they were all in the Hammersmith bed-sit. When she awoke it was nearly six-thirty and a steaming cup of strong tea with a digestive biscuit was beside her.

Surely she could see Ty now. She couldn't bear the thought of spending another minute without seeing his little-boy face, conscious or unconscious. Her mouth felt putrid, her hair like string. There was a rip in her skirt where she'd caught it on the taxi door in her feverish anxiety to get to the hospital. She went back to the cheerless, Lysol-smelling lavatory to splash some life into her face with water and comb her hair. Then she went with determination to the nurse's desk. It was no problem. They allowed her into the ward where Ty lay, tubes and wires linking him to life-support systems, a monitor recording his heartbeat. Sylvie chilled. He was so white, so motionless, only the monitor above the bed gave any indication that his heart *was* beating, that he *was* still alive. As she bent to kiss his hand he opened his eyes.

"Oh, my darling." She kissed his cold cheek. With his eyes he told her he knew she was there. She was allowed to sit with him for half an hour before a nurse came to take her away. He hadn't spoken but every so often she'd felt a slight pressure from his hand.

She agreed to go back to the hotel. She had to have a bath, had to put on the Blue Grass fragrance Ty loved so well so that *all* his senses would record her presence—and she had to find out why there had been no word from Nell or Johnny.

"My God, Sylvie—we've been frantic, out of our minds with worry. This country goes to sleep on New Year's Eve. We hadn't been able to find out a thing about you or your friends . . ." Natalie Forrester, Ty's old friend in Surrey, wouldn't let her interrupt.

When Sylvie was finally able to explain the terrible events of the past twenty-four hours she heard a gasp of shock down the wire. "You poor child. All alone in that hospital. Frank, Frank, come here, come here at once."

Sylvie could hear dogs barking, could imagine the scene in the beautiful sixteenth-century home where Ty had taken her one spring. Now there would be huge logs burning in the grate, Chippendale mirrors reflecting the *boiserie*, the silver; there would be the best champagne on ice in antique buckets and delicious tiny hot hors d'oeuvres handed round by Tuffit, the Forresters' dignified elderly butler.

Frank Forrester was all business on the phone. The name of the doctor? The ward number? He would come up to London at once to ensure all that could be done for Ty was being done. Sylvie tried to protest, but her heart wasn't in it. She needed the support of an influential man who would be able to get the best, even in a city that to all intents and purposes had indeed fallen asleep. As she sat on the edge of the Savoy bed, out of nowhere panic started to rise. She could feel sweat on her upper lip. Something was pulling her back to the hospital. She tried to calm herself. "Did . . . did Nell . . . Johnny arrive?"

"Nobody arrived." Now Natalie's voice was clipped, slightly offended. "We just couldn't begin to understand what had happened. We thought you'd had an accident on the road. We talked to the Surrey police but we couldn't find out anything." The aggrieved note hung in the air. It suggested the least Sylvie could have done was to telephone to say they weren't going to make the New Year's Eve party because Ty had been involved in a car crash. Sylvie heard the note but ignored it. She was far more puzzled over the whereabouts of both Nell and Johnny, whom she'd discovered had checked out sometime during the afternoon of New Year's Eve. The reception desk seemed to think neither of them had received her message—but if they hadn't gone to Surrey, where *had* they gone and why?

It was a nightmare of confusion, but again Sylvie pushed the queries out of her mind. None of them mattered. Nothing and no one mattered except Ty.

Frank came back on the line and this time she cried openly, mentally leaning against the strength of his voice.

In twenty-four hours Frank had brought in another specialist for a second opinion, had received a complete report of Ty's injuries and the way the hospital had dealt with them. He patted Sylvie's hand confidently. "They've done well, my little love. Have no fear. It's only going to be a matter of time before Ty will be back making beautiful music. Really, have no fear."

It was irrational, she knew, but fear as palpable as a tumor enveloped her sane thoughts, made her hands clammy, her breath short.

Ty had a pallor which she knew had to be expected but which still frightened her. To her it indicated his life's blood was oozing out of him.

Three days after the accident, as she sat in a chair at his bedside stroking his hand, Ty began to tell her what had happened. He spoke with difficulty. He was obviously experiencing pain, but although she tried to make him stop, he shook his head, gasping, "I must tell you. I'm here because of your best friend." He even managed a wry smile. "In fact your worst enemy, my little brown mouse. Nell Nesbitt . . ." He took a deep breath, closing his eyes, "should be burned at the stake . . ." He took fifteen halting minutes to tell her of Nell's lies, and as he told her the terrible story of their lunchtime meeting the pain came back to her abdomen. She was soaked in sweat, her hands alternately hot and cold. She wanted to faint but of course she couldn't, wouldn't faint. She had to show superhuman strength to support her husband.

Nell! Sylvie clenched her hands. What Ty had just told her that Nell had tried to imply was incredible—and yet a voice inside her told her it had always been that way with Nell. Her dream of a few nights before came back. Nell's leg beside Dick's leg . . . and if things hadn't been so wonderful, so strong and enduring between Ty and herself, it could have been Nell's leg against Ty's . . . but Nell had seen it wouldn't work this time, so she'd had to dream up a way to poison their relationship, not realizing that no amount of poison could affect Ty's love for her.

Sylvie's eyes filled with tears. Now here was her beloved husband suffering in hospital, suffering terribly as a direct result of Nell's lies.

Sylvie blamed herself, blamed her gullibility, looked back across the years and saw, for the first time, the evil in Nell—her lies, her callous attitude to her parents, even to Harry Pegler, who should have known better. But then everyone and anyone who had ever had any dealings with Nell should have known better.

It was like a chasm opening in front of her. Sylvie felt herself being pulled in, as she grappled to suppress the hate she suddenly felt for Nell.

"Sylvie . . ." Ty's fingers clutched hers, then slackened. His pupils rolled upward and a dreadful sound came out of his mouth, half snore, half yelp of pain.

"Ty . . ." she screamed. She was being ushered out of the room. There was a loud clanging of bells. People rushed by her in green coats. Someone was screaming "Ty." She didn't know it was her own voice. "Ty, Ty . . ." The chasm was opening wider. She was being pulled in by Nell, whose long fingers were clawing at her body, at her baby, at Ty.

~~~

"He died as I sat there, auntie." Sylvie's voice was flat, empty of all feeling. She lay as she'd lain since the morning of January the fourth, like a little old lady slowly withering away, no muscles in evidence to support her body, each limb appearing to weigh too much for her to lift.

She had lost her husband. She had lost her baby.

Gert blinked back tears as she stroked the pale forehead with a pad soaked in Blue Grass. Sylvie flinched. "Please . . . please throw that scent away. I can't stand it."

Gert flushed with pain. What a stupid idiot she was, hurting the human being she loved more than herself by reviving memories with fragrance, something fragrance had such an uncanny ability to do. What *could* she do to help her tragic niece? Gert felt she herself was bleeding with her inability to take any of the burden away.

The doctors had told her it was going to take a long time for Sylvie to recover from the shock of Ty's sudden death from a heart attack. He had been expected to recover from his injuries. When he died, Sylvie had been sitting by his bedside, optimistic, holding his hand. Again Gert's eyes filled with tears. Why had it had to happen to her niece, who always tried to do the best for everyone?

Nobody could answer that one. It had to be accepted as God's will . . . but it was *so* unfair.

Gert bit her lip. Sylvie couldn't stay at the Savoy forever. Where on earth was she to go? Where could she ever find happiness again?

Gert's thoughts went to the company she and Pierre were now well on the way to implementing. Perhaps Sylvie would like to become a partner. It was probably small potatoes to her—but at least it would give her something to think about, something to concentrate on, away from the terrible pain and ache caused by her void inside. Gert knew exactly how Sylvie must feel. She had been there. Was death worse to bear than betrayal and rejection? Whatever the answer, she could remember, could even conjure up, the agony of living with that huge, ugly, empty void.

Gert looked lovingly at Sylvie's pale face on the pillow. She would regain her strength, whether she wanted to regain it or not, Gert knew that. She was still young. She would meet someone else. Gert's thoughts thrashed about even as Sylvie opened her eyes to stare vacantly into space. There were ten more years on the young face Gert had welcomed back to England only three weeks before. It was inconceivable. Gert still didn't know what had happened—except that it involved Nell.

Nell. Bitter anger tightened Gert's lips. If only it had been Nell in the crash, Nell who had died. Why were the wicked allowed to triumph over the innocent every time? There was no justice—nothing could ever be bad enough to happen to Nell, and yet she had heard everything around Nell was blossoming, her company forging ahead, while she herself apparently was more beautiful than ever. There was no justice.

"Mrs. Caplan, may we inquire how much longer we can have the pleasure of accommodating you? And perhaps you would be kind enough to indicate when you will settle your account to date?" The day manager's voice needled her brain.

"I'll be leaving at the end of the week. Yes, of course I'll settle. How . . . how much is it?"

There was a discreet cough. "To date, madam, twelve hundred pounds."

Sylvie managed to stop a gasp of astonishment escaping. Twelve hundred pounds! How could it be? Yet of course it *had* to be. The Savoy wasn't a second-rate hostel. It was one of the leading hotels in London—in the world. She forced herself to think practically. Ty had to have had traveler's checks somewhere. She would gather up her strength to look in his suits, go through his music case. The last thing she'd given a thought to was money. Now she realized every moment she stayed at the hotel meant only money. She had to get out fast, but where should she go?

She spent the afternoon painstakingly going through Ty's things.

Every so often she had to stop to lie down, her trancelike state penetrated when she least expected it—by a rumpled handkerchief that she could see Ty pushing down into his trouser pocket . . . by a hastily written bar of music on the back of a book of matches. It was agony. In all she found about five hundred dollars and seventy-odd pounds. Could she write a check for the rest? She knew she had no money in her London bank. She had been about to close it. Would the Savoy take an American check? She worked out the rate of exchange. She wasn't even sure she had the remaining amount in her checking account in New York. She'd hardly written a check since her marriage to Ty. Whenever she'd needed or wanted anything she had used the stores Ty directed her to—stores where she could sign for her purchases. Then Ty's manager had taken care of all the household and travel bills. Sylvie sighed. How stupid and slow she was being. Of course Frank Forrester would know what to do. Ty's English manager was still away on vacation—somewhere in Europe. They hadn't even been able to locate him for the funeral and he obviously hadn't seen the English papers where Ty's death had been reported prominently, because there had been no word from him. Well, Frank would know how to handle everything.

It was an embarrassing conversation. Sylvie hadn't known how to begin it. She had never been adept at "getting around" to a subject in order to reach a main objective. It was an art she had never even tried to master. Her strength was in being forthright, but how could you be forthright about asking somebody else to settle your hotel bill? It was ridiculous, but she felt she was asking for charity. Charity—when obviously once the proper papers were filed she would be able to pay everything and everyone back without a thought. All the same she stuttered and stumbled, her head aching with the thought of the weeks ahead with managers, lawyers, sorting out Ty's affairs. Frank hadn't attempted to put her out of her misery. She'd had to come right out with it and ask for a loan, which he had quietly agreed to supply. It was Natalie Forrester who intimated later there had been other loans made to Ty . . . loans that had not been paid back.

Sylvie had never been smart about money. She'd always known it; had never particularly worried about it. Once she had even felt privileged to be paid for what she loved to do. Then had come the exhilaration of earning good, even excellent money for a woman, when

Smith Maynard had singled her out as a rare talent and dramatically increased her salary. On top of that she had had an expense account, which meant all the things she had seen others enjoy had become part of her everyday life—meals in the best restaurants, first-night tickets, chauffeur-driven cars, first-class travel. She had fallen into the trap she had seen others fall headlong into—she had taken the expense-account life for granted.

Ty, with his own brand of magic, casual, disdainful Ty, hadn't helped, deprecating any *show*, any talk of money, yet always buying, renting, even borrowing only the best. Ty had believed in signing his way through life and had shown her how to do the same, looking down his nose arrogantly at people who displayed the fact they carried large amounts of cash.

Back in the States, two weeks after her return from London and a week after the New York memorial service packed with the famous—most of whom Sylvie had never met—she looked out bleakly at a snow-covered Central Park, brooding on the harsh facts behind Ty's happy-go-lucky, let-tomorrow-take-care-of-itself outlook on life.

Now she knew the bitter truth—that for the past several years Ty had "mortgaged" his future away. Now he had no future—and neither did she. There was no money, no savings, no stocks or bonds or, for that matter, any "papers to sort out" to unravel Ty's estate. There were only debts and debtors.

"Leave it to me, little brown mouse." It had been Ty's favorite saying. With increasing panic she realized that she *had* left everything to him and she was now left with nothing.

"Where are all Ty's friends?" Gert hadn't been fooled by Sylvie's efforts to reassure her over the phone that all was going well. Sylvie knew Gert could not afford to make the transatlantic calls she was making to find out what was happening. "Please, Aunt Gert, stop worrying. I'll be all right. It's just that everything takes time to sort out over here. The lawyers . . ." She'd broken off, unable to lie, only too aware of other people's lawyers who were now writing terse, frightening letters and phoning to demand repayment on behalf of their clients for loans or advances Ty had received and apparently spent long ago.

Gert's question, "Where are all Ty's friends?" mocked her day and night. Well, where were they? Since their marriage there had been so many "yes men" and "yes women"—sycophants all—around them, so anxious to please, Sylvie had been astounded, even touched at first that Ty was obviously so revered. He had teased her about her naivete.

"I'm hot right now—and you're making me hotter, darling. My name means money at the box office. One flop and they won't even remember my name . . ." She hadn't believed him, had thought it was yet one more example of his modesty—and, worse, his lack of belief in his own extraordinary talent. Now she'd learned the hard way that he had been right all along. The cooing doves had turned into vultures.

Lying awake, the curtains open, the park turned into a deep grave pond, the twinkling lights of Central Park West, and Harlem far in the distance, Sylvie could imagine Ty's sardonic look as the letters of condolence continued to pour in, at the wilting baskets of flowers that had only just stopped arriving.

"Is . . . is that you, Cathy?" One afternoon on Park Avenue, Sylvie ran into an aristocratic brunette whom she'd often caught up with on the conveyor belt of lunches, cocktail parties, and dinners that she and Ty had jumped on in New York whenever Ty felt like it. The woman turned to give her a distant stare.

"Cathy?" This was the woman who had told her on their first meeting that she was one of Ty's greatest friends, and Ty hadn't denied it. She had been warm, if not a little too warm, but Sylvie had liked her, instinctively sensing that beneath the sophisticated exterior was a real person. She hadn't sensed that about many she'd met on the New York social scene. For a moment her heart raced uncomfortably. Was Cathy going to be a fairweather friend, too?

There was embarrassment in the hazel eyes. "Good God, Sylvie . . . I've just returned from Tokyo. I feel dreadful I haven't written. I'll call you, I promise. I was never so shocked in my life. You poor darling." Her long nails touched Sylvie's arm, bringing back a fleeting remembrance of Kitty Stein with her burgundy talons, her burgundy snood . . . and the terrible article she had written. Tears came to Sylvie's eyes. They were of course mainly tears for Ty, but they were tears for all the other things that hurt so dreadfully. Nell. Kitty; the emptiness; the loneliness.

Cathy didn't phone, but after a few days the absence of phone calls was if anything a blessing. When they did come they usually brought bad news.

"It's not a very happy situation." Jerome Mossop, the lawyer Sylvie knew Ty had always trusted and the man who had been most involved in his many problems with Brenda, put his rimless glasses down on his huge mahogany desk and leaned back in his swivel chair, a reflective look on his face.

"Ty died at an inopportune time as far as his finances were concerned. He died owing a great deal of money—with, unfortunately, much of his commissioned work uncompleted." The lawyer did not take his pale eyes away from Sylvie's face, flushed with distress.

"How much?" Her voice was choked with unshed tears. Mossop's expression of vague disinterest did not change.

"For a half-written score for Twentieth Century-Fox he received an advance of about a hundred thousand dollars. The California house has an outstanding mortgage for about the same amount. He owes two or three people a total of four hundred thousand. Unfortunately, he had already sold his royalties on *Olympic Fiesta* and *Holy Cow* and . . ."

"The apartment?" Sylvie interrupted.

"It's a rental—but there's little money in the bank for the rent. At a rough estimate I'd say that once everything has been evaluated, about half a million dollars will be outstanding."

Sylvie closed her eyes. When she opened them it was to find Mossop standing over her, uncomfortably close, looking down with eyes that appeared almost colorless. She shifted awkwardly. It was absurd, but she felt in danger. He put a pudgy hand on her shoulder. There was no benevolence, no pity in the gesture. It was a "pay attention" grip that said, "listen to me or else."

She tried to look unconcerned as she returned his steady, unwavering gaze. "What can I . . . what should I . . ."

He began to trace the pinstripe on her sleeve down to her elbow with one finger. It was extraordinarily suggestive. As if bestowing a rare accolade, he said, "There's a way I can help you, Sylvie . . ." She moved imperceptibly but enough to tell him she disliked his closeness, his touch.

He removed his hand, but still he continued to stand over her. Without changing his tone, he went on, "We should get to know each other. Ty selfishly kept you all too well hidden . . . and . . . in fact, why not have dinner with me tonight?"

When she remained silent, he again put his hand possessively on her shoulder, and with a trace of sarcasm said, "You look as if you could do with a square meal . . . and it will give me an opportunity to tell you what I'm prepared to do to settle Ty's debts." He paused deliberately, then added softly, sinisterly, "And what you have to do for your part of the bargain. For once Ty showed good judgment in his choice of women. I've always heard that English girls have the hottest . . ."

She bit him hard, astonished even as her teeth sank into the fleshy curve of his thumb that she could do such a thing, yet determined to put every bit of hate she felt into the bite. He let go of her with a curse and Sylvie raced to the door, only to find it locked. She pummeled on it, yelling, "Let me out, let me out," as Jerome Mossop strode back to his desk to throw the key at her.

He sounded as cool and as detached as ever, as he said, "You'll regret that, Mrs. Caplan. Yes, you will certainly regret that. Please don't bother me again with any of your considerable problems. You and I have nothing further to say to each other."

8

Assuming a sale is part of positive psychology, nod your head yes when you are talking to your customers. It's a mild form of hypnosis. Look them in their right eye because the right eye controls and is also a form of hypnosis. Phrase questions to get a *yes* answer. Touch the customer often, to show you care. And when it comes time to sell, give them a complete set of products. If they hold them all, they will want them all. Never forget when a woman says no, she means maybe. When a woman says maybe, she means yes. Above all, remember the key to being Ready to Change is self-motivation. To help you build your self-motivation, our leader, Nell Nesbitt, has created a series of easy-to-learn inspirational poems and songs. They are available on the left at the back.

There, too, you can register for special classes on positive attitude and self-motivation, which I urge you all to attend. Let us remind ourselves now how to stop procrastination ruining our drive, our lives. Let's repeat fifty times, "Do it now. Do it now. Do it now." And remember to repeat it every day. After only a week you will have an indelible tape in your brain that will automatically snap on whenever you put something off. Isn't that a comforting thought? Then, of course, there is the importance of daily Bible reading . . .

"Okay, turn it off." Nell didn't bother to stifle a yawn. As the screen went dark, the light went on immediately in the small viewing theater. "She's not bad . . . quite good, in fact—but is she good *enough*? Are her leadership abilities real or skin-deep?" Nell seemed to be asking the questions of herself, not looking at any of the tired men who occupied seven of the twenty plush theater seats. There was an audible sigh from the oldest member of the group.

Nell stared at him coldly. "What's wrong, Gordon? Past your bedtime? Shall I call your overpaid secretary to get your limo?"

The way Nell paused and coughed deliberately before saying the word *secretary* was unmistakably suggestive. Gordon Findon was so taken aback—despite the fact that on getting the Ready to Change account he had issued the order himself—"no smoking in the presence of Nell Nesbitt"—he started to light a cigarette with unsteady fingers. He jammed it into an ashtray the next second as Nell hissed, "Put that filthy thing out. And I think *you'd* better get out, too. My business is obviously getting too much for you to handle. You've lost your touch, Findon."

The aging advertising man looked haplessly at his colleagues. He knew it was counterproductive to answer Nell Nesbitt back, but how he longed to take her icy composure away with an appropriate sharp retort. What a bitch! Well, he would be taken off the account now, that was sure. Now that the ax had been swung, he felt a certain amount of relief. For the first six months he had been the blue-eyed boy. Now he was going the way of several others before him.

There was an uncomfortable silence after he left. Nell broke it with an unexpected earthy chuckle. "Has this shop turned into a morgue or something? Let's have a coffee break, then go over the other training films." She glanced casually at her watch as if it were the beginning of the day, not the end. "It's still not midnight. Let's resume at the witching hour. Goldo, I'd like to go over some of the things that aging moron Findon obviously never considered important."

Dirk Goldo, a slim young man with close-cropped, bright blond hair, as youthful and agile as Gordon Findon appeared decrepit and stiff, held out his hand to pull Nell to her feet. Bitch though he knew her to be, being close to her for one instant was undoubtedly exciting. He made a fast calculation as to how she must look naked. Was her pubic hair as silver as the hair on her immaculate head? Goldo could feel a tremor in his penis, for in her beautifully cut, light wool dress, it was easy to see the outline of her full round nipples. The word around the office was Nell Nesbitt bought her bras from "girlie" shops in Hollywood. Bras with holes in the right places to ensure a "finger-licking, fondling, fucking feeling in the opposite sex." Goldo shut off his wandering erotic thoughts. There was no way he was going to find out about this client's bras. Madame Chairman did not play around with the hired help, however pretty, and right now he was in the hot seat, Nell Nesbitt's oracle, taking over from veteran Gordon Findon.

Since Nell's return from England minus her family confidant and ardent fan, Johnny Nesbitt, the scuttlebutt was that she would be on a perpetual rampage because Johnny Nesbitt was the *real* motivating brain behind the incredible Ready to Change organization, and she was in a panic to hide the fact. After only a few hours working closely with the lady, however, Goldo had found that to be complete rubbish. Whatever anyone said about her, he knew Nell Nesbitt was the genius totally responsible for the Ready to Change business that was growing in the most incredible leaps and bounds—and along with it their own ad agency.

"Goldo, there are a number of things missing from that promo film. I want *facts*, not feminism. There's already too much feminism in this last version. We've got to get across facts—that there must *never* be any time for a customer to change her mind between payment and delivery of a product. My girls must learn that they *must* have enough inventory to fill customers' orders on the spot. The urge to buy and buy has to be satisfied immediately, not in fifteen minutes or a day or a week, but right then and there." Nell's voice was rising but she didn't care. "We've got to get the Ready to Change girl to understand that although she's obviously helping company profits, she's also helping her own. That doesn't come across. That addle-head Findon left out so many of the great pluses about becoming Ready to Change consultants—that because they're *independent* business people, they are entitled to tax deductions on any rooms in their homes used for business, plus depreciation on their cars, clothing, travel, child care, gas, and all the hundred and one things that can be legitimately considered as job-related expenses. Look how far Mary Kay has moved in only five years. We're keeping up with her here on the West Coast, but we're way behind in the Midwest—and nowhere in the East. We're not going to change anything with gimmicks in this hard-up economy. We've got to get across the incredible, amazing uplift in the quality of her life, once a woman joins the Ready to Change crusade."

Nell crossed her long beautiful legs, well aware that her skirt rode up to expose more of her thighs than the designer had intended. Let the beautiful boy drool. She needed to get him on heat to get the most out of his creative talent. She let her voice soften, knowing the contrast between her sensuous slouch in the chair and her sweet, almost motherly tone would disorient Goldo further. "As my beloved husband, Wallace, told me so often, the only rock a direct-sales business can be built on is its sales force. Our wonderful Ready to Change consultants need mental support"—her voice sharpened without her realizing it—"and it's not enough to *imply* rewards—freedom from the domination of a husband, the shackles of domesticity, acting as unpaid servants for unappreciative slobs. We should get people like Faye Dobson, Grace Darlington, Toby Mather to say on camera how much they are earning. What's the average?"

It was a familiar scenario. Nell knew very well what her top saleswomen were earning, but Goldo relayed the figures as if he thought she were hearing them for the first time. "On average about thirty-two thousand dollars annually. In fact I think Toby Mather will probably hit the forty-thousand-dollar mark this year—a record."

Nell bounced up and down excitedly, all contrived thought of her appearance forgotten. "Let's make an example of her. Use her in the last quarter on TV. Prove through Toby that any woman can share in the great American dream and become rich and independent of a man—without losing sight of the fact that we sell the best products for every woman willing, anxious, and ready to change her looks. Toby isn't bad looking—in fact she can run rings around that actress I've been staring at for the past four hours . . ."

Inwardly Goldo groaned. He would be blamed if Nell threw out the film they'd spent so long persuading her to accept. It was good, too. It would be a terrible waste of excellent material. He felt jaded, depressed. He wasn't used to dealing with a woman like Nesbitt. He didn't know whether she meant what she was saying or not. It was a hideous spot to be in. He had to prove his worth to the company— not just to the client. Goldo shook his head, trying to concentrate, suddenly keenly aware of his incarceration in a temperature-controlled environment on this, the first really good Saturday they'd had in Los Angeles in ages. Easter Sunday, at that! Everyone would have spent it at the beach—yet this tough broad had had no qualms about keeping them all at the office, intimating she expected some of them to be on call the next day, too. That would certainly mean him. She must be learning from Charlie Revson of Revlon who, Goldo had heard from the folks at Gray Advertising, liked nothing better than to start work about nine o'clock on a Friday night—but at least Revson didn't get to the office at the crack of dawn. He was a midday-to-midnight workaholic, whereas Nell Nesbitt apparently didn't need sleep at all.

Against his will Goldo's eyes wandered to the place where Nell's thighs crossed. She may not need sleep, but surely such a gorgeous piece of tail needed sex. Didn't everybody?

"Toby's told me she earns as much in a few hours as a Ready to Change consultant as she used to make in a week in her old job at the bank." Nell leaned forward earnestly. "We've got to tell the women of America we pay the highest commissions of all—that's what will attract them in the beginning, and they'll soon learn they don't have to work every day—almost thirty-five percent of our sales volume comes from reorders. Thousands live on reorder sales alone." Nell seemed to be addressing herself again, her eyes half closed, as she murmured, "Perhaps I should do a country-wide tour with Toby—explain to the women of America how easy it is . . ."

To Goldo's horror, as Nell lay back, apparently deep in thought, through the office partition he could hear Gordon Findon's voice bellowing into the phone. The man must have cracked, or was he drunk?

"Yes, that fancy fart, America's own Godmother, just gave me a lecture . . ." Gordon laughed unnaturally loudly. "Yep, that's what I call the tramp—Godmother. It fits. She is full of holy shit, yet about as godforsaken a person as it has ever been my misfortune . . ."

Goldo reddened with embarrassment, trying not to look at Nell. To his astonishment, however, Nell was smiling. She beckoned Goldo to come nearer, her eyes creased with real mirth.

She whispered, "If that's what he can come up with when the fancy fart 'lectures' him, she should do it every night." She sparkled with animation. "That's the name I've been looking for, Goldo. Godmother. It's perfect—a natural attention-stealer. I am the Godmother, that's the name to inspire all those women out there, who are, after all, my disciples. Why didn't I think of that?" She blew a kiss at the wall, then shouted, "Thank you, Gordon!"

There was a sound of a phone being crashed down in the next office. Goldo could just imagine Gordon's face, but he didn't have to worry. He might even have saved his bacon, for Nell Nesbitt was obviously enthusiastic about the name. Goldo was incredulous. Could it be true that, like the simplest of little starlets, Nell Nesbitt was beginning to believe her own publicity? His fear began to evaporate as he surreptitiously looked at her. It was true! She obviously believed she was destined to be Godmother to all the women in the world! What a joke, but where the hell was that going to lead?

⌒⌒⌒

"I slept with a man last week. It—he—was the first since . . ." A tear hovered on her lash, then plopped with amusing accuracy into the small basin in front of her—"since Alfie, my husband, died." Washed out and prematurely wrinkled from the sun, the thirty-eight-year-old mother of two, Monica Miller from Newport Beach, wondered how on earth the Godmother had extracted such a statement from her. She wished the ground would open to swallow her up.

A forceful hand maneuvered Monica's chin so she was forced to look into the eyes of the most beautiful face she had ever seen. She gasped. As part of a volunteer Ready to Change focus group, paid ten dollars an hour for her trouble, she'd been told the Godmother might actually put in an appearance, but she hadn't believed it. In the Burbank film studio—on a set described by the lady from the advertising agency as representative of a typical Ready to Change location—Monica was seated at a mahogany dining table in a pretty dining room. She had quickly been put at ease by Toby, apparently one of the main Ready to Change disciples, and had been enjoying the fuss as a mirror, a Styrofoam pallette filled with colors, and blobs of creams and powders had been put in front of her. At first it had *all* been fun and games as along with seven other volunteers (a "typical, happy, wanting-to-learn RTC group," a man called Goldo had stressed) she'd had her skin analyzed. "Dehydrated, I'm afraid. Next year you'll be able to use our new Silk Soothers to get back the baby-face bloom you should still have," Toby had told her, "but I'm afraid you've got to do some work with our Natural Dew line first . . ."

She'd followed Toby's instructions, forgetting after a while that cameras were whirring and apparently microphones overhead were recording everything they were saying. She couldn't think why. It hadn't been very exciting—at least she hadn't thought so. Things had begun to change when Toby slipped in a few odd questions about the lives they led, their hopes, their disappointments. She'd been terrific, really, confessing to some upsets of her own although, as they'd all been told, Toby had won the Ready to Change sales award of the year and was going to receive a real diamond "disciple" brooch at the October banquet in—of all wonderful places—the Bahamas.

With no warning, another voice had interjected, a warm, lovely voice that had a smile in every syllable. The voice had talked about a woman's responsibilty to herself and how in a man's world a woman owed it to herself to realize her own potential, to learn there was a life of quality that could be achieved not as chattel of a man, but for a woman alone, standing on her own two feet. They'd all realized more or less at the same time that it had to be the Godmother's voice, that she *had* actually come to the studio to meet them. The funny thing was the Godmother had started speaking just when they'd reached the makeup stage, so, a little flushed with excitement and the gorgeous RTC colors, they'd all looked so much prettier, healthier, *changed* than when they'd first arrived.

But how on earth had Monica opened her big mouth to mention, of all things, *sex?* Monica was mortified, but the Godmother was making her feel a bit better. Her words had just tumbled out, following the woman on her right from the Valley who told the Godmother how right she was, that a woman didn't need a man, that she'd been without one for six years and hadn't missed "it" one bit. Her meaning had been clear. "It" was sex. And hadn't the Godmother then gently asked a question? Monica tried to remember, blushing as the Godmother *herself* held her hand and looked—could it be?—admiringly at her.

"How long is it since Alfie died?" Her voice was caressing, soothing, hypnotic.

"Two years . . . well, eighteen months. I haven't been interested. But . . . but . . . this was different."

Monica now felt all America was watching her. The cameras seemed bigger. The microphones loomed nearer. If the Godmother hadn't been holding her hand she was sure she could have fainted right into her Styrofoam tray.

"You know it's the pubococcygeal muscle that is the key to feminine response in making love? Like all muscles in the body it needs exercise after a time, but you mustn't confuse muscle with matter." The Godmother had seated herself at the table now and Monica, not feeling so shy, studied the Godmother's beautiful sand-colored—no, she corrected herself proudly—oyster-colored suit, which complemented her incredible camelia-colored skin and somehow made her glorious hair look like a shining silver halo. Monica couldn't believe anyone could be so perfect. There wasn't a line on her face, and there didn't seem to be a trace of makeup, either.

The other women were hanging on the Godmother's words, longing for more. "Muscle, not matter—brain matter! Sometimes a man can trigger a release of phenylethylamine in the brain, a correlate to amphetamine. More to the point, it's what we call 'being in love.' It's a chemical condition—giving us a 'high' and too often a 'low' when something goes wrong and the phenylethylamine dries up. You've heard forever that being in love and loving someone are two different things. Being Ready to Change means learning to love yourself more and discovering the love of God."

Monica was impressed, although she'd come to the focus group in order to earn some extra money, determined not to fall into the trap of spending what she earned on any Ready to Change products. Nothing she'd used since Alfie's death had put any bloom back into her cheeks, but in one way the Godmother was right. Although making love with her next-door neighbor, who'd come in to help her fix her showerhead, had turned her cheeks and chin red, it was more from the stubble on his chin than anything else.

By the time the session ended, Monica was sold. She was going to become a Ready to Change disciple and start "spreading the word" about loving yourself, loving God, and—of course—using only the best products. The starter kit, which had convenient small sizes of all the major products, cost Monica thirteen dollars and ninety-nine cents. When she organized her first Ready to Change party—after she'd practiced pronouncing some of the long words the Godmother suggested they use for the motivational talk that apparently *followed* getting the "feel" of the products—she could sell the same kit to her "guests" for twenty-five dollars and fifty cents. Almost one hundred percent profit and—this she could hardly believe—she could keep it *all!* It seemed like the easiest way in the world to make money—except for the world's oldest profession.

Monica smiled all the way back to Newport Beach. How different her thoughts were since she'd left her small apartment that morning, when the sight of Amy Beard cleaning her windows had made her sick with guilt, yet also fiercely jealous that Tom Beard must have been putting "it" into his wife during the night. Well, she would make sure she never slipped again and let him put "it" into her! She *was* ready to change and she would make lots of money "changing." She felt more alive than she could ever remember feeling—mentally going through the list of women she could recruit into the movement. It really was incredible! The Godmother gave them an extra six percent commission on every order put in by those they recruited—that is, if eight or more were recruited. If she could recruit *twelve* disciples—not easy, since she didn't have that many friends—she could become a director, just like that, and get an even higher commission on unit sales, up to ten percent, depending on volume. A unit, she'd learned, consisted of the director and her recruits. Best of all there were fabulous prizes— better than those she'd seen on TV's "Let's Make a Deal"—handed out twice a year at sales meetings for all kinds of different reasons: the best example of self-motivation . . . the best example of kicking a bad habit . . . the best example of total independence.

As she turned into her drive, in her rearview mirror she saw Tom Beard's car right behind her. This was the first test. She parked badly, rushing up the stairs to her apartment where she not only locked the door but put a chair against it. She would prove to the Godmother she didn't need a man . . . didn't need "it."

⌒⌒

"What d' you think? Well edited, I think . . . don't you? This focus group produced some good stuff." Nell didn't reply, didn't like the way Goldo followed her into her bedroom. It was the first time he'd had the audacity to do that. Usually she let him cool his heels in the study while she got herself ready for the cat-and-mouse game they played. She never let him have her every time, only when she was so goddamned in need, every part of her body aching for Johnny, that Goldo's huge relentless prick could make her forget the pain—at least for the twenty minutes or so it took for her to drain the last drop of juice out of him. He was good at exercising her pubo all right. Four orgasms in twenty minutes . . . not many women could ask for more.

The light was flashing on the direct private line to the office, which made Goldo's presence all the more irritating. Did he think she was beginning to depend on him, need him? He would have to learn to think again.

"Goldo, go make yourself a milkshake. I have something urgent here to attend to."

He smirked, then reddened, reminding her of Sylvie. Why on earth did great literature dwell so much on the beauty of the blush? It was not beautifying. It was defacing. Now, the beauty of the *blusher* was entirely a different thing. Because she felt pleased with the day's work at the studio and because Goldo was leaving the room like a whipped dog, Nell picked up the phone with no sense of apprehension. The flashing light always did mean something important, which usually tightened her stomach and made her heart beat faster, but today she was relaxed, not even concentrating.

The sound of Joe Diaz's voice sent such a chill through her body that it was like being doused with cold water. Other than Johnny and her secretary, Diaz was the only one who knew the private number. "I'm in your neighborhood. I want to come over." For once Nell mentally thanked Violana, who had taught her how to remain cool even in the worst emergency. Before she replied she threw her head back to yawn, opening her mouth as wide as she could, feeling her lips strained to the splitting point. Then she lowered her head and began to smile her charmed-life smile. "Well, Joe, what a surprise. I thought you were going to be in Europe for the month. Is anything wrong?"

"Not if you can help it—which I figure you can. Can I come over now?"

Nell hesitated. It would probably relax her to have a good fuck before dealing with Joe. She could hardly believe that there was a time when she would have sent Goldo home and hoped to use Joe Diaz to get rid of her inhibitions. Now, the thought of his little finger even touching her arm made her want to vomit. "I have some of the ad people here . . ."

"*Some?*" His sarcasm was unmistakable. Why had she tried to get away with a lie? It was no good trying to hide anything from Diaz and his secret army. They knew everything, except her love for Johnny. Oh God, she prayed, never let them know that.

As the thought flashed into her mind, Diaz said his name. "Johnny Nesbitt—when did you last see Johnny?" It was such an invasion of her most secret thoughts, such a sickening shock to hear the man she loathed more than anyone utter the name of the only man she now felt she had ever loved, involuntary tears came to her eyes.

No yawn or smile could help her now. "New Year's Eve in London. He went . . . went to Australia . . . and hasn't returned. Lucy, his daughter, has been very ill—meningitis . . ." Her breathing was labored. She had to struggle to speak.

"He's getting in our hair, babe. He's no longer in Australia. He's in Nassau. Get rid of Goldilocks. I'll be over in an hour. It should only take you five minutes to come. Then get your pants on and be ready to talk."

Rage flooded through her as he put the phone down. Scum of the earth. She ground her feet into the carpet, longing for Diaz's face to be there to stamp on.

Experiencing so many emotions in such a short time drained the desire out of her. Without looking in a mirror Nell went into the study, where she noticed with added irritation Goldo had taken off his jacket and tie. "I've got business to attend to now—urgent business. I'll see you at the office tomorrow morning to discuss the silk campaign."

Damn and blast the little creep, he wasn't going to be shaken off so easily. Goldo continued to sit on the sofa sipping a glass of champagne, which really infuriated her. Who had given him permission to open champagne? He was getting above himself. He would have to go. Pity. He was the best ideas-man in the agency—if not in town, apart from his other outstanding asset. She couldn't avoid seeing the bulge at his crotch was larger than ever.

"What happened to the couple who tried to steal a march on you in London? Did they ever bring out their line of silk . . ."

"No." She cut across him. "No chance. We pinned them to the wall." She was incensed that he should have reminded her of Gert and Pierre, which meant reminding her of Sylvie for the second time that day . . . Sylvie, who for the sake of her peace of mind, she had decided she had to forget forever. "Please leave now or I shall be very angry."

There was studied insolence in the way Goldo got to his feet, a deliberate slowness in the way he put down his glass. Not taking his eyes away from hers, he began to stroke her shoulders, her arms, her breasts. Even though she still had on her jacket she could feel his fingers through the fabric, manipulating her skin. She stood ramrod straight, arms at her sides, not moving her eyes or her mouth when he began to kiss her, opening her jacket, the buttons on her silk shirt, assessing correctly that she wouldn't be wearing a bra. Now he used his tongue to stroke her neck, the hollows in her shoulders, her breasts, opening his mouth to draw her large nipples deeply inside. They began to ache with the suction, but she willed herself to stay unaffected, detached, stiff. It was just another version of cat and mouse. Could she still tell him to go once he slipped her skirt and briefs off? Her breath became labored as Goldo lifted her up, up, up with his powerful surfer's arms, his hands on her bare buttocks until his mouth met her cunt and she began to whimper and moan as his tongue probed her labia apart and she knew he was going to make her wait for "it" . . . wait and writhe until she was almost begging, and he also could stand it no longer. He suddenly threw her face-down onto the sofa to stab her with his enormous prick, first in the backside, then in front, over and over for an ecstatic, mind-bending twenty minutes.

"He's picking up the pieces, Madam Nesbitt." Joe Diaz blew a cloud of cigar smoke to the right of her shoulder, his tone as mocking as it usually was. Once she'd been fooled into believing his outwardly light-hearted mood meant he didn't care one way or another whether she agreed to help them or not. Once, before Lucy's kidnapping, she'd even thought he was approaching her for old times' sake, willing to do a "trade"—her help for their money, because she'd made something of herself which he respected. At first Wallace's death—which she may have been able to prevent if she'd turned to tow him back to shore when she'd heard his cries for help—had appeared to be a blessing, for two reasons. His death not only released her from a marriage that had become increasingly untenable but had earned her Joe's thanks in a hefty, tangibly financial way. There had been no way to avoid accepting "Joe's reward," as he'd first laconically described the money put on deposit for her in a numbered, unnamed, account in Nassau. Joe had presumed she had "engineered" Wallace's death and she'd let him think it, not fully comprehending what she was getting herself into, because she was desperate to get the funds she needed for her Ready to Change expansion plans.

It was hard to believe that only a year ago, when she'd received Joe Diaz's "reward for services rendered," she'd even thought Joe was keen on her. Now she knew differently. She was an expendable piece of tail, no more, no less. Expendable or useful. It was up to her to choose.

"What do you mean?" Goldo's services hadn't been wasted. As always after that number of orgasms Nell felt dead inside, still and dead. She knew she looked detached, even when the rat mentioned Johnny's name.

"Johnny Nesbitt, your boyfriend, is working against our interests again. He's meeting with the new Bahamian government today, giving Mr. Prime Minister Pindling and company the much-needed word that he and the Nesbitt money can be behind them if they can have a stake in the gambling expansion plan. Unfortunately we did Mr. Nesbitt a favor when we rattled the saber over Lucy. Now it looks as if the Nesbitts were never in cahoots with the old guard, the Bay Street Boys. 'We believe in majority rule—the Bahamas for the Bahamians' he's saying, and all that kind of crap . . ."

Diaz's vicious face looked more venal than ever. Nell shivered. What was really at the bottom of it all? Why was Johnny such a threat to men like Diaz, who could blow him away with one small silver bullet as effortlessly and casually as he now blew away a puff of cigar smoke? Nell found it hard to accept that Johnny was really interested in gambling concessions in Nassau. That had been Wallace's idea, not Johnny's. He'd told her often enough how much he loathed and detested Nassau after Lucy's ordeal.

As if Diaz read her mind, he snarled, "Your smart-ass boy wonder is an undercover guy for the American government, my dear. He thinks he can pull the wool over our eyes with his wheeler-dealer plans. He's not talking to Pindling because he wants a piece of the casino cake. That's just a ploy to get his feet in the door and his nose into plans that have been in the works for many, many months." Joe gripped her wrist painfully. "We have long-term plans for the Bahamas, baby, plans that will refill your coffers again and again and again . . . so you can end up the richest cunt in the country, but things are at a very delicate stage right now. We don't want mister smart-ass fouling us up, and we don't want to call attention to ourselves either. We want Johnny Nesbitt out of there . . . out . . . without fuss." Nell shuddered at the evil showing on his face as he said with heavy sarcasm, "without bloodshed . . ."

Even as she answered him, her mind raced frantically, trying to understand what long-term plans Joe Diaz could be referring to and what on earth Johnny was trying to "uncover" for the American government. It seemed like a farfetched James Bond story, yet she accepted Diaz's words without question. Everything he had ever told her had always turned out to be true.

"What . . . what do you want me to do? How can I help?" She knew she sounded whipped, defenseless. She was.

"We need another victim. Someone Johnny would not like to see get hurt. Lucy and her mother are in Australia. We want someone nearer to hand, someone more immediate." Diaz pulled an airline ticket out of his pocket. "You leave for New York tonight. Catch the afternoon plane to Nassau tomorrow. A car will be at the airport for your reunion with your 'stepson.' " Again he was heavily sarcastic.

"No!" There was no conviction in her cry. Johnny—to see Johnny again—her heart was leaping with joy. "But it doesn't make sense." She tried to sound composed. "Why would I go to Nassau? How am I supposed to know that he's even there?"

"The manager of the British Colonial Hotel told you, when you called to discuss details for your upcoming sales conference. He casually mentioned he'd seen Johnny on the island—and you decided you couldn't wait another minute to see him after the terrible way you parted."

Nell fell silent, not because she was asking herself how on earth Joe Diaz knew so much. She took that for granted. She was remembering the terrible scene in Johnny's suite at the Savoy on New Year's Eve months before, as she'd clung to him, trying to stop him from packing, trying to stop him from going out the door, hanging on like a leech, despite the fact that he had shown her the cable with the news of Lucy's illness. How ill she was neither of them had known then, but even if she had known, it wouldn't have made any difference. She would still have clung and screamed at him not to leave her.

Weeks later Charlotte had written, a letter that was typically Charlotte, packed with trivia, which Nell had recognized as an olive branch generated by Johnny. The letter and the olive branch it represented had burned in her brain, and so had the distant note in Johnny's voice when she'd finally buried her pride and called him in Perth. He'd sounded so like a stranger that she'd asked him if there was somebody listening. When he'd hesitated, she was sure that as usual he had told her the truth. "No, nobody."

How she'd managed to sound cool, matching his distance with hers, she would never know. After that he'd written once to see if she was interested in a factory he was selling. He'd called another time to ask how she was, still sounding like a stranger, no trace in his voice of the passion they'd shared, no sign he ever thought of their bodies meeting with such ecstatic abandon.

Johnny . . . perhaps if he saw her again. Nell felt sweat on her skin. She thought of the night she'd sat close to Johnny in Eddie Taylor's car, driving through the soft tropical air.

Joe Diaz knew he had her hooked.

"We won't need to kidnap you, Madam Nesbitt. You can tell him this—that for the last few weeks you've been bothered with strange, threatening calls . . . that when you heard he was back in Nassau you were sure the calls had to be from the same Mafia guys who kidnapped Lucy, knowing that part of the deal for Lucy's return was a guarantee the Nesbitts would *never* interfere in their Nassau enterprises again. You became terrified . . ."

Nell interrupted him. "Perhaps he won't care." There was no coquetry, no teasing in her voice. She was not sure Johnny would care.

"He'll care." Joe Diaz puffed out another cloud of cigar smoke. "You're terrified. You beg him to leave well enough alone. You know something terrible will happen if he doesn't." He leaned back and looked at her through half-closed eyes. "On another subject, Madam N, you will soon receive some more 'laundry.' We'd like the same excellent service you gave us before—and you will be rewarded as before—very, very well. I'm glad to see the TV campaign is working so well."

Nell shuddered. Laundry! It was an apt euphemism that Joe Diaz had had to explain to her the year before when, incredibly, again she hadn't really appreciated the significance of beginning such an arrangement. Not that she'd had any option.

As he'd told her then, "We've been dealing with a currency-exchange company, baby. Le Tucosa—does the name mean anything to you?"

Of course it had. Newspapers had been full of the story about Le Tucosa's chairman who'd refused to testify before the President's Commission on Organized Crime as to how his company had supposedly been used by criminals to conceal hundreds of millions of dollars obtained illegally.

There had been a hue and cry for Congress to empower the commission to subpoena the unwilling witness. Then Mr. Le Tucosa had disappeared, despite an extensive manhunt—and, along with him, all the files in his office.

"We obviously can't do business with that organization again," Joe had said as calmly as if he were discussing the most proper Ivy League investment-banking deal. "I suddenly thought of you . . . Ready to Change has to have a huge cash flow, doesn't it, baby? And a regular supply of cash available for your girls' floats?"

Nell remembered she'd groaned inwardly, without realizing how sinister it was all going to become. Of course Diaz was absolutely right. It was essential that her consultants always took a cash float along to their Ready to Change parties so that no sales would be lost because of the oldest excuse in the world, "I don't have any change." That and "I've run out of checks," were the time-honored ways women wriggled out of buying of products.

Joe hadn't waited for her answer. He'd gone straight on, "I don't know why I didn't think of it before. Your company is ideally suited for a laundering operation. It can work like a dream. . . . We'll deliver to you boxes of dough—always in small denominations, which you can use for your floats, commissions, too, petty cash . . . then you give back to us clean dough and"—he'd winked saucily—"we'll pay you a commission no Chinese laundry would believe."

So it had begun. The "dirty" money gained from corruption and evil, drugs, gambling, extortion, had arrived regularly in boxes marked for her personal attention, which she had exchanged for money as clean as donations from the pope.

In the beginning, the enormous fee Joe had paid into her secret account in Nassau had delighted her, but as the "laundry" had increased in volume, the idea of using dirty money for Ready to Change had slowly begun to revolt her. She had to break away, had to cut all ties with this ruthless evil swine, but how . . . how?

Thank God Joe Diaz seemed unaware of her desperate thoughts as, with her trained smile in place, Nell poured him a bourbon and soda. Not so long ago it would have been easy to smile naturally, even to thank God that Diaz had come back into her life, for as they drank together he told her casually that another hundred thousand dollars had just been added to her secret account in the Bahamas . . . money she would use for the continued growth of her business, her crusade.

Now Nell realized how deeply involved she had become—now she knew that as long as she allowed the involvement to continue, she was in danger, deadly danger.

~~~

They sat together, aunt and niece, in the tearoom at Lyon's Marble Arch Corner House. Thirteen years before, they had been there to talk about Gert's future bright with promise as she'd shyly admitted she and Pierre had discussed entering into a lifelong relationship—marriage—as well as the business partnership, which had appeared to be only weeks away from implementation and production.

Now, years later, they talked about the past, and Sylvie learned for the first time why one week after that exciting teatime meeting, she had arrived at her aunt's home to find everything finished, Pierre gone, the lab destroyed, no marriage, no business.

Gert's story of finding Nell and Pierre making love on the dining-room floor would have filled Sylvie's eyes with tears once, but for a long time she had had no tears left to shed. Instead, the smoldering anger she felt for Nell expressed itself in the way she clenched her knife and tightened her lips.

"I could kill her. I may have to kill her if I'm going to be able to go on living with myself." This wasn't an outburst. Sylvie spoke coolly, reflectively. Gert knew she meant every word she said.

There was no way Gert could protest, remonstrate, or even attempt to cool Sylvie's hate. She couldn't try to influence her for the good, rather than for evil, which she knew full well murder to be. Gert couldn't because she knew with certainty that, if she could get away with it, she would kill Nell herself—with pleasure.

It was tragic that here they were, two injured parties, so damaged by an infidel that their basically good, God-fearing natures had begun to change, to move nearer to Nell's own stop-at-nothing character. Nell was responsible for filling their minds with hate, when once hate had been an emotion neither had understood, let alone experienced.

As she looked at Gert, Sylvie marveled that after all her aunt had been through she still hadn't aged that much. Gert had to be nearing fifty, yet looked no more than forty, even younger on some days. Impulsively Sylvie clasped her aunt's hand. "I'm to blame for your unhappiness . . ." Then with sarcasm she stressed, "I brought my 'very best friend' into your life. If I hadn't . . ."

Gert interrupted. "I was a big girl, love . . . and in any case I should have known from the beginning that Pierre was a phony. Do you know something?" A glimmer of the old feisty Gert surfaced. "Although I'd have liked to be another Elizabeth Arden, in one way I'm not sorry that Pierre's grand plan has been scuttled by Nell and her heavyweight lawyers." The glimmer went, to be replaced by scorn. "It's his own bloody fault. The conceited bastard. If he'd taken the proper precautions and patented his formula—but then he says he couldn't because it was 'adapted' from a Rubinstein formula, already patented. But then if *he* couldn't, how could *she?*" Gert grimaced. "Don't answer that. The devil knows how to do everything. I'm 'Ready to Change' into a devil myself if it means getting even with Nell."

Neither of them spoke for the next few minutes as they sipped their tea and dwelled on the events of the past few months. Sylvie, bitter, mistrustful, remembered the scene with Jerome Mossop, the coolness of other supposedly good friends of Ty's, including his great and good friend Cathy, who had never called. She remembered the cold shoulders she'd received in New York, the articles that had used Ty's irresponsibility, spending money before earning it, to emphasize that saving for a rainy day wasn't to be despised. It was to be admired as an honorable way to live—pointing out that Ty Caplan, one of America's most talented composers, on his death, had left so many debts that it meant many rainy days for others.

Sylvie had returned to England determined to throw herself into the job of helping Gert and Pierre launch their skin-care at last. They had registered "GP" as the company name, using their initials in a clever way. The GP Better Skin Bureau counted on the fact that in England a GP, general practitioner, regularly makes house calls on request, just as Gert had been doing for Avon for years.

Everything had been all set to go. Such was Gert's popularity that at least a hundred of her Avon friends all over the country had been willing to desert in order to speed her company on its way. The small but compact line, using Pierre's "adapted" silk-from-the-silkworms formula, had been beautifully designed—simple, striking. They had been only weeks away from the first ad breaking on London's underground, in buses, and in Sunday newspapers—Sunday-newspaper reading being a ritual in England—when Nell had attacked with a restraining injunction. She claimed Pierre had violated her copyright by using the words "real silk" on the GP packaging, had stolen her Ready to Change real-silk formula, protected by patent worldwide, had contravened an agreement signed by him that should he ever start his own business he would never use the direct-sales method. He had denied ever signing anything, screaming and yelling his innocence. Neither Gert nor Sylvie had believed him, because only then had they learned that Pierre and Nell had lived and worked together for almost a year in Montreal. For Gert that knowledge had been worse to bear than all the legal entanglements Nell had begun to weave, which meant the postponement, if not the end, of the GP business before it even got off the ground.

Looking at the thin wedding band on her left hand Gert sighed. "I'd like to divorce him, Sylvie, but what's the point? He doesn't want me to, and he's generous up to a point. I suppose I'm doomed to live in warring wedlock for the rest of my life . . ."

"Can't you fight her, Gert? Remove Pierre altogether from the company, forget silk, and start afresh with another idea. You've got your hero worshippers out there, ready to sell day and night for you no matter what, and you know I'd be out there with them."

Gert sighed again. "I haven't got the heart. My enthusiasm's gone

—quite apart from the money. We don't have a penny to start over. Everything went to get GP off the ground. We owe the bank, the building society, quite apart from the lawyers. I don't even know if we will have enough to keep a roof over our heads. By the time it's all settled, I'll probably end up in the poorhouse like my grandparents."

Plucky little aunt. There were still no tears, no complaints, but now a look of anxiety clouded Gert's face, forcing a primeval note of rage out of Sylvie.

"Oh God, if only I could pay you back every penny. I can't stand it. There has to be justice somewhere in this rotten world . . ." Sylvie smashed her hand on the table. "I'm going to get revenge one day . . . one day . . ." How much more could Nell perpetrate, after stealing her early love, indirectly causing the death of her husband, and now the ruination of her aunt's business? Sylvie had an urge to throw the tea things on the floor, to run ranting, raving, screaming through the restaurant.

As if she knew what was going through her head, Gert put a restraining hand on Sylvie's shoulder. "Sylvie, love, I'm not beaten yet. I'm not going to let that bitch finish me off. She'll get her comeuppance. She has to—let's look on the bright side. What about you? You're a brilliant writer. Why don't you call Smith Maynard? He'd jump at the chance of having you back."

Sylvie shook her head. "I can't go back to the paper. I'm empty inside. In any case, I'm sick of journalism and what it can do to people —the hypocrisy, the innuendos, the manipulation of words that stay just on the right side of the law but imply everything, so the damage gets done. Anyway, I can't write anymore. It's gone. I can't even write a decent letter."

It was true. The sight of her typewriter sickened her. She didn't read the newspapers anymore. They all stood for the pain she'd suffered from the misrepresentation of her life with Ty. She would never call Smith Maynard again and prayed she'd never have the bad luck even to run into him. He had betrayed her, printing Kitty's piece packed with lies—printing it although he'd known she wasn't the despicable gold-hunting witch Kitty had depicted, printing it irresponsibly because it made a good story.

As they walked down Bayswater Road toward the house Gert and Pierre had bought a year after their marriage, Sylvie tried to match Gert's courage. "I'm seeing Frank Forrester tomorrow. He's taking me to lunch . . . says he has an idea he wants to discuss with me. I can't think what it can be." Depression swamped her attempt to try to look on the bright side. "I hope he's not going to ask me when I can pay him back. I don't owe him that much—but it's too much right now. I don't think he'll mention it, but you never know. Of all Ty's friends" —she stressed the word *friends* sarcastically—"Frank Forrester's been by far the kindest. In fact, except for Charles Strouse—he's a brilliant New York composer—Frank's been the *only* kind one."

Sylvie told him so the next day as they sat at one of the best tables in Claridge's main restaurant. She knew now that Frank's offhand manner was only evident when his wife, Natalie, was there, the cool, disinterested note in his voice only apparent when she was within earshot. Sylvie supposed Natalie was frightened her husband might be doing too much for others. She didn't know what to think about anything or anyone anymore.

Now Frank was warm, concerned, putting her mind at rest immediately when she tried to apologize for the fact that her debt to him was still outstanding.

"Before I tell you what I have in mind, I want you to know your debt with me is canceled. I don't want you ever to mention it again. It was peanuts anyway."

Her throat choked up in a way it hadn't since Ty's death. She tried to show him how she felt by clasping his arm. He talked in a desultory fashion at first—about what was new and exciting in the London theater: *Canterbury Tales*, never expected to make it but going strong at the Phoenix; the amazing, spiraling success of the Beatles; and John Lennon and Paul McCartney's latest collaboration in the movie *Yellow Submarine*. He reminisced about his long business association and friendship with Ty, telling Sylvie for the first time that when they'd first met Ty had called him from Rome to announce he had "met my Fate at last." Now the Olympic Games were on again, this time in Mexico City.

"Life goes on." It was a trite statement that would have irritated Sylvie if she'd heard it from anyone other than Frank, but she knew all he'd been saying was meant to encourage her and was probably leading up to his idea.

"Are you going back to Fleet Street or trying journalism in the States?"

"I'm through with it, Frank. Probably journalism is through with me, too. After all, I did go AWOL." She tried to laugh but it came out all wrong.

She looked at him anxiously, hoping now he would bring up the reason for their lunch.

"I'm glad to hear that, Sylvie. You're a talented, resourceful young woman who has been dealt a rotten blow. I've seen the way you deal with people. You have an air of hope, trustworthiness, honesty, about you without being a heavy. You've got a great deal of charm. And that's very appealing."

What on earth was Frank's objective?

The waiter cleared away their plates. Although Sylvie had looked forward to a delicious meal in a top restaurant, the first she'd had in ages, when the carré d'agneau she'd ordered appeared, she'd hardly been able to touch it.

The sweet trolley arrived. "Dessert?"

"No. Coffee, please."

Frank leaned forward earnestly. "It's time you went into something where you can earn *real* money. You can't expect to make a bundle as a salaried employee. Not even as a star writer in Fleet Street. You're not going to get any equity or stock options or even a commission however much you increase the paper's circulation. An annual bonus, handsome though it may be, is about all you can expect, and with the exorbitant tax situation in this country, there's rarely much left for those who earn top dollar. It's a no-win situation, particularly for a woman with no dependents. I want to make you rich, Sylvie dear . . ." Frank squeezed her hand.

"You and me both," Sylvie muttered. Then, alert and excited, she said fiercely, "Frank, I've got to settle Ty's debts. Apart from my survival, I've got to salvage his reputation. Those vultures over there . . ."

He didn't let her finish. "Sylvie, I know more than you realize. Now perhaps you're going to be able to get even."

"How?"

"I've been thinking about you a great deal recently. I happened to be talking to an old pal of mine who was in London last month—one of the most important men in the Bahamas. In fact, he's the real-estate king down there. He's looking for help of a very special kind."

Sylvie looked perplexed, totally unable to think what Frank had in mind.

"To everyone's amazement the old guard is out of power—the Bay Street Boys, the merchant government, who've been running things their way forever and lining their pockets beautifully at the same time.

Well, why not? They brought a lot of money to the islands. Have you ever been there—to the main island of Nassau?"

Sylvie shook her head. "No, Ty didn't like islands . . . resorts . . ."

"It's a paradise. In fact, Paradise Island—that's a tiny cay in Nassau harbor—will open early next year, a multimillion-dollar hotel and casino complex bound to attract hordes of tourists." Frank Forrester snorted. "The blacks—who forced the whites out at the last election—sure are the beneficiaries of that little caper, though they're getting on their religious soapboxes and talking about getting a Royal Commission down to investigate the corruption and the sinister Mafia connection of the old government let in . . ."

Sylvie tried to conceal her impatience. Okay, so what? Civil rights were the issue everywhere. So the blacks were now in charge of their own destiny in the Bahamas, and the Bay Street Boys—the white minority—were out to count their ill-gotten gains in the sun. Who cared? She'd read about it somewhere. How could any of this help her pay off Ty's debts and hold her head high again?

Her fidgeting brought Frank back to the main subject. "Harold Christie persuaded many powerful men to invest in the Bahamas, among them Eddie Taylor, a Canadian multimillionaire, who a few years back drained a swamp at the northwest tip of the island to create a Shangri-la called Lyford Cay, a club that's a haven for American snobs—who want the best there is overseas—and British tax exiles. There's no tax in the Bahamas. Lyford's an enclave of magnificent homes with a luxurious clubhouse at the center, a club with the most exclusive membership in the world. Money alone doesn't get you in . . ." Frank looked at Sylvie whimsically. "D'you see what I'm getting at?"

"Frankly, no."

"Well, Harold's one of the shrewdest wheeler-dealers in the world. He knows that with an untried, inexperienced black government in power for the next five years, the fellow with the big bucks isn't going to rush into buying at Lyford Cay—or anywhere in Nassau for that matter—not unless Harold is out there pitching the properties himself. Harold could sell ice cubes to the Eskimos."

"Are you thinking I could . . . you mean me . . . sell?"

Frank smiled at her warmly. "I called Harold in Nassau last night and told him I thought I had just the right sort of attractive young woman to help him. Someone whose feet are on the ground, who's unlikely to go 'native' on him, as so many Anglo-Saxons tend to do after a few rum punches and tropical nights."

Sylvie took a deep swig of the wine she'd left untasted until now. "Gosh, Frank, I don't think so. I just don't think I could. I've never sold anything to anyone in my life."

Frank put his hand, a strong steady hand, on her shoulder. "Yes, you could, my dear, you could and you will. It's a good time to go there. The club's growing pains are over. The main clubhouse is working like a dream, the golf course is finished . . . and the black government has only been in a few months. They've got to feel their way for a couple of years yet. Pindling, the new prime minister, isn't a dope. He knows he needs tourism to survive—and plenty of American investment. He won't do anything rash to scare the rich away—yet. You've got a couple of years to make a bundle. Who knows, you may also end up with a rich husband to look after your problems forever. That wouldn't be all bad, would it?"

Sylvie couldn't join him in his teasing laugh, but she managed a weak smile. "Frank, I appreciate everything you're saying, but truly—selling real estate—it's so foreign to me, so different from everything I've ever tackled . . . I just don't know . . ." He looked crestfallen that she hadn't immediately grasped the opportunity he was putting her way. Like the majority of men, Sylvie thought to herself, he had already taken for granted the fact she would be overjoyed with his idea —to go to some kind of banana republic or island in the sun to flog probably overpriced, uncivilized chunks of brick and mortar to spoiled, overrich people. All the same, Frank exhibited some sensitivity. He didn't press her, subtly changing the subject away from the anxieties of her future, trying to make her laugh or at least smile over the past and some of the eccentric antics that had earned Ty his "bad boy of Broadway" reputation.

But it was all too soon for her to reminisce—too painful to dwell on the charming but undoubtedly childlike aspect of Ty's complex nature that had now put her into such jeopardy.

She tried to appear at ease, but she was relieved when the long lunch came to an end.

She invented a nonexistent appointment in order to avoid a lift in Frank's car—"only a block away, I'd really like to walk my lunch off, thanks so much, Frank, for everything."

As the sky grew deeply overcast, she turned in the direction of Bond Street and walked resolutely as if she knew exactly where she was going. If only she did. Life was such a quagmire.

In Hanover Street she stopped to look in the window of a large real-estate company, reading the elaborate descriptions of the properties for sale, some marked with equally elaborate prices, others with a discreet "more inquiries inside or please call . . ." To her surprise there were a number of overseas properties featured: "a magnificent villa with inspiring views of the Mediterranean, with easy access to the best shops and restaurants in Cannes" . . . "a tropical Shangri-la, eight spacious rooms built around a heart-shaped pool, Montego Bay, Jamaica," and "Lyford Cay . . ."—wasn't that the place Frank had just been describing? Large hailstones fell as Sylvie studied the sunny photograph above the typed description. It was a poor photo, and an even poorer description. She dismissed them both as if she were considering them for the *Evening Mirror*. As she ran for cover she realized she was thinking she could certainly improve on the *words* used to attract potential customers.

Later that night, back at Aunt Gert's house, Sylvie curled up in the old armchair she had loved so much as a teenager. In her lap was a massive tome she'd taken out that afternoon from the local library. *Welcome to the Bahamas* was its unimaginative title. "Seven hundred islands, a thousand and one cays . . ." She'd wondered what a cay was —pronounced by Frank as "key." Now she knew it was a tiny islet, "lying in an archipelago of multihued seas west and south of the Florida coast . . ." The Bahamas certainly *sounded* like paradise.

Sylvie took the book to bed, reading late into the night about the British colony settled in 1648 . . . about the Duke of Windsor's governorship during the war . . . about the dreadful, still-unsolved murder of Sir Harold Oakes, one of Nassau's leading real-estate developers, and—echoing Frank Forrester—about the discrimination perpetrated against the black Bahamians up until the end of the war when they'd made a test case of the UN Declaration of Human Rights. Her eyes began to close as she tried to take in more facts: ". . . irrational and emotional stirrings automatically confronted the rising economic prosperity after the war, while the genius of Stafford Sands as head of the Development Board introduced two important and growing sources of income—tourism and foreign investment, very attractive in view of the Bahamas' tax-free status."

Tax-free. Her sleepiness disappeared as she remembered that was a fact Frank had emphasized. Everything she earned—*if* she ever earned a sou—would be tax-free! It seemed too good to be true. What had Frank said? She would receive a six-percent commission . . . a tax-free six percent on hundreds of thousands of dollars, for apparently no properties at Lyford Cay were less than one hundred thousand, and most, Frank had pointed out, cost much more. She would be able to pay off Ty's debts. She would be able to subsidize Gert's business. She would be rich enough to solve all her problems. But could she use the same tenacity to pursue potential clients that had come in such good stead when searching out stories for Fleet Street? Did she have the patience, the charm, the ability to sell that Frank seemed to think she had? The more she thought about the idea the more attractive it became, particularly when she contrasted the hailstorm she had been caught in that afternoon with the weather she could expect in the Bahamas. It had been thirty-six degrees or thereabouts all day in London and she was still chilled to the bone, whereas apparently it had been eighty-four degrees in Nassau. "A fairly usual temperature in winter," Frank had informed her.

She couldn't sleep after that. Around four o'clock—"the low tide of the night," as Ty had always described that bleak hour—sure she'd lost the chance to "give it a go," she felt bitter tears come to her eyes. When conscious thought was finally blotted out, it was nearly dawn and snow had taken the place of hailstones.

"Frank, I'd like to talk some more about Nassau—about the real-estate job . . ." Her anxiety over the phone made her sound unnaturally tense, but she needn't have worried. Frank sounded delighted, even relieved. "That's swell—another lunch?"

"Why don't I come to your office? I've got to get plugged into something fast . . ."

As she left Frank's office the next day, Sylvie was smiling as she reflected the only "sales" experience she could truthfully say she possessed had been gained when she was thirteen years old at a makeshift roadside stall selling her homemade (and too-bitter) lemonade one hot summer day. Luckily—incredibly—the subject of her experience had never come up. Frank had spent half an hour describing the way Lyford Cay real estate worked and then and there had placed a call to his old friend, real-estate tycoon Harold Christie, hoping to introduce them over the phone. He hadn't been there, but Frank assured her that he would "work everything out" and call her as soon as he contacted Christie.

As she arrived at the Bayswater Road house the phone was ringing and it was Frank. "It's all arranged. I've booked you an open ticket to Nassau. As soon as you've settled whatever you have to settle here, call me and I'll call Harold again with your date of arrival. He's willing to give you a three-month trial, all expenses paid, living in the staff quarters at Lyford Cay. I've never seen the staff digs—but I can tell you one thing—everything I have seen at Lyford Cay is five star and then some."

"I can't thank you enough. I hope I didn't seem ungrateful the other day, but the idea of selling real estate—houses, land, to multi-millionaires—the idea took some getting used to. All the same, the thought of earning six percent on those kind of prices. . . . I suppose I'm ready to give it a go. After all, what have I got to lose? I'll try my best not to let you down, Frank."

That night with sleep elusive again Sylvie's thoughts returned to the hot summer when she'd sold lemonade in the East End of London. That had been the first summer she had been proud to call herself "Nell's best friend"—Nell! If everything came to pass as Frank Forrester predicted—providing she worked hard enough (and she certainly would do that)—she would at least earn enough money to achieve the one objective that far outweighed all others. She would have enough money to get even and somehow to get her revenge against Nell.

9

Nassau,
March 28, 1969

A masterpiece of a house in immaculate condition, this residence with three hundred feet of ocean frontage has been designed by one of the world's leading architects to combine European style and elegance with the finest of modern construction and American efficiency. High ceilings, marble floors, wide corridors, all add to its very special charm, one gracious room flowing into the other—from the living room to formal dining room to sumptuous patio, which in turn leads to a spectacular pool and pool house. A step-down, dome-ceilinged library has its own secluded patio, as do all the guest rooms in the right wing of the house. The master bedroom, bathroom, and dressing room all have sweeping ocean views. Exclusive to the New Providence Development Company. Sylvie Caplan will be happy to answer your questions and arrange an appointment to view this unique property . . .

Sylvie pushed the proof of what was going to be an expensively printed brochure to one side. Through her office window she could see a tantalizing slice of aquamarine sea and occasionally a white sail sailing by. It wasn't easy to work on a day like this, but then nearly every day was the same in Nassau, with no sudden temperature drops, no impossible humidity, and, at Lyford Cay—where intensive spraying went on every dawn and dusk—not even many bugs.

Sylvie yawned sleepily. She felt she was living in a cocoon, a paradisiacal cocoon of bright green lawns, softly waving palms, green-blue seas and fragrant flowers of every hue. Sometimes before properly waking up, luckily for only one or two nightmare moments, she thought she was still in the upstairs guestroom of Aunt Gert's house off the Bayswater Road. But she wasn't dreaming. She was really living in the Bahamas and had the best of both worlds, living rent-free in a Lyford Cay staff cottage, yet not considered one of the staff, so not subject to the many rules strictly imposed on the employees of "the most exclusive private club on earth."

On her arrival four months before, Sylvie had been amused to be given the Lyford Cay staff handbook as a "courtesy" by the club manager.

"Here you will have the opportunity personally to meet distinguished people from all over the world. You were selected from a great many applicants because we feel you have the special qualities necessary to become a member of the Lyford Cay family. I sincerely hope you will enjoy your association with us for many years to come . . ."

It was, to say the least, an improvement on the welcome usually proffered to those in service-oriented businesses. No wonder every day or so Sylvie heard anxious mumblings that with the new black government, working visas would probably soon be revoked, which would mean the mostly white personnel—waiters, housekeepers, maids, front-desk managers—who had the opportunity "personally to meet distinguished people," were going to be sent home, away from Shangri-la. It hadn't taken more than a few days for Sylvie to understand why there was so much underlying tension about the situation. Who on earth would want to be sent away from paradise?

Although the beauty of so many things on the island—the birds, the exotic flowers, the sunsets, and the famous green flash that could sometimes be seen as Old Man Gold sank below the aquamarine horizon—occasionally intensified her aching loneliness and the loss of Ty's great love, at other times she found the beauty soothing, even remedial.

Best of all, however—to her amazement—Frank Forrester had been right. She *could* sell and enjoyed selling. It was therapy. She'd gone to an intensive real-estate course in London for a month before arranging her passage. From the first day she'd asked more questions than anyone else, pursuing the subject as if she were on a hot scoop, and she had found herself thoroughly engrossed.

Instead of the lonely occupation of the writer, selling real estate was a "people business." She didn't have time to mope, to dwell on the past. She was constantly viewing, searching, arranging, trying to match client to property. And she'd quickly found the job was much more fun than the training course. Much more educational, too, as she confided to Madge Riskin, an Australian of uncertain age who supervised the brigade of maids for the fifty-one bedrooms and seventeen cottages that comprised the club accommodations.

"Some of the 'distinguished' people I've been showing around lately could do with a fast course in basic good manners." It hadn't taken her long to recognize "old money," the breeding and quiet unostentatiousness that went with it. It was apparent in the courtliness of one multimillionaire from a place she'd never heard of outside Chicago, who rushed to open doors, apologized for taking up so much of her time, and sent her flowers the day he signed to buy a hundred-thousand-dollar plot of land on the bay.

"Madge, it's so ironic! As he comes from Chicago I'd expected the worst, but he was a dream. In direct contrast, I might say, to the banker I'd been asked to be especially nice to—because of his millions and what is apparently called an Ivy League background and Mayflower antecedents. He turned out to be a bully. Unfortunately he will be the neighbor of Mr. Nice Guy from Chicago—if big mouth ever actually builds a house. You soon learn who the *real* people are—to separate the wheat from the chaff."

With two commissions, one following the other, just a month after she started work, she had been ecstatic, thinking how easy it was to sell. Since then, however, business had been in the doldrums. Now two or three "special" houses had suddenly come on the market, the owners sure the Bahamas' first black prime minister, Pindling, was going to make life impossible for any nonblack. Harold Christie was bringing down a charter-load of possible buyers from the States, so Sylvie had been told to expect "a good end of season."

The house she was featuring in the brochure was one of her favorites. For the first time since Ty's death, Sylvie felt a surge of her old adrenaline. If she worked around the clock, and could get permission to show properties in other parts of the island, not just at exclusive Lyford Cay, she felt she was bound to make sales. She had already made reconnaissance trips to get to know Nassau by car, just as once she had set out to discover the City of London on foot.

There was no time for sunbathing on the glorious golden beaches, no time to play tennis or golf at Lyford Cay's magnificent new facilities. No time, and no invitations either, to the lavish parties Sylvie heard about through the staff grapevine—parties that went on night after night in the palatial clubhouse and private homes scattered throughout the four-thousand landscaped acres. She didn't care. She was consumed with paying off Ty's debts and proving she didn't need "favors" from loathsome men like Jerome Mossop. There was also hardly a day that went by when she didn't vow retribution against Nell.

The day she was late for an appointment to show her favorite house to one of the tycoons brought down from the U.S. by Harold Christie, was the day she met Oliver Burt. She had been delivering an urgent package for Eddie Taylor in town—volunteering when no one else was available in the manager's office.

Her watch had stopped. Then as she passed the turnoff to the airport and started to pick up speed on the one straight stretch of road to the club, the old Ford she'd been using from the development office started to wobble precariously. A puncture! She couldn't believe her bad luck after being such a good samaritan. Tire changing hadn't been part of the real-estate course either.

Sylvie sat on the curb, close to weeping for the first time in months, visualizing Mr. Tycoon cursing her under his breath for cutting short his golf or tennis game or curtailing his time on the beach. All chances of the fat commission she'd dreamed about—six percent of four hundred thousand dollars—went down the drain in front of her.

Her misery was replaced by fear as she became aware of someone standing over her. With large scared eyes she looked up to see an exceptionally tall black man with a ferocious-looking scar indenting his chin. She got up hurriedly. He started to laugh. "I'm not going to bite, missy. What's your trouble—got a flat, have you?"

She nodded, not sure whether to start running down the road. Little good it would do against his long legs. He took no more notice of her, lifting up the trunk of the old Ford to take out the spare tire. Within fifteen minutes she was back in business, the car roadworthy again.

"I don't know how to thank you, Mister . . . Mister . . ." She knew she was blushing.

"Burt. Oliver Burt at your service, ma'am."

There was no other car parked on the road. No bike. No mule cart. Mr. Burt had appeared out of nowhere. "Can I . . . give you . . . a . . . . a lift?"

"As a matter of fact you can. I'm going to the Lyford Cay Club to meet a fat cat or two. Do you know where that is?"

Now she laughed with him. "I certainly do. That's where I'm living —working—selling real estate. Hop in."

Where he'd come from she didn't know or care, and he didn't offer any explanation. By the time she dropped him in front of the lofty clubhouse pillars, she realized her puncture could have been a lucky break, for Oliver Burt was a back-bencher in Pindling's new government and, it appeared, like Premier Pindling, was a lawyer, "educated overseas—in London, where I would like to hazard a guess you come from, ma'am. Would you like a beer one evening?"

Yes, she would. She gave him her card. He probably wouldn't call, she told herself as she hurriedly drove back to the main club road, but if he *did*, then it could present a wonderful opportunity to find out what was really going to happen to all the white landowners and club employees on the island.

She was intrigued, looking through her mirror, to see the club's usually condescending manager give Oliver Burt an effusive welcome. Sylvie decided then and there that if Oliver didn't call her for a beer, she would call him for an interview. Why not write an article . . . she stopped the thought before it took hold. How on earth had that idea come into her head? She was through with journalism. She had to thank Frank Forrester for introducing her to real estate. As he'd predicted, she'd made more money with two sales in two weeks than she'd taken home in six months even during her heyday at the *Evening Mirror*.

Sylvie had been right. Mr. Tycoon—more usually known as Alec Boyar—had been cursing Sylvie Caplan vociferously for being late.

Alec Boyar's temper had a short fuse even on the best of days, and this had not been one of them, starting with the atrocious hard-boiled egg he'd been served by a half-witted maid at 7:00 A.M. If there was anything he abhorred it was hard-boiled eggs, and he'd even brought down his three-minute egg timer, too. Dealing with the infernal Bahamian telephone system for the next five hours and getting nowhere had convinced him he should never have come. Well, what else had he expected? How Christie had ever talked him into coming he didn't know . . . well, yes, he did know. Good times in the Bahamas were not over yet by far. He'd missed getting in on the Freeport deal where profits for the developers, Wallace Groves and Lou Chesler, had been phenomenal. He was lucky that Groves and Chesler owed him one—at least he'd *thought* he was lucky. He wasn't a hundred percent sure now that he'd actually arrived on this so-called jewel of the Caribbean to take his first real look-see at an investment he'd persuaded Groves and Chesler to let him make in Bahamas Amusement Limited. That was another genius accomplishment chalked up by Groves, who in 1964 had been given by the Bahamian government the exclusive right for ten years to operate casinos on the entire island of Grand Bahama. The company was also to own, operate, and control all gaming equipment and furnishings. Wow! It was a license for making money, or it had been during the rule of the United Bahamian Party, who until the last election had successfully kept the blacks out of office, despite the fact that blacks made up eighty percent of the population.

Now it was a different deck of cards. The blacks were in and the white Bay Street Boys were out. God knew, they'd had a long run.

No conflict-of-interest act had ever been passed in the Bahamas, a fact so incredible it was laughable. No wonder the Bahamian government had been known forever as the "merchant government." All the motherfucking ministers, thought Alec with a grimace, even the prime minister, had had their own thriving businesses on Bay Street and had seen "no conflict of interest" in giving themselves lucrative government contracts—one hand helping the other.

But the introduction of gambling had been the most lucrative move of all, attracting all kinds of gate-crashers to the party. Well, they'd dealt fast with Old Man Nesbitt, and luck had been on their side. It had been helpful that Stafford Sands, the minister of finance and tourism, had received the brunt of criticism from the world's press for under-the-table dealings with mobsters. The *Saturday Evening Post* had called it "Shadow of Evil on an Island in the Sun." But had old Nesbitt's adopted son Johnny stopped interfering in their long-term plans as Diaz seemed to think? Only time would tell . . . and, he for one, didn't intend to let *much* time elapse.

All these facts passed through Boyar's meticulous mind as he waited, fumed, and fretted for Christie's salesperson to arrive. She was twenty-five minutes and forty-two seconds late when he saw her Ford arrive outside at last. In another three minutes and eighteen seconds Alec Boyar had decided he would call Harold Christie and demand Miss Caplan be fired and replaced by someone "who knows who I am!"

Unwittingly Sylvie saved herself from this condemnation with her opening remark. "Oh, sir, I know how terribly valuable your time is. I had a puncture. I am so sorry for the inconvenience . . ." Perhaps if she hadn't sounded so English, so sincerely apologetic, a black mark would have gone against her name in Harold Christie's evaluation book, but as Frank Forrester had accurately predicted, there was something about Sylvie's open, trusting, freckled face—which Pa and Ma O'Halloran had been comforted by back in the fifties in the East End of London—that touched Alec Boyar's usually totally suspicious mind.

He believed her story of the puncture and she was cute-looking, not exactly pretty, but cute like a kitten. There was something about her that reminded him of his mother sitting in a Miami condo surrounded by all the good things his money could buy—which was a great deal.

Sylvie didn't know she had been magically exonerated. "This man —as sleek as a seal," as she described him in a letter to Aunt Gert, "wasn't about to let me off the hook. He lectured me for about ten minutes on the importance of expecting the 'unexpected' in life." Sylvie appeared to hang on his words, which Alec Boyar also liked. He didn't know that long ago Sylvie had learned when it was more important to listen than talk.

"He 'allowed' me—that's the only way I can describe it, Aunt Gert, to show me that glorious house on the beach I told you about in my last letter. Although it has a price that's just a telephone number, for all the sense it makes to me, if any *house* can be worth four hundred thousand dollars (yes, you read me right), this one is. It was obviously built by people in love with this magical island. The ocean, the colors, the scents, everything comes *inside* without any of the problems. It's the easiest, most practical house to run, too. Well, to get back to Mr. Boyar, he's apparently the largest box maker in America. I haven't dared ask if that means coffins. I don't think he has a sense of humor."

Alec Boyar had nearly married three different women, all of whom had paid for the mistake of thinking his sense of humor did exist. He had laughed a lot when they'd presented him with unexpected bills for exotic furs, limo hire that often seemed to include the cost of the limo itself, room extensions, and even the latest bathroom gadgetry (turning tubs into Roman spas for "neat sexual experiences").

He'd laughed. He'd paid. He had then moved them out of his life, one by one. They had all been showgirls with similar statistics and

lack of vision, although they'd disguised it so well—or so he'd thought
—he'd imagined he'd chosen three very different women until Judgment Day.

"Expensive, Sylvie, but thank God I never got really hooked." It
was the third time she had shown him the house on the beach, holding
her breath that six percent of four hundred thousand dollars was now
within reaching distance. She had hardly opened her mouth since
their first encounter, sensing Alec Boyar was a man who had either
never met a woman of intelligence—and so didn't expect a woman to
be able to hold a decent conversation—or who wasn't prepared to
listen to any woman, however bright.

It was a bit of both, she decided, after the third visit when they
watched the green flash together from the porch of the tiled patio—
or rather she watched the extraordinary sunset phenomenon, while
Alec Boyar held forth on "all that the white leaders of this nation have
accomplished." He meant the Bahamas, she quickly learned, at first
thinking he must mean either the U.S. or the U.K.

"Who would have come to this swamp—because that's what it was,
Mrs. Caplan, a swamp—until the likes of Harry Oakes, Harold Christie, Eddie Taylor, Wally Groves, and Lou Chesler put in their hard-
earned money? They put it in because dedicated guys like Stafford
Sands gave them an assurance they'd *make*, not lose on their investment. And why am I here, you ask?" He turned to look at her accusingly, although she hadn't said a word, let alone dared to ask such a
question. "Because someone of my standing, my leadership, my
wealth, my commitment to sanity has to continue the work started by
those enlightened fellas—someone has to counter the lack of confidence in the Bahamas now that these black morons are in, morons
who haven't a business brain between 'em."

"I met Oliver Burt . . ." It was Sylvie's first remark in at least ten
minutes of uninterrupted soliloquy.

"Oliver Burt?"

"The seal," as Sylvie described Boyar to her aunt, to Madge, and to
herself, seemed to see her as a person for the first time. "How d'you
know Burt?"

Some instinct told Sylvie not to be too forthcoming, not to imply a
knowledge of Burt she didn't possess, but in any case Boyar didn't let
her answer. "I'm aware of Burt"—and then—"I s'pose if you work for
Christie you're bound to know a lot of people I know. Still, I'd like to
hear your opinion of Burt sometime. I can tell you're pretty smart for

a woman. Like my mother, you have that weirdo second sense some broads have . . ."

Despite his incredible statements and the mixed-up language that Sylvie knew would irritate most people she knew, for some inexplicable reason she felt sorry for Alec Boyar. He may be a multimillionaire maker of boxes, someone she and other people in the development company had been told to make a fuss of, but underneath she felt he was really a lonely, misguided little boy.

Oliver Burt called one night when she'd just washed her hair and was soaking her feet in a hot salt-water solution. It had been a particularly trying day, dealing with a series of would-be house buyers and no takers, despite hours of stair climbing, marble-hall traversing, garden walking, and beach strolling.

Her voice reflected her exhaustion, although she tried to hide it. Surely a month had passed, if not two months, since their chance meeting. She'd almost forgotten about him.

"I'm here at Lyford," Burt said, "but I can tell it's the wrong night. How about a beer on Wednesday?"

A reprieve. "Yes, I'd love it."

When Boyar came by the office the next day to look over brochures of other available properties, she made a point of telling him she was going to see Oliver Burt. By now Sylvie had decided Boyar wasn't serious. Why would he want a house on the beach anyway? He never seemed to go near the ocean, and although the house she loved was one of the few with its own dock for a good-sized boat, he didn't seem interested in sailing, fishing, or anything except getting back to his boxes. She threw out the news of the Wednesday-night invitation in the hope of keeping in contact with him. If he was intrigued, perhaps in some way she could interest him in another property. She wasn't too hopeful, but she wasn't giving up entirely—yet.

To her disappointment Boyar didn't react, except with a grunt. Perhaps it was just as well.

Would she be shocked when she saw Burt again? Was he as black and tall as she remembered him? By the time Wednesday came around she was thoroughly sorry she had agreed to the beer. She felt she already knew enough about the corruption in Bahamian politics and endless infighting for position. What she didn't know, she could live without.

All day she tried to think of an excuse to get out of what was just an innocuous meeting over a beer. All the same it bothered her. If it hadn't been for Madge egging her on to find out what she could about the revoking of foreign work permits, she would have called the date off by lunchtime.

By four o'clock when she usually left the office she was still thinking she'd plead a migraine headache, when the phone rang and Alec Boyar was on the line. He didn't waste any time getting to the point. "Are you seeing Burt tonight?"

"Yes."

"Find out if he's still in touch with Johnny Nesbitt—or Nesbitt with him, then come to see me about the beach house at nine sharp, tomorrow morning. I've decided to take it." The line went dead, as Sylvie, numb with shock, stared out at the sliver of aquamarine sea.

~~~

"What's sauce for the goose is sauce for the gander. The old-boys' network, godfather-mentor approach has worked for men as they've moved up the corporate ladder, but I believe although able, hardworking women need male mentors, there's a *greater* need for corporate 'godmothers' who know what the corporate unspoken scenario can be on the way to the top, because they've *been there*. They know what works and what doesn't work, when to be aggressive and when to let a matter pass."

Barbara Walters received the signal it was time to bring the interview to a close. She wasn't the most successful woman on television for nothing. She chose not to ask her last question, sensing the Godmother would answer it without being asked.

"Women have come a long, long way, but only when corporations show in deed as well as in memo that the upper reaches of management are open to females will women be integrated into higher job slots in more than isolated instances. Ready to Change isn't a philanthropic course. It is a viable, eminently successful business, selling the finest beauty products in the world. I am proud of being the founder, chairman and chief executive officer, but I am prouder still of being viewed as Godmother to my RTC disciples who know my main objective is to help prepare them for *any* career opportunity."

Barbara Walters led her on. "Even if it means an opportunity with one of your competitors—with Avon, Mary Kay, Revlon, Estée Lauder?"

Nell's now-celebrated smile came to her face. She used it straight into the camera. "Even if my disciples leave to go to one of my 'competitors,' as you call them—if it means true advancement."

"You were wonderful, Nell. Inspiring, motivating. Everyone at Ready to Change will have tears in their eyes."

Nell squeezed Johnny's hand as they sat closely side by side in the Cadillac taking them out to Kennedy Airport. His praise was music, but Nell wanted more, much more. After all this time Johnny still displayed a restraint that frustrated and baffled her. She deprecated herself for the one weakness she was unable to master. It meant she wasn't in total control of herself, which had to have an effect on her performance as Godmother to the increasing number of women, now in the tens of thousands, who were willing to show her in myriad marvelous ways that they were ready to change. As far as Johnny was concerned, she obviously was not. If any of her girls ever knew . . . Nell could feel herself shudder deep inside. She knew she shouldn't allow the slightest kink in her will power. It had taken her years to build up a barrier against feeling *anything* for a man again, feelings which once had demonstrated themselves in a servile willingness to give herself so totally that her body had been violated and she had given birth to a child who would never know it had inherited her genes of genius.

Although it was like pulling a piece of her flesh away, Nell deliberately shifted her position to move into the corner of the car, turning her legs to rest against the car door.

Johnny regarded her quizzically. "Now, what's troubling you?"

She knew her expression didn't reveal the passion of her thoughts. Quietly, calmly, as if she were indeed talking to a stepson who needed a stepmother's guidance, she replied, "I'm thanking God yet again for making you listen to me—and deciding to give up your your . . . mission in the Bahamas . . ."

Johnny didn't answer, turning to look out at the uninspired dreary dwellings on the airport route. She didn't mind his silence. At last she felt sure after his return to the U.S. that he meant what he said. He would no longer pursue his "business interests" in the Bahamas. He would give up what he had admitted to her had been the real reason for his return to the island he actually loathed—to find out what lay behind Lucy's kidnapping and what he suspected was a link to Wallace's death, despite a neatly signed death certificate stating his step-father had "accidentally drowned."

Their "reunion," as Joe Diaz had sardonically predicted, had been emotional, tearful. It had not been sexual. Johnny hadn't given her one opportunity to be alone with him, and because of her anxiety, her sense that one of Diaz's men if not Diaz himself was somewhere watching, waiting to pounce, she had repressed her desires, putting all her energies into her story of persecution by phone, fear for her life, for his life, fear of the unknown.

"What are you trying to do, Johnny?" She hadn't had to pretend that she was anxious. She wasn't only trying to penetrate Johnny's phlegmatism for Diaz's sake. She had to know for herself what he was really after, in order to protect him. She had to find a way to make sure he realized dangerous people were aware of his intrusion, his interference, that they were on to the fact he was an undercover man.

Johnny had answered her frantic questions with questions of his own, veiled in what he kept expressing as "my very real concern for your safety." He seemed to swallow whole her explanation for her sudden appearance in Nassau. He knows I love him, Nell had told herself bitterly as he'd moved his hand away when she'd attempted to cover it with her own. Her command of herself had never been so perfect. I'm a true graduate of Violana's academy, was her next bitter thought. She'd gone on, persistent for real answers. "I don't understand, Johnny. You told me that part of the deal for Lucy's return was a promise the Nesbitts would stay out of the casino business, wouldn't try to undo any of the deals these shady characters had set up. Why are you back here again when you told me how much you loathe the place?"

He hadn't answered her then, but in only twenty-four hours it seemed he'd come to the conclusion that whatever he was pursuing wasn't worth it. "I'm going to cut my losses and come back with you," he'd said.

It was only on their way back to California that he'd started to unbend, to lose the tense control showing on his face, even to squeeze her hand a little during the long journey. "For some time now, Nell, I've been working with a brilliant young guy in Nassau, trying to find out who was really responsible for Lucy's"—he'd hardly been able to get the word out—"disappearance." His grim expression had churned her up inside. If he ever found out about her involvement . . . she'd stopped the train of thought before it could show on her face.

Johnny had gone on, "Lucy was taken as a warning—but it wasn't only because of dad's interest in the casinos. The money in gambling is chicken feed in comparison to the money the Mafia are going to get from other plans they've set in motion . . ."

"What plans?"

Johnny had shaken his head, increasingly leaden, gloomy. "I can't tell you about it, Nell. Now that I realize how much danger I've put you in, I've got to reassess everything. I'm going to step back—let my contact down there follow up on the very real leads I've found that can—and *will*—upset the bloody swines' apple cart . . ." He'd refused to say much more, except she'd then learned he'd been back to Nassau far more often since the kidnapping than she'd ever realized. Terror had frozen her tongue, immobilized her limbs. Johnny had never returned to the subject again, moving easily back into his old slot as her most trusted advisor and comforter at the Ready to Change headquarters, making her realize in only one day how much she needed him, not only for her emotional health, but for every practical reason too.

She hadn't heard a word from Diaz in the nearly seven months since they'd returned together to Los Angeles. The more time that passed the more relaxed she'd grown. She had done the job Diaz had asked her to do. Why should she hear from him further? Certainly not to receive any thanks. All she longed for was endless silence from that quarter, the silence of the dead.

Nell had a speech to write on the plane, a balance sheet to study of a manufacturing plant she was considering buying, and the résumés of two experienced international sales executives, one of whom she intended to hire to start up the Ready to Change operation overseas, first in England, then in Germany. Not France. From observations and her own instincts she knew France was a poor bet for a direct-sales company. The French didn't open up their homes easily to their nearest and dearest, let alone acquaintances and people they hardly knew—not even for profit.

As Nell settled back for the lengthy journey west, she longed to put her head on Johnny's shoulder and let everything go to hell. This time she didn't ask herself what was wrong with her. She knew. She was tired, physically and mentally tired of the responsibilities of her life. The feeling would pass. She was becoming one of the most powerful women in America, which automatically meant one of the most powerful woman in the world, self-made, self-taught, not powerful because of any inherited empire. She had fought for her power, was still fighting, would probably always have to fight.

It was the attraction she felt for Johnny, a festering canker, that made her tired, clogged her spirit, choked her strength. Did she have to "kill" him, as in her own mind, she'd "killed" his stepfather, to gain her release and grow as she was destined to grow?

"Why are you laughing? You're in such a strange mood today." Johnny covered her hand with his, making her laugh still more as she thought how incredulous he would be if he could read her thoughts. "I'm laughing with happiness." Nell smiled deeply into his eyes.

"Are you happy? No longer scared of things that go bump in the night?" Johnny's voice was light, but there was an intensity about his expression that unnerved her.

She was right to be unnerved. For the first time since her rush down to the Bahamas, Johnny started to interrogate her, and it went on and on during the five-hour flight. "When was the last call?" "What exactly was it that frightened you so much that you decided to fly down to see me?" "Was it always the same voice—the exact words—the exact threat?"

There had been few questions from him in the Bahamas. Now he was asking her all the things she'd expected to have to answer months before. Then she'd been prepared, schooled. Her Violana training, thank God, still held her in good stead. Her voice was steady. Her expression was troubled but in no way betrayed the extent and reason for her anxiety. She tried to wriggle out of answering most of his questions. "I'd like to forget, Johnny. Can't we put it behind us, now that you've decided not to dwell on the past, now that you're out of the line of fire?"

It was a nightmare trip. Nell felt sure she hadn't handled the situation well. Johnny knew what an extraordinarily retentive memory she had—almost as good, Wallace used to joke, as his own. So how could she expect him to believe her when she pleaded she couldn't remember exactly what was said or how the voice sounded? Was it her imagination that he sounded increasingly suspicious?

She tried to change the subject, but Johnny wouldn't be budged, returning to it like a dog nibbling at every vestige of flesh left on a bone. Worse, he insisted on going over with her step by step the day of Lucy's kidnapping and then the days before Wallace's death. Had there been anything out of the ordinary? Anything she'd noticed that made Wallace act differently? Only when the pilot announced they were getting ready to land in Los Angeles did Johnny stop his relentless questioning, leaning back in his seat with his eyes shut, his lips tight together in a grim line.

The cold tone of his voice rang in Nell's ears all night as she tossed and turned in her king-sized bed, no sleeping pill able to shut out the torment of her thoughts. Her bed had never seemed so huge or so empty.

~~~

Why were they both so interested in Johnny Nesbitt? Sylvie was mystified as Alec Boyar refilled her glass and repeated, "Tell me *exactly* the way Burt phrased that remark about Nesbitt."

Sylvie wrinkled her brow in concentration. It had seemed such an innocuous remark. Had she missed a key word, a key phrase? "He said . . . I think he said . . . Johnny Nesbitt is a good man . . ." She couldn't help a trace of sarcasm creeping into her voice. "He is one of the few who can see the wood for the trees—that he's clever enough to know when to be overlooked and when to be looking over . . ."

Boyar leaned back, puffing on his second Havana cigar of the night. He enjoyed looking at this cherub-faced girl with the freckles on her nose and such amazing knockers on her slim, trim body. Over the months he'd begun to be fond of her, impressed with her neat mind. She didn't give him any B.S. and he loved that. What luck she'd met up with Burt and passed on everything he asked about the arrogant bastard. Burt had it coming to him, but only at the right and proper time. Not until they knew exactly what Nesbitt was up to would Burt receive his—and young Nesbitt meant trouble, that was for sure.

Unfortunately, Nesbitt and his oversure asshole of an informer couldn't just be put away—poof, poof—in the good old ways of the past. Nassau couldn't afford another scandal, let alone another unsolved murder. There couldn't be anything like the brouhaha that had smirched Nassau's reputation following Sir Harold Oakes's bludgeoning back in the forties, when even the governor, the effete Duke of Windsor, hadn't been able to curb the probing of the world's press. Now, more than at any other time in their history, the Bahamas *had* to present an impregnable aura of stability. It was difficult enough to present *any* picture of stability to a suspicious world with Pindling in power. They had to scare Nesbitt away, and perhaps through this little chick, Sylvie Caplan, he could make sure Burt got the message to head Nesbitt off for good.

Joe Diaz had reported he had a fancy lady friend, who had influence of some kind over Nesbitt, but Alec knew better. Nesbitt was still sniffing around, playing both sides of the fence, friendly on the surface with Pindling, yet supporting Burt in his effort to split Pindling's party. God knew, it wasn't difficult. The blacks liked nothing better than fighting among themselves. Idiots that they were, they couldn't see that they'd never had it so good, that by bringing more havoc to the island they'd be killing the goose, the golden goose of tourism, and their better standard of living along with it. But just why was Nesbitt so busy? What was he *really* after? It was inconceivable that he was on to their real game . . . and yet . . . Boyar ran his hand nervously over his well-cut jacket, so well-cut that no one could guess his gun was beneath it—with him, as usual, wherever he went.

As the evening went on and a glorious full moon turned the velvety night into a silvery day, Alec felt unusually relaxed, even expansive. This little Sylvie had an uncanny ability to lull his fears, take his insecurities away. He felt smarter, taller, totally in command—even in this crazy place—in her presence. He found himself telling her about his early days, his struggles with his father, who had "never understood him." He painted a fascinating picture about his way to the top and how he got into the "box business," conveniently forgetting the number of people who—in his way—had had to be carted off in his larger-sized cartons.

Sylvie was enthralled. Alec exuded power, vitality. Even his roughness—which frequently broke through the all-too-thin veneer of what he imagined was sophistication—touched rather than appalled her. She knew about rough times all right. She knew about struggling to the top. She was about to tell him that flinty, pencil-sharp stiletto heels could inflict just as much damage as the kicks he told her he'd received from steel-tipped cowboy boots, when some inner caution told her to stay quiet.

They stayed up talking till one o'clock. Alec could hardly believe the time. It was easy to stay up all night in air-conditioned Vegas, gambling, fucking, eating, and gambling again, but here on this godforsaken island, sitting on a patio with sweat streaming down his face, just *talking* to a good-looking broad without even touching her hand, let alone anything else, he couldn't believe time could pass so quickly.

It was the first of many such evenings when, constantly amazed at himself, Alec found he looked forward to seeing Sylvie—to confide in her, going endlessly over past victories, always victories, settling old scores. He no longer fixed up dates simply because he wanted to ensure he wouldn't miss anything she might learn from her meetings with Burt. In fact, the more he thought about them, the less keen he was on the tête-à-têtes taking place at all.

Sylvie was increasingly touched by the way the tough little man was mellowing and starting to trust her. There was a childlike quality about him that in some extraordinary way reminded her of Ty.

Ty. She quickly dismissed any thought of tender, brilliant Ty. It was still too painful. How could she compare a rough diamond like Alec Boyar to someone as special and sensitive as Ty? The sooner she stopped that peculiar train of thought the better for her peace of mind.

There was plenty of work to occupy her and no end to what she was learning about the island in the sun she was beginning to think was as full of intrigue and suspense as Moscow or Washington!

Occasionally she jotted down notes. The writing bug was still there. She wasn't sorry. It was as if she were living in a state of suspension. On hold. Waiting for something—or was it someone?—to give her the impetus to start living life to the full again. Could she? Could she ever rekindle her old spark without Ty?

As she showered a couple of evenings later, getting ready to drive into town to meet Oliver Burt, she felt strangely apprehensive, jumpy. She tried to analyze why. Was it because she felt guilty, knowing she was expected to relay to Alec Boyar anything Oliver said that was relevant to what she now knew was Burt's obsession, his antagonism to the government he was supposed to be part of?

He had implied more than once that "Pindling's boys" were worse than the Bay Street Boys ever had been—"Hypocrites, every one of 'em . . . blasting off about corruption in one breath, congratulating themselves in the next for the millions of tourists coming to the is-land . . ." Eyes blazing, he had gripped her wrist. "You can take my word for it, they're lining their pockets as fast as the Bay Street Boys ever lined theirs."

What Oliver intended to do about it—"firebrand back-bencher" as he was now regularly called by the local press—Sylvie couldn't guess, but she believed in his sincerity. There was something about him that struck her as honest and determined to do the best for his fellow Bahamians, no matter what the cost to himself.

As she left the staff bungalow, the reason for her unsettled feeling became blazingly clear. It wasn't guilt about being an "informer." It was Burt's so-far-unexplained link with Johnny Nesbitt—and so once more a link to Nell.

Sylvie shivered, although, as usual at six in the evening, there was little breeze, let alone a cool draft. She would never be able to think of Nell again without a feeling of dread and a slow-burning determination for revenge.

As she drove toward the broad iron gates set in pink-coral stone walls at the club's entrance, she asked herself if she still hated Nell with the same passionate hate. Probably not. The hate she'd felt tearing away her insides as she'd sat at Lyon's Corner House with Aunt Gert, hearing for the first time about Nell's early affair with Pierre, had died a necessary death. Necessary because it would have destroyed her. She no longer wanted to _kill_ Nell, but she _did_ want revenge, yearned for it, and along with revenge the public revelation that the holy image Nell was creating for herself with every tick of the clock was utterly base and false.

Now that Sylvie was living in the Western Hemisphere, close to the United States, hardly a week went by without her learning something superlative about Nell, universally described, without a trace of hypocrisy, as the Godmother. When Sylvie first heard Nell's self-appointed title she'd burst into cynical laughter, only to realize those around her were genuinely put out that she appeared to be ridiculing a patron saint.

The Godmother, it was reported, had set herself the superhuman task of helping women all over America—and eventually the world—"find" themselves in careers that would build their self-respect, independence, and—if they had the "seed"—motivation to become leaders in their communities.

More and more as the weeks passed it was impossible to avoid hearing or reading about this "amazing, extraordinary woman," whose crusade to help women move away from being "mere appendages or chattel of their husbands"—and become self-motivated disciples of the movement so well named Ready to Change—was succeeding beyond her wildest dreams.

Sylvie's rage grew in proportion to Nell's fame—and, undoubtedly, fortune. If only those who talked about the Godmother with stars in their eyes were told—if only they knew, if only the world knew what an evil hypocrite Nell Nesbitt really was. It was incredible, if not impossible, for Sylvie to believe people were actually describing Nell O'Halloran Nesbitt when they talked about the selfless woman who worked so tirelessly for womankind. It was as crazy as believing night was day and white was black!

With every mile Sylvie drove closer to town, she listed Nell's evil acts in her mind. Nell was an infidel who had forsaken her aged parents, had stolen from them, breaking her father's heart, causing his death. She had stolen her best friend's boyfriend, had a baby with him, then abandoned the newborn child on a hospital doorstep. She had seduced one man after another, ruining Gert's love life and then Gert's business through her affair with Pierre. She had lied all her life . . . she had lied to Ty, causing him to . . . Sylvie abruptly pulled over to the side of the road, tears clouding her vision.

Only once had she erupted and let others in Nassau know how she felt. She'd overheard Madge, the Australian housekeeper, read aloud from *Ladies' Home Journal:* " 'the Godmother even gives special bonuses to widows.' Poor woman. It says here she knows only too well how widows feel. She lost her own husband unexpectedly and suffered terribly. He drowned and . . ." Before Madge could go on Sylvie had snatched the magazine out of her hand, crying, "Don't believe a word of it. She's a phony. A crook, a terrible woman. She probably murdered old Nesbitt. In fact I'm damn sure she did . . ."

Sylvie remembered the horrified look on the housekeeper's face, a look that said Sylvie had to have gone out of her mind—sweet, unassuming, hard-working Sylvie, of all people—attacking a national heroine. Before Madge could ask her what on earth her outburst was all about, Sylvie had rushed out to the beach to try to swim her torment away. Swimming always soothed her. It was then that she would try to think of a way she could write the truth about Nell. What a story it would make—but who would believe her and, more important, who would back her up? Kitty Stein? There would be no help from that quarter . . . and even if for her own reasons Kitty did support her, the memory of what Nell's battalion of lawyers had done to extinguish every vestige of hope for Gert's business to start, let alone survive, was all too fresh in her mind. And yet, as she swam with slow steady strokes through the turquoise waters out to the reef, Sylvie would tell herself she wouldn't give up . . . would never give up her objective to tell the world one day the whole truth and nothing but the truth about Mrs. Wallace Wainwright Nesbitt!

As she proceeded on toward town she switched on the radio . . . better to listen to anything to stop the torture of thinking about Nell. "Raindrops Keep Falling on My Head" blasted her eardrums. Raindrops . . . sea water . . . Wallace Nesbitt's death by drowning . . . *murder.* Had she actually made that accusation? If she had, it was because now she *was* sure Nell had had something to do with her husband's untimely end.

In the three years since her husband's death, Nell's business had prospered astonishingly, amazing even the most hard-bitten Wall Street pundits. Nell had poured money into national advertising and promotions, money she'd obviously inherited from Nesbitt's estate. Sylvie realized she was gripping the wheel so tightly her wrists were beginning to ache. It was doing her no good at all dwelling on Nell's ill-deserved success. She had no way to redress the situation at the moment. No ammunition. No one to help her unmask the monster. If there was a God, He would do it Himself, without any help from her.

In this preoccupied frame of mind Sylvie met Oliver as arranged in the parking lot of the E.P. Sassoon Building in Shirley Street and walked with him through a now-sultry, thundering night to what he had described as a "hot new club." It was apparently modeled on Freddy Munnings's famous Cat and Fiddle, where the first rumblings of Lynden O. Pindling's arrival on the local political scene had been told in outrageous native junkaloo songs.

Oliver Burt was preoccupied, too. It was unusual for him to be silent, locked into his thoughts, but tonight he only answered Sylvie's comments with monosyllabic grunts, affirmations or negatives. She gave up trying to coax him back into his more usual genial mood. Even when he was at his most belligerent, Burt usually flashed her expansive smiles and patted her cheek to make sure she realized his venomous remarks in no way reflected his regard for her.

Tonight was different. Sylvie was different, too, in so low a mood for no real reason, as she tried to chastise herself, that she sank to his level of noncommunication.

A cheeky junkaloo song—about Eight Mile Rock, a shanty town of broken-down huts that Pindling had used as an example of stupendous white indifference to black suffering—suddenly snapped Burt back to normal. As the balladeer whipped together a rhyming patter that implied Pindling hadn't helped Eight Mile Rock one bit since his election . . . and knows "he canna hock it cos nobody want it," Burt covered Sylvie's hand with his massive black one. "Sorry, love." He flashed a big white-toothed grin at her. "Lots on my mind. You know Johnny Nesbitt, don't you? You told me so."

In the middle of sipping a rum and soda Sylvie was so taken by surprise she started to splutter. Oliver slapped her firmly on the back. "I didn't expect such a violent reaction to my friend's name . . ."

The dreaded blush followed. Sylvie felt angry, first at herself, then

more at Burt for causing such an unexpected mixture of pain and
discomfort to surface. Although she felt hot and bothered, she was
pleased her voice sounded so disinterested, even icy. "What of it? I'm
surprised you haven't wanted to discuss our 'association' before this."

Burt didn't appear to register her frigid tone. He went on talking.
"He wants to see you. He's coming down this weekend . . . wants to
ask you a few things—to understand something about . . ." Sylvie saw
the big man's Adam's apple move rapidly, as if he were consciously
gulping to show he knew he was moving into a sensitive area—"the
day your husband had his regrettable, totally regrettable accident."

Sylvie couldn't understand how she could be smiling. She couldn't
be drunk on one rum and soda, yet the farcical side of the situation
made it impossible for her not to smile. When Burt tried to be diplomatic, he sounded like a ventriloquist's dummy, repeating platitudes
for effect, revealing his lack of sophistication, despite his natural
street-smarts. If he had a white skin, Sylvie decided, his last "totally
regrettable" remark would have made him sound like an elderly un-
dertaker who had never ventured far from his undertaking parlor—
but Oliver wasn't white, or in any way elderly. He was a passionate
jet-black man, in his late thirties who had never learned the special
brittle language of extending unfelt commiseration, smooth unemo-
tional condolences. Her blush over, Sylvie exerted the charm Frank
Forrester had spotted, in order to put Oliver at ease.

Releasing her hand from his, she gently touched his scarred chin
and, smiling into his eyes, was about to speak when a camera flashed
in their faces. "What the . . ." Oliver was on his feet, but whoever had
taken the picture was nowhere in sight.

Sylvie tugged at his shirt. "Sit down. What does it matter? You're
up and coming in Bahamian politics—I'm sure I'm not even in the
picture. It's you they wanted."

Their usual spontaneity and warmth were gone for the evening,
however, no matter how many junkaloo songs satirized world events:
man landing on the moon while Teddy Kennedy landed in the Chap-
paquiddick drink and—nearer to home—the wonderful two-headed
Cecil Wallace Whitfield in charge of culture *and* education, "who
never goes cultivatin' the friendship of boss Prime Minister Pindling
and who's not particularly educated either . . ."

At the end of the evening as they approached the old Ford in the
Shirley Street parking lot, Oliver Burt began to indicate why he'd
acted so morose and out of character.

In the badly lit courtyard of the finance building he clasped Sylvie by the shoulders. "Things are going to change here soon, Sylvie. Our history has long been involved with pirating, buccaneering, ship-wrecking, blockade running. Until the right people are in power, who *really* care for our people—who don't just pay the white kind of lip service to the idea—I believe some of us still have to be pirates, buc-caneers, blockade runners." He was so intense that Sylvie felt steam was about to come out of his wide nostrils. He was like a nervous thoroughbred getting ready for a race, as he went on. "Some of us must pirate good ideas to lead us all to the safe harbor of true freedom. Some of us must shipwreck prejudices that spell the breaking of any link in our chain of democracy, and some of us must buccaneer every lofty idea Mr. Pindling seeks to impose for his self-aggrandizement but to the detriment of everyone else in this beautiful place."

His tone sharpened. "Be careful whom you associate with, Sylvie. There are evil elements that can harm you. This Mr. Boyar friend of yours"—Sylvie again felt a blush heat up her skin, but she stayed silent —"he thinks he's very clever, spreading the word that the Mafia, the very source of *his* evil influence"—Burt paused dramatically, then virtually hissed—"are responsible for a plot to overthrow this present unpardonable government." Still Sylvie remained silent. "In fact, it is Boyar's cronies, Joe Gallo and Meyer Lansky, who are ruining the endeavors of our brave black new world." Sylvie's head was spinning. What did it all mean? Where did Johnny Nesbitt fit in? Could Nell have anything to do with the revolt Oliver implied was about to hap-pen?

She eased herself behind the wheel, but as if he read her mind, Oliver bent his long body down to whisper sinisterly into her ear, "Your best friend is on *their* side . . . and *their* side is Mr. Boyar's side of evil . . . evil . . . evil. Why do you think he bought that fine palace on the beach? Because he likes your pretty face?" Oliver laughed ironically. "Why does a man who never gets out of his business suit buy a house on the beach with a deep-water dock for a good-sized speedboat?"

Later Sylvie could have kicked herself for interrupting at that point, but she was getting tired of ignoring Burt's mysterious innuendos. She turned off the ignition to ask coldly, "What exactly do you mean?" She started to open the car door, but Oliver leaned his bulk against it. "Don't get mixed up with the wrong crowd, child, that's all I mean." Child was an endearment he had begun to use, one that amused, even touched her. Child at thirty-four years old! Until now Sylvie had rather liked it. Now she wasn't sure. He cupped her face in his hands as he hissed through the car window, "There's going to be a parting of the ways—to build a movement—to look after our people the right way!"

"A parting of the ways for the good of the people." Burt hadn't said it quite like that, but those words rang in her head like a junkaloo song as she navigated her way back along the bends and curves to Lyford Cay. "A parting of the ways for the good of the people . . ."

Next day Oliver Burt called her at the office, half apologetic, half bombastic. "Will you bury the hatchet and meet my friend this weekend? He really wants to talk to you . . . to ask you . . ."

"No, absolutely not." Sylvie was adamant. She could feel the wound that she had hoped was finally healing straining to open as she spoke. Even the thought of *seeing* Johnny Nesbitt again, let alone talking to him, immediately raised the specter of Nell. "I have nothing to say to him. Nothing."

"You're wrong." Burt's voice was controlled, but Sylvie knew she had angered him. "You have a *lot* to say and a lot to learn." He put the receiver down before she could retaliate.

That night Alec Boyar made his first pass, and later, tossing and turning, unable to sleep, Sylvie could hardly believe what had happened. Worse—or better (she was so confused she didn't know how she felt)—she was aghast she had responded as she had, almost giving herself to a man she merely felt sorry for, a man she hardly respected . . . or did she?

Boyar had opened a second bottle—or was it a third bottle?—of wine because it was his mother's birthday. Then he had insisted she speak to the unknown woman; Sylvie felt embarrassed, responding to a tiny little voice that ebbed and flowed with the vagaries of the Bahamian telephone system, platitude following platitude with Mama Boyar rarely getting away from the subject of her darling little boy, Al.

Al? Alec had beamed as Sylvie tried in vain to bid Mama a tactful farewell and pass the phone on to the "best boy in the whole wide world." She hadn't meant to drink so much, but it was the finest wine Alec had ever poured. She was surprised he even knew a St. Emilion from a Chateauneuf-du-Pape. She'd felt nervous, mainly because at the last minute she'd decided not to tell Alec about her evening with Burt, even though it meant not telling him the all-important news that Johnny Nesbitt was arriving in Nassau that weekend.

By midnight her head had kept falling cozily onto Alec Boyar's shoulder, although she'd fought to keep her eyes open. Boyar's favorite Glenn Miller records hadn't helped, the soporific beat merging hypnotically with the lazy lap of waves against the dock.

Back in her own bed, staring at the ceiling, willing sleep to overtake her, she nevertheless found herself reliving what had transpired, even recalling the heady male cologne Boyar always wore. Why on earth was it still in her nostrils? Caron pour un Homme—Alec's handkerchief was the culprit—crumpled up on her nightstand, the handkerchief he had handed her to wipe perspiration from her face. At the same time, his arm had encircled her, one hand cupping her breast as if it were a rare treasure. He'd murmured, "Baby, baby, you're turning me on . . ."

It was humiliating to realize now she hadn't moved away—hadn't actively wanted him to go on but hadn't resisted either, when he'd slipped the elasticized top of her dress down to her waist and had even unhooked without any apparent trouble what was usually the irritating, difficult clasp of the one bra she owned which fastened in front.

She'd slid lazily down on the long, pale-blue linen sofa, feeling safe, protected, even while Alec was exclaiming on the beauty of her naked "tits." He'd pulled her nipples, gently at first, then harder and harder as they had hardened and pointed up. His mouth had gone to work like a terrier, biting, sucking. . . . It had been a good feeling and when she'd felt his hand on her bare thigh, she knew she'd begun to open her legs, enjoying the sensation of his thick fingers stroking, stroking, pushing aside her panties, already wet with the tropical heat—and her own heat.

What had abruptly stopped the drift into sex? And it would have been urgent, pulsating sex, she knew that, as Alec had established a steady rhythm inside her, his fingers probing in, out, in, out, even making her moan a little.

She'd seen his other hand, pudgy, well-manicured, and the memory of Jerome Mossop had made her sit up so quickly that Alec had lost his balance and fallen to the floor.

The scene had ended ungracefully with her pulling angrily away from his hands clawing to get back, as she'd tried to fasten her unfastenable bra to make a quick exit, as Alec groaned, "Baby, baby, don't do this to me. You've got to let me come . . ."

Whether her near acquiescence to his advances made her more desirable, Sylvie didn't know, but there was no question that Alec began to pursue her after that evening.

"So near and yet so far," he said suggestively, arriving unexpectedly at the real-estate office the next day. She was embarrassed when he placed a hibiscus flower on her blotter. "Dinner tonight?" She shook her head. "Why not?" She couldn't think of an excuse and ended up at the house on the beach, half afraid he'd pin her to the wall and not sure how she'd react if he did—but he didn't.

Instead he circled her like a wary matador, then extravagantly bowed her through the door into the patio at the end of the dinner, sitting with exaggerated care at the opposite end of the long pale-blue sofa. At midnight he kissed her hand, led her to her car, and kissed her hand again. "I've got to attend to some urgent business next week . . . got to go to Miami. Why don't we get to know each other's habits? Let's go to Eleuthera for the weekend. I want to see what they're doing with the Windermere development over there. I hear they've got a few royals who bought—and Annie Orr Lewis has done the place up to look like Buckingham Palace . . ." Sylvie smiled. The little man really thought she'd be lured by titles, just as he was. Should she go? She was in an agony of indecision, confiding to Madge, who thought she was crazy to waste even a second weighing the pros and cons.

"He's loaded, Sylvie. What have you got to lose? After all, you're not a seventeen-year-old virgin, are you, ducky? What are you saving it for?"

All the same, on Friday afternoon at the thought of the forty-eight hours ahead Sylvie felt panicky. She sat in close proximity to Alec on the small plane he told her had been furnished by Frank Christie, Harold's brother.

In fact, Alec behaved like a gentleman. Well, almost.

On Sunday morning she languished in a hot foamy tub, her anxiety lulled by hours of noneventful behavior, reflecting with some surprise that Alec hadn't even attempted to enter her luxurious twin-bedded room, a corridor away from the master suite he occupied in one of the most modern houses on the windswept but majestically beautiful Windermere Estate Beach.

There was a tap on the door and she looked up to see Alec bound over to the side of the bath, the same look of excitement and awe on his face that had been there the night of his first pass.

"Let me study you." It wasn't a request. It was an order.

"No, Alec, really. Please go away." She slid under the foam, feeling a blush climb up to her forehead. He yanked her up by her shoulders, soaking his shirt-sleeves, laughing happily, getting his mouth full of foam when he bent to suck her nipples. It was all over in seconds. He threw a towel over her head and left.

As he dropped her back at the Lyford Cay staff bungalow that night he placed a small parcel in her lap. "Open this later. See if you like it. If you do, be wearing it when I come back from Florida Thursday."

In her tiny bedroom Sylvie stared at the still-unopened box. It had to contain a ring. It was a ring box. She felt sick. Minutes passed. She heard the phone but couldn't move to answer it. She was being ridiculous. It was the easiest thing in the world to say she couldn't accept a gift, any gift from a man. She didn't even need to open the box— yet the thought of hurting the little man, who acted so tough but who was, she felt deep down, as vulnerable as she was, was impossible.

With trembling fingers she tore off the white shiny paper and gasped as a dark blue square-cut sapphire ring was revealed inside the aquamarine Tiffany box. It was magnificent. She slipped the ring on the finger on her right hand. It slipped up and down. She placed it over her thin wedding band on her left hand. It fitted.

She took it off as if it were poisonous. Where could she keep such a valuable ring until Thursday? It was unfair of Alec to give it to her without warning. On impulse she went outside to her car and drove over to the main clubhouse. "I'd like to rent a safety-deposit box," she told the receptionist. "Just for a week."

She had to return it. A ring, even without one word being said, was a commitment—whichever finger she wore it on.

The events of the next few days, one following upon the other in quick succession, were so disturbing that Sylvie kept forgetting the existence of the ring. To begin with, suddenly the tables were turned. There she was, sitting, enjoying a quiet drink with Oliver Burt when he started questioning her about Alec Boyar. It was bizarre, but she saw nothing wrong in telling Oliver the few facts she knew about the "largest box manufacturer in the East . . . why do you want to know?"

His answer surprised and, without her quite understanding why, delighted her. "I may have misjudged him by the company he keeps."

"Me?" She grimaced in mock displeasure.

Burt hastily patted her cheek. "No, no, no. Johnny Nesbitt distrusts him, thinks he's in with the Mafia crowd—the Canadian Mafia in Miami, but now I'm not so sure. I met him today. We talked for an hour or so . . ."

Sylvie was flabbergasted. "But he told me he was leaving for Florida —is he still on the island?"

"Nope. He left on a chartered plane about ten minutes after I left him. He doesn't trust Pindling and company either. He's on to something about him—says he doesn't want his investment to get dirty. I know he could have been in at the beginning of the Freeport deal. There was a lot of talk but no one could ever prove any under-the-counter dealings. Sure, the Bay Street Boys lined their pockets, but they also brought prosperity to the islands. Gambling doesn't hurt anyone. Drugs, that's another thing." Burt's expression was so fierce Sylvie was momentarily shocked.

"Drugs . . . what d' you mean?"

"It's what Johnny and I have suspected for some time now." Burt looked at her whimsically. "You know, child, we are a nation of seven hundred islands. For some time there's been whispering that with our beloved PM's blessing we're about to become a major refueling and transport spot for smugglers carrying drugs to the States from South America . . ."

"Why are you telling me this?"

He eyed her carefully. "I don't like not being sure about a man. I thought I knew all there was to know about Mr. Boyar. Now, after our meeting I am not sure anymore. He told me too much. Why did he tell me anything? Why did he say he wants my help in getting the bastards?" Oliver looked at her directly. "Tell me why?"

Sylvie was flustered, confused. "I don't know anything, Oliver, really I don't. We went to Eleuthera."

"For the weekend, yes, I know. I thought there had to be a connection—perhaps something you told him—about Johnny Nesbitt's arrival . . ." He studied her so carefully she had to force herself not to look away.

"I didn't tell him anything, but you're right. He has asked me questions about you in the past." She was relieved to be able to tell him at last. "But, I promise you, I decided not to tell him about Nesbitt. By the way, did he arrive?"

"No." It was obvious Oliver wasn't going to elaborate. "It wasn't necessary. When I passed on the information that you had gone island-trotting with Boyar and refused to see him anyway he decided not to take the risk . . ."

"Risk?" Sylvie was more mystified than ever.

"Yes, risk. These are dangerous times, child. I've told you so. I want you to tell me if Mr. Boyar is an ally or an adversary. Tomorrow you will know why it's so important."

As Sylvie listened to the six o'clock news the next night she began to understand what Oliver Burt must have been referring to. "An international plot to overthrow the government is imminent, claimed Senator Henry Bowen today at the opening of the Progressive Liberal Party convention. The statement was greeted with derision by certain well-known dissident members of the party, among the most vocal being the Minister of Culture and Education, Cecil Wallace Whitfield, long regarded as an opponent to Prime Minister Pindling and contender for the party's most senior position . . ."

Two days later Cecil Wallace Whitfield announced his resignation, followed shortly after by that of Dr. Curtis McMillan, the Minister of Health. The _Tribune_, long-established supporter of the Bay Street Boys, gleefully speculated as to who would be next to jump Pindling's party.

As rumors swept through the club about international payoffs involved in the party eruptions, the names of Mafia-connected operators were whispered too. Sylvie tried to get hold of Oliver Burt, but there was no reply from any of his numbers. For the first time since Ty's death she began to feel an urge to hunt down the news, to find out what was really behind the mysterious liaison between Johnny Nesbitt and Oliver Burt . . . to discover just why Alec Boyar was now willing to talk and listen directly to Burt and perhaps cooperate in whatever he was up to, which certainly seemed to be a scheme to scuttle the government, a scheme that was already under way, according to the latest reports. Then there was the ring. Why had Alec Boyar's ring arrived so suddenly? Perhaps it had nothing to do with his emotions at all? Perhaps it had more to do with business, shady business? Somerset Maugham's famous line about the south of France came to mind: "a sunny place for shady people." Nassau was sunny, all right —but was Alec "shady"? Was Oliver?

She felt more alive than she had in months, her news "antennae" reacting to the myriad stories circulating in and around Lyford Cay. She remembered that Johnny Nesbitt's daughter had been kidnapped in Nassau, that a huge ransom had been paid, and that not even a year later Johnny Nesbitt's stepfather had suddenly drowned. Johnny Nesbitt's stepfather and Nell's husband. Were these all pieces of the same puzzle? If so how did they fit together?

Sylvie was excited. She sensed a big story, one that could resurrect her reputation as the savviest writer-reporter in the Street. She decided she would start to ask questions, listen, sift through everything.

It was odd how the reappearance of Alec Boyar the next day destroyed her enthusiasm for the idea. Again she recalled with bitterness how the press had treated Ty and herself—the hypocrisy of the fourth estate. How could she have felt so eager to be part of it all again only the day before?

That evening she dined with Alec on the patio outside the magnificently proportioned domed library. As they reached the dessert stage without any mention of the ring, Sylvie purposefully opened her bag and took out the small box.

"Do you like it?" Alec looked nervous, sounded so timorous, she couldn't do anything but nod her head affirmatively. The look of relief on his face made her stomach turn over. She had to make him understand she couldn't keep it, couldn't wear a symbol of a relationship that didn't exist. He put his tanned hand firmly over hers. "Don't worry. It isn't an engagement ring. We won't get engaged. We'll skip that and go on to the main event . . ."

She blushed, trying to interrupt, trying to get up from the table to walk away from a situation she found too embarrassing to deal with, but the pressure of his hand increased. "You're the first woman I've ever met who doesn't give me any bullshit . . . and . . ." A crafty smile broke across his face, "I'm crazy about your tits." He immediately looked so sheepish she had to smile.

"Alec . . . thank you. I don't know what to say, but all I can say now is it's too soon. Please take the ring back. I can't wear it out. It's too good . . . too expensive . . . too dangerous to keep at the bungalow . . ."

"Why don't you move in here with me, as my personal assistant . . ." He was smiling broadly, but she wasn't entirely sure he was joking.

"That's impossible. People would say . . ."

"Who cares? Didn't your late husband teach you people talk whether you give them any reason or not?"

It was the first time he had ever mentioned Ty in such a familiar way. She sat staring down at the table, her ambition and excitement of just an evening ago about renewing her work dissipated, leaving her feeling useless, a chattel. Against her will she could hear Madge say, "not just as an appendage of your husband but as a self-motivated member of the community . . ."

She had to change the subject. "I hear you saw Oliver Burt. I'm glad. I like him. He told me you and he think alike after all—that possibly members of the government are turning a blind eye to drug smuggling—receiving payoffs, bribes." She'd said much too much. She hadn't meant to mention the drugs, but she'd had to think of something to get away from the subject of their emotional involvement.

"Did he say that? What else did he say?" Alec asked the questions like a father talking to a child, disarming, gentle.

"You know there's been an upheaval since you left . . ." Sylvie's self-confidence was oozing away. Something told her she was on treacherous ground. She felt she was betraying Burt, despite Alec's recent overtures to him.

Alec reverted to form, lecturing her. "I told you before, young woman, my influence is considerable. There's a lot of my money down here in this tropical no-man's-land. A lot of dough of my friends, too. D'you think we want this government unseated? D'you think even those numbskulls would be fool enough to get caught up in a drug scheme when they've only been in office three years . . . three years of trying to convince the money men, the big shots, that they're responsible, caring people? The time was right, young lady, for me to sit down with Mr. Burt. I knew what was coming up. I wanted to test the waters—to see just how dangerous he is—to decide what measures, if any, have to be taken. If anyone's involved in receiving payoffs, I'd say it's Mr. Honorable Burt himself. Now, Sylvie . . ." Alec pulled her to her feet and drew her close to him, his breath hot on her cheek. "I don't want you to see Mr. Burt anymore, unless I specifically request it. He and the other dissidents have to watch it. Shooting off their mouths about illegal drug operations going on down here . . . about members of the government taking bribes . . . Burt especially better watch it, m'dear . . ."

If an offensive letter hadn't arrived the following week from one of Ty's last remaining creditors, Sylvie realized later, she might have reacted differently to Alec Boyar's increasing interference in her life. He was slowly drawing her into his luxurious net, checking up on where she went, whom she saw.

When they met he was amazingly considerate, even gentle, stroking her, kissing her in a way that meant she could draw back without feeling she was insulting him—but a pattern was being set. There was a difference she couldn't quite pinpoint in the way people at the office reacted to her. There was a certain reserve, not exactly suspicious, but the camaraderie and joking that usually went on around the clock would stop whenever she came into the office.

One day when she went to the parking lot, a brand-new Thunderbird was in the spot where the old Ford had been. "For your exclusive use, Sylvie . . ." The memo from Harold Christie explained it all without dotting any *i*'s, crossing any *t*'s. The inference was pleased approbation from the management. She was keeping a very important resident happy and perhaps would make him still happier . . .

She began to feel uneasy, except ironically whenever she was with Alec, which happened more and more—dining with him at least four nights out of seven, looking out over the immaculate lawns to the shimmering sea. Then a kind of euphoria took over. She wanted to lean on someone—to hand over the bills, the summonses, the creditors' letters—which, without prompting, Alec seemed to expect her to do.

"You still haven't slept with him?" Madge was incredulous. Sylvie didn't blame her. It wasn't natural. She felt herself to be a fraud. Perhaps one day she'd succumb and find herself asking him into *her* bed.

The months were slipping by in the never-never land of languorous waving palms, the soft breezes never changing into the icy winds that Sylvie read were sweeping through New York with a windchill factor of minus twenty degrees. "It's hard to believe, Aunt Gert, it isn't that far away, yet this morning when it was snowing in Central Park, I was out snorkeling to keep cool."

She hadn't told Gert about Alec Boyar. The ring was back in the safety-deposit box, but the creditors' letters were being dealt with by one of Alec's legal advisors. For the last two months, to her astonishment, she'd hardly had to show a house or a piece of land, yet sales were being phoned in to her. Her commissions were piling up without her having to lift a finger . . . or move a foot.

Of course, it was all because of Alec—her indebtedness to him was growing. He was sweet, considerate, openly admiring of her—yet all he seemed to want was the right to play with her naked breasts, to nestle his face between them, to stroke them and pull her nipples until he felt her withdraw, when without complaint he would take her to her car.

She hadn't seen Oliver Burt since Alec's return from Miami when he had asked her not to see him and given her the lecture on being too trusting, but she read about Burt frequently. As a member of a group called the Free PLP, Oliver was now openly antagonistic to the government, and on a beautiful spring day he supported a vote of no-confidence against the prime minister, encouraging all dissident members to vote with their former bitter opponents the UBP—Use Black People Party—as she'd heard Oliver himself call them—the Bay Street Boys!

Oh, be careful, Oliver, Sylvie said to herself as she heard on the news that Oliver's attempt to oust Pindling had only failed by a slim margin. She didn't think about Oliver for long. She was too excited, too anxious to get over to Alec's house to thank him for one more sign of his feelings for her . . . and his great influence in the island. A memo had arrived that afternoon telling her that starting the following weekend she had new accommodations—a pretty little bungalow all to herself on the edge of a half-moon-shaped beach. It was like having a permanent Santa Claus!

She didn't bother to call ahead to tell Alec she was going to be early. She put on a new strapless white-lace top with matching skirt, which showed off her tan perfectly, then raced off in the Thunderbird, not wanting to lose a second to express her gratitude. It was the first time she'd ever arrived at the house without finding Alec in the doorway to welcome her. She entered the cool, arched hallway, looking for one of the servants to announce her, but no one was about. As she went toward the library where they usually had predinner drinks, she could hear Alec's voice on the phone. Her excitement and gratitude died, to be replaced with fear as she heard him say sharply, "tonight, yes, there's no more time to waste. He's being set up tonight. He'll be caught red-handed with the stuff. In the car. He'll be stopped on the highway. Of course he'll fight—where d'you think he got that bloody scar? In a nunnery? But he won't get away . . . we don't want him dead. We want him disgraced. Tommy will just down him in the leg . . ."

Sylvie didn't know how she managed to get out of the house to the world that had looked so beautiful, had been so joyful only seconds before. "Set up . . . red-handed . . . planted . . . scar . . . disgraced . . . down him in the leg." She stifled a scream she longed to let out, bit her lip so hard she could taste blood. Her hands trembled so much she could hardly steer the car as she left the driveway, not knowing where to go, but sure of one thing. She couldn't let it happen.

Her true instinct about what was right and what was wrong surfaced. She had been in Alec Boyar's cocoon too long. It had slowly sucked the fire out of her, taken away her courage, turned her into a zombie with no brain of her own. She had to have been mad not to have seen it before. Well, it was over, but before she paid attention to her own life she had to get to Oliver . . . to warn him . . . no matter what the cost to herself . . .

10

Los Angeles,
December 4, 1971

In the Supreme Court

Divorce and Matrimonial Side

To the Supreme Court dated the 5th day of September, A.D. 1971

The Petition of Charlotte Nesbitt shows that

1. On the 16th day of January, 1958, the Petitioner was lawfully married to Jonathan Owen Nesbitt at St. Thomas Church, North Sydney, Australia.

2. After the said marriage the Petitioner lived and cohabited with the Respondent in Sydney and Perth, Australia, until 1961, when the Respondent returned to the country of his birth, Canada, where the Petitioner and Respondent continued to live in Montreal and Vancouver.

3. The Petitioner now resides at Peppermint Grove, Perth, Western Australia.

4. The Respondent is a company director, whose domicile is now Cable Beach in the western district of the island New Providence, Bahamas.

5. There is one child of the marriage, a daughter Lucy.

6. There have been no proceedings previous hereto in any court with reference to the said marriage.

Nell heard a door open and close softly as she leaned back with her eyes closed in Johnny's chair. She didn't have to explain her presence in Johnny's office, sitting at his desk, to his secretary whom she was sure had just looked in. She didn't have to explain her actions to anyone.

So the settlement with Charlotte had finally been reached. Before he'd left for New York, Johnny had attempted to tell her about it; but maintaining the posture of someone "removed" from the world and its earthly pursuits and pleasures—a deeply ingrained, trained habit by now—Nell had convinced him she wasn't interested in the financial details. Now, however, her hand shook slightly as she turned the pages of the lengthy legal document dissolving Johnny's marriage. Charlotte was getting a bundle. She didn't deserve a cent in one way, although in another way Nell had to admit that by claiming desertion Charlotte had ensured the sanctity of her Godmother reputation. Not that Charlotte could have come up with any real evidence to despoil her image.

Nell smiled bitterly. It was ironic that the day Johnny had finally succumbed to the forces she knew she stirred in him, Charlotte had sued for divorce on the grounds of his continued and deliberate absence from home.

As usually happened when she recalled the dull, sullen Sunday when Johnny had taken her completely by surprise in the office, suddenly kissing her neck as she sat at her desk going over the latest overseas figures, she began to feel physically weak as if he were actually in the room with her now, about to take her as he had taken her that ecstatic day.

This time, however, the yielding weakness of her body was swiftly followed by rage, unrelenting rage as the bitter fact pounded in her brain that she was powerless to respond in the way she longed to respond and in the way Johnny obviously, at the moment, took for granted.

As soon as the decree was granted he expected their partnership, their relationship, to be sanctified by marriage. For a second, not realizing what she was doing, Nell saw to her horror that she had stabbed her palm with a paper knife. As she saw the blood ooze out, she was back for the first time in years in poverty-land, recalling a scene on a dirty park bench, the stench of soot in her nostrils as she bullied Sylvie into following the rites of their blood pact—Sylvie who, unwittingly, was now the cause of her frustration and rage. Well, at least they were quits. *Now*, she had no reason to feel any guilt over Ty's death in London. Not that she'd ever seriously considered herself responsible. The crazy, unstable composer had simply overreacted to her attempt to take the smug, self-satisfied look off his face and destroy the holy thought in his head that he'd married an angel. Ty Caplan had simply overreacted and died as a result of his own lack of control.

As if in a trance, Nell watched her blood drip onto Johnny's rich brown mahogany desk. Blood *was* much darker in color than most women realized . . . That was why her dark blushers were so clever. For a second in her mind she recalled Faye Dobson, one of the top RTC training directors, teaching the color training sessions: "It resembles the color of your own blood . . . blend it, blend it, and you will get the most natural blush of health on your cheeks." She switched off. Sylvie! Her thoughts relentlessly returned to Sylvie, who would never know she had scored an incredible revenge through a series of events that were entirely coincidental. If! If! If! If Sylvie hadn't gone to work for Harold Christie in Nassau . . . if Joe Diaz's mentor Alec Boyar hadn't bought a house from her . . . if they hadn't become as friendly as, according to Diaz, they had . . . if Sylvie, with her natural nose for news, hadn't found out from Oliver Burt that Johnny—despite everything he'd said to her—was still trying to upset Diaz's deals with the black government down there—if Sylvie hadn't then reported it "innocently" back to Boyar, who then passed it on to Diaz . . .

Nell shivered. There had been an unmistakable menacing note in Diaz's voice the night before. Staring at her with his dead, fishlike eyes, he'd said, "So at last you've got what you've always wanted, have you? Johnny Nesbitt's going to be free to marry you, isn't he?" Insultingly he'd let the ash from his cigar drop onto her lap as he brought his face closer to hers. "You'll be a widow again, before you've grown used to being a bride, my dear. Do you think we could ever trust you again once you'd achieved your heart's desire? D'you think you would ever be able to hide from your husband"—the way he'd pronounced "husband" had sounded like a threat in itself—"our very special business arrangement?"

She'd tried to talk her way out the way she could talk her way out of or into anything and everything she wanted with everyone—except him. She'd pleaded, no, *begged* Diaz to believe her that, once married, she would make certain Johnny never interfered in his plans again—

but she was in a hopeless position and Diaz knew it. Even now she found it hard to believe that Johnny, despite his promises, had never given up his quest for the truth in Nassau—that, in fact, he was actively behind Burt's attempt to form a dissident group to topple the Pindling government, which he now distrusted more than he had ever distrusted the Bay Street Boys. According to Diaz, Johnny had even sworn in a private memorandum to the U.S. authorities that members of the Bahamian government were receiving payoffs in return for shutting their eyes to setting up a new distribution center for drugs in the islands, drugs destined for the U.S. mainland.

"How do you know all this?" she'd cried, a question she had long ago sworn she would never ask Diaz again—as he always knew *everything*.

The door opened wide this time and Johnny's secretary came in, affecting surprise on seeing the Godmother slumped in the president's chair.

"Oh, Mrs. Nesbitt, I hope I am not disturbing you. I just wanted to check on . . . things . . . can I help you in any way?"

Nell shook her head wearily. She hadn't even the energy to reprimand the fool with a dose of her special intimidating disdain, which showed the recipient she had caused displeasure.

"Can I turn the light on?"

"Leave me," Nell said. The secretary backed out anxiously. Nell hoped the woman's anxiety would last and cause her a sleepless night. It probably would. None of her employees wanted to see a frown on her face, let alone be the cause of one.

As the day slipped into night she stayed almost motionless in Johnny's chair. She searched in vain for a solution—for a way to get out of the tightest corner of her life. Her mind twisted this way and that way. Even if she got rid of Diaz there would surely always be another Diaz behind him. But would there be? Since that terrible confrontation in Nassau back in 1966 she'd never seen any of his gang. They'd been shadows then—they had been more shadowy since—shadows who left parcels in post-office and safety-deposit boxes. They weren't even voices on her phone. Diaz and Diaz alone phoned and then arrived whenever he wanted to arrive. She now hated him so intensely that she had to spend hours after his departure on self-hypnosis to make sure none of it showed on her face, marring the vision of loveliness that her disciples gathered strength from. How could she get rid of him? How, how? The question gnawed at her all that night and well into the next day.

~~~

"To be protected forever . . ." Alec Boyar's softly spoken sentence haunted Sylvie as she swung herself in a hammock under the palm trees in her favorite part of the garden, where the green met the gold of the beach.

On the horizon a three-masted schooner, shiny white in the sun, was preparing to enter the Lyford Cay Marina. It wasn't easy getting in over the bar on a day like today with a choppy sea, waves rearing up like white horses over the reef. As she moved her body rhythmically from left to right, right to left, in a soporific indolent haze, she could imagine the activity on board, the sweat, the exertion.

"To be protected forever . . ." and "learn to separate the good guys from the bad guys." That was another Alec Boyar expression—childlike, simple—totally at variance with the man himself. Sylvie shuddered her lethargy away. Separating wheat from chaff was one thing —the talented from the untalented. When it came to *power* exerted by governments, who in turn were influenced by big, *big* money men, then it was essential to know if they were motivated for the good of the people or for themselves.

Had Alec finally received the message that she could never be part of his life—not in any shape or form? Despite the fact that she would never trust him again and wanted desperately to cut off the "social fraternizing," the dinners *à deux* at the house on the beach, even the cozy telephone calls—daily when he was on the island—that had become part of her life for the past year, face to face she'd found it impossible to say what she had to say outright.

Instead she'd resorted to what she'd always deprecated in others, half truths instead of whole truths, and inferences as opposed to the straight-out sentences she had prepared.

The evening before had been the deadline date she had set for herself—positively the last dinner, the last time she would ever accept an invitation, the last time she would ever knowingly see him again. She'd had her well-chosen sentences ready, explaining that for both their sakes it would be better to stop seeing each other, that she had never meant to encourage him to think she could be more than a good friend, and in order to avoid any hurt feelings this was to be their last meeting.

As she'd driven over in the Thunderbird she'd reflected grimly she could hardly tell him how she really felt—that she longed to hear he was leaving Nassau for good, that she was convinced he was evil, that she was beginning to fear him and all he stood for. Sitting with him in the beautiful library, insisting on only grapefruit juice for a cocktail, as so often happened Alec's demeanor became that of "boy-on-best-behavior." The shy way he spoke and looked at her sideways with quick, timorous glances had taken away all her resolve to tell him fast and if necessary leave before dinner.

Dining outside in the bougainvillea arbor with a breeze murmuring across the ocean, ruffling his usually sleek hair, the tall white candles in the hurricane lamps softening his expression, she'd frantically tried to think of a way to say gently what had to be said.

Instead he had taken her hand, sensing its constant urge to withdraw, but not allowing it to.

"I know you're upset with me, Sylvie. I don't know why, but I can guess. Rumors, stories, always someone out there trying to ruin me, to get me—it's always been like that—but you know me better, Sylvie, don't you?" His voice had grown softer, sweeter. It had been an agonizingly embarrassing moment. "Just know that I want to protect you forever . . . forever . . . and I will."

She'd had enough presence of mind to ask, "But why do I need to be protected, Alec?" She'd wanted him to hear a note of reproof, of suspicion, but somehow it hadn't come out like that.

He'd let her hand go, saying as he'd so often said, "You'll learn to separate the good guys from the bad guys, Sylvie. Where there's big money, big rewards, there will always be little guys—bad guys—trying to muscle in without doing the work . . ."

Only when she'd insisted she leave after dinner without their usual hour over coffee and Tia Maria in the pale blue patio had he looked unhappy, even angry. Instead of explaining as she'd meant to explain, she'd said quickly, uncomfortably, "Alec, I can't come to dinner again. It's better we . . . we . . ." She hadn't been able to look him in the face and say "never meet again." Instead, she'd ended lamely, ". . . meet less often." He hadn't answered, had simply gripped her so hard before opening the car door that in the shower later she'd found a bruise on her shoulder.

Now it was Sunday. All morning she'd expected his call—or even his arrival, although that would have been unusual. As he'd admitted once, thank God, some deep-rooted insecurity dating from his teenage years meant he could never arrive at a girlfriend's house unannounced, "in case I find the broad is being unfaithful."

Her feeling of somnolence gone, Sylvie fidgeted in the hammock, her mind concentrating on all that had happened in such a short time.

Alec had never guessed she had been instrumental in getting the word to Oliver Burt that his reputation was about to be ruined, that even his life might be in danger. No one had apparently seen her arrive and then leave the house on the beach.

Even swinging in the warmth of a perfect Nassau day, there were goose pimples on her arms as Sylvie relived her agonized drive to the nearest phone booth outside the club. When Oliver answered, relief had drenched her clothes with sweat so thoroughly it was as if she'd been caught in a sudden tropical downpour.

After her call somehow Oliver had eluded the trap, had left for the U.S. on official business, reported in the local newspapers in a small paragraph.

The reason she'd gone on seeing Alec during the week or so that followed was to ensure that he didn't think she was in any way involved in Oliver's "escape" . . . and it was she, not Alec, who'd brought Oliver's name up the week before, apprehensive that never mentioning a name that had once been a regular part of their conversation could be suspicious. That Alec had seemed so disinterested that Oliver Burt had ever been born had finally convinced her that, despite all outward appearances, Alec was the ultimate con man. She had been conned by him just as she'd been conned by Nell, his female equivalent in evil. If she didn't learn from this lesson, she would never learn!

It had been a nightmare waiting for the deadline date she'd set to arrive—and still she hadn't handled it as she'd planned, but one thing was certain. She would never go near the house on the beach again.

Now as she shifted position to stretch her legs out into the sun, she thought about Oliver. Was he evil, too? Was the news on the front page of the *Tribune* the past week bad for the island? Oliver's name had figured in it prominently; the dissident group he belonged to, the free PLP, as it was called, was definitely going to merge with the opposition, the UBP, led by the old Bay Street Boys Oliver had once hated so passionately. There was no stopping the merger, according to the paper. It was only a matter of days before a new political entity, the Free National Movement, was born—with one major objective: to oppose the Bahamian prime minister in every possible way.

Squinting against the sun, Sylvie watched a beautiful yacht make a slow approach to the harbor. It took her a minute to register the fact that the yacht she had been watching casually but with pleasure suddenly seemed to be in trouble. One moment it was moving serenely toward the harbor entrance, the next moment Sylvie saw it veer sharply off course, as if some hidden force from the sea bed was attempting to keel it over.

She jumped off the hammock so quickly she fell and scraped her knee. Through the telescope Alec had bought her—when she'd told him how she loved to study the island's birds—she could see the yacht was really in trouble.

It was out of control, at the mercy of the sea, which through the lens she could see was sending towering waves over the stern. She rushed to the phone to call the harbor master's office. "Something's happened to a yacht on the way in. One minute it was on course, the next minute something seemed to snap . . . it's drifting on to the reef fast."

Like watching a movie, Sylvie anxiously watched what happened next through the telescope. Endless minutes seemed to elapse before the Lyford Cay launch emerged from the harbor for the rescue attempt. She could hear her heart beat fast as she saw it move powerfully alongside the drifting yacht where hands pulled and attached ropes. From the shore every movement looked agonizingly slow, but Sylvie could almost feel the sharp spray on her face, the tilt of the deck, imagining the tense fear on board until, like a chastised maiden, the yacht was finally linked to the launch and towed toward the safety of the marina.

On impulse she threw a cotton shift over her bikini and drove over to watch the arrival at close hand. She felt responsible until the yacht was safely moored and tied up at the quay. What a beauty it was. Thank God, she'd seen the disaster and acted so swiftly, but what could have happened to cause such a trauma?

"Tiller broke," a deckhand yelled out in answer to her query.

The yacht was called *Volition*, an inspired name, she thought, for the eighty-foot, superbly crafted vessel. Talking to the people in the development office she'd learned enough about the yachts coming in and out of the club to recognize a masterpiece of design when she saw one. This was it.

She was about to walk back to her car when a man's voice called out, "You there, were you our guardian angel?"

She looked up to see a man so tanned he was almost black, an areole of unruly gray-black hair giving him the look of a gypsy.

She stared at him. Her heart missed a beat. She looked at the ground. It seemed to be spinning around her. What was wrong with her? Too much sun? Too much excitement? Why was she reacting so strangely?

She threw her head back and laughed. "Yes, I suppose you could say I was—are you the captain? You certainly had an unlucky arrival . . ."

Now the man was staring at her intently, fiercely, in a familiar way that she knew yet she didn't know.

As if he read her thoughts he cried, "I know you—at least I think I do. Can you come closer? Come and have a drink. It's the least I can offer you, unless you want to come for a cruise if and when the blasted tiller's fixed."

Before she could answer, the most beautiful young girl appeared beside him, a golden brown vision in a minute white bikini that showed off her silky skin and exquisite figure so dramatically Sylvie could do nothing but stare in wonderment. Was this a daughter? More likely a mistress.

As if to confirm it, the gypsy put a familiar hand around the beauteous one's waist. "Connie, persuade this all-seeing eye to come on board and get acquainted."

Why did she feel so torn—not indifferent, as she usually was to invitations from visiting yachtsmen, but apprehensive—as if once she set foot on board, something awaited her there that she didn't want to know.

All the same she climbed the gangplank to the salt-splashed teak foredeck to shake the hand of the gypsy who'd had such an extraordinary effect on her.

As soon as she stood before him, she knew why. And as she knew, so did he.

They looked long and silently into each other's eyes, the girl-vision disappearing as quickly as she had arrived.

"Sylvie . . . Sylvie Samuelson . . . no, that's not your name now, I know . . . but Sylvie, the same sylphlike Sylvie, the same freckles . . . is it really you?"

The pain attacked so fast and was so searing in its intensity that Sylvie had to turn abruptly away to look toward the harbor entrance where the waves thrashed the stone wall. She didn't trust herself to speak. Tears were in her eyes, her throat. He must not see—must never know how much he'd hurt her, yet just the way he had said her name, "Sylvie," had been enough to turn back the clock. She was a young girl again, in love, hurt, abandoned, betrayed not only by him but by her best friend in the world.

He put a firm hand on her shoulder. She prayed it was steady, not trembling as she felt her whole body was. Now along with the pain came anger, an unreasonable anger that she could have been so wrong, so terribly wrong about a man who obviously still sought out the most beautiful girls as his companions, who perhaps really was a fiend, who had abandoned Nell for newer, fresher loves as Nell had told her that night long ago in London.

Her anger helped her composure. She moved her shoulder slightly, so that he knew it was a rebuff, a silent request to remove his hand. "Dick, is it really you?" She repeated his question, hoping her tone was as cool and as indifferent as possible.

Her flinching had annoyed him. She could see that and she was pleased. Calmly she curled up on one of the side bunks, even managing the kind of smile one would naturally give an acquaintance of long ago.

There was a tremendous difference about him. What exactly was it —apart from the gray-flecked hair, which he still didn't seem to be able to control?

It was his look of assurance, of command.

"What an incredible coincidence. How long is it? Twelve, thirteen years?" Of course she knew. It was almost sixteen years since they'd set eyes on each other. She supposed it was surprising they had recognized each other at all, although she knew she'd kept herself in good shape. "The same sylphlike Sylvie . . ." It hadn't been difficult to stay sylphlike. Her problems had kept her weight off.

Was he going to ask her about Nell? She hoped not. All at once she couldn't wait to get herself off *Volition* and back to the safety of her own little bungalow. She could feel her fear growing like a tumor inside her. But fear of what?

"Is she on charter? Out of Miami?"

Dick Kolinzcky nodded, not taking his eyes from her face, studying her as if she were a specimen from another planet.

Self-consciously she was about to take her mirror out of her purse, certain perspiration was streaking her face, then thought better of it. Connie, the vision, was back and Sylvie felt strangely relieved. She took a glass of champagne from the tray the girl presented. Only two glasses. "Aren't you going to join us?"

Connie smiled, shaking her head. "Too much to do, but I hope I see you again later." She looked expectantly at Dick as if to say, "Why don't you ask her for dinner?" but there was no response. When she went below again Dick started to ask Sylvie questions. Luckily he didn't ask about Nell.

"I'm so out of touch. I just can't believe you saved our guts. It's fate, isn't it, Sylvie? I read about your husband's death. I'm sorry, so very sorry."

Why did she have to sound so acerbic, so out-to-wound, when she answered him. It wasn't like her, yet she could hear her barbs herself. She bit her tongue. She was being unfair. Dick owed her nothing and she owed him nothing. The least she could do was act like an old colleague.

It was only when he began to ask about her writing that she felt uncomfortable again. "I've given it up. I'm disenchanted with Fleet Street—with all the press . . ."

"But you were so _good_—I heard even in the wilds of Canada how successful you became. You were the best and probably still are." He went on, reminding her about her early ambition. It was warming, yet unsettling.

She cut across him. "What about you? Did you 'make it'? If you can charter a yacht like this beauty, I guess you must have done . . ."

Dick laughed. "I suppose you could say I made it in some ways." He didn't elaborate, coming straight to the subject she was dreading. "What about Nell, your 'very best friend'?" Sylvie could hardly believe the lightness, the indifference of his tone. How could he ask about Nell so casually after all that had transpired between them?

"I'd sooner not talk about Nell. I think you must know, as everybody does, all there is to know about her today. She's a very famous lady. She's the . . ."

He interrupted her irritably. "The Godmother, yes, I know. An amazing irony . . ."

Sylvie stood up. "I'd really rather not continue this conversation. I can't understand why you would want to either. I must be going. It was great seeing you. You haven't told me what you're doing, but then what else is new . . ." There was a barb again. She dug her nails into her hand.

"Are you glad you saved me?" He was laughing at her, his eyes twinkling. "Can't we have dinner together while I'm here? I want to ignite that old ambition of yours. You've not become a beach bum, have you? I'd hate to believe that of my fiery little Cockney sparrow . . ."

The blush, the old dreaded blush was invading every inch of her skin. She felt if she looked down she'd see her feet turned blood red with the rush of blood his words had produced. "My little Cockney sparrow!" How dare he say "my."

"Yes, I've become a beach bum. I sell real estate, but not much. I lie around and drink rum punch all day."

"Not with that smashing figure, you don't." He laughed again, ignoring the ice in her voice. "I bet you know everything that's going on here." His voice became serious. "Knowing you, I expect you're really here to do a long overdue exposé of all the rottenness beneath the exotica . . ." He smiled down at her as if to take away the sting of his words. "Once an ace always an ace, and your nose for news was one of the best."

She remembered Dick Kolinzcky's words two days later as she saw _Volition_ leave the marina and head out to sea. He hadn't tried to get in touch with her and she wasn't sorry. She didn't know how to cope. He was obviously on board with his beautiful girlfriend, his mistress. Connie could even be his child-wife for all she knew. Nothing had changed, except that her eyes were open now, whereas they'd been closed so tightly long ago. Now she realized all along she'd hoped she'd been wrong about Dick, that there had to have been another explanation for Nell running off with him, that her first, early impressions had been right. But Kolinzcky was no different from the majority of men. He was more attracted by beauty than brains, and when it came together in one dazzling package as it had with Nell, who could blame him for being bowled over?

"Are you glad you saved me? You've not become a beach bum, have you, my fiery little Cockney sparrow . . ." The words rang in her mind. There had been a challenge inherent in everything he'd said to her. She had to admit he still stirred her in a way she couldn't explain. She forced herself to acknowledge there was something about Dick she reacted to in a way she had never reacted with any man—not even to her beloved Ty—but obviously a relationship was never to be.

Volition's arrival with Dick on board had been like a message from fate—reminding her of another world of news, views, deadlines, data . . . a world that demanded quick thinking, action, _living_.

Although during the forty-eight hours he'd been in Nassau, Dick— the new, assured, masterful presence of Dick—had lurked somewhere in the back of her mind, she had been confronted with too many pressures to think about the possibility of seeing him again or even ponder what might happen if she did.

Early Sunday evening a huge sheaf of tuba roses, orchids, and lilies had arrived with a note from Alec that was more a command than an invitation. "Seven o'clock dinner tomorrow. Wear the white lace dress I love so much. Your protector forever, Alec." The flowers were glorious, the arrangement atrocious. It would look good on one of his boxes—the coffin kind. Was she being deliberately ghoulish? She'd taken the arrangement apart, stem by stem, filling all her vases, wrapping up a big bunch of those left over to drop off at Madge's place.

She hadn't realized how tense she was until she'd called the house on the beach the next morning to say thank you for the flowers and no thank you to dinner. Alec had been out, and her relief had been so great she was drained of all energy after leaving the message.

It was energy she couldn't afford to lose—for when she went to the parking lot after work that afternoon the Thunderbird was no longer where she'd parked it. She had rushed back to the development office with the news, thinking it had been stolen, but the manager of the real-estate office had obviously known what to expect. He hadn't even been able to look her in the eyes, as he shuffled through papers, mumbling that the car had been "requisitioned for something important in town . . . we'll have to find you something else . . . but the Ford's gone in for inspection." The implication had been she would have to walk home, but Madge had dropped in at that precise moment to thank her for the flowers and had given her a lift back to the bungalow. Sylvie hadn't been sure what to say. She wasn't even sure her key would still fit the lock and she wondered if her possessions would still be there. A Sword of Damocles was obviously hovering perilously over her head.

She'd decided to put on a brave front. "Madge, I'm without transport for a few days. Do you think I could borrow one of the club's bikes?"

She would show Alec Boyar what she was made of, Sylvie thought, as she pedaled furiously to work the second day after *Volition*'s departure.

There had been no word from Alec, but there had been other ominous signs the day before—as she put it cynically to herself, of her lack of cooperation in keeping one of the most important club residents happy.

"We want a weekly report on your clients and your calls, Sylvie . . ." Again the manager hadn't been able to look directly at her. He'd coughed apologetically. "We're looking for a certain increase in sales . . . the figures are being worked out now." He'd reddened, aware Sylvie was looking at him with barely concealed, amused contempt. "You've been—hm—very lucky, Sylvie . . ." He'd straightened up, assuming a new mantle of self-importance. "This office is under my authority now. I've decided everyone's being too slack. We've got to get more systems going. Anyone who doesn't meet the target I set is going to be out . . ."

"That's all right, Ted. I understand." Sylvie had even felt sorry for the pompous little pipsqueak. "I'll do my best, but obviously I can't perch prospective buyers on my saddle. Are you going to supply me with any wheels or are you going to supply my clients with bikes? Will the Ford be available for my use again soon?"

He'd mumbled and stuttered but in effect had refused to give her a straight answer.

As she approached the office her anger grew. She would show the Alec Boyars of the world she couldn't be intimidated. She would work herself to a standstill and embarrass those who were, for some reason, licking Alec Boyar's boots. If no transport were available she would say so loud and clear, and when the richest and most illustrious names came looking for their Shangri-la in Nassau she would borrow Madge's decrepit old station wagon to show them around. That would soon bring a blush to the wrong cheeks!

There was another gargantuan monstrosity of flowers propped up by the bungalow door when she returned. There was also another note from her "protector." It simply said, "Nassau can get awfully lonely without you. Don't turn your back on those who love you. Come to dinner tomorrow night." This time she didn't bother to bring the flowers inside, but left them to wilt in the hot afternoon sun. She didn't call to say she couldn't make dinner either. She was living on the edge of a volcano about to erupt and she knew it, but unsettling and frightening though it was, she infinitely preferred it to resuming the life she had allowed herself to slide into all too easily.

The atmosphere in the office was horrendous. She was given little information, no leads, no clients; she obviously was deliberately going to be kept from getting even near the "target." The other agents stopped talking as soon as she entered. It was as if she had contracted an infectious disease that was going to bring them all to their knees.

Surely it couldn't go on, Sylvie told herself. She had to think positively. If worse came to worst should she call Harold Christie and ask for an explanation—or call Frank Forrester and ask him to talk to Christie on her behalf—but how could she explain it all over the phone?

After a week of being "in Siberia," the blow she had been expecting daily came. A memo told her to vacate the bungalow by the end of the month and report to the club manager for new accommodations, at which time there would also be a reappraisal of her work, her company status, and her work permit.

Instead of being upset, Sylvie felt the old bit between her teeth. To hell with Alec Boyer and his phony-baloney influence. Okay, so perhaps her days in the sun were now numbered, but who cared? She would go to New York or London and write the definitive story of what was really going on in Nassau, helped with the truth by Oliver Burt.

Boyar and all those under his influence would rue the day they ever tried to coerce her. Rereading the terse memo made the adrenaline race through her veins. She felt ready to take on every sycophant, every hypocritical hustler in the world. She wasn't made of British grit for nothing.

Her bravado didn't last. She woke up in the middle of the night, and fear of the unknown flooded through her. She was scared. She had to admit it—she was scared to death of starting afresh. She even felt she wanted to stay cocooned in Nassau, never too cold, never too hot, never overexerted . . . never _anything_ much—existing, not living. But Dick had rekindled her ambition. "You were one of the best," he'd said.

She relived the minutes on his yacht. They had been uplifting, inspiring. _Volition_—even the yacht's name carried a message. "Of my own volition," she whispered to herself as she looked out at the sea, now colored a deep indigo. She had been drifting for far too long. Without realizing it—he would be beside himself with anger if he knew—in giving her no option, except a life with him, Alec Boyar had actively pointed her in the right direction. She would go back to the work she had been born to do—and write the exposé of all time about life under the sun in the Bahamas.

But there was something she had to write _immediately_—a letter to Alec expressing what she _really_ thought of him and the infantile tactics he'd employed to rein her in.

She spent most of the morning writing it. It wasn't easy, particularly as she saw in the sharp clear light of the sun how her passivity had been a form of encouragement. As she tried to find exactly the right words, she remembered some of Alec's remarks over the months, remarks she hadn't bothered to fathom. Now they had new meaning. "Move in with me, baby," he'd said more than once. "It will save me checking up on you . . . will save the expensive phone job . . ."

Phone job. She looked at the phone in her bedroom. For the last couple of months she'd heard odd noises on the line but hadn't paid much attention, knowing how poor the island's system was. She dialed the clubhouse and listened intently. Click. Click. Click. Were they "normal" clicks or were they related to the kind she'd read about in a police report on phone taps?

All at once she *knew* her phone *was* being tapped. Probably there was a microphone somewhere in her bedroom.

"Save me checking up on you . . ." She shuddered. It was obscene. She climbed on top of the bed to look for a microphone on top of her wardrobe. She looked under the bed, in drawers, but even as she searched, she knew it was futile. Anyone working in that line of business for Alec would be so professional they would make James Bond look like an amateur.

Sylvie reread her letter. Even in terse, simple language it was far too good for him. She found an envelope, sealed it, and with new resolve cycled over to the main clubhouse. She would pay for a bellboy to deliver the letter along with Alec's ring.

Sylvie hadn't been in the development office for more than ten minutes later that day, when Alec Boyar marched in, his face white with anger, holding the letter out in front of him. "What the motherfucker is this all about?" He seemed oblivious to the stares of the other realtors.

"Alec, please . . ."

"Come with me or I'll break the place down." He looked as if he would, too. Sylvie followed him outside, his hand pinching her arm so tightly she could feel her blood constricted. "Alec, this is ridiculous. There's no need for this outburst. It's only demeaning you . . ."

"What are you made of? Ice? Oh, baby . . ."

To Sylvie's horror, at the end of the path, in full view of those looking at them through the window of the sales office, Alec went down on his knees, looking up at her with a piteous expression. "Baby,

I've missed you so much. Come back and let's fuck ourselves silly. It's because I waited too long. I was crazy. I should have fucked you the first time I saw you. You're going to love it. I'm going to give you the moon, the stars . . ." He held onto her legs.

"Alec, Alec, please, *please*—everyone's looking. Think of yourself, if you don't think of me."

He refused to leave her until she promised to come to the house that evening to "talk things over." He dropped her back at her bungalow, saying he would call for her himself around seven.

How could she have allowed herself to get into such a situation? Sylvie castigated herself. What could she do now? She had no intention of being there at seven, but where could she go?

She felt like running anywhere to get away from Alec. But where —to England? To worry Aunt Gert, who already had so much to worry about? No.

To Florida where her mother and Ed had recently bought a retirement condominium? She shuddered. Never! She looked around the bungalow she had loved so much. Now she saw it for what it was—a luxurious cage with hidden taps—phone taps, microphones. Oh God, please let Dick return and take me on that cruise . . . if only she knew where he lived—if only she'd taken his phone number.

On impulse, she asked Madge if she could borrow her station wagon for an hour or so and drove outside the club to the same phone booth she had used the night she'd warned Oliver Burt. Oliver— where was he? Should she try to reach him? Wouldn't that add to her problems, if not to his, too? She was a marked woman—of that she was sure. She was in terrible danger. Suddenly she thought perhaps she should go to Harold Christie or Eddie Taylor and tell them what was *really* going on. Who knew what Alec Boyar had told either of them, bringing about such a tour de force and cessation of so many privileges? They seemed like decent men. They would surely listen, but Sylvie discarded the idea. Alec Boyar was a valuable client who during recent months had spent a prodigious amount of money in the islands, investing, so he'd told her, in all kinds of deals. She was lost, staring at the phone.

On impulse she drove on to the airport. She would check into flights to New York and to London. She had to make a plan. Perhaps she would go and visit Aunt Gert after all, without telling her why; she hadn't been back since she'd taken the job, but even the thought of London in February deepened her gloom. She shivered, thinking of the cold guest room in Gert's house. The trouble was she was spoiled rotten.

She drove back despondently. The phone was ringing as she came in, with news of a reprieve, which cheered her up instantly. Alec had had an urgent call from Miami and had to leave that afternoon. He would call her on his return.

To go back to the development office was out of the question. Sylvie decided she would try to find a solution to her problem while she was swimming. She would swim out to the reef to clear her mind. She had just changed into her bikini when her patio door swung open and there stood Alec, his face strained and taut. "I'm late but I can't leave without you. You'll disappear. I know you will. You're coming with me."

"No, I'm not." She screamed. He came toward her like a tornado, tearing off her bikini top, savagely fastening his mouth on her nipple. She could feel his teeth making a mark. She threw her body about to avoid his hands, one diving down inside her bikini pants, his fingers clawing for her vagina, the other clutching her behind. Again he repeated, "I'm not leaving you here. Get dressed unless you want me to send the boys in to take you topless."

It was a new Alec, one she had never seen before, ominous, threatening, and adamant about being obeyed. Through the screen door Sylvie could see two of the men she had always thought were manservants. Now they looked like bodyguards—thugs. Alec was grunting, panting, his fingers caressing, but probing deeper, deeper in front and behind, his mouth suddenly covering hers, his tongue down her throat. He was about to force her over to the sofa when one of the men coughed and called out loudly, "You're going to miss your plane, boss."

He released her, staring angrily into her eyes. "Do you want to go in a sack or go dressed like a lady? You've got one second to make the choice." She knew he meant it. She could see herself tossed into burlap and thrown over one of the thug's shoulders to be checked as luggage. Without a word she headed for the bedroom to dress.

Alec followed her. "Don't forget your passport."

All the fire and revolt had gone out of her. What was the good of fighting him? Alec was too powerful, too influential in Nassau, if not everywhere in the world, a world that was rapidly closing in on her. She was lost. She was about to be "protected forever" by a Mafia boss, for that was Alec's real role in life. Of that she was now sure.

All the way to the airport Alec kept his arm tightly around her shoulder, one hand pinioning down her knee. As the car rounded the bend at the airport entrance and started to slow down to pull up at the curb, Sylvie's frantic prayers for a savior were answered.

Ahead of her, of all people, she could see Oliver—Oliver Burt himself—about to get into an official car with flags on the hood, following a tall, regal-looking gray-haired man.

As Alec released her to lean forward to give instructions to the driver, she opened the car door and leaped out. The car was still moving. She screamed, "Oliver, Oliver, Oliver . . ."

She expected to hear the crack of a gun as she ran blindly toward the tall black man. She expected to fall to the pavement with a bullet in her back, but nothing happened. Nothing.

As if in slow motion she saw Oliver, a puzzled look on his face, straighten up and look back toward her as she ran panting, still crying out his name. The puzzled look gave way to his usual wide, warm smile. He stretched out both hands and then, looking over her shoulder, he swiftly pushed her into the back seat of the car and almost into the lap of the startled-looking gray-haired gentleman sitting there.

~~~

"Missing!" So now Sylvie was missing, was she? Nell allowed herself a deprecating snort as she pushed the English newspaper to one side and moved her body so no rays of the sun could possibly bypass the large umbrella shading her.

It had been a shock to see Kitty Stein's by-line, even more of one to see the photograph of Sylvie touching the cheek of a monstrous-looking black man. Trust Kitty and the salacious English press to deliver a clumsy innuendo that Sylvie was having it off with Mr. Black up-and-coming politician, Oliver Burt. Knowing Sylvie, as Nell did all too well, she knew the story was trumped up from beginning to end. She started to read the last paragraph again. "Last seen being pushed into a large limousine by her intimate friend, Oliver Burt, one of the leading members of the opposition party, Sylvie Caplan has mysteriously disappeared from her Lyford Cay home. According to the Honorable Member Oliver Burt, Mrs. Caplan sought his protection at Nassau airport from a so-far-unnamed Miami mobster, who was attempting to shanghai her to his gangland headquarters. After forty-eight hours Oliver Burt announced, 'Mrs. Caplan has left the island for an unknown destination.' Questioned at the Lyford Cay development office, Sir Harold Christie described Mrs. Caplan as one of the most able and trusted members of his real-estate team. Mrs. Caplan joined Sir Harold's organization in 1968 following the death of her husband, the celebrated American composer Tyrone Caplan."

Again Nell pushed the newspaper away. It was ironic that she should arrive in Nassau just as Sylvie left. Had Sylvie really had to seek protection? Had she, too, been living in fear? If so, their lives—despite the enormous disparity between them—were eerily reflecting each other's once again. Nell hoped Sylvie knew what it was like to live with fear—hoped she knew how one's breath could freeze and guts could shrivel when a certain voice came on the phone.

Here she was in Nassau, loathing every minute of it, her only moment of relief the whole agonizing week coming when she had desultorily flicked through the English newspapers to find the highly suggestive story of Sylvie Caplan and her relationship with Oliver Burt. She had to hand it to Kitty. Kitty never gave up.

As Nell lay with her eyes closed, looking, she knew, infinitely tranquil, meditative, as the Godmother in repose was supposed to look, she mused on the amazing fact that her life and Sylvie's had somehow always been destined to intertwine. For of all the teeming thousands in the islands, she had discovered that Oliver Burt was Johnny's undercover man, who'd been working to unseat the first black government of the Bahamas—a corrupt black government at that—and to blow wide open the neat "receive and distribute" drug operation Diaz and Boyar had set up with very little trouble, once a few hundred thousand dollars changed hands.

Money was the ultimate weapon, whereas sex was the ultimate deterrent, a negative force that she was at last beginning to conquer and deal with on her own terms.

Her need for Johnny was no longer so great. It was still there but had lessened since her refusal to marry him. She had found she almost believed in the reason she'd decided to give him with many tears: that it would deal a terrible blow to her reputation to marry not only a divorced man, but a man who was, after all, her stepson, despite the similarity in their ages.

His initial mystification and obvious misery had affected her own feelings. It had assuaged her pain to know she had the power to wound him, too. Soon after, he had become withdrawn, had started to repress the feeling she now knew he possessed for her, but it no longer upset her in the way it once would have done.

When she drew near him, putting her arms lightly around his neck, she did so to test him, satisfied when she felt his erection, satisfied she could arouse him with the slightest bodily contact. It was enough for the moment; perhaps it would be enough forever.

The adulation of her people—her disciples—was akin to having an orgasm. She prayed it would always be so. Then there was still Violana. She'd paid Violana an unexpected visit only three months before. For a reason she couldn't explain to herself she'd felt in need of the old crow's admiration . . . for her confirmation that even without regular sex with a man her body could remain alluring, desirable.

Violana had half undressed her in her usual demeaning way and then to Nell's surprise and delight had made her body throb and sing as much as ever.

Unfortunately there were still times alone in her vast bed when her whole being cried out for Johnny.

Then her rage against Diaz would take over, rendering her weak, useless until it subsided. The wish for revenge because he had rendered her immobile was still there, but she was calmer about when she could achieve it. Now she knew the time, place, and person to carry out everything that she wanted carried out would come eventually. As the Godmother, she could achieve *anything* and *everything* she wanted, even the extinction of somebody as powerful and cunning as Joseph Diaz. For a long, long time Diaz had held the upper hand. Now it was unthinkable that the Godmother would have to endure this situation for much longer.

Violana had taught her patience and Nell could employ it with no trouble at all, but now it was patience with an end in sight.

She shivered despite the heat of the Nassau sun. "Your lover boy is going back to Nassau. *This time I want you to go with him.*"

As usual, Joe Diaz's call had come like an earthquake, collapsing the foundation she'd built for her life, wrecking her painstakingly acquired equilibrium.

"He's not. I'm sure he isn't planning . . ."

Diaz had cut across her icily. "He won't tell you. You tell *him* that you're going down to the island. It will give you a chance to check up on your secret funds. You'll find out that I keep *my* word, baby." There hadn't been the slightest letup in his freezing tone, despite the apparent friendliness of his words, and as usual Diaz had been right.

Johnny had told her he was going to Florida, and she had asked him if she could go with him. Looking at her searchingly, he had immediately admitted he wasn't only going to Florida. He was getting near to the truth. He was going on down to the Bahamas to meet his secret agent, the man who had become a friend, a trusted and true confidant working with him and the U.S. government to try to unravel a new and circuitous drug ring. His change from reticence to revelation had been astounding. Along with it had come signs of the old laughing Johnny. "I'm glad you want to come to Florida with me— and come down to Nassau, too. It will do you good to get some sun . . ."

"Sun!"

He'd laughed at the real dismay in her voice. "You can practice what you preach, dear GM . . ." She'd flinched. It was a contraction she loathed him to use, meaningless when *Godmother* meant so much. She couldn't bear anyone, not even Johnny, to talk about it lightly, let alone make fun of the name. He'd been oblivious. "Avoid the direct rays and protect your precious skin from summer's major snare, just as you wrap up your body from winter's woes . . ."

Again he had been making fun, mimicking their latest sales-promo language—which, as was so often the case, *pioneered* a new thought: the use of sun protection as an anti-aging device. Now that she was able to afford such experienced, talented research-and-development chemists she was always pioneering new ideas, even unpopular ones like avoidance of the sun; but unlike most inventors, creators, and pioneers, she made money immediately. Once she put her seal of approval on an idea and released a new product, a whole brave new world of women accepted it. *She was their Godmother. She knew.* She didn't give them bullshit. *She* cared, so Johnny could tease, mimic, could even sneer. But he knew more than anyone how much her public cared for her. Even if he hadn't been a sensitive soul and appreciated the *caring*, the businessman in him knew it because of their profits—enormous and growing more so every day.

She'd withdrawn into the safety and sanctity of her Godmother role and he'd quickly moved to take her in his arms. It didn't happen often these days. He'd asked almost brokenheartedly, "Nell, are you afraid of going to Nassau with me?" His question had alarmed her as much as the intensity with which he had asked it, even to the extent that she'd backed away, out of his arms, an action that would have been unthinkable not so long ago.

"Why, Johnny, what on earth d'you mean? There's nothing to be afraid of. But Nassau nauseates me . . . because of . . ." She couldn't bring herself to mention Lucy's name; she hadn't once since the divorce. "I've never wanted you to get burned . . ." As soon as the words were out she'd known they were the wrong words.

Johnny had taken her by the elbows angrily, if hungrily, half shaking her. "What does *that* mean? How do you know I'll get burned? Who are you referring to . . . who will do the burning? What do *you* know, Nell?"

She had smelled his suspicion of her. It had all been too much—first from Diaz, then from Johnny. She was sick of it all but she had remained calm, quietly rebuking him. "We both know it's a troubled place, Johnny. Whatever Wallace was trying to accomplish there, somebody wanted to obstruct him and you, too. From what I've read and what you've told me—the *little* you've told me . . ." There was a deliberate trace of hurt in her voice—"nowadays it's even more troubled. 'Evil under the Sun' . . . 'Drug Running' . . . you've seen the headlines. You probably know more than the papers do. Why are you so suspicious of *me?* What have I done to deserve that?" It was always the best way to deal with nonbelievers. Challenge their doubts, their insecurities. It worked with RTC nonbelievers. By taking the initiative it could give her time to deal with whatever doubts Johnny had about her. It had worked. He had apologized and now she was with him in Nassau, aware of what she had to do, receiving from Diaz in person a definite directive to report on the real reason for Johnny's visit, not the superficial meeting with Oliver Burt and some of his "trusted colleagues," some influential bankers on the island.

She *had* checked on her own investments, too, and been staggered by the amounts Diaz had added in the last few months. It was millions. If Johnny knew. . . . She had felt choked up as if she'd wanted to cry, seeing what was there.

There was nothing to cry about; the money was protected by the Bahamas' strict bank-secrecy laws, something Diaz had assured her about long ago, a guaranteed fact that had whetted her appetite, and encouraged her to go along with all that he had proposed in those early days. Now she had the millions and was making more for Ready to Change, but she had paid a high price for it, too high a price.

Was she going to be able to tell Diaz what he needed to know—that Burt knew more than they thought he knew—that there was a trap being set up by the U.S. Feds with the blessing of the British government, who wanted Bahamian politics clean and fresh before the islands moved to independence in 1973?

It was a trap for Boyar, one of the leading boys in the drug-distribution racket with close ties to the Canadian Mafia, already well in residence and operating real-estate businesses in South Florida. If Diaz was right, it was the kind of trap that could backfire and puncture the whole covert·U.S. investigation. "If, as we think," Diaz had told her silkily, "Burt is in cahoots with Fed agents, it's a violation, baby, of the sovereignty of the Bahamas. It's a conspiracy against the Bahamian government, and against that special fellah, Lynden O. Pindling, the prime minister." His sarcasm had been thick and unmistakable. "We'll make sure the Bahamian government gets to know what Mr. Smart-ass Burt is trying to do, with the help of those American assholes. It will put a stop to their snooping around in a way that bullets can't do—but we've got to be *sure*, baby. We've got to be sure. We think there's a plan to get a high Bahamian official into a very embarrassing spot—to take him into international waters and try to get him to accept a bribe on camera."

"What about it?" Nell had been short, sharp, not wanting to be any part of Diaz's plan, yet resigned to knowing she had no alternative.

"If what we think is right, the whole operation will be on film. Not your ad-agency type film or anything glamorous from Hollywood, but filmed by the FBI—as proof." He'd shut up abruptly, leaving her with just one more admonition. "It's up to you to get us the proof from Nesbitt and Burt. Call Boyar if you need any help."

She hadn't needed it, and in any case Boyar was "off the island." She guessed why after reading Kitty's venomous piece about Sylvie, "hobnobbing with those she thinks are going to hold the reins—no matter their color, creed, country, or credentials." Boyar was obviously off the island trying to locate his missing treasure.

Nell's lip curled disdainfully as she sank deeper into the richly upholstered wicker chaise lounge. It wouldn't matter how much clout Mr. Boyar had or how many millions were at his disposal; Sylvie wasn't a respecter of that kind of person. She had never understood the true value and power of money, which was the reason Sylvie had ended up having to scratch a living selling real estate, although Nell had to admit she'd chosen the right climate in which to do it.

It was such a heavenly day . . . if only . . . if only . . . in the distance Nell saw Johnny's car turn into the driveway, saw his sensitive face above the wheel come closer into view.

Her stomach lurched and she closed her eyes to try to dismiss the knowledge that she wasn't over him—even yet. This was the day she had to give the most convincing performance of her life, the day when she had to get Johnny to tell her what Diaz needed to know. It was no longer a fear of blacl mail, no longer greed to amass money. Long ago she would willingly have given up receiving another cent from Diaz. No, she was "following orders" to save her own skin. Deep within her a voice said, "It's your life that's in jeopardy." She would always be in jeopardy until Diaz was dead.

Johnny had been away since yesterday—to the "outer islands," he'd said, intimating that by the time he returned he would know whether all the time and money he had invested during the past few years had been worthwhile.

He was frowning as he approached to kiss her. It was easy for her eyes to fill with tears. She had trained herself to do it, following Violana's cruel tuition, but in any case with Johnny the softness that only he could evoke in her made it child's play. He cupped her chin. "Why tears?"

"Of relief." Her voice was so low he had to bend closer to hear her, kissing her eyes as if to take the tears away.

"I told you I wouldn't get burned. See?" He put out his hands, turning them over to show her his palms, too. "No burns, no scars, no danger . . ."

"Did you . . . was everything okay?"

He laughed a bitter but satisfied sound. "Yep. I'm going for a swim, then I'll fill you in on some of what transpired."

"I'll come with you . . ." Now she laughed, seeing his wry expression. "If you don't mind swimming with a blubber baby . . ."

He knew what she meant. She didn't allow a single ray of sun to get to her perfectly smooth, camelia-colored skin. She had had a special rubber suit made that covered every inch of her up to her chin. The new Ready to Change Sunblock covered her face in a thin opaque veil and over her hair she wore a hat with a large brim.

The water was like a drink for her body, and for the first time in months she felt carefree, young, as she tried to keep up with Johnny's strong crawl.

Later, showered, sprayed with her favorite lilac scent, in a flowing Mexican robe, she sat with Johnny in the Polynesian *tupa*, a lookout point on high stilts that was one of the many special features of the house Johnny had rented for the week. She knew she looked younger, rested, her beautiful hair like a luminous halo framing her head, her lace robe revealing her full bosom, the darkness of her nipples, darkness between her legs.

"Nell, you *do* look like an angel. Are you an angel?" It was the old

Johnny, affectionate, teasing, with no hidden suspicion in the question.

She nodded gravely. "Of course, I am, Johnny—your guardian angel."

They sat like loving friends—he stroking her hand, or every so often her hair, her face. He told her even more than Joe Diaz had expected to know—that Oliver Burt had indisputable proof Alec Boyar had been recruiting Bahamian blacks to replace the depleted ranks of the Mafia; that it was highly likely Boyar was involved in the death of Joe Gallo, who along with six others had recently been gunned down in New York; and that a major gangland war would possibly soon erupt between members of the Canadian and American Mafia, both fighting for a piece of the big new drug business being routed through the Bahamas. To sit surrounded by such beauty, listening to stories of so much ugliness, was, for Nell, unreal.

She closed her eyes as if to push it all away. When Johnny stopped speaking she opened them to murmur, "Go on. I can't believe it. What are you—what is Burt . . . or anyone, going to do?"

"I can't tell you any more, Nell, but believe me there's a plan that will prove to the world this government *is* corrupt, that money—big money—is changing hands, and high officials here are involved in helping move drugs more efficiently, faster into the States. The drug-enforcement guys are here—Burt is working with one of the most brilliant of 'em all. When the lid comes off this stew, believe me, the smell is going to be enough to gas every bloody gangster and politician living in this island in the sun."

"Is the plan all arranged? . . ." There was a charming little-girl hesitancy to her question.

"All it needs is the okay of the American ambassador. There's always some political busybody, lobbying for something or other, who doesn't want to upset the apple cart with a local government, but I don't think we'll have any trouble."

Inwardly Nell groaned. It was all as Joe Diaz had predicted—a plan that could be viewed as a violation of sovereignty.

When Diaz knew, all the work of years would be negated—*when* Diaz knew—*if* she told him. . . .

Again she groaned inwardly. She had no choice. Too much was at stake. But she vowed this was the last time the Godmother would bow to Diaz's commands. Following this, the Godmother would exercise her divine right and appoint an executioner. There would be no more time lost.

"*The School for Scandal* dramatizes the importance, even the necessity of gossip. We are, after all, to some extent a composite of what different people say about us—their views, their opinions of our personalities, our characters. It is fair to say, I think, that talking—gossiping—about people, constitutes an enormous part of what is known as 'social life.' " The talented director leaned back as he spoke, obviously measuring my reaction . . .

The phone rang and this time Sylvie decided to answer it. If she let it ring three times her answering service picked up, but it was time to be interrupted.

She had "broken through" the most difficult part of the interview with the brilliant movie director. When she returned from Marietta Tree's dinner party she was confident she would be able to finish the piece.

"Sam?"

"Yes, Helen . . ." Sylvie was delighted she'd answered the phone. It was Helen Gurley Brown, editor of *Cosmopolitan*, one of the wittiest, kindest, and most efficient women she had ever met. In a few quick sentences in her husky, sexy voice, Helen outlined an article she wanted Sylvie to write—on friendship. "Fast. Have you got the time?"

Sylvie sighed. It wasn't the deadline that worried her. It was the subject, fascinating though Helen's suggestion was. "It's not for me, Helen. I have the time, but not the heart for it. I'll explain that to you over one of our anticipated lunches sometime . . ." It was a year-old joke. They both tried to avoid the time and the food that "lunch" involved. They were forever promising to make a lunch date, which so far had never happened.

As Sylvie ran the water for her bath and heard the phone ringing on and off every few minutes in the other room, she wondered whether she had been too hasty turning down the opportunity to write the friendship article for *Cosmo*. She, of all people, was qualified to write a book on the subject, not only an article! Perhaps one day she would.

As she relaxed in the tub, happily aware that for once she wasn't running against the clock, she mentally counted how many people she considered were her close friends. Not many. Five or six at the most. They included Oliver Burt as the newest friend and Aunt Gert, her oldest, who was also her most-loved relation.

What a friend Oliver Burt had turned out to be—putting up with gossip-column innuendo at such a sensitive time in his political life, shielding her in the most literal sense of the word from real danger when he himself was a wanted man.

In the end it was Alec Boyar who'd received the bullet in the back, not more than a month after Sylvie had arrived in the U.S. and gone into hiding with one of Oliver's cousins who lived in Queens.

At the time she had been ashamed that the news of Alec's death had left her so unmoved. It was almost as if she had never known him. Perhaps in many ways she never had, because certainly the man she encountered during her last terrifying hours in Nassau had not appeared in their relationship during all the long months before. Her only emotion had been relief, a huge sweeping relief that she no longer needed to be in fear of her life, that she was away from the island of intrigue and corruption, and that her "cocooned" days were over. She had a fair amount of money—enough anyway to live on for a few months until she found a job.

One good thing after another had started to happen. She had been shopping for a thank-you present for Oliver's cousin when she'd run into the manager of the St. Regis, where she'd stayed with Ty when they'd first returned to New York, before they'd found the apartment overlooking Central Park. She had totally forgotten the article she'd written about the honesty of the valet on the fifth floor of the St. Regis who, gently reprimanding her, had brought back the diamond brooch in the shape of a musical clef that had been her first present from Ty. It had been attached to a dress she had sent to be dry-cleaned.

Smith Maynard had liked the piece, published it; and in the hope that the management would reward the valet, Sylvie had sent the manager a copy of the story headlined, "Honesty Is Alive and Well in Skyscraper City." From then on, whenever they had checked into the hotel until the apartment was ready, the manager had made an enormous fuss over them.

"What have we done?" Sylvie recalled wryly that these had been the manager's first words that day on Madison Avenue. "We haven't seen you in years!"

It had been the first real smile of welcome from somebody she knew, although Erica, Oliver's cousin, had tried to make her feel at home. Before she could stop herself, tears had coursed down her cheeks as she'd remembered the wonderful old days with Ty.

Over a Bloody Mary in the King Cole Room the manager had learned how troubled her life had been since Ty's death. He'd insisted she stay at the hotel for a pittance in a small room on the top floor. "At least until you've found what you want . . ."

It was an incredible act of kindness, which had been followed by an even bigger one—an introduction to Jim Brady, the brilliant newspaperman who was about to leave *Women's Wear Daily* to take over the editorship of *Harper's Bazaar*. He had encouraged her to write an account of her life on the island in the sun—not from the current tensely political angle, but from the vantage point of "getting to know people when you're trying to sell them a million-dollar property in a totally foreign climate."

Other pieces had followed. She'd compared New York's *shortest* building with its tallest—when the World Trade Center opened. She'd written an amusing account of celebrities' comments which accompanied their photographs taken with a new type of camera called the Polaroid SX–70, which produced an instant print developed outside the camera.

Then had come her big breakthrough piece in December 1972 when she'd written a kind of retrospective, referring to a piece she'd written ten years before that had predicted fame and fortune for a young man just starting his TV career—a young man called Johnny Carson. And Johnny had liked—no, loved—the new piece. He'd also been a great admirer of Ty Caplan's work, which meant Ty had occasionally been persuaded to go on the show. He'd always said he hated "that kind of thing"—until he actually sat in the guest chair, when he'd so obviously enjoyed every moment of thrust and parry.

Like Cinderella, Sylvie had found herself on a Pan Am golden coach flown to the West Coast to appear on the "Tonight Show." The exposure had been just the spur to start her ride to a top spot in journalism again.

As she switched on the news to see her favorite, Walter Cronkite, go into action, Sylvie marveled yet again at what a land of opportunity America could be—*if* you were prepared to work until you dropped; if you had a point of view that showed those in command you knew exactly who you were; and if you didn't just take pot shots at people, but wrote thoughtful, reflective articles based on what you perceived as the truth.

After her appearance on the "Tonight Show" she had received an invitation from total strangers to a black-tie dinner. "Mr. and Mrs. Ivo Carruthers request the pleasure . . ." She'd seen their names so many times in the gossip columns, she'd already appreciated how much they *liked* seeing their names in print. She had mentally labeled them with Ty's "insect" description . . . they had to be "no-see-ums," people of no account, no sense of their own identity, who lapped up their newspaper mentions as proof of their existence.

A letter from Aunt Gert had arrived the next morning. Sylvie had seethed at a paragraph describing the BBC's coverage of Nell, the Godmother's arrival in England and her triumphant Ready to Change pageant at the Albert Hall. "I hope you're meeting people, darling," Aunt Gert had written. "I know you're enjoying getting back to your writing, but if you stay cooped up with your typewriter, only your behind will get big, not your bank account or your opinion of yourself. Don't seek out loneliness, pet."

She had been about to chuck the Carrutherses' invitation away, although she liked the feel of its engraved surface. Rereading her aunt's letter, although she was sure Ty was probably smirking at her somewhere, she'd decided "what the hell." It was a miserable month —she only had two commissioned pieces to write and nothing else on the horizon except a book idea she wanted to try out on someone. Aunt Gert was right. If she didn't get out and about she wouldn't meet anyone to help her move on. She accepted.

Lady Luck had played right into her hands. She'd been seated next to Doug Tattersall, a lookout man for the N.A.N. News and Feature Syndicate, one of the nation's largest. He'd seen her on the Johnny Carson show and vaguely thought he remembered her pieces from the old days, although she doubted it. "Send me some ideas," he'd said.

Two days later to her amusement, Oliver's cousin Erica had called to say her name as a guest at the Carrutherses' "bash" was in both Suzy's column and Eugenia Sheppard's—in the former as "Ty Caplan's stunning widow, the writer Sylvie Samuelson . . ."—in the latter as "that bright new talent in town, the freckle-faced, laughing-eyed Sylvie Caplan . . ."

As Sylvie finished her makeup and slipped into a hot-red, ruffled short evening dress that Scaasi, a wonderful New York designer, had insisted she borrow from him, Sylvie reflected that for the first time in six years she felt like her own person. Perhaps it was for the first time in thirteen years, because after meeting Ty she had been so absorbed by him, so much a part of his life and personality, that her own persona had thinned into a shadow.

She had sent Tattersall some ideas, which he'd commissioned her to do, and after only a few months he had signed her up to do "people pieces" for the N.A.N. Syndicate on a regular basis. She had been writing "people pieces" ever since, deciding to use a contraction of her surname for her by-line, which ran as "Sam Says."

It was her own "in-joke." Interviewed as an up-and-coming talent on the "Dinah Shore Show," she'd laughingly explained, "I can't get over how people are daily chronicled in the gossip columns here, particularly in New York. If Samuel Pepys, England's most famous diarist, were to come back to life, he surely would have to be reborn here."

By now, "Sam" had totally obliterated Sylvie Samuelson—Sylvie Caplan, too. She was delighted. It was like being given a new life, a new chance to stand successfully on her own two feet—as if by shedding her old name she had also been able to shed all the grief and anguish that had been part of it. She had found a delightful little apartment on East Seventy-first Street with a small secluded balcony where she persevered trying to grow some plants. She had discovered an Italian wizard with scissors called Imo, who'd given her a brand-new look with a snappy new haircut. She had adopted a stray cat which she'd delighted in calling "Kitty," and she'd concentrated on becoming a typical New Yorker—hard-working around the clock, not conscious of weekends or holidays, striving only to do her best work.

In six months she had become the hot new rage. She knew herself that her writing had more depth, more perception. Smith's blue pencil might still be needed occasionally, but not very often, for she knew when a story was going off on a tangent and she could pull it back. She was happier than she had ever been in Nassau, which seemed like a bad dream.

Although she wrote five columns a week for a fast-expanding audience of readers across the country, she didn't accept many dinner or party invitations. There was no need to go and mingle with people like the Carrutherses anymore—although she'd read with amusement in *Women's Wear Daily* that they'd taken credit for her success.

Her phone had begun to ring almost as soon as her first N.A.N. "people" piece appeared in print. In a week, mail had started to arrive, and in a month she'd asked the syndicate if they could supply a secretary. How naive she was. If she wanted a secretary she would have to pay for one herself. As with the majority of syndicated writers, the arrangement was that she was paid a percentage of the manuscript fee paid by the papers who took her column. The syndicate handled basic editing, cursory checking of facts, and the mailing costs, which soon escalated as her column began to be picked up by newspapers across the country.

It didn't take long for Sylvie to remember and now thoroughly understand why Ty had avoided the "social conveyor belt" so assiduously. She was soon inundated with invitations from strangers and, worse, people who swore they knew her, had known her, were "sisters under the skin" and insinuated that without their help she couldn't really succeed.

"Don't worry, I've been there already," she dryly told Lad Myers, a young man sent along to her apartment by the St. Regis manager to help her out when a series of girls sent by a secretarial service proved they could touch the typewriter keys only at random. "Lad's creative but not overly so," the hotel manager told her. "He lacks the charm his hotelier father thinks he has. I tried to train him for his father's sake, but he's not cut out for front-desk work. Don't worry, he's hard-working and reliable. He just doesn't seem to know how to smile!"

Despite the hotel manager's warning, Lad's grave countenance suited Sylvie. She didn't have to worry about his moods because his temperament always seemed to be saturnine. The manager was right. He _was_ hard-working and reliable. Although his expression became neither less nor more pained, he also knew how to convey concern when a particularly persistent social-climbing hostess called to say that "unless Sam accepts my invitation to dinner and says she's been to my brownstone with one of the prettiest gardens in the world she'll just never _make_ it in this city!"

Make. Break. They were Nell's words, although Nell probably never used them anymore. Now that Sylvie was actually living on Nell's own turf—the good old U.S. of A., the land of opportunity— she was even more appalled to find how far Nell the Godmother had traveled. Hardly a week went by without some breathless accolade being paid to her in print, on TV, or the radio.

Nell had just been to the White House to receive a citation from the president for her tireless, selfless work; for now her philanthropy had been "discovered," a well-kept secret that had "miraculously" been ferreted out by a couple of reporters, who were being congratulated, Sylvie bitterly observed, as if they had done the country a huge favor.

Sylvie longed to stem the tide of adulation—and then finish it forever with words that would expose Nell as she knew her to be— worthless, scheming, immoral, utterly ruthless, and without conscience. She didn't dare. Even implying the Godmother had feet of clay was too dangerous. The revenue from Ready to Change advertising, Sylvie knew, had to be enormous. Any _suggestion_ in her columns that Nell was considerably less than honorable, let alone downright evil, could be enough for advertising to be whipped away from the papers carrying the damning words—and that would be only the beginning.

Sylvie knew only too well how fast Nell's lawyers could move. Aunt Gert's travail had shown her that, and then Nell hadn't been anything like so powerful. In five years the Ready to Change movement had thundered across the States like an eagerly awaited express train. From Maine to Miami, from Seattle to Syracuse, Nell's evangelistic "Be Ready to Change" message was being lapped up by women of all ages and backgrounds. The president had congratulated Nell on the spirit behind the movement in a televised meeting Sylvie had seen beamed out from a TV set in a Madison Avenue shop window, as she'd rushed to mail off a week's supply of columns to the N.A.N. headquarters in Philadelphia.

The only way Sylvie could let the anger out of her system was to get down on paper the story she longed to write. She tried, failed, tried again—then knowing it still wasn't right put it away in a drawer. One day, she promised herself, one day justice would be done. It just had to be.

She "separated the wheat from the chaff" in myriad ways in other columns, ones that were beginning to build her name for spotting talent early or conversely predicting when an apparently fast-zooming star would splutter out and disappear almost overnight. She seemed to have a divining rod for spotting the phonies. With her ability to spot sensitive issues, to pry loose the one sentence that gave her insight into an otherwise mysterious personality, the "Sam Says" column began to take on an extra dimension. In little over a year it was appearing in over three hundred newspapers—and "that's just the beginning," Doug Tattersall told an exuberant Sylvie over lunch at "21," where every so often someone would come over to say something like, "Hi, Sam, you look great. How's everything? Can you make my party next Tuesday—Wednesday—Thursday? . . ."

Sylvie took it all calmly, without fuss, winking at Doug whenever a particularly fulsome individual tried to butt in.

"Glad to see you're not fazed by all this attention."

"It's invisible ink," Sylvie quipped. "Doesn't leave anything in my mind because no one means what they say." Although she was incredibly busy, she was often consumed with a strange, wistful loneliness she had never experienced before, not even in Nassau. She tried to analyze what it was. It had nothing to do with missing a man. She was, if anything, intolerant of the women she knew who had to have an escort to go anywhere. English girls, she decided, had more self-reliance, perhaps because they'd had to put up with English men, who in the main were infinitely more self-centered than American men. No, it wasn't the lack of a man in her life; so what was it?

She came to the conclusion it was postconvalescence. It had taken her at least a couple of years to get over the shock of Ty's death and the abrupt change in her fortunes that had accompanied it. Then she'd been living in the cocoon spun by Alec Boyar and had had to fight her way out of it, with all the resultant trauma. She'd really been living a sick kind of life since Ty died. Now she was recovered but was going through reentry symptoms. She believed wholeheartedly in what she had written one day, based on Helena Rubinstein's celebrated remark that "work is the only excitement that lasts." But there were still moments, usually late at night or when she first awoke in the morning, when desolation took over, a mood that made everything seem pointless, joyless. It didn't last—but it didn't go away for good, either.

The first time Sylvie learned about the change in the ownership of the N.A.N. Syndicate came as she sat reading the *New York Times* one Tuesday, sipping her first cup of coffee of the day. She couldn't believe her eyes.

A. R. Kaye was not available for comment yesterday, following an announcement that he had obtained controlling interest in the N.A.N. News and Feature Syndicate, the nation's third largest. As part of the company's communications orientation, the announcement stated, it will investigate the possibilities of many projects, from satellite mail to business-intelligent information services, including joint ventures with other concerns. The company will also expand its electronic news operation.

A. R. Kaye, who has never given a press interview, is known to be one of the world's most powerful men. Industry sources say the transfer of stock involved little cash, that N.A.N. was acquired with other valuable considerations, described by a Wall Street analyst as extensive contacts in the journalistic, political, and financial communities, and Mr. Kaye's ability to obtain funds if necessary for continued operations.

One source said that Mr. Kaye had made only an insignificant investment of money and that officers of N.A.N. had yielded control to give the new owner the best possible chance to turn the company around and make it profitable. It was commented that with this transaction N.A.N. freed itself of a financial drain and from such continuing obligations as pension liabilities. According to an internal memorandum, by the end of 1975 the company will have a satellite receiver in every community it services, which is expected to translate into a five-million-dollar savings over standard telephone lines . . .

Sylvie had never easily understood financial reports, and as the story continued with a profit-and-loss statement she put the paper down and drained her coffee cup to stare out across the rain-streaked rooftops of East Seventy-first Street.

Did a change of ownership mean her column was in jeopardy? Why hadn't anyone, Doug or her editor in Philadelphia, told her about this? Would it affect her in any way? By the time she was dressed and on her way to interview Stephen Sondheim, she had forgotten all about the ownership change. It took another three months before anyone at the syndicate bothered to send her an official letter on the subject.

~~~

"Direct selling adds eight-point-five billion dollars annually to the U.S. economy. It offers about five million people income opportunities, mainly people who need little experience or capital to get started and who want to tailor their sales efforts to personal and/or professional commitments." Nell paused and turned slightly, as if to tell the pretty woman standing on her right the next piece of information more personally. "About seventy-five percent of all households in America are contacted by a direct-sales person each year and half of those households make a purchase of some kind . . ."

The pretty woman, whose face in just a few months had become the most famous in America, nodded and smiled as if the news delighted her.

Nell brought her speech to a conclusion. "As thousands of women all over America and in many parts of the world today know, direct selling offers self-employment with many, many advantages—flexible time, excellent earning potential. It has been a boon to women reentering the work force after raising families, as it does not require previous work experience for success. Direct selling allows people to meet new friends and provides a second career opportunity for those whose previous jobs no longer exist. Perhaps most important of all, it builds self-confidence and self-respect . . ." The applause and cries of approval from the thousand-strong specially invited guests seemed to be caught by the wind to echo in Nell's ears like parts of a familiar symphony.

As she turned to ask the new First Lady of the United States to cut the ribbon and declare the new 350,000-square-foot Ready to Change plant and research laboratory officially open, a stronger gust of wind caught the dark green hat that Givenchy had specially designed to go with her sleek green and silver coatdress. It lifted it high into the air to land with amazing precision on top of the Ready to Change flagpole. Nell joined in the laughter, which again ebbed and flowed in her ears like music. She was fully aware Johnny was looking at her—or rather *studying* her, a word that better described how he looked at her nowadays. She didn't give him the satisfaction of returning his concentrated gaze.

Although she was irritated that her hair was now blowing over her face, with her usual control she made no move to push the wisps away but thanked Mrs. Ford eloquently for her presence and for encouraging women everywhere to be ready to change. She then indicated the steps to the left of the platform which would lead to the new staff cafeteria where a celebration lunch was going to be served. Cafeteria! It was an absurd name for such a tastefully decorated dining area. No one working in a factory could ever have had it so good—nor would anyone working in a factory ever be able to find anything to equal it.

Nell surveyed the airy, peach-colored room, specially laid out today with tables for eight or ten. The tablecloths matched the walls, and the lighting was subdued, soft and flattering, so that even after a tiring shift the workers wouldn't look as jaded as they might feel. Betty Ford murmured how pleasant it was to look out on such a pretty garden, and Nell felt a surge of pride as ripples of appreciation continued through the room as the guests slowly entered.

It had cost plenty to blast out rock to build an extra patio adjacent to the cafeteria, but it had been worth it. It was tranquil, as if miles away from the nearby expressways, toll booths, and industrial parks. Banks of flowers and a gentle waterfall would encourage workers in good weather to sit outside under giant umbrellas and listen to good music, improving their tiny minds, opening up their souls—if people working conveyor belts had souls. Nell looked at her watch. Twelve-forty-five. They were exactly on schedule. A smile of satisfaction escaped as she took in the happy scene. Everything was moving smoothly, serenely, with her key people—saleswomen with the fastest-growing productivity—escorting the honored guests to their tables. Her best Ready to Change disciples were being introduced and, where it made sense, seated either next to or near someone of importance.

Seating was the most important factor in any event that involved feeding guests. Nell had learned that just from being at Wallace's side, when she had been appalled to see how few women who had all the help and money in the world knew how to be good hostesses.

By studying the success stories of the great ladies of cosmetics, Elizabeth Arden, Helena Rubinstein, and now Estée Lauder, Nell had also learned that they had one thing in common—a total awareness of the *importance* of the person actually selling their products. By making that person feel like a member of the family—sending birthday cards, regular presents, and invitations to significant events—the saleswoman was motivated to sell more and more and more. With the exception of Charles Revson, men never seemed to grasp that simple fact. "Business is business and friendship is friendship" was apparently in an embroidered motif framed and hanging in the Revson office dining room, but as far as his sales force was concerned, the two had always been intertwined.

What a fool Sylvie had been not to accept the invitation to the opening of the new plant. Nell was surprised by her reaction: Sylvie's curt "no interest in attending" message relayed to her by her public-relations people still rankled.

Didn't Sylvie understand how important the Godmother's friendship could be, how many doors the Godmother could open? She magnanimously had decided she *would* open those doors—where appropriate and mutually helpful—to the columnist who was, after all, her oldest childhood friend. Sylvie had apparently even *snubbed* the head RTC public-relations girl, who quite correctly had called her again in case there'd been some misunderstanding and Sylvie hadn't realized what an honor it was that she had been invited at all. They had had to cut down drastically on the number of press invited, so eager had *everyone* been—and that meant everyone who was anyone —to be present at the ribbon-cutting ceremony, performed so graciously by Mrs. Ford. Didn't Sylvie realize that the wife of the president of the United States rarely performed opening ceremonies of industrial plants—that her presence was an accolade of a very special kind? It was recognition of Nell's enormous influence on the women of America and a reward from the White House for giving her—the Godmother's—support to the administration after the agony of Watergate. Didn't Sylvie *know* by now how invaluable her support was to any endeavor? In two years' time she would be worth millions of female votes in the 1976 election.

As Nell had gone over the final list of acceptances—without a trace of irritation showing in her voice—she'd asked the only questions that really mattered regarding Sylvie. "This column, 'Sam Says,' are you certain it's now appearing in over four hundred papers, important papers . . . and that that figure is increasing every month?"

The overanxious, too-thin RTC vice-president of media nodded vigorously. "Yes, Godmother, I'm afraid so. I can't understand why she turned down our invitation. It was made perfectly clear that she could have an exclusive—that you had graciously agreed to a private interview before the press conference . . ."

As the VP leaned forward, Nell saw the stupid wretch had a smear of foundation cream on her collar. An RTC public-relations expert! What a travesty!

Wrinkling her nose fastidiously but without raising her voice, Nell drew the woman's attention to the stain on her collar, reducing her to tearful silence before dismissing her.

The PR maven could thank her lucky stars she hadn't been fired. As it was, Nell had made a mental note to start checking the collars of all the administrative staff. If they weren't ready to change, she'd decided, she was ready to get rid of the lot!

One thought had led naturally to another . . . if Sylvie was going to be "difficult . . . uncooperative"—Nell didn't waste time on the notion that Sylvie might be stupid enough to be antagonistic (she wouldn't dare!)—if Sylvie didn't want to *acknowledge* the Godmother's importance to the women of the world in those four-hundred-plus newspapers, well, then, Nell had made up her mind she would give a little of her valuable time to studying just how Sylvie Samuelson Caplan had achieved such a remarkable position in apparently double-quick time. Then she'd decided she would give even more time to the interesting task of stopping "Sam" from saying anything further. She'd buzzed the VP of media on the intercom. "Give me a list of the papers that carry 'Sam Says' and also Ready to Change advertising." She'd paused, then added, "Then give me the name of the competing newspaper in every town."

Looking around the vast room, before she started to eat her avocado and grapefruit salad, Nell checked that her instructions were being carried out perfectly. Where a saleswoman had an unfortunate, overbearing, or overtalkative personality, or was the reverse—too shy and uncommunicative—a key member of the RTC staff separated her from the VIP to avoid any embarrassing moments.

By accident Nell caught Johnny's eye. He winked at her in a way that once upon a time, even a year ago, would have affected her emotionally—sexually. Not anymore, although he could never know it. His inquisition of her the year before, following the collapse of the scheme to frame the Bahamian government, had been too harrowing and thorough for her to forgive. She had been put on the spot too often by him, and she had decided once and for all she didn't like it.

It had suddenly come to her who she was . . . *the Godmother* . . . *a revered and special member of the human race.*

She didn't need any man and certainly not one who looked at her with suspicion, who questioned her movements, her values, her contacts.

As she smiled her trained and lovely smile back, in exchange for the wink, she mentally felt herself grow taller, stronger as she saw how hungrily Johnny received her sign of approval. Even Johnny Nesbitt, the man she had carried a torch for since the day she'd first seen him in May of 1961, was an easily persuaded fool. He'd come running to her like a repentant, naughty little boy, when through his own method of investigation, he had decided he'd been wrong to doubt her, wrong to think in any way she would have passed on the plan he'd, in any case, only partly divulged as they'd sat by the ocean in Nassau.

Just as Diaz had predicted, the plan had been stopped by the American ambassador, but not before it had been "leaked" to Pindling who, snorting and shouting with indignation, had told the world press that America was interfering in Bahamian affairs and *daring* to insinuate that Bahamian officials were involved in an illegal drug scheme.

It was all part of an effort to discredit and destabilize the Pindling government. . . . Pindling was still making "outraged statements," even though he had been returned to office with no trouble and had achieved the independence from Britain he'd promised his voters.

Diaz, whom she loathed for circumventing her for so many years, was nevertheless head and shoulders above most men in getting things right. The Feds had not only been stopped short in their endeavor to break the ring but, according to Johnny, whoever had leaked it to Pindling had put back any progress for at least ten years. As if she cared.

For the last year she had realized she was at last in control. She could even be celibate if need be, although it wasn't necessary. Johnny would never grovel like the rest, but she knew that the more reserved, mysterious, and single-minded she became, the more he would be at her side, believing in her goodness, her purity. How puerile men really were.

Diaz was an exception and she was about to deal with him. She wanted him out of the way because of his opposition to her marriage and love life with Johnny. In a curious way she supposed she should almost be grateful to him for making the marriage impossible. But Diaz stood for the part of her past she had to be rid of forever.

At last she had it all worked out—even the date of his "disposal," as

if he were one of her product lines that could no longer be relied upon
to bring in the right return on investment. By her estimation, in early
1975 she would no longer need the extra "secret" funds that Diaz
supplied. By God, she couldn't wait to get rid of the mental hassle that
had always accompanied them.

Just as she had worked out Plans A, B, and C to become Mrs.
Wallace Nesbitt, so she now had Plans A and B for the extinction of
Mr. Joseph Diaz.

The First Lady was getting to her feet, the Secret Servicemen beside her to spirit her away. As Nell chatted to the wife of the new
president of the United States as they made their way toward the exit,
she mentally applauded her on her makeup, discreet but effective. All
thought of anything or anyone, however, swiftly disappeared as she
began to hear in the background her own special anthem—"Financial
security, emotional maturity, God-fearing, God-willing, we're Ready
to Change the world . . ." Proud tears pricked her eyes as the message
grew louder and more fervent.

Betty Ford turned to wave at the crowd before she disappeared from
view, but Nell knew nobody really cared that she was leaving. It was
the Godmother they cared about, the Godmother they loved.

As if to assure her of that fact the crowd now sang at the top of
their voices the Ready to Change call to duty, the song of allegiance
to her—the Godmother—to all the women in the world.

~~~

"It's your turn, Sam. He wants to meet you—not surprising as you
provide one of the most stable sources of revenue." Doug Tattersall's
words hung in the air. Taken by surprise, Sylvie couldn't think what
to say. Her old insecurity surfaced. Doug's words were meaningless.
She knew the anomalies, inconsistencies, and lunatic decisions taken
at the top in the publishing world—in every world, for that matter.

"Are you still there, Sam?"

"Yes, Doug, but . . . I don't really understand. Why can't he come
here? Why do I have to go to his office in Miami? D'you think one of
my columns offended him, or one of his protégés or projects? Oh,
God, what _are_ his politics? He's probably taken exception to my 'Cold
Water on Watergate' piece . . . and America's hair-shirt complex . . ."
She stopped, realizing she was thinking out loud. She didn't want even
Doug to know how quickly she could lose sight of her value to the
syndicate.

He sighed. "I can't answer you, Sam. I agree, you can never know what the top guys are thinking when they do what they do." He was saying all the wrong things.

To stop him making her feel worse, Sylvie interrupted him. "I've got to rush, but thanks for telling me in advance about the invitation. I'll wait till I get the letter before I torture myself further."

It wasn't so much an invitation, more a command appearance, Sylvie registered three days later, when a letter from A. R. Kaye arrived with an open airline ticket, giving her three suggested dates for their meeting. An economy-class ticket. Sylvie was amused. The little she'd heard about the man, it made sense that his worker bees, even a columnist who added so much lucre to his coffers, should be made to understand the value of money. She called the number she was directed to call and told one of his secretaries she would be in his office on the second date suggested for a "free-ranging exchange of ideas, a chance to explore new possibilities, and to get to know each other."

She phoned Aunt Gert in London before she left New York. Gert was really the only person Sylvie felt she could confide in about her fears, her trepidation that her newfound sense of security and confidence was yet again going to be decimated.

Sylvie had called Gert when she'd received the invitation to the opening of the Ready to Change plant, astonished that even Nell could have the gall to expect *her* to write glowingly about the Godmother's good works.

Gert's down-to-earth sense of humor had made her realize that Nell was beyond all normal comprehension and her value system now so seriously out of sync that she was—or thought she was—truly a law unto herself. "Stay away from the subject—stay away from danger." As if she'd *needed* Aunt Gert's explicit warning.

Now Sylvie said anxiously, "Takeovers always cause problems. There's another syndicate after me to work for them, auntie, but I hate change. Still I suppose it's good to know I won't be jobless if Mr. Mystery Man takes an instant dislike—just when my luck has finally changed, too. Wouldn't you know something like this would happen."

Aunt Gert was really helpful, as she somehow always knew how to be where Sylvie was concerned. "You're so good at what you do, Sylvie, and so modest—certainly in comparison to all those trumped-up Americans you're surrounded with. Just be yourself, darling, that's all you need to be." Gert was as reassuring as Sid had been the day she'd gone to the Ivy to have lunch with Smith Maynard. Sylvie gulped, an inexplicable lump of nostalgia in her throat. All the same, she reflected the day of her trip down south, I wouldn't go to *this* interview with a button off my coat.

She'd gone shopping the day before and found a cheeky school-girlish jacket and skirt by Kasper, one of her favorite American design-ers, which perfectly emphasized her tiny contours, and a white-lace shirt, which emphasized her femininity.

But she hadn't expected it to be so hot in Miami in February. She'd chosen all the wrong things. That fact, and her natural inclination to nervousness, meant she could feel beads of perspiration on her nose, even in the perfectly air-conditioned, towering office block overlook-ing the ocean. It was ridiculous to feel so nervous, she told herself one more time as she waited for Mr. Kaye's secretary to come out to escort her into "the presence." Perhaps he was going to ask her to cover world events, news, instead of the people stories that had be-come her trademark.

Five minutes passed into ten minutes that felt like ten hours, before a freckle-faced, snub-nosed pretty blonde in Bermuda shorts with matching shirt came toward her, hand outstretched. Sylvie was shocked. Obviously the big boss wasn't one for formality. She had expected a high-powered, suited secretary, not someone who looked like a high-school kid turned model. Instead of relaxing, Sylvie be-came more and more uptight, pleased in a perverse way she was "prop-erly dressed for an office," even though the office was a stone's throw from the beach.

It *was* a magnificent office all the same—that opinion surely had to be universal, Sylvie thought, as Prue Bailey, the secretary, ushered her into a small anteroom, its walls covered with beautiful old nautical maps. Prue suggested she make herself comfortable in one of the dark leather library chairs. "Mr. Kaye will be with you in half a minute. He's just finishing a long-distance call."

An archway with no apparent door led to what Sylvie imagined was Kaye's inner sanctum. Through the arch she could see floor-to-ceiling windows with panoramic views of the Florida keys and ocean, a group-ing of oatmeal tweed–covered sofas on one side, an antique mahogany drink trolley on the other.

There was a decisive "Yep, no, glad you see it my way." A click on the telephone.

Sylvie got up and smoothed down her skirt as she heard Mr. Kaye's chair creak and footsteps approach. He came toward her, hands outstretched, and for a second, with sunlight in her eyes, she couldn't see his face. When she did, her own outstretched hand flew to her mouth to cover her involuntary cry. His grin grew wider when she recoiled as if in fear and repeated, "Oh, my God . . ."

He didn't stop coming toward her. He gripped her shoulders fiercely, laughing joyously. "Forgive me, Sylvie. I couldn't resist it. In any case, I wasn't sure you'd come if you knew it was only me. I thought you might resign on the spot and go to King Features."

Dick Kolinzcky. It was Dick Kolinzcky. Sylvie looked behind him as if to say, "Is Mr. A. R. Kaye here? Is he behind you in the office or are you one and the same person?" She expected to feel her skin grow hot, the way it always did grow hot and red from blushing whenever something overwhelming happened, but instead she felt as if every drop of color had drained out of her. She was speechless. She didn't know whether to be furious at his deception or ecstatic that the new boss was someone who had already told her she was "always the best." But a lassitude was creeping over her limbs. If he hadn't been holding her, she could easily have fallen to the floor.

He led her into his office, stunning in its simplicity, a Paul Klee dominating the wall behind his desk, which was a large slab of blue-gray slate, quarried, as he told her later, at the place where he'd made his first real money, near Lake Athabasca in Alberta.

"Well, Sylvie—Sam—shall we have a drink to celebrate that we will be working together again?"

She shook her head. Alcohol would be a disaster until she recovered herself—if she could *ever* recover. In a wobbly voice, she said, "I guess you could say you've made it all right, Dick. But why did you change your name?"

"No one could pronounce it." He laughed, and she was struck by how boyish he still sounded, how he still brushed his hair back unnecessarily, although now it looked neat and controlled, infinitely shorter than when she'd seen him on the yacht at Lyford Cay.

The thought prompted a question that really was silly, but she had to ask it. "Was *Volition* on charter? Or do you own her?"

He snorted self-deprecatingly. "What does it matter? Yes, yes, she's mine—I had her built to my specifications. I'm hoping you're going to stay down for the weekend and come for that sail."

Now the beetroot-red blush came after all—ruining her appearance of composure. She didn't know what to say. She knew her answer depended upon whether the beauteous vision—Connie—was still on board, or perhaps another one just like her in her place.

Dick didn't press her. He started to talk about N.A.N., his new business, and his fascination with the news-and-features service side of it. She began to relax as he moved onto familiar ground; she was even able to ask him after a few minutes whether it was true, as reported, that he hadn't put out much cash for the purchase, despite the millions it involved.

Again he laughed, throwing his head back and looking for one quick moment like the wild Czech gypsy, as Kitty had always called him. "I've never used what you may call orthodox methods, my Cockney sparrow. Like many of Europe's displaced children, remember, I had no formal education. I realized in England I would never catch up in the academic sense, as much as I longed to—*that* I've reserved for my old age." Although his tone was light, Sylvie knew he meant what he was saying, remembering he'd always talked like that back in the days when both of them earned only a pittance. Three pounds, three shillings a week!

She glowed with pride in his accomplishments. To think that Dick Kolinzcky was the mysterious multimillionaire A. R. Kaye! Everything he'd set out to achieve he *had* achieved and then some! She felt an odd, motherly sense of pride, but even as he explained more about the N.A.N. deal, the pride was contaminated by another realization.

"Paying money for a property is just one way to acquire it, but it's not necessarily the best for either party . . . and as far as N.A.N is concerned, where a trust is involved, the sale eased the way toward making provision for the trust dissolving, as it must in the next five years . . ." Sylvie tried to look as if she were paying attention, but her mind was racing on another course. How could she ever write the true story about Nell now? How could she ever carry out the grand exposé she had promised herself, to right the wrongs of so many people?

Dick Kolinzcky was the father of Nell's child. He was just as much to blame for the child's abandonment as was Nell. What had happened to Nell's vow that "one day we'll get our baby back"? Who had decided to forget the past so completely? Obviously Nell, but obviously Dick, too, in his relentless climb to the top. A cold chill went through her; her pride in Dick's accomplishments was doused out.

Nell and Dick—both had reached the top, all right. They really *had* been meant for each other, after all. Sylvie didn't know what had happened to their relationship, but who knew if one day they wouldn't get back together again? They were both ruthless, uncaring. Perhaps one had to be in order to get to the pinnacle. As if it were yesterday she could hear Nell saying, "Why bother with millionaires, when there are multimillionaires? Why go for less, when you can go for *more?*"

She decided for once she would be clever, too. It titillated Dick to think he was now in a sense her boss, so she *would* go along on a short cruise . . . and once on board she would make it clear she would sign a new contract, but only for much more money, or she would go to the opposition. She would extract as much from him as possible, and what was more important, she would make sure she had a good time doing it.

During the next twenty-four hours she had to keep reminding herself that Dick was a ruthless, stop-at-nothing mogul . . . it was hard, because he was going out of his way to be kind, to be charming, to be fun!

He took her shopping in Coral Gables for some clothes to wear on the yacht. He introduced her to a Cuban friend, who served black bean soup that tasted the way he told her his family cook had made it back in Prague. They combed old bookstores together, and then he sent his car away and they walked the two miles or so back to her hotel —Dick holding her arm and answering his own questions just as he'd always done in the old days whenever they'd met for coffee at Jimmy's Sandwich Shop.

If she felt nostalgic, it was obvious he felt more so, although every so often she sensed him withdrawing into a world of his own, when he would stare into space and remove his hand from her arm, acting as if she weren't there.

Now she began to dread the yacht trip, hesitant to ask who would be on board, certain in some uncanny way that the beautiful young creature she vaguely remembered was called Connie would be there . . . and there she was, as exquisite as ever, waving to them from the top of the gangplank as they left the car on Friday evening, Dick's face eager and excited as he began to run toward his yacht.

He must be dying to make love to her, Sylvie thought bitterly, for she had to be one of the most beautiful girls she had ever seen away from the pages of *Vogue.*

Dick bounded up the gangplank and gave Connie a quick kiss on the cheek. He doesn't want me to see him really kiss her—but before that thought could show on Sylvie's face, Dick turned to propel her forward. "You met Connie in Nassau, didn't you, Sylvie? Then she was just a fledgling member of the crew, a substitute cook, as a matter of fact—but can you believe it, she cooked her way right into the heart of my confirmed-bachelor captain. Too bad you missed their wedding a few months ago. You can imagine what an ugly bride she made, eh?"

For the second time that week, Sylvie was speechless. Connie shyly looked at the deck as her husband, Captain Tony Booker, came up to shake Sylvie's hand vigorously.

Her head was spinning. Would another beauty suddenly appear? Surely there had to be *someone* as divine and as young (Sylvie estimated Connie to be no more than nineteen or twenty), who would appear as mistress of the master cabin? But no—Sylvie was the only guest, shown to an amazingly spacious stateroom with a white linen sofa and white linen cover on a queen-sized bed, Mozart's score for the Overture to the *Magic Flute* framed in alpaca frames on the walls, huge white fluffy towels piled up beside the adjoining full-sized tub in the bathroom.

That night, as the captain and Connie joined them for dinner—a delicious seafood concoction known as Connie's Delight, consisting of crab, conch, lobster, and ginger sauce—Sylvie saw the years fall away from Dick's face. He looked again like the boy she'd once known. She decided she would live a fantasy weekend, pretending everything she had once thought and dreamed about had come true, pushing to the back of her mind all thoughts of Dick's betrayal, going off to Canada with Nell.

They fished and snorkeled, swam in the magical turquoise waters off Abaco, sat in the sunset's glow to toast their new "partnership" and the new contract that would be signed on their return. When Dick took the wheel, obviously in his element as the wind got up and the vessel seemed to fly over the water, Sylvie tucked herself in a corner with Connie to talk about the free and easy life the girl had lived for the past three years.

She was as unspoiled and beautiful inside as she appeared on the outside, Sylvie decided. Whether it was the freedom of life at sea that had produced such a remarkable creature she didn't know, but in only twenty-four hours Sylvie felt a strong attraction toward her. She noticed Connie's kind little gestures, the thoughtfulness she exhibited toward others, her devotion to her husband, who, Sylvie noted with some irritation, treated her more like a favorite child than his wife.

And Dick, she realized with even more irritation, was treating her like a child, too, a favored child with brains! There only seemed to be affection in his attitude to her—the kind of affection he'd bestowed years before with pats on her hand, a casual arm thrown around her shoulders. It hurt. Didn't he know she'd grown up, that she knew now what shared passion was, that she'd been adored—no, *worshipped*—by one of the most talented men in the world of music?

On Sunday afternoon Dick announced he'd decided to take a day off, that instead of returning to Miami that night, they would "loaf a little. How about it, Sylvie? Can you put off turning into Sam until Tuesday?" Before she could reply, he did it for her, laughing, "I'll put in a good word with your editor."

She knew she should go along with his childish humor, but she felt strangely out of sorts, irritable.

When she came on deck that evening in a tailored shirt and slacks to see the captain take Connie fiercely into his arms to kiss her neck, she rushed back to her cabin, a pain she knew only too well invading every inch of her. Jealousy! It was ridiculous, but the sight of two people obviously in love was too painful to observe. It was no good dreaming about a relationship with Dick. She knew only too well what kind of man he was. A man may change his name, but a leopard doesn't change his spots!

She decided to dress up, to look not sporty but alluring. She was glad she'd slipped a favorite dress into her luggage. It was so simple that on a hanger it looked like lingerie; but its cherry red color lit up her looks, and the high demure front, closing at the neck with a Peter Pan collar, gave no indication of the back, which was cut so low that it barely covered the crease of her buttocks.

"Whew!" said Connie with huge appreciative eyes as Sylvie came back on deck, "don't you look smashing. Wait till the boss sees you in that."

Dick's eyes lit up, Sylvie noted with pleasure, but he said nothing. All right, don't pay me any compliments, she thought angrily; I've lived without them to this date, I'll survive.

For a change she had two rum cocktails before dinner, which was delayed with a call for Dick that came through the ship-to-shore radio. Whether it was the balmy night, the cocktails, or the champagne the captain poured while they were waiting for Dick's return, Sylvie didn't know, but as Connie started to tell her shyly how happy she was they'd met, that the "boss" had told her what a brilliant writer Sylvie was after their first meeting in Lyford Cay, Sylvie started to reminisce to Connie about her first meeting with Dick in Fleet Street, her eyes shining with tears as she looked out over the sea as the yacht rocked gently on its anchor.

The two Filipino cooks on board were preparing dinner that night, so Connie was relaxed, listening intently, not going below to check on things as she usually did. As Sylvie stopped in midsentence, Connie whispered, "You're still in love with him, aren't you?"

Sylvie blushed. She couldn't stop herself. "Of course I'm not."

Connie touched her apologetically. "Don't be angry." She wasn't angry. Who could be angry with Connie? There was such an appealing innocence about the girl, but she was wrong. She *had* to be wrong.

She squeezed Connie's hand. "Of course I'm not angry. You're right, I did love him once when I was very young, but he loved my best friend . . ." Connie was about to answer when Dick reappeared, shouting, "I'm starved. Come on, children." They went to the dining galley for a wonderful Eastern dinner.

A crazy quarter moon hung in a perfect sky like a child's toy. Sylvie knew she'd drunk too much champagne, that she wasn't making much sense, but she felt she had to get through to Dick, had to make him understand something—what it was, she wasn't sure . . .

When Connie and her husband made their excuses and left, Dick took her by the hand and said "Let's go aft . . ." She followed him meekly, aware how tall and strong and powerful he was now. He made no attempt to touch her as she looked up at him in the moonlight, talking, talking . . . what was she saying? She didn't care. It had to be said. She was telling him about the column she had wanted to write for years, the one she *intended* to write one day, the exposé of the Godmother, the most important piece of writing of her career, of her life—"to put the record straight . . . to see justice done . . . for Mr. and Mrs. O'Halloran's sake . . . for Aunt Gert's sake . . . for the baby's . . ." Before she could finish the sentence, the most important sentence of all, his mouth was on hers, eating her, sucking her mouth into his, all the power of him pouring out to envelop her slender body.

He lifted her off her feet, carrying her down below deck to his cabin. She could hear herself feebly protesting, but she didn't mean it. She wanted him, oh, how she wanted him more than she'd ever wanted anything in her life. He was kissing her gently now, her eyes, her ears, her chin, not touching her body, when she longed for him to rip her dress off, to ravage her, to have him in her as once he'd poured himself into Nell.

Instead, to her hurt and disappointment, he moved away, stood up from the bed where he'd laid her down like a precious piece of porcelain.

He looked down at her cryptically. She couldn't read anything into his expression. "I'm not going to make love to you now, Sylvie." His voice sounded strange, taut. "Have I proved to you that I'm not the worthless creature you believed me to be all those years ago?" She remained motionless, not understanding, her head still spinning with the champagne and her own emotions. "Sylvie, do you believe in me now," he repeated, "as I thought you once did when I was just a dreaming young boy?"

"Of course, I do . . . but . . ."

"There's no 'of course' about it. Sylvie. I want you to marry me. That's why I asked you down here. I'm not interested in renewing your contract. I don't want any more columns, any more 'Sam Says' . . ."

She jumped up. She felt tawdry, unclean, as if she'd walked into his cabin and lain down asking to be raped.

"You don't want any more columns," she repeated stupidly. "No more 'Sam Says' . . ." Rage came from out of nowhere. Did he think she was an idiot, a stark raving idiot who couldn't see what he was getting at—when only minutes before she'd poured out her long-burning ambition? Would he go to those lengths—actually ask her to marry him to stop her writing the truth about Nell? She lurched as she tried to reach the cabin door. "You must be out of your mind. You must think I'm out of _my_ mind. How dare you try to shut me up like that? You haven't changed. Don't worry! I'm not going to sign another contract with you. You can't pull the wool over my eyes . . ."

She rushed along the passageway to her cabin, throwing herself onto her bed, hot angry tears soaking the pillow. "How dare he. How dare he." The same words reverberated in her throbbing head until she was aware the yacht was moving. They were sailing, when Dick had said they wouldn't set sail till the morning. As the motion increased, Sylvie began to feel very ill. She spent most of the night retching, resolving never to drink champagne again or to set foot on _Volition_.

She finally fell into a disturbed sleep about 4:00 A.M., waking when a sharp streak of sunlight blazed into her eyes, and she looked through the porthole to see they were tied up once again in Miami.

She hastily showered, only wishing she could go straight to the airport and back to New York, but she'd left most of her things in her hotel room. There was no one about on the top deck, and it was only when she stood forlornly on the dockside that one of the Filipino boys told her he had been detailed to take her back to the hotel.

No sign of Connie or her husband, the captain. No sign of the boss.

They were back to start a new work week, after all. Mr. Kaye had obviously had a change of heart. No wonder, after the events of the previous evening. Sylvie felt a blaze of anger start again, but she submerged it. She had to extricate herself from N.A.N. and get over to King Features before they changed their minds. If only she didn't feel so ill.

When she reached her hotel room, she decided to lie down for a few minutes after she'd booked herself on an early-afternoon flight to New York.

She awoke with a start, not knowing where she was, sweating, nervous, aware the phone was ringing. It must have been the phone that woke her. Good God, it was three-thirty in the afternoon. Was it Dick calling? She didn't want to answer, in case it was, but when the phone kept on ringing and ringing, she cautiously picked up the receiver.

"Sylvie . . . Mrs. Caplan . . . it's me, Connie Booker . . ."

Her relief was audible. "Oh, Connie, I'm so glad you called. I felt terrible leaving without saying good-bye . . ."

What on earth had Dick told the captain? Probably nothing. It was, after all, his prerogative to change his mind, to put out to sea, to put back to dock—whenever he felt like it.

"Oh, me too, Mrs. Caplan . . ."

"Oh, please, call me Sylvie . . ."

"Can I come to see you, Sylvie?" There was a note of urgency in her voice.

"Why . . . yes . . . but I've got to get back to New York. I wasn't feeling well . . ." Sylvie tried to laugh apologetically. "Too much champagne and too many spices . . . too much excitement. I fell asleep. I don't know if I can make a connection now, but I'd like to. I've missed the plane I booked when I came back to the hotel."

There was a pause, then Connie said hesitatingly, "I think there's a late flight going into Newark. Would that suit you? About seven-thirty? I really would love to see you for a short bit, but I could book you on that flight first, if you like . . ."

"Oh, Connie, that would be wonderful. Would you? When could you get here?"

"In about thirty, forty minutes—shall I come straight up?"

"Why not . . ." Sylvie groped for her glasses to read the number on the telephone. "Room 1146 . . ." She still felt groggy when she went into the bathroom, but a quick shower would fix that. She decided to wash her hair too. She had about three hours before she had to get to the airport. It would dry in time. She didn't want Connie to see her looking so depressed and hung over. Whatever the dear girl wanted, probably an exchange of addresses, Sylvie hoped she wouldn't sing a paeon of praise for her boss—or even mention him. She felt too exhausted to entertain even Connie for long. Her spirit was broken. The old joylessness was back, every time she thought of the lengths to which Dick had been prepared to go to stop her telling the truth about Nell.

About four-fifteen she tried to read through some notes on an interview with Gloria Steinem, knowing she was reading the same paragraph again and again without taking it in. There came the expected tap-tap on the door. Thank goodness. Now she badly wanted to see Connie . . . somehow *wanted* to mention Dick's name . . . probably, she admitted to herself, she wanted to interrogate the young girl.

She didn't bother to put her shoes on as she went to open the door. "Dick . . ." He pushed her back into the room, now really towering over her, his face angry, in pain.

"Yes, Dick . . . Dickie . . ." he mimicked. "I don't really know what persuaded me to come to give you one last chance . . ."

"Me! How dare you . . . me, one last chance! What gives you the right . . ."

"This . . ." He swung her into his arms again, his mouth hungrily searching for hers, his hand somehow under her skirt on her bare thighs. Oh, she groaned inwardly, how could she fight him, how could she leave him? She was in a turmoil of misery.

He threw her down on the bed, covering her with his body. She could feel him, big, enormous against her, as he kissed her more and more passionately, but again it was he who desisted, who broke away. "It's time you and I had a long-overdue conversation. You told me once I was an opportunist. You told me not to bother you anymore, remember? I was down on my luck. You believed everything that half-witted Stein told you."

It was incredible, Sylvie thought, that it still bothered him. He had made the biggest success of anyone on Fleet Street, probably in Britain, for that matter; he was richer than Croesus, yet he still remembered word for word what a silly little girl had said to him twenty years before.

"Yes, I was wrong." The fire had gone out of her. Connie was right.

She was still in love with him, perhaps always had been, if it was possible to love two men at once—Ty, who had loved her, and Dick, who never had. She looked up at him, her eyes full of tears. "I loved you, Dick, but you loved Nell . . . so much . . . you had a secret love affair." He put his hand over her mouth.

"Don't say any more, anything you may regret. Connie was the one who told me what you told her on the boat last night. I couldn't believe my ears—that you could have thought I loved Nell, but then I started to see it through your eyes. I started to realize how it could look, but then you see, Nell told me how you used to laugh at me behind my back, about Kitty's influence, about . . ."

She interrupted him. "But you and Nell . . . the baby? . . ."

Dick sat back looking at her, then let out a long whistle. "You thought . . ."

"Nell told me so!"

Dick pulled her to her feet as she went on talking. "And last night, when I told you in my tipsy state that I wanted to expose her in a column, hoping for your backing, your support, I thought you were trying to shut me up for obvious reasons, asking me . . ."

This time he stopped her with his mouth, probing, loving, until she responded with more and more passion.

He pushed her away gently. "I've got to control myself somehow. Don't ask me how. I've got to show you something. Not another minute of life must tick away before you know the truth, the whole truth. Come to the office with me now."

Sylvie looked at her watch and said halfheartedly, "I've got a plane to catch . . ." She paused and looked at him with a shy smile. "At least I thought I had."

He simply shook his head and tucked her arm in his.

They went back to his office, up to the twenty-second floor where only five days before, Sylvie had sat in such trepidation about her future prospects. Now events were moving at such speed she felt she was on another planet.

Purposefully, Dick went to his desk and pressed a switch. In the far corner of his office a section of the wall swung open to reveal a safe. "I keep any number of odd-related things in here," he said over his shoulder. "I've always known one day this would be useful. Sit down, Sylvie. You'll need your strength to read this." He handed her a cheap airmail envelope with one word, "Dickie," scrawled across the surface. It was Nell's writing. Sylvie's hand shook as she took out a letter, written on yellow lined notebook paper.

*Dickie dear . . . I should hate your guts but I don't—yet.
You'll probably hate mine when you discover I've taken
your savings. What a creep you are, always pleading poverty when you had that nice chunk of cash stashed away.
Well, you'll make some more and I'll pay you back in
spades one day. The fact is, I can't stay around here any
longer with you away and not showing any more interest
in me now than you did when I persuaded you to help me
escape from that rat, Smith Maynard. As I told you on
the ship coming over, all I want is a chance in life to
prove to that bastard that when he got me in the family
way he should have married me, and not pretended the
kid wasn't his. He salvaged his conscience, getting the
kid adopted, although Big Boots Stein thinks it's because
it was her idea. Let her think it! I'm going off to the States
to make it big myself. Don't try to find me. You never
will, but I've just got to prove I'm someone to Smith so
he'll suffer the pangs of hell as I've done over him, the rat.*

Sylvie turned the paper over. "SWALK, Nell . . ." Tears brimmed
over as she put the tatty paper down. Seeing Nell's old sign-off greeting.

Smith Maynard! She couldn't believe it. Dick took her to the oatmeal tweed sofa to dry her tears with his handkerchief. "She paid me
back, too." He showed her a check that she hadn't noticed stapled to
the letter. It was for five hundred dollars to A. Richard Kolinzcky,
signed Nell Nesbitt. "I never cashed it," Dick told Sylvie. "It was a
lesson I wanted to remember forever."

Sylvie turned her face away. How could Dick ever forgive her for
all the things she'd thought about him, all the things she'd said? Her
instincts *had* been right . . .

He took her in his arms, then said, "Hell, wait a minute . . ."

He went over to his desk and pressed the intercom. "You can leave
now, Prue. Lock the outer door. I'll let myself out." He pressed a
switch and Sylvie saw a door in the archway slide out. He came back
to the sofa. "I'm short on control, Sylvie. We've wasted too many
years . . ."

She held out her arms. "Oh, please, please, don't have any control
left. I can't stand it either."

He knelt before her, his hand carefully unfastening her skirt, placing it neatly over the chair, pulling down her panties, as she much more carelessly pulled off her lace shirt and bra and threw them to the floor.

He looked at her nakedness for a long minute before he opened her legs and started to suck her slowly, deeply, until she was writhing in ecstasy and crying out for him to enter her.

Palm Beach,
April 25, 1975

AMBASSADOR AND MRS. GUILFORD DUDLEY

REQUEST THE PLEASURE

OF YOUR COMPANY

AT A SMALL DINNER DANCE

ON THURSDAY, APRIL 24, 1975

9:00 P.M.

TO CELEBRATE THE FORTHCOMING MARRIAGE

OF

SYLVIE CAPLAN

AND

RICHARD KAYE

R.S.V.P.   Black Tie

Sylvie carefully put the engraved invitation on top of all the others in the file marked "wedding parties." As Dick had predicted, the Dudleys' party—the last they would attend before their marriage—had indeed been the best of the lot. There had been a marvelous mixture of guests as attractive and as intelligent as the hosts, swinging music, and a glorious setting on the wide terrace of the Dudleys' beautiful old Mizener-designed mansion between the lake and the ocean.

Although there were now maids to "tidy up" for her, from habit Sylvie picked up the Oscar de la Renta chiffon sheath she'd worn the night before to hang it neatly in the huge walk-in closet of the room now designated as madame's dressing room.

She could still hardly believe the number of new clothes she saw hanging there, most of them bought on Worth Avenue, the most tantalizing, tempting street she had ever visited in her life. She felt a sense of adventure every time she went to the closet, although she was well aware her taste wasn't really adventurous. The evening dresses she'd bought weren't "entrance clothes," but in any case she was also aware that whatever she wore would cause comment, that there would always be those who wanted to find fault rather than pleasure from the happiness radiating from her face.

Since she'd accepted Dick's proposal (actually while lying on the twenty-second floor of his spectacular office building), the world had turned into an enormous cake, filled with slices of pleasure, messages of good will, extravagant presents from big names—leaders of industry, influential politicians, stars of TV, screen, and radio—arriving by every known conveyance, even by helicopter, as yesterday's "his" and "hers" exercycles from Johnny Carson had put in an appearance. There were endless hypocritical loving and truthful loving messages from skywriters, telegram boys, and singing telegram girls in can-can costumes.

Dick had said more than once he couldn't stand it. Twice he'd escaped, taking *Volition* out to sea with only the captain for company. Several times he'd suggested they change their plans and elope, instead of being married with all "pomp and ceremony" in the garden of the Palm Beach mansion. He'd always changed his mind the next minute, and Sylvie understood why a big wedding was important to him.

It amused and touched her to realize that underneath all Dick's assurance, sophistication, and air of command, there was still a little boy who wanted to "get even," who, for the first and probably the last time, was willing to reveal a little of his private life to the five hundred invited guests in order to show only two of them a sample of what he had achieved—as well as to exhibit his enduring love for her.

As he had put it himself, he wanted both Kitty and Nell at their wedding reception, so they could see their shining happiness, "to make up for all the years we've wasted—all those miserable lost years without you."

Kitty had actually phoned from London to say how thrilled she was to be invited, that she had some riveting news herself—"that I can't wait to tell you. How wonderful it will be to see you both again—to let bygones be bygones . . ." If Dick was expecting Kitty to eat "humble pie," Sylvie thought he would be lucky!

It was from Kitty that Sylvie had learned, of all amazing coincidences, Nell's annual Ready to Change convention was taking place in Boca Raton only days before their wedding—and Kitty had managed to arrange to interview Nell. If Kitty only knew how she was going to be preempted . . . Sylvie couldn't stop smiling. Long before Kitty's article on the Godmother was in print, her own last column would be a major topic of conversation all across America—and probably the world.

As the helicopter lifted off to take them to the yacht for their honeymoon in the Caribbean and the Galápagos, the "Sam Says" column that would set the record straight, that would topple Nell the Godmother from her lofty God-fearing perch, would be released. The truth would be out at last.

Her trusty old typewriter, on the beautiful Hepplewhite desk in the middle of the huge bay windows, challenged her. As usual she had a love-hate feeling toward it. Should she wash her hair before she started once again to try to find the right words, so the reader could learn in the simplest way the evil that lurked behind the most beautiful façade in the nation? Sylvie knew she was vacillating.

Dick's words rang in her ears. "Write fearlessly, my darling—the whole truth and nothing but the truth about Nell Nesbitt and her evil ways. You need fear nothing. I promise I won't allow anyone or anything ever to harm you again."

~~~

The drive from Boca Raton had taken its toll. Nell grimaced at her reflection. The wretched Kitty Stein would be with her in less than two hours and she looked and felt an utter wreck. She examined her face minutely in the magnifying glass.

Dr. Joseph Hoffman had been right when he'd written in his famous treatise on skin that losing your temper can age you. Her temper tantrum on seeing the photographs of Sylvie and Dick together had unexpectedly blown a fuse. The shock had been too much. Although to the outside world she still presented an enviable serenity, inside she seethed at the injustice of it all . . . that the mysterious tycoon Mr. Richard Kaye should be none other than Dick Kolinzcky. It hadn't taken her more than a second to realize it after seeing the newspaper photograph. In an eerie way it was as if she'd *known* that one day she would see Sylvie and Dick together again.

She brooded how she had been unaffected by the marriage announcement in the *Times*, the supposedly investigative piece about Mr. Mysterious Multimillionaire Kaye in *Women's Wear Daily*—which hadn't revealed anything. She had been indifferent to the fact that not only had Sylvie landed on her feet again, but this time had made a remarkable catch. Once she would have been angry—yes, she had to admit it, even jealous—but she had thought all those kinds of emotions, experienced by ordinary mortals, were behind her, beneath her. For she was extraordinary, a giant among women—and men. She had been amazed—amused—to receive an invitation to the wedding; she had decided to accept just for the hell of it, in view of the fact that she was going to be in Florida the weekend before anyway.

She'd thought at the time it would give her pleasure to outshine Sylvie even on her wedding day. Who would look at the bride, whoever she was marrying, when they could see—even meet—the Godmother in person?

Photographs, like fragrances, provoked memories that could destroy. In this case, photographs had broken through *her* colossal self-discipline. Thank God it had happened in the car where only Fizz had been a witness. As usual Fizz had swallowed whole the explanation—that for the first time in her life she felt she was coming down with the flu! Nell decided she would use the same excuse to postpone her interview with Stein until the following day.

As Fizz stood by her bedside with a worried expression, she refused to consider canceling the interview altogether. "No," Nell whispered, "I've known this journalist for many, many years. Once, long ago, she was kind to me. I don't want her to think I've forgotten her kindness." Nell could see with a detached kind of acceptance that Fizz was marveling anew at her strength . . . Fizz, who had never once heard her boss complain about being sick . . . who had had the extraordinary experience of seeing the Godmother throw up on the roadside.

The next afternoon Nell soaked in a hot tub, steeping her silky skin in lilac oil–laced waters. Water always relaxed and refreshed her. She applied one of her new ginseng masks and allowed herself a five-minute drift away from the world. She drifted to a place where there was no intrigue, no competition, only lilacs and lilacs when . . . without warning . . . the thought of Diaz broke through the indolence and relaxation of the moment.

Did Diaz know she had tried to kill him? That the bomb that had blown up his car had been placed there by her orders? The bomb had exploded too soon. If Diaz suspected her, he had given no indication. There had been other killings in Miami soon after, but her secret ally, the traitor in Diaz's camp, had survived, and knew only too well to stay away from her. Their plan had been that if anything went wrong they could not talk again for six months. Six months! Nell sighed. It was a lifetime, but next time she would not fail.

It was strange that Diaz hadn't bothered her in quite a while. He hadn't called or arrived for three weeks, two days and, now, six hours. There had been other periods of silence. Instead of worrying, she decided it was more beneficial to be grateful.

The Meissen clock showed her it was time to get out of the bath. She still felt oddly apprehensive, totally different from the day she'd received the request from Kitty Stein for the interview and believed she would enjoy showing the sleazy, snood-covered sneak what a supercolossal power she had become. She had had no fear that Kitty was coming to remind her of the past—of the baby in her past. There was no way Kitty could get very far with that. She still worked for Smith, was a slave to him as she had always been. Nell's lip curled. Her secret was safe.

For a second her thoughts went to Lucy. Strange how any thought of the baby she'd lost invariably turned her thoughts to Lucy. The pain came back as it always did, as if she'd lost Lucy, not the nameless lump of flesh she had given birth to.

She shook her head vigorously to lose the pain. Where was Johnny? He should have arrived after the meeting with the new supervisors in Miami—and he hadn't even called. She had been overly sharp to him. It wasn't the first time, although it didn't happen too often, but he'd always called—especially after such a successful meeting. Oh well, he probably thought by leaving her alone for twenty-four hours she would revert to her old sentimental ways and be all the more anxious to see him on his arrival. She wasn't sure about that.

All the same she was irritated that she was *waiting* for his call. Once upon a time she would have been incapable of operating. She'd spent too many years waiting and yearning for Johnny, only to find out she didn't need him after all. She didn't need any man, nor would she ever need a man again.

There was a tap at the door just as she was going to call Fizz to send in Mary Muller, the self-important little hair stylist who, Nell knew, threw her weight about with the other staff members because she had the honor to comb out the Godmother's hair. "Who is it?" she called out crossly. Surely Kitty Stein wouldn't have the gall to arrive early. Knowing Kitty, she would have the gall for anything.

"An important letter, ma'am . . ."

Nell frowned. There were strict instructions at the desk never to bring anything to her directly. Someone would pay for countermanding or ignoring her orders. "Slip it under the door."

She recognized Johnny's handwriting even from where she was standing, waiting with a sense of apprehension as the envelope came into view. She clutched the chair. Without opening the envelope she knew what the letter contained. He was saying good-bye again, just as he'd said good-bye in London on New Year's Eve over eight years before. But this time—this time—she shook her head as if to throw away all negative thoughts, and then opened the envelope. Yes, it was all there as she expected—he was going away to spend some time with Lucy. Only one paragraph made no sense unless . . . unless all along Johnny had known. "I can't bear to stay around and see you destroy yourself, Nell. While there's still time, make a clean break with the past. Put yourself in an impregnable position while there's still time. I can't say more. I'll always love you. Good-bye."

Love you! Yes, she knew he loved her, and because of that fact, very much in doubt in 1967, she could live with his disappearing act this time—wouldn't suffer, knew that now she had a much more important calling in life than to be at the emotional beck and call of a man. She needed all her energy for her disciples. Johnny would come back. She gave him six months maximum, before the yearning for her meant his will power would ebb away. But what did the last paragraph mean? "Make a clean break with the past"? How did he know she had a "past" to break with? It had an ominous sound.

She would have to discuss it with Diaz. The thought that she was now contemplating talking about Johnny with Diaz sent a chill through her.

She caught sight of her face in the looking glass. It was grim—and her hair! Oh God, her hair. The ingratiating Mary would have to be summoned after all. She had no time to do anything to it herself.

At the appointed time Nell was more than ready for Kitty. If Kitty was ready for Nell she didn't show it. She looked flustered, embarrassed, not at all like the Kitty Nell remembered from—when was it, could it really be almost twenty years ago? Kitty was still a Fleet Street hack, while she . . . well, it was impossible even to describe what she had become in comparison. She was as great a personality as Eva Peron, and even more revered; she was at least as important as Elizabeth Arden and Helena Rubinstein had ever been in their day. They had been incredibly successful, but they had never been as loved (adored she decided, was a more accurate description) as she was.

To Kitty, Nell's air of tranquility was—she racked her brain to think of the right word—supernatural. She had expected to find a link, *something* related to the headstrong Sarah Bernhardt she remembered in the fifties, but Kitty decided after twenty minutes there was nothing visibly left of the old Nell in the poised, exquisitely dressed woman who had welcomed her with such a clever mix of warmth and careful restraint.

Kitty longed for Nell to ask the question that would enable her to release her own marvelous news, but Nell gave her no help.

For the first time in many years Kitty was tongue-tied. After her first question, she needed to say very little because once she mentioned witnessing the magic of the Ready to Change annual meeting, it triggered off one of Nell's many "mini-speeches," although Kitty didn't know it. On and on Nell went about the vitality, the enthusiasm, the heartwarming sincerity of her "disciples."

Kitty kept her tape recorder rolling, since every word Nell said she knew would make wonderful copy. Cynic though she considered herself to be, even *she* felt Nell's words were uplifting and would certainly inspire the women of Great Britain.

"Shit," Kitty thought, "this isn't really what I came here for." She didn't mention the baby. What good would it do? Part of the agreement had always been that Nell would never know who the parents were, and that the parents would never know the truth about the mother.

Kitty had almost given up the thought of telling Nell that, despite *her* incredible mind-boggling success, beauty, wealth, and obvious happiness, at last she, too, had a reason to look on life with anticipation and joy. Then Nell provided a much-needed segue.

Turning to her desk Nell opened a small box to take out a bottle of what looked like pearlized liquid. "Kitty, I see you're wearing a pretty ring. I think you should try this new product of ours to make your nails live up to it. It isn't just a nail color. It's extraordinary nail care, a builder of strength—you see, all my products have a dual purpose to care as well as to color. I believe only in products that give a woman real benefits."

Kitty put out her hand proudly to show off more clearly the diamond she was wearing. "I'm glad you noticed, Nell . . ." It was the first time she had said her name and she was strangely timorous about using it, as if they had never met before. "Do you by any chance remember Smith Maynard, the man who used to be called 'the wolf of Fleet Street'—your old boss, in fact, and still mine?"

Nell nodded, smiling coolly, apparently with little interest as Kitty went on, gathering steam. "Well, at last he's going to be tamed! We're going to be married when I return home from the States. He's been a hard man to pin down, but now that he wants to put his feet up occasionally and look forward to retirement, he's decided I'm not so bad after all. Aren't you going to congratulate me?"

Nell's hands went slowly to her throat. Instead of thinking of Smith, she thought of Violana, her old coach. Violana had inconveniently died three months before . . . but her memory would _never_ die. Now Nell thought how proud Violana would have been to see how her star pupil followed her instructions without conscious thought. No one would ever have been able to guess that Nell's graceful movement was used to allow her to take a deep breath to send a much-needed shaft of fresh oxygen to the brain—a "diversionary tactic, my dear, in times of stress." She could hear Violana's grating voice in her brain.

Smith Maynard and Kitty! Dick Kolinzcky and Sylvie! A hideous, familiar silent scream was building inside her—and Johnny gone to Australia! It was the same scream that had threatened her sanity as she'd walked into the Savoy Restaurant beside a smug, complacent composer praising his wife, "your very best friend"; the scream had made her so sick with anger she'd had to tell a lie to take the smile away from his face. Now she didn't need to tell a lie. The truth would be enough to take the smile away from Kitty Stein's face forever.

Nell leaned forward to switch off Kitty's tape recorder. There was an embarrassing silence before Nell turned to look at Kitty straight in the eye, watching her look of joy disappear as she said in a clipped tone, "It's impossible for me to congratulate you, Kitty. Smith Maynard nearly ruined my life. He was the father of my child, the child he forced me to abandon for adoption. He is a wicked man, who only in recent years, with God's help, have I learned to pray for. I think you should reconsider your decision. He doesn't have the ability to give love . . . he's an evil man."

Kitty stared at Nell openmouthed, paling, as Nell's words seeped into her brain like the poison Nell intended.

Who knows what might have happened if Fizz hadn't come into the room at that moment, exactly at the time Nell had asked to be interrupted in order to get ready for her next appointment. Aware that something untoward had happened, Fizz acted with her usual presence of mind. As angry tears spurted from Kitty's eyes, Fizz maneuvered her by the elbow in the direction of the exit, while Nell slipped into her bedroom and firmly closed the door.

Like a sleepwalker Kitty was led to the Ready to Change car that had brought her over from the Colony Hotel. The driver returned her there—like delivering a parcel, Kitty thought. She looked at her watch. It was almost ten-thirty in London. Where was Smith likely to be? The Garrick? Playing cards? Even if he was sitting watching TV in Montpelier Square, what could she say to him on the telephone? Whatever she said was bound to ruin all that had only recently come to pass, as little by little he'd given in to getting older, a little grayer, more tired every night after a lifetime of service in the front line of Fleet Street. It was only in the last six months that he had begun to believe her—that she no longer drank, that she was a responsible, caring woman who had spent a great part of her life loving him and asking little in return.

Kitty sobbed and sobbed in the hotel bedroom, a bleak unfriendly room with no view except onto the rooftop of a garage below. She had looked forward to a good eight hours' sleep before the wedding the next day, but that was no longer possible. She knew she wouldn't get a wink. Who could she turn to? Who would know the truth? The father of Nell's baby couldn't have been Smith! He couldn't have been so deceitful all those years ago when she'd rushed to him with the idea of the adoption crusade for the baby on the doorstep. If he was the father, looking at her as he had then, straight in the eye as if he knew nothing whatsoever about it, then he had to be the biggest liar ever to set foot on God's earth!

Only one person would know the truth, and that was tomorrow's bride. Sylvie. Sylvie owed her one. Surely Sylvie must realize that. She hadn't been grudging; she had been generous, phoning Sylvie to thank her for the invitation. Sylvie's life had always had a magic carpet in it to fly her out of trouble. Now Sylvie had to see her for old times' sake—to settle old scores—to make up for the terrible betrayal she'd perpetrated when she'd taken over her Kit Carson column behind her back.

~~~

"Missus Caplan, it's a lady in the hall wants to see you urgently . . ."

"What's her name, Lizzie?" It was the daughter of Dick's housekeeper who, like so many of the staff, seemed overwhelmed by all the wedding preparations

There was a pause, then Lizzie's voice came over the intercom, strong and true. "Miss Kitty Stein, Missus Caplan. She says she has to see you. It's a matter of 'streme urgency . . ."

Sylvie sighed. Dick wasn't home yet. They'd decided the night before that they wanted a quiet evening before the wedding, sharing it only with Connie, who was to be her matron of honor, and her husband, Tony, the captain. They were expected at any moment.

There really was no reason not to see Kitty, as much as she felt put out. How could Kitty expect her to welcome her with open arms after all that had happened? She had imagined she would just shake hands with her at the reception the following day and then never have to see her again. Well, there was nothing she could do, except see her for a few moments—but that was all. "All right, Lizzie. Show her up—into my private sitting room—but interrupt us after thirty minutes, please. Explain that I'm very busy."

She glanced at herself briefly before she went through the latticework doors into the small room adjoining the master bedroom. She looked fine—certainly better than could be expected after all Kitty Stein's poisonous articles. Was Kitty coming to apologize? She doubted it. If so, something monumental must have happened to her soul, her conscience.

Sylvie was totally unprepared for her first reaction on seeing her old boss again. Pity, total pity, washed away the bitter memories as she saw the once-immaculate and colorful Kitty follow Lizzie into the bright airy room overlooking the pounding ocean. Kitty had aged so much! There was still feisty defiance there, but her once-sharp, neat features that the severe hairstyle had shown off to such perfection— the chiseled cheeks, the aquiline nose—now had a sharp, birdlike look, while a fine network of lines etched from forehead to temple gave away Kitty's sleepless nights, the endless cigarettes, the overdoses of gin and tonic.

"Hello, Kitty, would you like a drink?" How banal a greeting after so much travail and so many years had passed, but Sylvie couldn't think of anything else to say. She didn't need to think of anything else, because as Kitty came toward her, her hands trembling, tears rolled down her cheeks.

"Sylvie, Sylvie, my little Sylv . . oh, thank you for seeing me now. I know it must be inconvenient." Kitty hadn't meant to sound so grateful, but seeing Sylvie standing there, the same Sylvie she remembered so well from the past, courteous, a sweet look on her face, made Kitty realize how much she had once cared for her. Disappointment in herself made the tears flow faster.

Sylvie clasped Kitty's hand and led her to the window seat where Kitty put her head on Sylvie's shoulder and burst into noisier tears. Even as Sylvie was wondering what on earth to do, Kitty blew her nose and drew herself up tall, some of the old spark reignited and the real reason for her "urgent business" pouring out. It was like turning the clock back. Sylvie remembered for the first time in years how uninhibited Kitty had been in her description of Nell, following Nell's departure with Dick, and before Smith had taken steps to replace Kitty on the Kit Carson column with her own assistant.

"She's a bitch, still a bitch . . ." Kitty's voice quavered, but she sat erect, eyes blazing directly at Sylvie. "Despite her own success, she still can't bear to see anyone else happy." Kitty paused as if a thought had struck her for the first time. "Perhaps she's not happy after all . . . perhaps living on a million dollars a month or whatever she earns hasn't brought her the happiness she deserves . . ." The last syllables came out in a sarcastic sneer. Then everything poured out in a steady flow as Kitty screamed, "She even used the baby's adoption campaign as proof of Smith's involvement. . . . She tried to say he all but ruined her life when he refused to accept the responsibility, that he readily agreed to *my* idea because the baby was *his* . . ." It was the old Kitty, Sylvie thought, half amused, half saddened to hear how Kitty still had to make sure she got the credit for the adoption idea.

Kitty finished her story and once more looked pathetic. She put out a trembling hand to touch Sylvie's arm. Sylvie wanted to recoil in disgust, but she didn't move, pity uppermost in her mind for the old war horse, still battling away on the unrelenting newspaper front, trying to keep up appearances, probably terrified of growing old and having to cope with a man as dissolute and emotionally unreliable as Smith Maynard.

"Lop-sided halo"—that was the description Smith had once used about Kitty. It fit, Sylvie realized. They all had lop-sided halos, but despite what Kitty had tried to do to her, Sylvie sensed that once more her early instincts had been right. Kitty was basically a decent person, who had had to put up with too many bad breaks.

With Kitty breaking down in front of her, drawing a picture of a solitary, lonely Nell who perhaps, after all, did yearn for the baby she'd once screamed she never wanted to see again, Sylvie's thoughts were in confusion. There was only one constant. The sense of being loved again by a dear, sweet man. How on earth had God singled *her* out to be so lucky, to be loved twice in such a fashion, when the two women who along with Aunt Gert had once meant the whole world to her, had never wholly been loved at all?

Whose fault was it? In Nell's case certainly Nell's own fault. Good God, Sylvie asked herself, could she be pitying Nell? It was *impossible*. She forced herself to remember how both Nell and Kitty had tried and had nearly succeeded in destroying her happiness.

Focusing on the past made her stronger. It was her duty to confirm what Nell had said. Why should Kitty go through life with any doubt? Wasn't it better for her to face up to the truth, and if she still wanted to marry Smith, then that was her affair, but at least she would have no illusions? She was about to answer Kitty's agonized plea, "Only you know the truth—I'm sure of that, Sylvie. Tell me, *please*, tell me the bitch lied . . . that the father was . . ." Even Kitty didn't have the gall to come right out with it and say Dick's name.

Sylvie was about to speak, picking her words with care in her mind, when there was a light tap on the door and Sylvie heard Connie's voice say excitedly, "Can I come in, Sylvie? I can't wait to see the bride-to-be . . ."

Sylvie threw her hands up in mock aggravation, whispering to Kitty, "We'll talk in a few minutes." She then cried out, "Come in, come in, darling."

If anything, Connie looked more of a vision than ever, but seeing Kitty sitting by the window with a set, grim expression she backed away awkwardly. "Oh, I'm sorry. I didn't know you had a visitor."

Sylvie shook her head, beckoning Connie forward. "Come in. You look like a bride yourself. Well, you are, of course . . ." Sylvie was amazed to see Connie blush as vividly as she herself had ever blushed. It was something she hadn't seen before and some instinct told her why. "Excuse me for a moment, Kitty . . ." Sylvie got up and, taking Connie's hand, led her into the bedroom next door. "You've got 'big secret' written all over your face. Is it . . . is it what I think it is?"

Connie blushed still more. "Oh, I feel dreadful interrupting you, but I wanted to tell you before the excitement got under way. Yes, the doctor has confirmed it. I'm pregnant . . ."

Sylvie felt a lump in her throat, looking at the beautiful girl who was little more than a child herself. "I'm thrilled, thrilled! Look, my old friend Kitty Stein will soon leave. Let's have a glass of champagne together, then we can really celebrate. Is Tony with you? And my husband-to-be?" Happiness radiated between them like something tangible.

"No," Connie said with pride. "Tony didn't want me to fly in the helicopter. He sent me ahead in a limo. Said I had to be sure to feel one hundred percent for your big day . . ."

Sylvie hugged Connie, then they both returned to where Kitty sat looking out to sea, morose, slumped, obviously very unhappy.

Sylvie tried to lighten the atmosphere, saying, "Connie, this is Kitty Stein of the *Evening Mirror*, one of the most famous journalists in England and my old boss." As she spoke she picked up the intercom. "Lizzie, bring up some champagne. Yes, cold, of course."

She laughed, turning to Connie, and went on, "Kitty has some great news, too. She's going to marry the editor-in-chief of my old paper, Smith Maynard . . ."

There was considerable tension in the room with Kitty looking as if she were once more going to burst into tears, while Connie, usually so happy-go-lucky and able to defuse difficult situations with her warmhearted smile, looked as if she, too, were going to break down.

She threw her hands up to her face, screwed up her eyes tightly, and muttered, "Oh, my goodness, my goodness . . ."

"Whatever's wrong, Connie? Here, you'd better sit down. You look as if you've seen a ghost or something . . ."

Connie allowed Sylvie to lead her to the window seat, where she stretched out a trembling hand to Kitty. "I'm sorry, Miss Stein, to be acting so peculiarly. Congratulations . . ."

Sylvie felt a lump in her throat as she saw Connie blush again. Connie smiled tremulously. "I've never told you this but, meeting

Miss Stein, well . . ." Connie gulped, "it's like meeting my fairy god-mother. I can hardly believe I'm actually sitting here beside her . . ."

At Connie's use of the now-so-familiar word, Sylvie and Kitty exchanged grim glances, but Connie continued, "You see, I was adopted . . . and when I was growing up, hardly a week went by without my mum and dad telling me about Miss Stein and the *Evening Mirror* who somehow helped get me adopted . . . and how they had been chosen out of thousands and thousands of people in England to be my parents." Connie looked down at the carpet. "I used to get fed up because my folks could never tell me anything about who I really was. All they would say was that I came beautifully wrapped in a silk shawl with an S embroidered in the corner. S is for Smith, my dad used to say, and out of the forty-eight million people in England, forty million of them are named Smith! He nicknamed me 'Smithy' because of that. . . . Smithy after the 'S' and I think after the editor of the paper who got up a trust fund to help them look after me." Connie, still looking down, was oblivious to the fact that Sylvie had sunk down into an armchair, her eyes never leaving Connie's face, her hands nervously twisting the tassle on a cushion, while Kitty had turned so pale her lipstick looked like an ugly red slash across her face.

Lizzie came in with the champagne and, as usual, as if she were on duty on the boat, Connie stood up to pour it into the crystal glasses. "My mum didn't like it, but the name stuck. When my dad died, mum married a man I didn't like, so I joined my girlfriend, cooking her way around the Caribbean—that's how I met Mr. Kaye. I decided it was time to make a fresh start and use my real name, Constance—Connie . . ."

Kitty and Sylvie's eyes locked in a look of mutual understanding. It was an agonizing moment. Connie suddenly realized something dramatic was happening, something she couldn't fathom.

She faltered, "Have I said something wrong?" The door opened again and in came her husband, Tony, followed by a beaming Dick, carrying a magnum of champagne. He cried out boisterously, "So much to celebrate, Sylvie . . . so much to celebrate. You'll never guess what I have to tell you . . ."

For the first time in weeks Sylvie woke to find herself alone in the king-sized bed. She hugged herself as she had been doing since she was a small child, so full of joy she could hardly contain it. Oh thank you, God, for sending Dick back into my life. She had attended the

Catholic wedding of one of Dick's close business associates a month before and beautiful, telling words from the mass came into her mind: "Lord, I am not worthy to receive you, but only say the word and I will be healed . . ." She was healed and she had God to thank for it.

She laughed softly, remembering Dick's face the evening before when they had agreed to sleep apart the night before their wedding. He had sworn they would never sleep apart again. "I'm going to be so lonely in the guest room . . ." he'd said, only half jokingly as he'd turned to kiss her good night one more time before walking with exaggerated gloom down the passageway to the guest wing.

Before that they had drunk a great deal of champagne. "So much to celebrate . . . you'll never guess what I have to tell you," he had said on arrival, stopping short when he'd seen his old enemy Kitty sitting there with tear-filled eyes. Then Sylvie hadn't known Dick's big news, although *he* had thought he knew all of theirs—that he was arriving to toast the beautiful mother-to-be Connie and her handsome captain husband. He still had to learn of the enormous revelation that Connie had inadvertently made.

It wasn't until Connie and Tony took Kitty back to her hotel that Sylvie had been able to tell him, "I can hardly believe you never knew, Dick . . ."

"Neither can I. It's the most amazing coincidence of my life, and there have been plenty. I really *can't* believe it . . . yet, of course, I don't know the life histories of most of my employees. There are almost nine thousand of them, you know." He had looked like a little boy as he'd spoken, half proud, half ashamed, feeling he was boasting—". . . let alone the case histories of my crew! It's their expertise I care about, not who their mothers and fathers happened to be."

Without another word on the subject he had handed Sylvie a memorandum marked, "Strictly confidential—for your eyes only." It wasn't the first he'd shared with her about a delicate business matter involving the government.

Sylvie had gasped as she'd read: "Joseph Diaz, long-time member of the Canadian Mafia arrested a week ago as he left his Miami residence, agreed today to a plea-bargaining deal with the National Narcotics Task Force Organization, closely affiliated with the F.B.I., the Coast Guard, Customs Service, and Central Intelligence Agency. In turning state's evidence, Diaz has implicated Nell Nesbitt, the world-famous head of a major cosmetics organization, Ready to Change. In the next twenty-four hours it is believed the Godmother, as Mrs.

Nesbitt is more commonly known, will be called in for questioning . . ."

Sylvie walked to the window to look out over the ocean toward Nassau. Her wedding day was going to be beautiful. Even as she stared at the horizon, the soft mist, which caught the spray to hold it for a second like tiny glittering pieces of crystal, started to lift until it disappeared to leave behind a perfectly blue sky.

～～

The line of guests stretched from the terrace at the back, where Sylvie and Dick were welcoming their guests, all the way to the front of the colonnaded mansion, where Nell, flanked by an entourage of beautiful girls in different shades of blue, had just arrived. She dispensed her beautiful smile to those who managed to catch her eye, an appreciative murmur running through the guests as one after the other realized who was now in their midst.

From the terrace even from a distance Sylvie caught sight of a look of smug satisfaction on Kitty's face, which, shaded by an enormous brim, once again looked like the Kitty she had once admired so much. Sylvie knew exactly what the look meant. Kitty had added two and two and come to what in her mind made the only sense of the situation —that _Dick_, not Smith Maynard, _had_ to be Connie's father, after all. Otherwise, how had she managed to end up on Dick's yacht, married to Dick's captain, and, today, be in the privileged position of matron of honor?

No one could fault Kitty for that conclusion and, on this, the happiest day of her life, Sylvie smiled all the wider as the thoughts flashed through her mind. What did it matter? There was no need for Kitty to know the truth, even if she would believe it, which she probably wouldn't without a blood test! Kitty had had enough trouble and probably would have plenty more dealing with Smith Maynard in the years ahead, without carrying one more painful piece of knowledge into her marriage.

As congratulations and compliments poured into her ears and she felt, without even looking, Dick's constant beam of pride on her, his hand continually seeking out hers, Sylvie saw Nell turn the corner of the mansion flanked by her entourage in blue. Her breath quickened and she looked away, tears pricking her eyes, not understanding why, despite everything, her first thought on seeing her was "poor Nell."

Nell had brought everything on herself. She had been given life's greatest gifts, exceptional beauty and extraordinary brains, and yet she had done everything to destroy the happiness of those who loved her the most. Perhaps that was why she was "poor Nell," and would always be, because she would never know the joy of giving for giving's sake. Nell had been born a "taker." She had taken and taken and taken and been left with nothing.

As Nell and her group of beauties came nearer, Sylvie looked at her carefully. She was still incredibly beautiful, but now she could see the uneasiness and the look Sylvie recognized from the old Hammersmith days. Nell *was* unhappy, desperately unhappy, although as Sylvie had learned from Dick only that morning, Nell still did not know the devastating blow about to be delivered to her some time later that day.

Suddenly Sylvie realized there was another reason for Kitty's smug look, which became more evident as she came nearer. Kitty must have found a way to tell Nell what she had learned only the night before.

Of course Kitty had had to tell Nell—that the exquisite girl, the matron of honor, now standing beside Sylvie in the receiving line, was her own daughter, the daughter she had abandoned, the daughter she had never known, could never know and could never acknowledge. Knowing Kitty, she must have accepted Connie's incredible, innocent revelation as a truly heaven-sent message . . . one to use for retribution.

As she slowly approached, Nell could see what everyone could see —Connie's constant look of love and admiration at the bride and groom.

It was the Kitty of old who offered her congratulations profusely and eloquently before striding on with head held high into the first of the giant marquees, no sign of last night's travail on her face.

After twenty or thirty more people, came Nell. As Nell approached Sylvie felt Dick's arm go round her waist and gently propel her closer to his side.

Sylvie could sense the bitter emotions fighting beneath what the world knew as the Godmother's usually phlegmatic, serene expression. Like a painful jolt in her stomach Sylvie could also see—and was astonished she had never seen it before—the resemblance. Connie was *obviously* Nell's daughter. At that precise moment Sylvie knew how right she had been to choose another subject for her last column. She had torn it up—the one that had exposed Nell so thoroughly, even though by tomorrow Nell's indictment would be front-page news all over the world, and she would have had the greatest scoop of her career for a grand finale.

Dick had only asked her once the night before if she was sure of what she was doing, not because she was passing up an extraordinary journalistic triumph, but—"are you sure you don't want *Nell* to know that at last you've put the record straight to revenge all those she's hurt so much?"

On impulse, just before Nell reached them, Sylvie turned to kiss Dick's cheek. He was *such* a great man. He had accepted her decision without comment that, apart from the fact she couldn't risk hurting Connie in anyway, Nell's doom was, in any case, near at hand. Justice was going to be done in the right and proper way.

As Nell came sharply into focus, Sylvie realized with a blast of pain and sorrow that it hadn't been necessary to write one word to exact revenge. No revenge could be as devastating as that which was about to be meted out. At that moment she was intensely aware of Connie, so lovely, standing so proudly beside her and, having seen the God-mother moving closer and closer, reacting the way most young girls would react—with a certain shy awe and excitement that she would soon be shaking the hand of one of the most famous women in the world. She would never know that she would actually be shaking the hand of her real mother.

Nell was before them, a half circle of pretty maidens around her like leaves around a flower. She put out her hand and started to proffer her congratulations. Her words were cool and carefully chosen, although Sylvie hardly listened, so acutely aware was she of Nell's uncontrollably trembling hand.

· The anticipated moment had arrived, and with it Sylvie's mind flooded with memories. As she saw Nell turn slowly to Connie, Sylvie smiled her own untrained, cherubic smile and said, "Connie, I don't believe you've ever met the world-famous Godmother, have you? Nell Nesbitt, who was one of my very best friends . . ."